<u>MAX</u>

Enjoy the read.

Stafford

Stafford
Vance

1

2

GALACTIC YETI
PUBLISHING

info@galacticyetipublishing.co.uk

Copyright © 2024 by Stafford Vance

All rights reserved. No part of this book may be reproduced, distributed, or transmitted in any form or by any means, including photocopying, recording, or other electronic or mechanical methods, without the prior written permission of the author, except in the case of brief quotations used in reviews or other non-commercial purposes.

Galactic Yeti Publishing

info@galacticyetipublishing.co.uk

GALACTIC YETI
PUBLISHING

First Edition

CW01501674

Discl

This is a work of fiction. Names, characters, businesses, places, events, and incidents are either the products of the author's imagination or used in a fictitious manner. Any resemblance to actual persons, living or dead, or actual events is purely coincidental.

Acknowledgments:

A big thanks to Paul, your advice and encouragement
made all the difference

Table of Contents

Chapter One

Max loved London. The city was like a vast, sprawling playground, full of hidden treasures and secret spots only a savvy terrier like him could appreciate. From the cracks in the pavement to the smells wafting out of bakeries, London was his kingdom.

Well, maybe not quite a kingdom. More like a republic where the citizens were busy and unaware of their scruffy ruler. But Max took pride in his domain anyway. And what a domain it was! The streets were a maze of possibilities: discarded food, friendly faces, and the occasional adventure. Sure, there were some dangers, minicabs being the most immediate threat, but for the most part, Max had learned to navigate the city's quirks with ease.

He padded along Brick Lane, dodging around the legs of tourists taking photos of the street art that adorned the walls. A couple snapped a picture of a particularly detailed mural of a dragon, oblivious to the small terrier weaving through the crowd. The air was thick with the scent of spices, and Max's stomach growled in response. Curry was always tempting, but it was tricky business getting near a restaurant without being chased off.

Max trotted past a group of friends laughing outside a café, their voices mingling with the clink of coffee cups and the hiss of the espresso machine. The tables were littered with half-eaten pastries, and Max's nose twitched as he caught the scent of buttery croissants. He eyed a piece of fallen pastry on the ground but decided against it, too close to the café door, and the barista with the sharp eyes had a habit of throwing water at any dog who got too close.

No, today was about the fish market. It was Wednesday, after all, and that meant Roger would be there, waiting for him. But first, Max had a city to explore.

As he made his way through the streets, Max's mind began to wander. It wasn't uncommon for him to day-dream on these little walks, after all, the life of a street dog wasn't exactly luxurious, and sometimes it was nice to imagine something… more. When it came to imagined patisseries or sausages…. a lot more.

Max often dreamed about the big houses he sometimes saw from afar, the ones with perfectly manicured lawns and little garden gates that squeaked just the right amount. In his ideal world, Max would live in one of those houses. He'd have his own big bed, the kind with cushions that never flattened and blankets that never smelled like wet dog (no offense to himself, of course). And there would be cheese. The finest cheeses that humans could offer, brie, gouda, maybe even a bit of stilton if he was feeling adventurous. Oh yes, he'd have a whole fridge stocked with cheese, just for him.

Also, no showers. Not a single one in sight. Baths were one thing, but showers? They were like being caught in a never-ending rainstorm, with water attacking you from all sides. No, Max's dream house would be a sanctuary free from showers. Maybe a nice big tub that he could laze in, with bubbles, of course. Not that he was one to indulge in such luxuries often, but hey, a dog could dream.

Then there was the matter of reading material. Most dogs weren't readers, but Max wasn't most dogs. In his ideal home, there would be a subscription to *Accountancy Monthly* waiting for him by the door every month. He could picture it now: lounging on his big bed, flipping through the glossy pages filled with spread sheets and tax advice. There was something oddly comforting about numbers. They were predictable, dependable. Unlike humans, numbers never lied. Numbers were dependable.

Max sighed contentedly as he wandered through a small park, the sound of children playing nearby bringing him back to reality. He watched them for a moment, humans, so carefree in their youth. If only life could stay that simple. No worries, no responsibilities, just play and snacks whenever you wanted them.

But the city was calling him back to reality, and Max had to focus. The fish market wasn't far now, and he could already smell the salty tang of the sea drifting on the air.

The fish market was a bustling hub of activity, filled with vendors shouting over each other to sell their wares. Fishmongers in aprons stained with the remnants of the day's catch moved quickly, their hands expertly filleting fish and wrapping them up for eager customers. The air was thick with the smell of fresh seafood, salt, and a hint of diesel from the delivery trucks parked along the curb.

Max had been coming to this market for as long as he could remember. It was one of the few places in London where a dog like him could find a decent meal without too much hassle. The fishmongers had long since learned to tolerate his presence, so long as he didn't cause any trouble. Flushing out and chasing off the occasional rat always 'netted' him a fish head to chew on.

And then there was Roger. Roger was a seagull, as large and loud as any you'd find along the coast, but with a bit more of a city attitude. He perched on a crate near one of the stalls, his white feathers slightly ruffled and his beady eyes scanning the crowd for any sign of an easy meal. Roger was a regular here, just like Max, and over the years, they'd developed an understanding. Sort of.

"Caw Caw!" Roger squawked as Max approached.

"Morning, Roger," Max greeted him, settling down beside the crate. "How's the fish today?"

Roger flapped his wings in a half-hearted display of authority before squawking again. Max nodded thoughtfully as if Roger's caws were full sentences.

"Yeah, I know what you mean. Pickings have been slim lately," Max said, glancing at the humans bustling about. "The economy's taking a hit, and people are holding onto their scraps more than usual. It's tough out here."

Roger let out another series of loud caws, eyeing a particularly large fish on the stall nearby.

"You and me both, mate," Max replied with a sigh. "I heard some blokes on the street talking about inflation. Prices going up, fewer people dining out, it all trickles down, you know? Fewer leftovers for us."

Roger squawked in agreement, though his attention was now fully on the fishmonger who had just turned his back on the stall.

"Right, time to make our move," Max said, his tail wagging in anticipation. "You distract him, I'll grab the goods. Fair split, as always."

Roger gave a final *caw* of affirmation before launching himself into the air, his wings flapping noisily as he swooped down toward the fishmonger. The man cursed loudly, waving his arms to shoo Roger away, and in that moment of distraction, Max made his move.

He darted forward, quick as a flash, and snagged a piece of fish from the edge of the stall. Without missing a beat, he ducked back into the safety of a nearby alley, the fish clutched firmly in his jaws.

Moments later, Roger landed beside him, looking rather pleased with himself.

"Well done, Roger," Max said through a mouthful of fish. He tore off a chunk and nudged it toward the seagull. "As promised."

Roger squawked in approval and quickly snatched up his share, swallowing it whole before flying off to find his next target.

Max settled down in the alley, savouring his meal. Life in the city might be tough, but moments like this made it all worthwhile. He chewed thoughtfully, glancing out at the bustling market.

"One day," he murmured to himself between bites, "one day I'll have that big house, that big bed, and all the cheese I could ever want. A nice big calculator too, one with the roll of paper, the fancy type."

But for now, he was content with a belly full of fish and the quiet satisfaction of a successful day at the market.

Max wasn't sure how long he'd been asleep when the sharp poke of a boot against his side jolted him awake.

"Oi you!" a gruff voice barked.

Max blinked groggily, looking up to see a man in a high-visibility vest standing over him, one hand on his hip, the other holding a notepad. A traffic enforcement officer. Though more often Max heard other people in the city refer to them as, traffic enforcement bastards. The man glared down at him, clearly unimpressed with Max's choice of nap spot.

"This ain't a place for dogs," the officer said, waving his notepad like it was some kind of official decree. "Off you go. Go on, scram!"

Max let out a low growl but stood up anyway, shaking the sleep from his body and giving the man one last withering look before trotting off. There was no use arguing with these types. 'They never listened. Don't have the right equipment up top you see.' Thought Max

As he made his way back toward the streets, Max glanced up at the sky. The clouds were thickening, and a light drizzle had begun to fall, the kind of rain that wasn't enough to soak you through but just enough to be thoroughly irritating.

"Great," Max muttered to himself. "Just what I needed."

Realizing that time was slipping away and the evening would soon be upon him, Max decided it was time to head back to one of his many stashes and hide-holes. He couldn't be caught out here in the rain with nothing to wear when it happened, that just wouldn't be proper.

"Not only would it *not be proper,* it would I am sure result in a night in the cells." He mused to himself as he trotted along the pavement.

As he weaved through the streets, Max couldn't help but eavesdrop on the conversations of the humans around him. London was full of stories, all playing out at once, and Max had a knack for tuning into just the right snippets.

"…he never called me back. Can you believe that? After three dates…"

"…I'm telling you, mate, if you don't ask her out, someone else will…"

"…love? Who's got time for love? We're all just trying to survive…"

"… yeah, and they ate the last Jammy Dodger…"

15

Max listened to it all, his mind wandering as he padded along the damp pavement. Love. That was something he hadn't thought about in a while. Not since… His mind clouded over.

Beneath his soft fur and wagging tail was a mind tangled in questions. There were moments, fleeting, almost cruel, when he thought he remembered something. A warm touch, a soft voice calling his name. Was it a previous love? Memory, for Max, was a lot like chasing his tail, it felt like progress until he stopped to wonder what he was even chasing.

Max's memories hovered just out of reach, like the scent of something delicious drifting on the wind, a hint of warmth, familiarity, and longing that he could never quite pin down. Had he loved before? He thought he might have. Sometimes, when he closed his eyes and let his thoughts drift, he could almost feel it, a connection, a bond, but it slipped away as soon as he reached for it. It was maddening, like trying to catch a shadow in the moonlight.

He thought he knew what love was, or at least he was pretty sure. It had something to do with sharing warmth, protecting someone, and perhaps bringing them things they didn't ask for. Socks? Maybe. Old shoes? Probably not. But he wasn't entirely sure. Had he gotten it right before? Did he know how to love at all?

Max liked to think he did. Love, he figured, was like curling up in a sunbeam, it felt right in the moment, even if you couldn't explain why. And yet, there were times when he wondered if that was all it was. Was love supposed to be just a feeling, or something more?

Sometimes it felt like he was on the brink of remembering, the pieces of his past almost snapping into place, but the harder he tried, the more the picture blurred, leaving him chasing after something he couldn't even name.

It was funny, in a way. Here he was, a creature who could navigate the city with the ease of a seasoned local, dodge trouble like a pro, and even outsmart a particularly wily seagull named Roger, and yet, he couldn't figure out the one thing that seemed to matter most. Maybe that was the point of it, he mused. Maybe love wasn't meant to be remembered but rediscovered, over and over again, no matter how many lives you lived.

The thought made him pause, tilting his head as if the answer might fall into place if he looked at it sideways. It didn't, of course. But that was fine. If there was one thing Max was sure of, it was that some mysteries were worth the chase.

There had been a time, back when he was just a pup, when life had been simpler. Before the streets, before the transformations. Back when he'd roamed a different part of the city with a pack of dogs that had taken him in. And among them had been a beautiful black spaniel with eyes that sparkled like the Thames at dawn. She had been graceful, quick-witted, and had a bark that could make even the toughest dogs pause.

Max sighed, his tail drooping slightly as he remembered those days. She had been his first love, his only love, really. But like all things in his life, it hadn't lasted. She had moved on, found a new pack, and Max had found himself alone again. That was the way of things. Life in the city didn't leave much room for romance when you were living day to day, paw to paw.

Still, the memories lingered, like the faint scent of a summer breeze long gone. Where they memories though? Were they his memories? So many things seemed foggy.

Max shook his head, pushing the thoughts aside. No use dwelling on the past. He had clothes to find and a box to get back to before the rain really started coming down.

By the time Max made it back to his alley, the drizzle had turned into a steady patter, the kind that drummed against the pavement and soaked everything in a dull, grey mist. His little alley was as he had left it, quiet, tucked away from the main street, and just out of sight enough to avoid unwanted attention. Bins lined, one of the walls, a few old pallets standing like sentinels and of course the obligatory graffiti. 'What was it about humans and drawing on everything?' He thought as he pee'd up the post at the entrance.

Max nudged aside a few old newspapers and found his stash, a small pile of clothes he had carefully hidden behind a stack of boxes. He nosed through them, checking to make sure everything was still there: a pair of jeans, a slightly faded shirt, and a battered but perfectly serviceable jacket. It wasn't much, but it was enough to keep him decent later.

Satisfied that everything was in order, Max settled down inside his cardboard box, curling up against the damp chill that was beginning to seep into the air. The rain continued to fall, a soft, rhythmic sound that lulled him into a state of calm.

The city might be full of noise and chaos, but here, in this little alley, with the rain gently tapping on the cardboard above him, Max found a rare moment of peace. And for now, that was enough.

Chapter Two

The shrill buzz of the alarm clock broke through the peaceful silence of Stephanie's bedroom, dragging her out of a dream she couldn't quite remember. She groaned and reached for the snooze button, but in her half-asleep state, she knocked over her water glass instead. It tumbled to the floor with a loud clatter, splashing water onto the rug and sending Oliver, her cat, bolting from the foot of the bed.

"Sorry, Ollie," Stephanie mumbled, rubbing her eyes and sitting up. She pushed her red hair out of her face, glancing at the clock. The numbers blinked back at her: 6:45 AM. Too early. Far too early for someone who had stayed up late reading romance novels and eating chocolate. But there was no time for regrets, she had work to get to.

Stephanie dragged herself out of bed, heading for the kitchen, where the ritual of making breakfast awaited her. As she shuffled through the apartment, she couldn't help but feel a small pang of pride despite her morning grogginess. The flat was far from luxurious, but it had character, what some might call "shabby chic," though Stephanie preferred to think of it as "well-loved with a touch of vintage charm." A home, rather than simply a place of living.

Her apartment was in a Victorian-era building in East London, one of those grand old houses that had been divided into smaller flats years ago. The ceilings were high, with ornate plaster mouldings that had long since lost their original lustre, similar to that of a Brighton hotel but still added a touch of elegance. The walls were painted a soft, warm cream, with little nicks and scratches here and there from years of tenants before her. Stephanie had tried to cover up the imperfections with art, mostly framed prints of her favourite paintings and a few quirky pieces she'd picked up at markets and second- h a n d shops. The result was a space that felt lived-in, comfortable, and uniquely hers.

The living room, which opened directly onto the small hallway, was the heart of the apartment. A faded, floral-patterned sofa dominated the room, its cushions plump and inviting. Stephanie had found it in a second-hand shop a few years ago, and though it was a bit worn around the edges, it was the perfect place to curl up with a book and a glass of wine at the end of a long day. A mismatched armchair sat in the corner, draped with a soft, knit throw in a deep shade of burgundy. The coffee table in front of the sofa was cluttered with magazines, a half-finished embroidery project, and a few empty mugs, evidence of late nights spent lost in novels or catching up on work.

Beside the sofa was an old bookshelf, its shelves sagging slightly under the weight of too many books. Stephanie's collection was eclectic, romance novels jostled for space alongside legal textbooks, cookbooks, and travel guides to places she hoped to visit someday. A few small potted plants sat on the top shelf, their green leaves adding a splash of life to the room. She wasn't much of a gardener, but she did her best to keep them alive. So far, they were thriving, unlike the cactus in the kitchen, which had mysteriously withered after a particularly long weekend at the office.

The kitchen itself was small but cosy, with painted white cabinets that had seen better days and a chipped enamel sink that added to the flat's vintage charm. The countertops were cluttered with jars of tea, half-used candles, and a few colourful mugs that didn't quite match. A small, round table sat in the corner, just big enough for two, with a pair of mismatched chairs pushed under it. It was at this table that Stephanie often sat in the mornings, sipping her tea, trying to get motivated for the day ahead.

As she reached the kitchen, Stephanie was greeted by the sight of Oliver sitting on the counter, staring at her with wide green eyes, his tail twitching expectantly. He was a handsome tabby, with sleek fur and an air of superiority that made it clear he believed he was in charge of the household.

"Alright, alright, I'm coming," Stephanie said with a smile, reaching for his food. She opened a can of cat food, the familiar *click* of the lid causing Oliver to purr loudly. She poured the food into his bowl, and Oliver immediately dived in, chomping away.

"At least someone's happy this morning," Stephanie muttered as she started to prepare her own breakfast. She pulled a croissant from the bag on the counter, cutting it in half and popping it into the toaster to warm. As she waited, she set the table and poured herself a glass of orange juice. The blouse she'd planned to wear that day was neatly draped over the back of a chair, waiting for her post-shower routine.

Stephanie loved mornings like this, the quiet before the rush, the few precious moments when it was just her, her breakfast, and her thoughts. But that peaceful moment didn't last long. Just as she was reaching for her tea cup, Fiona stumbled into the kitchen, looking decidedly worse for wear.

"Steph, are you awake?" Fiona's voice was slightly hoarse, probably from yelling over loud music the night before. She had long, wavy blonde hair that was currently tangled into a messy bun, and she was wearing an oversized t-shirt which she had undoubtedly liberated from a suitor. She looked like she had just stepped off the set of a hangover commercial, but she still managed to look effortlessly chic in her oversized shirt and leggings.

Fiona had been living with Stephanie for the past three months, ever since the breakup with David. The flat wasn't large, but it had two bedrooms, and Stephanie had been happy to offer Fiona her spare room. It was supposed to be temporary, just until Fiona got back on her feet, but Stephanie wasn't holding her breath. David had been a nightmare, possessive, controlling, and always lurking just beneath the surface of every conversation Fiona had with him. The breakup had been messy, with Fiona moving out in the dead of night to avoid any more of David's accusations and attempts to control her. Now, Fiona was determined to reclaim her life, and if that meant a few months, or more, of living in Stephanie's flat, then so be it.

"Morning, Fi," Stephanie said, grabbing her tea and taking a sip. "Rough night?"

"Don't even ask," Fiona groaned as she collapsed into the chair at the table. She immediately reached for half of Stephanie's croissant and took a big bite, chewing thoughtfully as she grabbed the glass of orange juice.

Stephanie raised an eyebrow but said nothing. This was a regular occurrence. Fiona had a habit of appropriating half of whatever Stephanie was eating, and by now, Stephanie had learned to accept it.

"You look like hell," Fiona said bluntly, though not unkindly, as she leaned back in her chair.

"Thanks," Stephanie replied dryly. "You're not looking too fresh yourself."

Fiona chuckled, taking another bite of the croissant. "Met this guy last night, tall, dark, and handsome. Absolute dreamboat. I think his name was James? Or maybe it was Jamie. Anyway, he was hot. Took me to this club in Soho, bought me drinks all night. We danced, we kissed… well, you know how it goes."

"Of course," Stephanie said with a knowing smile. "How was the club?"

Fiona waved her hand dismissively. "Loud. Over-priced. Full of people who think they're way more interesting than they actually are. But it wasn't the worst night I've had."

She took a sip of the orange juice and then turned her attention fully to Stephanie. "And you? I'm guessing you spent the night with your cat and a rom-com?"

Stephanie blushed slightly, stirring her tea. "Well… yes. It was nice. Relaxing."

Fiona rolled her eyes. "Steph, you can't live your life through books and tales written by others and your cat. When's the last time you went out? Met someone new? Had fun?"

Stephanie sighed. This was an old conversation; one they had had many times before. "Fi, I'm focusing on my career right now. I need to, "

"Oh, please," Fiona interrupted. "You hate your job, and you know it. That Alistair guy is a total prick. You're too smart, too beautiful, and too full of life to waste your time working for that overgrown man-child."

Stephanie grimaced. She couldn't argue with Fiona on that point. Alistair was… difficult, to say the least. He had a way of piling on the work without ever acknowledging the effort, always expecting more and more while giving praise to Amy, the golden girl of the office, who seemed to do half the work that Stephanie did.

"I know," Stephanie said quietly. "But… I need to prove myself. I need this job, Fi. Besides, I think I'm finally being noticed."

Fiona sighed, her frustration softening into concern. "I know you do, babe. I just don't want to see you burn yourself out. You're always taking care of everyone else, but who's taking care of you?"

Stephanie smiled despite herself. Fiona was a whirlwind, but she meant well. And she wasn't wrong. Stephanie *did* dream of a life that was more… more something. She wasn't even sure what, exactly, but it involved less stress, less Alistair, and maybe, just maybe, a little romance. The kind of romance that didn't involve spilled tea and wrinkled blouses.

Speaking of which… Stephanie glanced at the clock. She still had time for a quick shower before heading off to work. She excused herself from the kitchen, leaving Fiona to nurse her hangover and finish off the croissant.

As Stephanie stepped into the bathroom and turned on the shower, she allowed herself a moment to daydream. The steam rose around her as she closed her eyes and imagined a different life. A life where she didn't have to deal with Alistair's constant demands, where she didn't have to rush to the office every morning, where she could take her time, read novels in cafes, maybe, just maybe, find someone special. Someone who understood her, who saw the world the way she did. Someone who made her feel… well, something more than just stressed.

She smiled to herself as she rinsed the shampoo out of her hair. It was a nice thought, but it wasn't her reality. Not yet, anyway. For now, she had to focus on the day ahead.

The journey to work was as miserable as ever. The tube was packed, hot, and smelled faintly of sweat and damp newspapers. Stephanie stood squeezed between a man who was entirely too invested in his morning crossword and a woman who was yelling into her phone about some drama with her boyfriend. A beggar moved through the carriage, rattling a cup with a few coins in it, while a group of teenagers nearby played music loudly on their phones.

Stephanie did her best to tune it all out, focusing instead on the familiar rhythm of the train as it rattled through the tunnels. This was the worst part of the day, every day. The journey from her cosy little flat to the harsh fluorescent lights of the office felt like a descent into another world, one that was entirely devoid of joy.

When the train finally pulled into her stop, Stephanie hurried out, grateful to be back on solid ground. But the relief was short-lived. The office loomed ahead, and with it, the promise of another long, exhausting day.

Castel and Fink was located in a tall, nondescript building in the heart of the financial district. The office itself was modern enough, glass walls, sleek furniture, the usual, but it always felt cold to Stephanie, like the kind of place where people came to lose their souls, not find and fulfil their dreams.

As she walked through the door, Mrs. Bellwether, the firm's receptionist, greeted her with a curt nod. Mrs. Bellwether was an intimidating woman in her mid-fifties, with sharp features and a permanent air of disapproval. She had a knack for making everyone feel slightly out of place, as if they were intruding on her carefully curated domain.

"Good morning, Stephanie," Mrs. Bellwether said in her clipped tone, barely glancing up from her computer screen.

"Morning," Stephanie replied, forcing a smile as she headed toward her desk. She could already feel the familiar knot of anxiety tightening in her chest. She hadn't even sat down yet, and already she could sense the looming presence of Alistair.

As if on cue, Alistair appeared in the doorway of his office, his eyes scanning the room until they landed on her. He was a man in his early forties, with slicked-back hair and an expensive suit that he clearly thought made him look distinguished. In reality, it only made him look like he was trying too hard.

"Stephanie," he called out, his voice dripping with self-importance. "I need the new information that came in on my desk by noon. The Alcott divorce! Make sure they're thorough this time, alright? We can't afford any mistakes."

Stephanie bit back a sigh. "Yes, Alistair. I'll get right on it."

He gave her a curt nod before turning his attention to Amy, who had just walked in looking fresh and perfectly put-together. "Ah, Amy! Just the person I was looking for. I wanted to talk to you about the McKenna case, great job on that, by the way. We'll need to present to the partners next week, but I'm confident you'll knock it out of the park."

Amy smiled, her perfectly white teeth gleaming. "Of course, Alistair. I'll make sure everything's ready."

Stephanie watched the exchange, a familiar mix of frustration and resignation settling over her. It wasn't fair, but then again, life rarely was. She just had to keep her head down, do her work, and hope that someday, things would change.

With a sigh, she sat down at her desk, opened her laptop, and got to work. Another day at Castel and Fink had begun.

Chapter Three

Stephanie fumbled with her keys as she reached the front door of her apartment, exhaustion weighing heavily on her shoulders. The day had been long, endless emails, tedious meetings, and Alistair's never-ending demands. All she wanted now was to get inside, take off her heels, and have a quiet evening to herself.

When she finally pushed the door open, she was greeted by the familiar warmth of her little flat, the scent of lavender from the diffuser she'd left running that morning drifting through the air. She dropped her bag by the door, kicked off her shoes, and sighed in relief as her feet met the reassuring feel of the wooden floor. It was good to be home.

Her stomach rumbled, reminding her that she hadn't eaten since lunch. She headed for the kitchen, expecting to find the leftovers she'd been looking forward to all day, a pasta dish she'd made the night before, just enough for a second helping. But as she opened the fridge, she was met with an empty shelf where the container should have been. Instead, there was a note taped to the fridge door.

Steph, I'm sorry! I was starving and didn't think you'd mind. I'll make it up to you! Be back late. - Fi

Stephanie groaned, crumpling the note in her hand. Fiona, of course. Fiona, who had a knack for eating whatever she could find and then disappearing into the night for yet another spontaneous adventure. Normally, Stephanie didn't mind, Fiona was her best friend, after all, but tonight she was too tired and hungry to feel forgiving.

She glanced at the clock. It was too late to bother with cooking, and besides, she didn't have the energy for it. Maybe she could order something... but the thought of scrolling through endless delivery apps, trying to decide on a meal, made her stomach turn. She hated ordering apps. They always took forever, and half the time, the food arrived cold. No, what she needed was something quick and satisfying. Something that didn't involve waiting around.

Chinese, maybe. There was that little place a few streets over, Mr. Chan's. She hadn't been there in a while, but she remembered the food being delicious. It was close enough that she could walk, and at least she'd get some fresh air in the process.

Decision made, Stephanie headed to her bedroom and changed into something more comfortable: a pair of loose jeans, an oversized sweater, and her trusty trainers. She pulled her hair back into a messy ponytail, grabbed her keys, and slipped out the door, locking it behind her.

The night air was cool against her skin as she made her way down the street, the faint hum of the city all around her. London at night was different from London during the day, quieter, yes, but also full of hidden life. She liked it. There was a certain comfort in the city's steady rhythm, as if it were alive, a living entity of its own.

She walked quickly, her footsteps echoing softly against the pavement, and within a few minutes, she found herself standing in front of Mr. Chan's. The familiar neon sign buzzed overhead, casting a warm red glow over the entrance. The smell of soy sauce, garlic, and ginger wafted out each time the door opened, making her stomach growl in anticipation.

With a small smile, Stephanie pushed the door open and stepped inside, not knowing that this simple decision would set her on a path that would change her life in ways she couldn't yet imagine.

Max loved the night. It was the time when the city seemed to breathe differently, quieter in some places, livelier in others. After spending the day as a scruffy little terrier navigating the chaos of London's streets, transforming into a man at night felt like stepping into another world.

There was something about London at night that felt utterly magical to Max, in a way his daytime self could never quite grasp. By day, the city was a relentless machine, all honking cars and hurried footsteps, its people marching like ants in suits and ties, armed with coffees and scowls. But at night? At night, London exhaled. The air felt thicker, almost alive, as though the city had shrugged off its buttoned-up façade and thrown on a leather jacket.

Max loved how the streets transformed when the sun dipped below the horizon. Neon lights cast garish reflections in puddles, making the rain-slicked pavement look like it had been dusted with stardust. Even the noises changed. The honking gave way to laughter, sometimes joyous, sometimes the hysterical kind only a tipsy person could muster, and the hum of distant music weaving its way through alleyways.

He'd seen it all: the late-night revellers stumbling out of pubs, arm in arm, singing something vaguely resembling a football anthem. (One particularly memorable group had tried to harmonize "Bohemian Rhapsody" and failed spectacularly, but with such gusto that Max had almost along in support.) There were couples whispering sweet nothings, or not-so-sweet nothings, on street corners, and lone figures standing under flickering streetlights like characters from a noir film.

People let their guard down at night, and Max found that endlessly fascinating. During the day, they were armoured in their professionalism, walking billboards for stress and routine. But after dark, all of that fell away. It was as if the night gave them permission to be messy, to be real. Lovers argued as loudly as they kissed. Friends laughed until they cried. Strangers danced with strangers, even when there was no music.

And then there were the quiet moments, the ones Max treasured the most: the stillness of a near-empty street, the soft click of a cyclist's pedals, the glow of a warm light spilling from a bakery where someone, somewhere, was already preparing for tomorrow. Night-time London wasn't just a city; it was a theatre, with every kind of story playing out in its streets.

For Max, it was a spectacle he never tired of, even if most of the humans around him wouldn't have given him a second glance. And that was fine. In fact, it was perfect. He could slip through the city's heartbeat unnoticed, a spectator to the strange and beautiful chaos of the night.

But the night also held its shadows. Max had seen those too, the figures huddled in doorways; their blankets pulled tight around them as they tried to ward off the cold. The ones who had been forgotten by the city, indeed by the world, invisible during the day but painfully present at night. He'd heard the quiet sobs of a man sitting alone on a park bench, his head in his hands, the weight of whatever he was carrying too much to bear. Max had a soft spot for those people, the ones who felt lost, who had nowhere to go when the world went quiet. He understood that feeling better than most.

Then there were the workers, the unsung heroes of the city who toiled away in the small hours, keeping London running while the rest of the world slept. The cleaners, the street sweepers, the late-night shopkeepers. Max admired them, the way they moved through the night with purpose, their lives unfolding in the spaces between the city's more glamorous moments. They were like him, in a way, existing on the fringes, unnoticed but essential.

Tonight, as he made his way to Mr. Chan's, the familiar sights and sounds of the city at night washed over him. The hum of distant traffic, the clinking of glasses from a nearby bar, the muffled laughter of a group of friends walking down the street. London felt alive at night, as if it was a different city entirely, one that thrived in the darkness and revealed its true colours only when the sun went down.

Max rounded a corner, passing a couple leaning against a wall, lost in each other. He smiled to himself, wondering what it would be like to have that kind of connection with someone. The kind that made the rest of the world fade away, even for just a moment. He had seen it before, that unspoken language between two people who fit together like puzzle pieces. It wasn't something he had ever experienced, at least, not that he could remember.

His thoughts drifted as he continued down the street, his senses heightened in a way they never were during the day. The night sharpened everything, sounds, smells, even emotions. He could smell the faint scent of jasmine coming from a nearby garden, mingling with the more familiar scents of the city: car exhaust, fried food, and the dampness of the Thames lingering in the air. He could hear the soft strains of music coming from an open window above, a melancholy tune that seemed to echo the undercurrent of loneliness that always lingered at the edges of the night.

Max loved the city at night, but he also knew its darker sides. The joy and the tragedy walked hand in hand here, and you had to be careful not to get lost in it. There was a kind of raw honesty to the city after dark, a vulnerability that wasn't always present during the day. It was both beautiful and heart-breaking, and Max had learned to navigate it with the kind of care that came from years of living on the fringes.

As he approached 'Mr. Chan's', the familiar scent of soy sauce, garlic, and sizzling meat filled the air, making his stomach rumble. The neon sign buzzed overhead, casting a dim red glow over the pavement. Max pushed open the door and was greeted by the warmth of the small restaurant, along with Mr. Chan's usual gruff nod from behind the counter.

"Evening, Max," Mr. Chan said in his thick accent, flipping a wok full of noodles with practiced ease. "You're late tonight."

"Busy day," Max replied with a grin, sliding into his usual spot at the corner table. "You know how it is."

Mr. Chan chuckled, shaking his head. "Always busy in this city. What'll it be? The usual?"

"Please," Max said, pulling out his notebook and pen. As he waited for his food, he started going over the numbers for Mr. Chan's accounts. It was mindless work, simple, repetitive, but Max liked it that way. Numbers were predictable, reliable. Unlike the rest of his life, which was anything but.

As he scribbled in his notebook, the door to the restaurant opened, and a woman walked in. Max glanced up out of habit, his eyes catching on her for a moment longer than usual. She was striking, not in an over-the- top way, but in that natural, effortlessly beautiful way that seemed to glow from within. Her red hair was pulled back into a loose ponytail, and she had that slightly frazzled but determined look of someone who had just survived a long day at work.

She approached the counter, her shoulders hunched as if trying to make herself smaller. Max couldn't help but notice how she seemed to blend into the background, even though she had a presence that demanded attention.

It was an odd combination, shyness and quiet confidence wrapped up in one person.

"Evening," she said softly, giving Mr. Chan a small smile. "Can I get a sweet and sour chicken with rice, to go please?"

Mr. Chan nodded, taking in her order and immediately started a ballet of throwing ingredients into a well-seasoned wok. The woman sighed, her shoulders relaxing just a bit as she waited.

Max, who had never been one to resist a good conversation, or any conversation, for that matter, cleared his throat and offered a warm smile. "Long day?" he asked, his tone casual but inviting.

The woman, clutching a plastic bag that bore the unmistakable red-and-white logo of Mr. Chan's Takeaway, blinked in surprise. For a moment, she seemed caught off guard, as though she hadn't expected anyone to talk to her. "Oh, um… yeah," she said, her voice soft but laced with a tired honesty. "You could definitely say that."

Max chuckled lightly, leaning forward a little as if to bridge the distance between them. "I get it. The city has this way of keeping you on your toes, doesn't it? Never a dull moment."

She glanced at him, her expression shifting into something gentler, less guarded. "No, it really doesn't stop. Sometimes… it's like it's too much, you know? Like it's going to swallow me whole."

"Absolutely," Max said with a nod, settling back into his chair like they'd been sharing late-night thoughts for years. "The endless grind, the noise, the people, don't even get me started on the pigeons. But hey," he added with a grin, "at least you've got excellent taste in takeaways. Mr. Chan's is the real deal."

Her lips curved into a soft laugh, one that made Max's chest feel warm in a way he wasn't entirely prepared for. "Oh, I couldn't agree more," she said, relaxing into the moment. "It's nice after a day like this. Some people have bubble baths. I have sweet and sour chicken."

Max raised an approving eyebrow. "A woman of refined taste, clearly. Sweet and sour, though? Risky move. I'm more of a chow mein loyalist myself."

That earned him a fuller laugh, the kind that crinkled her eyes at the corners. "Well, to each their own," she said. "I'm Stephanie, by the way."

"Max," he replied, offering her a small, polite nod. "Pleasure to meet you."

"Likewise," she said, brushing a stray lock of hair behind her ear. She hesitated for a moment, then smiled again, a little brighter this time, as if the weight of her day had lifted just a fraction.

Max returned the smile, resisting the almost instinctual urge to wag his tail. Old habits, he thought, died hard. Even in human form, he couldn't quite shake them. Instead, he simply leaned back and let the quiet comfort of the moment linger between them, feeling, for the first time in a long time, like he wasn't just a part of the city's chaos, he was a part of its stories.

Mr. Chan returned to the counter with Stephanie's order, placing the steaming container of sticky sweet chicken and rice into one of their red and white bags. He took her offered note and placed it in the till, handing her a small collection of coins to go with her bag of food "Here you go. Have a good night."

"Thanks," Stephanie said, taking the bag and offering Mr. Chan another small smile. She glanced back at Max, as if debating whether to say something more, but then seemed to think better of it. "Nice meeting you, Max. Have a good night."

"You too, Stephanie," Max replied, watching as she left the restaurant and disappeared into the night.

As the door swung shut behind her, Max couldn't help but feel a pang of curiosity. There was something about her, something that made him want to know more. But for now, he had work to do. He turned his attention back to his ledger, though he knew that his thoughts would keep drifting back to the red-haired woman who had just walked out of his life as quickly as she had entered it.

Chapter Four

Stephanie hugged the brown paper bag to her chest as she walked down the quiet street, the warmth of the food seeping through the bag and into her hands. It wasn't much, but it was enough to chase away the lingering chill of the night air. The streets were quieter now, the late-night rush of city life starting to wind down, but there was still a hum of energy that buzzed in the air, as if London itself was refusing to sleep.

She smiled to herself, replaying the brief conversation she'd had with the man at Mr. Chan's. Max, he had said his name was. There was something about him, a kind of easy charm that made her feel comfortable, even after their extremely brief encounter.

She wasn't used to that. Most of the time, Stephanie felt like she was stumbling her way through social interactions, trying not to trip over her own words or make a fool of herself. But that had felt… easy. Natural.

She shook her head, trying to brush off the thoughts. It had been a long day, and she was tired. That was all. Still, as she walked through the dimly lit streets, her thoughts began to drift back to her life and the tangled mess of work, home, and the ever-present feeling that something was missing.

Work. The very word made her shoulders tense. Castel and Fink wasn't the worst place in the world, she knew that much. She had friends who worked in even more stressful environments, some at firms where they were lucky to get a weekend off every few months. But still, something about her job at Castel and Fink just didn't sit right with her. Every day felt like an uphill battle, and no matter how much effort she put in, it never seemed to be enough. Alistair's endless demands, Amy's constant praise from him, the feeling of being overlooked, it all weighed on her, more than she cared to admit.

She had gone into law because she wanted to help people. She had dreamed of making a difference, of fighting for those who couldn't fight for themselves. But now? Now she spent most of her days buried in paperwork, managing endless deadlines, and navigating the minefield of office politics. There were moments, rare as they were, when she caught glimpses of why she had chosen this path in the first place. But they were fleeting, drowned out by the constant noise of day-to- day survival.

-

Stephanie let out a sigh as she passed a small park, the faint scent of damp earth and fallen leaves mixing with the night air. What was she even doing with her life? She wasn't miserable, exactly, but she wasn't happy either. She was stuck in this strange limbo, moving forward out of sheer momentum but with no real direction. It was as if she was waiting for something to happen, something that would shake her out of this monotony and give her a sense of purpose again.

And then there was Fiona. Stephanie's thoughts drifted to her best friend and current roommate, the whirlwind of energy who had swept into her life like a tornado and…hadn't left. Fiona had always been a force of nature, bold, confident, and utterly unapologetic about who she was. Stephanie admired that about her, even envied it sometimes. But lately, having Fiona around was starting to feel more like a burden than a blessing.

It wasn't that Stephanie didn't love her, she did, more than anyone else in the world. But living together had changed things. Fiona's spontaneity, her habit of disappearing for days on end, her carefree attitude, it all clashed with Stephanie's need for order and routine. Fiona was supposed to be getting back on her feet after her breakup with David, but instead, it felt like she was spiralling further out of control. She was always out late, always chasing the next thrill, while Stephanie was left behind to pick up the pieces, whether it was the dishes Fiona forgot to wash or the rent she sometimes forgot to pay on time.

Stephanie knew Fiona was hurting. David had been a nightmare, and their breakup had left scars that Fiona wasn't ready to face yet. But Stephanie couldn't help but feel like she was losing herself in the process of trying to hold Fiona together. She didn't know how much longer she could keep this up without completely burning out.

She turned a corner, her footsteps echoing off the cobblestone street, and her thoughts drifted to the one thing that had been nagging at the back of her mind for months now, the *something* missing in her life.

It wasn't just work, and it wasn't just Fiona. It was deeper than that, something that she couldn't quite put into words. There was a hollow space inside her, a place that longed for… *what*, exactly? Love? Maybe. Or perhaps it was something more abstract than that. A sense of belonging, of truly being seen by someone else and wanted for her. She wanted a connection; something that made her feel alive again.

But where was she supposed to find that? Between the demands of work, the responsibilities at home, and the ever-present weight of the past, she barely had time to think, let alone pursue something as nebulous as fulfilment. Yet, the longing was there, gnawing at her in quiet moments, reminding her that life was passing her by while she was too busy trying to keep everything together.

She sighed again, feeling the weight of it all pressing down on her shoulders. As she walked past a row of darkened shops, the familiar neon lights of a late-night convenience store flickered in the distance. Life in London moved so fast, always something happening, always something pulling you in a million different directions. But right now, all Stephanie wanted was a little peace, a moment to breathe.

She turned onto her street, the familiar sight of her building coming into view. The warm glow of the streetlights softened the edges of the world around her, making everything seem a little less harsh, a little more bearable. She could see the faint light coming from her apartment window like a lighthouse in the dark, but instead of warning of danger, it was instead a promise comfort and warmth.

As she reached the front door, she paused for a moment, taking in the quiet of the night. She didn't have all the answers, she didn't even have most of them or as it happens know what many of the questions were. But at least tonight, she had a warm meal and a cosy apartment waiting for her. It wasn't everything, but it was something. And for now, that would have to be enough.

Stephanie slipped her key into the lock, pushed the door open, and stepped inside, the comforting warmth of home wrapping around her like a familiar embrace. Tomorrow, she would face the chaos again, work, Fiona, and the endless search for that missing piece. But tonight, she allowed herself to simply exist in the quiet, content with the small comforts she could hold onto.

-

Max leaned back in his chair, stretching his arms above his head as he closed the ledger with a satisfied snap. Numbers didn't lie, and for that, he was grateful. In a world full of chaos, spread sheets were his sanctuary. He glanced over at Mr. Chan, who was busy dishing out a massive portion of curry and chips to a customer who looked like he'd just had the longest day of his life.

"Books are all squared up, Mr. Chan," Max said, sliding the ledger back across the counter. "Everything checks out, I would suggest a new supplier for your dry goods, the current one's pricing seems to be constantly on the rise."

Mr. Chan nodded, barely glancing at the ledger as he handed the customer his takeaway bag. "Good. Good. You always do good work, Max. Thank you."

Max grinned, knowing full well that Mr. Chan was more interested in efficiency than compliments. "Appreciate it. I'll take my payment now if I may."

Mr. Chan raised an eyebrow, wiping his hands on his apron as he plucked a handful of coins from the register and slid them into a small paper bag. "Always with the coins. You're a strange one, Max."

Max grinned. "They're dependable. No sudden crashes, no getting locked out of an account because you forgot your password, and definitely no awkward emails about suspicious activity. Plus," he added, holding up a coin and giving it a deliberate shake, "they make that lovely clinking sound. It's like music, but portable."

Mr. Chan stared at him, unimpressed. "Music, huh? What are you, a busker without a guitar?"

Max ignored the jab and held out his hand eagerly as Mr. Chan dropped the bag into his waiting palm. The weight of it made Max's grin widen. Coins were solid. Honest. The world could spin out of control, but a coin was always a coin.

"Strange man," Mr. Chan muttered, shaking his head. "You keep hoarding these coins like you're preparing for some sort of apocalyptic vending machine scenario."

"Maybe I am," Max replied with a wink, pocketing the bag. "Or maybe I just like the sound they make when they jingle. Can't say the same for those pigeons out there."

Mr. Chan cracked a number of eggs into a metal bowl and began to whisk furiously, the man could multitask like no other.

"Speaking of which, could I get a handful of bean sprouts? Just the sprouts, nothing else." Said Max.

Mr. Chan gave him a suspicious look. "Bean sprouts? You want me to cook them?"

"Nope," Max replied, casually leaning on the counter. "They drive the pigeons wild."

Mr. Chan paused, mid-scoop, and looked at Max as if he'd just sprouted a second head. "Pigeons? Bean sprouts drive pigeons wild? What kind of nonsense is this?"

Max grinned, shrugging. "You'd be surprised. Toss a handful of these into the middle of a pigeon gathering, and you'll see chaos like you've never seen before."

Mr. Chan shook his head, muttering something in Cantonese under his breath as he handed Max a small bag of bean sprouts. "Strange man," he repeated, this time with a bit more conviction. "Take your bean sprouts and go drive the pigeons crazy then. Just don't do it near my shop."

"Don't worry, I keep my pigeon-related activities far away from respectable establishments like yours," Max said, grabbing the bag and stuffing it into his coat pocket. "Thanks, Mr. Chan. I'll see you next week."

With a final wave, Max pushed open the door and stepped out into the night. The familiar hum of the city greeted him, a constant background noise that felt as much a part of him as his own heartbeat.

Chapter Five

Max wandered through the dimly lit streets, the bag of coins jingling in his pocket and the bean sprouts tucked away for later use. London was a vast, sprawling beast at night, with endless possibilities and no shortage of strange encounters. He loved this time of night when the city's pulse seemed to beat just for him.

As he made his way through the quiet streets, Max kept an eye out for his next target: pigeons. He had a bone to pick with them, though not literally. They were the bane of his daytime existence, arrogant, strutting around like they owned the place, always cooing like they were discussing something important when in reality, they were probably just gossiping about which statue to poop on next. He couldn't stand them, and yet, he couldn't resist messing with them when the opportunity arose. But recently he's noticed, a change, a change in their behaviour, he dismissed the thought.

Then, as if the universe had granted his wish, Max spotted them: a massive flock of pigeons gathered in a square, pecking away at crumbs left behind by late-night snackers. They were clustered around a bench, their feathers puffed up against the chill of the night, bobbing their heads in that infuriatingly smug way pigeons always seemed to do.

Max's grin widened as he reached into his pocket, pulling out the crumpled paper bag of bean sprouts. He gave it a gentle shake, the soft rustle of the sprouts inside enough to draw the attention of every pigeon in a three-meter radius. They turned their heads in that jerky, suspicious way pigeons do, their beady eyes locking onto him like tiny feathery missiles primed for launch. Max chuckled to himself. He'd told Mr. Chan the truth, these little green tendrils were pigeon kryptonite. For reasons known only to some cosmic prankster, pigeons absolutely adored the sight of them.

To a pigeon, bean sprouts were the holy grail of street snacks. The long, pale stems, the wiggly ends, they looked like the juiciest, most delectable worms that ever wriggled. Max could almost hear their little bird-brains screaming, *Look at those beauties! Fresh! Plump! Gourmet worms!* He tossed a handful of sprouts into the air, watching as the pigeons immediately descended upon them like frenzied shoppers at a Black Friday sale.

But then came the betrayal.

The first brave pigeon lunged forward, beak snapping up a sprout with all the enthusiasm of a diner at an all-you-can-eat buffet. It took a moment, and then, oh, the horror. Max could practically see the realization ripple through the bird's body as it froze mid-chew, its head jerking back in a motion that could only be described as a dramatic avian gag. The sprout, far from being the juicy worm of its dreams, was bitter, fibrous, and worst of all, tickly.

The pigeon tried to cough. It hacked. It spat. Well, it tried to spit, but pigeons can't spit, so it just stood there, flapping its wings in outrage, desperately attempting to dislodge the offending sprout from its throat. Another pigeon swooped in, undeterred by the first victim's obvious distress, and repeated the process. More gagging, more flapping. Soon the whole flock was in chaos, birds hopping and flailing about like they'd stumbled into a wasabi-eating contest.

Max leaned casually against a lamppost, thoroughly enjoying the spectacle. "Every time," he muttered to himself, shaking his head. "You'd think they'd learn."

But pigeons, for all their urban cunning, had the memory span of a bean sprout itself. By the time Max had strolled to the next corner, they were back at it, pecking and choking like this was some kind of bizarre endurance challenge. Max couldn't help but laugh as he turned to go, leaving the pigeons to sort out their life choices, and their throats.

Looking back the pigeons had stopped pecking, their feathers ruffled in indignation as they spat out the offending sprouts. Slowly, almost as if on cue, they turned their heads in unison to glare at Max. The murderous intent in their eyes was unmistakable. If looks could kill, Max would have been deep-fried and served with a side of chips by now.

Max simply smiled, unfazed by the avian death stares. "What?" he said with a shrug, his tone mockingly innocent. "You didn't like the healthy option?"

The pigeons continued to glare at him, their beaks twitching in what Max could only assume was pigeon fury. One particularly large pigeon at the front of the flock puffed up its chest, clearly preparing to lead an uprising against their enemy.

Max didn't flinch. Instead, he did what any reasonable man with a mischievous streak and no fear of pigeon retribution would do. He raised his hand, extended his middle finger, and gave the pigeons a cocky, unapologetic salute.

"Enjoy the sprouts," he called out with a laugh, before turning on his heel and striding away from the square.

Behind him, he could hear the furious cooing of the pigeons, but he knew they wouldn't follow. Pigeons were many things, persistent, annoying, and oddly smug, but they were also lazy. Revenge required effort, and Max was confident that within a few minutes, they'd go back to their usual routine of loitering and terrorizing statues and hapless late-night tourists.

Max chuckled to himself as he continued down the street, his footsteps echoing in the quiet. There was something deeply satisfying about messing with pigeons. It was the little victories in life that made the bigger struggles feel more bearable.

As he walked, his thoughts drifted back to the more cosmic questions that always seemed to creep into his mind during these late-night wanderings. The vastness of the universe, the infinity of it all, how small he was in the grand scheme of things. But tonight, he wasn't focusing on his usual philosophical musings. Tonight, he was content with the simple joys of life: a handful of bean sprouts, a bag of good food, and the knowledge that somewhere in London, a flock of pigeons was plotting his downfall.

As the echo of the pigeons' angry cooing faded into the distance, Max continued his journey through the city. London was a vast playground, full of hidden nooks and crannies, and Max knew them all. He had spent years exploring every inch of the city, both as a man and as a dog, finding places that most people overlooked. The thrill of discovery never faded, even after all this time.

Tonight, like so many other nights, Max found himself visiting his usual haunts. There was the narrow alley behind the old cinema, where the smell of popcorn lingered in the air long after the final screening. And the tiny courtyard hidden behind a row of terraced houses in Shoreditch, where Max often sat on the old stone bench, pondering the universe or just enjoying the quiet. But tonight, Max was on a different mission: tending to his secret stash of coins.

He'd been doing this for years, hiding coins all over London. Why coins Mr. Chan and others before had asked, why not notes? Coins didn't blow away in the wind or get easily stolen. They were heavy, bulky, and a bit annoying, but they were also incredibly easy to hide. The muckier the bag, the more people ignored it, and in a city where everyone was too busy to notice anything that didn't affect them directly, a carefully hidden bag of coins could go untouched for decades.

Max had no illusions about his strange habit. He knew that, realistically, he'd never be able to walk into a bank, open an account, and apply for a mortgage. There wasn't a box for "part-time dog, part-time accountant" on those forms, and he doubted they had any special policies for individuals with his unique… condition.

But he had a dream, and like all good dreams, it required some planning. He wanted his own home one day, a place he could call his own, where he wouldn't have to worry about transformations, late-night street sweepers, or people stealing his clothes. A house with a big bed, a cheese-filled fridge, a large gate and a warm fireplace. It wasn't a grand dream, but it was his, and that was enough.

And so, the coins. He'd been collecting them for years, stashing them in hidden corners of the city like a secret treasure. Behind loose bricks, under floorboards, tucked into forgotten crevices, he had coins all over London, waiting for the day when he could finally put them to use. It wasn't the most conventional savings plan, but it was the best he could do under the circumstances.

As he wandered the city, he occasionally slipped his hand into his pocket, pulling out a few of the coins Mr. Chan had given him. He glanced around, making sure no one was watching, and then casually bent down, tucking the a few pounds behind a loose brick in a nearby wall. It was a practiced motion; one he had repeated countless times over the years.

He knew every spot by heart. There was the loose panel in an old phone booth near Leicester Square where he'd stashed a bag of twenty-pound coins. And the gap between two paving stones near the Thames, where he'd hidden a handful of 50p's. There was even a particularly weathered poster for a long-forgotten concert covering an alcove in a dark alley, behind it lay a small plastic bag filled with pound coins, hidden so well that even he had trouble finding it sometimes.

Max didn't know how much he had saved by now, he had never counted. The idea of piling up all the coins and trying to tally them was overwhelming, and anyway, it wasn't about the exact amount. It was about the possibility. Maybe, just maybe, if he kept saving, one day he'd have enough to buy something, even if it wasn't the house of his dreams.

He chuckled to himself as he dropped another coin into a hiding spot behind a flowerpot outside an old café. *Who knows?* he thought. *Maybe I'll be the first dog in history to buy a house outright. No mortgage required.*

It was a ridiculous notion, but it made him smile. And in a life as unpredictable as his, a little bit of ridiculousness was necessary to keep going.

As the night wore on, Max made his way back to his usual sleeping spot, a quiet alley tucked away behind an old pub, shielded from the main road by a row of dumpsters. It wasn't glamorous, but it was safe, and that was all that mattered.

The sky was starting to lighten, the deep blue of the night slowly giving way to the pale grey of dawn. Max glanced up, watching as the first hints of sunlight began to creep over the rooftops. The transformation would come soon, he could feel it in his bones. It always started with a tingling sensation, a sort of hum that vibrated through his skin, signalling that his time as a man was coming to an end.

Max undressed quickly, folding his clothes neatly and tucking them into his usual hiding spot behind the dumpsters. He wasn't the type to leave things to chance, clothes were hard to come by when you spent half your life as a dog, and Max had learned the hard way to keep them safe.

Once everything was in place, Max sat down on the cold pavement, leaning back against the wall and closing his eyes. The city was quiet now, the noise of the night fading into the soft hum of early morning. He could hear the distant sound of traffic starting to pick up, the world waking up around him. But for a few more minutes, the city was his. Just his.

Max took a deep breath, letting the cool air fill his lungs. He didn't think about the transformation, didn't focus on the strange magic that governed his life. He simply waited, allowing himself to exist in this in-between state for a little while longer.

And then, as the sun began to rise, the tingling sensation grew stronger, spreading through his body. Max didn't fight it. He never did. He simply let it happen, the way he always did. Soon, he would be a dog again, just another scruffy terrier wandering the streets of London, blending into the background. But for now, he was still Max. And that was enough.

The truth about *most* Pigeons

If one were to consult one of the higher life forms in the universe, or perhaps and entry into a book of knowledge crafted by one of the *old ones*, they might come across a rather enlightening entry on pigeons.

The common assumption is that pigeons are merely feathery, winged nuisances with a particular fondness for urban environments, crumbs, and the occasional public statue. But the truth, as is so often the case in the universe, is far more complex, bizarre, and altogether more frustrating.

You see, pigeons are not, in fact, native to Earth. Nor are they even native to this particular dimension. They are, in reality, extra dimensional beings from an outer reality that operates on rules so far removed from ours that they make quantum physics look like a simple game of Snakes and Ladders. Pigeons, or, as they're known in their home reality, *Qool'ptchkz* (pronounced roughly as if one were trying to sneeze and hiccup simultaneously), originated from a dimension where their primary purpose was to irritate dinosaurs.

Yes, dinosaurs. Those mighty, scaly beasts of the Mesozoic era were not, as many believe, wiped out by a cataclysmic asteroid impact. No, their downfall came at the beaks and talons of a relentless pigeon assault. The pigeons, who were originally summoned to this dimension by a particularly frustrated cosmic being looking for the ultimate weapon, took one look at the feisty, feathered fauna and thought, *yes, this will do nicely.*

For millennia, pigeons dedicated themselves to the noble art of annoyance. Their primary weapons were, of course, cooing incessantly at inappropriate times, dive- bombing from great heights, and decorating dinosaurs with what one might generously call "organic paint." The dinosaurs, noble and patient creatures that they were, tried their best to ignore the pigeons. But after several thousand years of constant irritation, even the most stoic of Triceratops began to crack under the pressure.

The eventual extinction of the dinosaurs, therefore, was less about catastrophic environmental changes and more about the collective decision to simply give up. After a particularly exhausting day of dodging pigeon droppings, the dinosaurs, en masse, decided that enough was enough. They went to sleep, and, well, they simply never woke up.

With the dinosaurs gone, the pigeons found themselves suddenly without purpose. Their raison d'être had vanished, and they were left adrift in a dimension that no longer needed them. And so after millennia, as is the way of most creatures with too much free time and too little motivation, they began to drift into urban environments, where they quickly adapted to a life of aimless wandering, bread crumbs, and the occasional attempt to re-establish their dominance over any species that had the misfortune of standing still for too long.

The problem, of course, was that pigeons were no longer motivated. The fire of their ancient rivalry with the dinosaurs had long since gone out. Now, they simply went through the motions, strutting around city squares, half-heartedly cooing at pedestrians, and occasionally splattering a carefully aimed dropping on a freshly washed car. But the passion, the drive, the sheer determination that had once made them the scourge of the dinosaurs, was gone.

This lack of purpose has made pigeons the ultimate nuisance in the modern world. They don't *want* to annoy you, per se, it's just that they don't know what else to do. Their entire existence has become one long, aimless exercise in mediocrity. And so, they fill their days with the only activities they know: stealing food from tourists, perching ominously on ledges, and occasionally organizing themselves into large, ominous flocks that seem to be planning something sinister, but in reality are just trying to remember why they gathered in the first place.

Every now and then, a particularly ambitious pigeon will attempt to rekindle the ancient fire that once drove their species to greatness. These pigeons are the ones you see dive-bombing street performers, stealing sandwiches from the hands of distracted office workers, or staring down pedestrians with an intensity that suggests they're planning something far more complex than they actually are. But even these ambitious pigeons eventually tire of their futile efforts and resign themselves to the monotonous life of the average urban pigeon.

And so, the pigeons continue to exist in a state of eternal apathy, trapped in a dimension they didn't choose, half-heartedly trying to recapture the glory days of annoying beings far larger and far more dangerous than the average human. They remain a persistent, mildly irritating presence in cities across the world, forever driven by a vague, lingering sense that they should be doing something important… but never quite able to remember what that something was.

If you ever find yourself face to face with a pigeon that seems to be staring at you with unsettling intensity, know this: it is not plotting your demise. It is simply reminiscing about a time long past, when its ancestors waged war against mighty dinosaurs and creatures from beyond. And perhaps, just perhaps, it is wondering if it will ever feel that sense of purpose again.

But until then, it will settle for your sandwich.

Chapter Six

Stephanie was not a morning person. This was a fact she had come to accept long ago, somewhere between her first university all-nighter and her first real job that required her to show up at the ungodly hour of 8:30 AM. But today, as her alarm blared its usual obnoxious tune, she felt a particular reluctance to get out of bed. It wasn't just the typical dread of another day at Castel and Fink; it was something more, something heavier that seemed to press down on her chest as she lay there, staring at the ceiling.

She couldn't shake the feeling that she was stuck in a loop, wake up, work, come home, sleep, repeat. The weekend parties and fleeting dates with Fiona's friends felt like they belonged to someone else's life. Somewhere along the way, she had lost track of her own dreams, and now she was just going through the motions.

With a sigh, she rolled out of bed and shuffled into the bathroom, where she splashed cold water on her face in a futile attempt to wake up. The reflection staring back at her in the mirror looked tired, tired but determined. She couldn't afford to let herself wallow in self-pity, not when there were deadlines to meet and clients to appease. She would just have to power through it, as always.

Fiona was still asleep when Stephanie made her way to the kitchen, her hair a tangled mess on the pillow as she snored softly. Stephanie smiled fondly at the sight. Despite the occasional frustration of living together, Fiona was still her best friend, and seeing her so at peace, if only in sleep, made Stephanie's morning a little brighter.

Oliver, her cat, greeted her with a loud meow as she entered the kitchen. He was already perched on the counter, his green eyes wide with expectation. Stephanie shook her head, smiling despite herself. "Yes, yes, I know. Breakfast first."

She opened a can of cat food, the familiar sound causing Oliver to chirp with excitement as she poured it into his dish. He immediately dove in, his purring vibrating through the small kitchen as he ate.

Stephanie reached for the kettle and filled it with water, setting it on the hob to boil, everyone used electric, but there was something ritualistic about popping an old kettle on the stove. She'd always preferred the slow, deliberate act of making tea over the rush of coffee. There was something soothing about the ritual, the way the water heated, the tea steeped, and the steam curled lazily upward. It was one of the few moments of calm in her otherwise chaotic life.

As she waited for the water to boil, Stephanie's mind wandered back to the previous night. The conversation with Max at the Chinese takeaway lingered in her thoughts longer than she expected. There had been something about him, something easy, comfortable. He didn't seem like the kind of guy who took life too seriously, which was refreshing, considering how many people she knew who seemed to wear their stress like a badge of honour.

"Max," she said softly to herself, rolling the name around in her mind. It was a good name. Solid. Uncomplicated. Unlike most of the things in her life.

The kettle whistled, abruptly snapping her out of her thoughts. She reached down to turn off the knob on the hob, listening as the shrill whistle slowed, then faded into silence.

Crossing to one of her shelves, she opened one of the neatly labelled jars and searched for just the right tea. Something soothing. After a moment, she smiled and selected a fragrant blend of chamomile and mint.

Carefully, she spooned the loose leaves into an antique, ball-shaped tea infuser she had found at a local vintage shop. Its tarnished surface hinted at stories of many cups brewed before hers. She lowered it into her favourite cup, watching as the water swirled around it, the deepening amber wake following each movement.

Steam curled lazily into the air as she gave the tea time to steep. Finally, she took a sip, letting the warmth spread through her like a soft blanket. For a brief moment, she allowed herself to sink into the stillness, savouring this small act of comfort.

But the moment didn't last long. There was always something that needed doing, always another task waiting for her attention. As she gathered her things for the day, her phone buzzed on the counter, pulling her back into the reality she had tried to escape for a few minutes.

It was a message from Alistair, of course. She didn't need to open it to know what it said, something about needing a report by noon, or making sure a client was prepped for their meeting. It was always the same, and somehow, it always managed to feel urgent, even when it wasn't.

Stephanie sighed, pocketing her phone and glancing back at Fiona, who was still snoring softly in the spare bedroom. She envied her friend's ability to sleep through the morning, to wake up whenever she felt like it, and to live her life without the weight of a demanding job pressing down on her. But Stephanie knew she couldn't live like that. She had responsibilities, goals, things she had to achieve if she wanted to make something of herself.

And yet, that nagging feeling of something missing refused to go away.

With one last glance around the apartment, Stephanie grabbed her handbag and headed out the door. The morning air gave a gentle chill against her skin, a subtle reminder that autumn was just around the corner. The streets were already busy, filled with people hurrying to work, students rushing to class, and tourists looking slightly lost as they tried to navigate the city. It was the same as every other morning, and yet today, something felt different.

As she made her way to the tube station, Stephanie found herself thinking about Max again. She wondered what he did during the day, where he worked, and whether he lived nearby. It was strange, she barely knew him, and yet she couldn't stop herself from wondering about his life. Maybe it was because he seemed so at ease, so unburdened by the kind of worries that weighed her down.

Or maybe it was because, for the first time in a long time, talking to someone hadn't felt like a chore. It had felt… natural. Why was she thinking about a man whom she had said a total of ten words to?

The sound of the approaching train pulled her from her thoughts, and Stephanie stepped onto the platform, joining the crowd of commuters waiting to be whisked away to their various destinations. As the train pulled into the station and the doors slid open, she filed inside with the others, finding a spot by the window where she could watch the city pass by in a blur of motion.

Today would be just like any other day, she told herself. But deep down, she couldn't shake the feeling that something was about to change, no, it needed to change.

The tube hurtled through the dark tunnels beneath the city, and Stephanie found herself staring out of the window at the occasional flashes of dimly lit stations, though her mind was elsewhere. The early morning commute always had a way of making her feel small, just another anonymous face in the sea of commuters, all crammed together yet utterly disconnected from one another. The hum of the train and the soft rustle of newspapers created a strange kind of background noise that made it easy for her mind to wander.

She thought about the day ahead, more meetings, more deadlines, more of Alistair's condescending remarks. The thought of it all made her stomach twist, and she found herself questioning, not for the first time, if this was really what she wanted. When she had started out in law, she had pictured herself making a difference, helping people, and standing up for those who couldn't fight for themselves. But that dream had been buried under piles of paperwork and endless phone calls, until now it felt like a distant memory.

It wasn't that she hated her job, exactly. It was just... draining. Soul-sucking, even. Every day felt like a battle against a tide that kept coming, no matter how hard she pushed back. And then there was Amy, always so put together, always so perfect in Alistair's eyes. It didn't matter how much work Stephanie did, Amy always seemed to get the credit, and it gnawed at her.

The train lurched slightly as it pulled into the next station, and Stephanie snapped out of her thoughts just in time to avoid getting jostled by a man with a large backpack who was trying to squeeze past her. She offered him a polite smile, but he didn't even notice, too busy staring at his phone, scrolling through whatever was demanding his attention at that particular moment.

As the doors slid shut and the train began to move again, Stephanie found herself thinking about Max. It was odd, she barely knew him, and yet there was something about him that she couldn't shake. He seemed so carefree, so at ease with himself and the world around him. It was refreshing, and in a way, it made her feel a little more hopeful about her own life.

Maybe it's just because he was kind, she thought. *It's rare enough to meet someone who's genuinely kind, especially in this city.*

She tried to push the thought of Max out of her mind, but it kept creeping back in, like a song she couldn't quite forget the lyrics to. As the train sped through the tunnels, she wondered if she would ever see him again. London was a big city, after all, and it wasn't as if she could just walk into Mr. Chan's every night, hoping to run into him.

But it wouldn't hurt to pop in again sometime, a small voice in her mind suggested. *Just for the chow mein, of course.*

Stephanie smiled to herself, feeling a little silly for getting so wrapped up in thoughts of a man she'd met only once. Still, it was nice to have something to look forward to, even if it was just the possibility of a chance encounter.

The train finally pulled into her stop, and Stephanie joined the throng of people exiting the carriage. As she made her way up the escalator and into the bustling street above, the familiar rhythm of the city began to take over. She blended into the crowd, becoming just another face in the sea of busy Londoners rushing to work.

-

"Shit, oh shit, oh shit!" Max barked in his small terrier voice as he bolted down the street, his paws barely skimming the pavement. He sprinted through the bustling market square, weaving between stalls and startled shoppers.

Behind him, the furious shouts of a man echoed through the air. "Stop that dog! Someone stop him!"

Max didn't dare look back. He could still feel the sharp

tug of the man's hand trying to snatch him up. What had he even done wrong? He was just following his nose, and his nose had led him to the most glorious roast chicken sitting unattended on a picnic blanket. How was he supposed to know it was part of someone's prized market display for "artisanal photography"? A chicken left out in the open was practically begging to be claimed.

"To be fair," Max muttered under his breath as he dodged a fruit stand, sending a cascade of oranges to the ground, "they're the ones leaving food around like bait."

The man chasing him clearly didn't see it that way. "You little thief!" he roared, his footsteps pounding closer.

Max darted between two women laden with shopping bags, narrowly avoiding a basket of tomatoes. He glanced over his shoulder for just a second, catching sight of the man, who was now waving his camera strap like a battle flag.

"Great," Max panted. "I'm being hunted by the world's angriest food blogger."

The fish market was just ahead. If he could make it there, he might have a chance to lose his pursuer. The market was always noisy and chaotic, a perfect maze for a dog with nimble paws and an eye for opportunity. And Roger was usually hanging around there, too. If anyone knew how to outsmart a human, it was Roger.

"Hold on, buddy," Max muttered to himself as he dashed past a fishmonger yelling about fresh mackerel. "We're almost home free."

He just hoped Roger was in the mood to help, and not busy stealing someone else's lunch.

Max skidded around the corner and dashed into the market, his nose assaulted by the overwhelming smell of fish, saltwater, and wet wood. He slowed his pace slightly, weaving between the stalls as he searched for his feathered friend. But as he trotted through the market, his heart still racing from the chase, he realized something was wrong.

Roger wasn't there.

Max came to a halt in the middle of the bustling market, his sharp eyes darting upward toward the familiar wooden beams that stretched across the fishmonger's stall. That was Roger's spot. At this time every day, like clockwork, the obnoxious seagull would be perched there, his beady eyes scanning for unattended fish or distracted vendors. His wings would twitch every so often, ready for the perfect moment to swoop down and make off with his prize. But today, the perch was empty.

No loud caws, no flapping of wings, no snide remarks about Max's less-than-impressive stature or his tendency to get caught up in ridiculous escapades. The absence was almost louder than the market's usual chaos.

"Where the hell is he?" Max muttered, his tail twitching anxiously behind him. He glanced around the market, hoping to catch sight of Roger's tell-tale white feathers and smug grin. But the only birds in sight were the usual cluster of pigeons, lazily pecking at discarded crumbs near the edge of a vegetable stall. They barely flinched when a barrel was rolled past, too engrossed in their feast to care about the hustle and bustle around them.

Max's ears flattened as he let out a frustrated growl. This day was rapidly sliding from bad to worse. He'd already been chased halfway across the city by an overzealous foodie with an inflated sense of justice, been kicked not once but *twice* by an irate woman, and narrowly avoided getting squashed by a careless pedestrian. And now, of all times, Roger, the one creature in the city who somehow managed to be both his partner in crime and his most exasperating critic, was nowhere to be found.

"Typical," Max grumbled, weaving his way through the market stalls. "Of all the days to pull a disappearing act..."

The air was thick with the mingling scents of seafood, spices, and the occasional waft of something roasting from a vendor down the street. Max's nose twitched as he tried to pick out Roger's distinct fishy odour amidst the sensory overload. Nothing. Just haddock, mackerel, and a particularly aggressive pile of prawns that smelled like they'd been sitting out for a bit too long.

"Oi! Keep away from the fish, ya mangy mutt!"

The booming voice of a burly fishmonger cut through the market noise. The man, all grizzled beard and beefy arms, waved a filleting knife at Max as he passed.

Max barely spared him a glance. He had bigger problems than a cranky fish vendor today. Roger had a habit of getting himself into trouble, usually the kind that involved dive-bombing tourists for their sandwiches or picking fights with larger birds who weren't inclined to back down. Max had lost count of how many times he'd had to intervene, dragging Roger out of yet another ridiculous situation. But today felt different. The seagull wasn't just in trouble; he was outright missing.

Max's ears twitched as the distant cry of a newspaper seller cut through the chatter of the crowd.

"Earthquake in Peru! Thousands dead! Read all about it!"

The words hung in the air, momentarily pulling Max out of his search. He stopped, his paws frozen on the cobblestones, and tilted his head toward the sound. The sharpness of the announcement felt jarring against the backdrop of the market's usual cacophony. He shook it off, forcing himself to focus.

"Not my problem," he muttered under his breath. The world was full of tragedies far beyond his control. He couldn't even keep track of one loud-mouthed seagull; he wasn't about to start worrying about global disasters.

Ducking under a cart loaded with crates of oranges, Max pressed on, sniffing the air with renewed determination. The longer Roger stayed missing, the more uneasy Max felt. Roger might be infuriating, but he was reliable in his own strange way. Every day, at precisely this time, he would show up at the market, ready to cause mayhem. The fact that he wasn't here now meant something was wrong.

Max's thoughts swirled as he pushed past a group of children giggling over a comic that they were reading. What if Roger had gotten himself into something he couldn't squawk his way out of? What if he'd tangled with the wrong group of pigeons, or worse, a hawk? Roger's bravado was unmatched, but his common sense was, well... let's just say it was on the light side.

"C'mon, Roger," Max muttered, his voice tinged with irritation and worry. "You're not allowed to just disappear. You've got a reputation to uphold, remember?"

The pigeons near the vegetable stall barely acknowledged him as he passed, pecking away with single-minded focus. For a brief moment, Max considered asking them if they'd seen Roger. Then he shook his head. No point. They'd just ignore him or, worse, pretend they didn't understand. Pigeons were always playing dumb, but Max knew better.

The market stretched out before him, alive with the clatter of pots, the hum of haggling voices, and the occasional bark of a street dog trying its luck near the food stalls. But to Max, it all felt strangely empty without Roger's familiar presence. He didn't like to admit it, but the seagull's absence left a void.

As he darted past a stall selling roasted peanuts, Max's nose caught a faint whiff of something familiar. Fish? No, not just fish, Roger's *particular* fishy smell, mixed with that odd tang of salt and mischief that always seemed to follow him.

Max's ears perked up. "Gotcha," he murmured, his tail giving a quick wag. If Roger was anywhere nearby, Max was going to find him, and then, of course, he was going to give that bird an earful. Not because Roger had done anything particularly wrong (this time, at least), but because it was Roger, and that's just what they did. A good-natured squabble here, a sarcastic jab there, it was practically their love language.

As he trotted toward an old and faint whiff of Roger's unmistakable fishy scent, Max let his mind wander, the way it often did when things got quiet. He'd never been able to recall exactly where or how he'd first met Roger. Maybe it had been near the docks, or during one of his escapades in the park. He liked to imagine it was something dramatic, like saving Roger from a particularly angry cat or rescuing him from a seagull- sized net. But no matter how hard he tried to pin down the memory, it always slipped away like a soap bubble bursting in the wind.

And yet, there was a connection, a bond that felt far older than any single meeting could explain. It wasn't just that they looked out for each other (in their own peculiar, bickering way); it was something deeper, something Max couldn't quite put into words. Sometimes, when Roger perched nearby and they both fell into an uncharacteristic silence, Max would get this strange, almost haunting feeling. Like they'd been doing this, this odd dance of partnership and mischief, for far longer than either of them could possibly remember.

Max shook his head, trying to dislodge the thought. "Getting sentimental," he muttered to himself. "Next thing you know, I'll be writing him a thank-you note for all those times he stole my lunch."

Still, the feeling lingered, warm and inexplicable, as he sniffed his way through the market. He had no doubt he'd find Roger soon, because, really, that was how it always worked. Roger would appear, full of smug commentary and bad jokes, and Max would roll his eyes (figuratively, of course, dogs weren't great at that) and grumble   about how   much   trouble   the   seagull   had caused. And then they'd carry on as they always did, because that was their thing.

It wasn't about the trouble or the teasing. It was about something Max couldn't quite name, something that made him feel like he wasn't alone in the vast, chaotic swirl of the city. And for a scrappy terrier who'd seen more of life's twists and turns than he cared to count, that meant everything.

Chapter Seven

Stephanie stood in the middle of the office kitchen, clutching a crumpled sheet of paper covered in hasty scribbles, the evidence of what had started as a simple task. "Can you grab lunch for us?" someone had asked, a seemingly innocent question that, like a harmless snowball rolling downhill, had grown into an avalanche of orders from every corner of the office.

It began with Amy, who barely glanced up from her monitor before rattling off her request. "Don't forget the sushi from Sato's! And I want extra wasabi." Her tone implied that the fate of the entire department hinged on her spicy condiment.

Then came Alistair, ever the connoisseur of complications. "Oh, could you swing by that vegan place? I'll have the quinoa bowl with the turmeric cold-pressed juice. They only make it fresh in the afternoons, so don't be late." His voice carried the gravity of someone who believed that missing the juice window might cause the collapse of civilization.

From there, the list had snowballed. Carl wanted a burger from Big Al's. Karen insisted on a salad from the Mediterranean spot. Amy's interns piped up with requests for overpriced smoothies from the health food café. And every time Stephanie thought she'd wrangled the last order, another colleague popped up like a human Whack-A-Mole to add another item.

Now, standing in the fluorescent-lit kitchen, Stephanie looked down at the chaos of orders scribbled in every direction. It was a logistical nightmare, and she wasn't even out the door yet. Her stomach growled, a harsh reminder that in the flurry of everyone else's demands, she hadn't even had a chance to think about her own lunch.

"Alright, everyone!" Stephanie called out, trying to sound more cheerful than she felt. "I'm heading out now to grab everything. Back in... hopefully less than an hour!"

As she turned to leave, the office chatter continued unabated, her colleagues entirely oblivious to the fact that she was about to embark on what felt less like a lunch run and more like an endurance sport. With a resigned sigh, she stuffed the list into her bag, braced herself for the chaos of the city streets, and wondered, not for the first time, why she had agreed to this in the first place.

Her co-workers barely glanced up from their desks, most of them waving her off with distracted murmurs of thanks as she shuffled toward the elevator. As the doors closed behind her, Stephanie let out a sigh of relief. At least in the elevator, she could take a breather.

But her reprieve was short-lived. As soon as she stepped out onto the street, the chaos of London greeted her with open arms. The lunchtime rush was in full swing, with people spilling out of offices and shops, all of them in search of food, coffee, or a momentary escape from their daily grind.

Stephanie squared her shoulders and tightened her grip on her bags. She had ten different restaurants to hit in less than an hour, no small feat in a city as sprawling and congested as London. She made a mental map in her head, plotting out the fastest route to each location, and then set off at a brisk pace.

First stop: Sato's sushi bar, where Amy's extra-wasabi order was waiting. The tiny shop was packed with people, and Stephanie had to squeeze her way to the counter, narrowly avoiding being elbowed in the face by a man waving his credit card.

"Order for Stephanie!" she called out over the noise.

A harried-looking server handed her a neatly packed bag of sushi, and Stephanie thanked him before pushing her way back through the crowd and out into the street. One order down, nine to go.

Next, she dashed over to the Mediterranean spot for Karen's salad. She had just grabbed the takeout bag when her phone buzzed with a message from Alistair.

Make sure the juice is cold, the text read. *No room-temperature juice.*

Stephanie rolled her eyes as she shoved her phone back into her bag. "No pressure," she muttered to herself, weaving through the lunchtime crowd as she headed toward the next restaurant on her list.

By the time she reached the health food café for the interns' smoothies, Stephanie was starting to feel the strain. Her arms were loaded with bags, and the weight of it all was beginning to make her shoulders ache. She had to balance two bags in one hand while grabbing the smoothies with the other, all while trying to avoid bumping into the endless stream of people on the sidewalk.

"Why the hell am I getting lunch for the interns!" She thought to herself, a little anger creeping into her thoughts.

Just as Stephanie exited the café, carefully balancing three precarious smoothies in one hand, a sudden blur of motion caught her attention. A small, scruffy brown- and-white terrier came careening around the corner ahead of her, its paws skidding comically on the pavement as it made a sharp, frantic turn.

The dog was moving at breakneck speed, weaving through the legs of unsuspecting pedestrians like an urban slalom champion.

She stopped mid-step, her attention completely captured. The terrier briefly paused near a lamppost, glancing back the way it had come, a voice shouting behind him. For a split second, Stephanie could have sworn it looked right at her. Then, it happened. The dog winked. Or at least, she thought it did.

"Did that dog just... wink at me?" she muttered aloud, her voice barely audible over the hum of the street.

A couple of passers-by gave her curious glances, but she

barely noticed them. Her brain was already spiralling into overdrive, trying to process what she'd just seen. Was it possible? Dogs didn't wink… did they? And yet, there was something about the way it had looked at her, something oddly familiar, like a face you couldn't quite place.

Before she could dwell on it, the terrier darted off again, disappearing around another corner and vanishing into the crowd like a ghost. Stephanie blinked, the weight of the smoothies in her hand dragging her back to reality.

"Right," she muttered, shaking her head as if to clear it. "I'm officially losing it. It's just a dog, Steph. Dogs don't wink."

Still, as she turned her attention back to the task at hand, namely, not spilling three expensive drinks all over the sidewalk, her thoughts kept drifting back to the little terrier. There was something about it, something that tugged at the edges of her memory like a thread waiting to unravel.

By the time she collected the final order, a vegan bowl so complicated it might as well have been a science project, her arms were trembling from the effort, and her patience was hanging by a thread. All she wanted was to get everything back to the office in one piece and be done with this ridiculous errand.

But as she hurried down the street, dodging pedestrians and silently cursing the uneven pavement, the image of that dog lingered in her mind. It wasn't just its scruffy charm or the absurd wink, it was something deeper. Something that felt like it mattered, even if she couldn't say why.

"Get a grip, Stephanie," she told herself. "You've got deadlines, co-workers waiting for overpriced lunches, and no time to obsess over strange dogs."

With one final burst of energy, Stephanie made it back to the office, balancing the bags and containers as she pushed open the door with her elbow. The sight of her co-workers casually chatting and sipping their coffees made her want to scream, but she swallowed her frustration and forced a smile instead.

"Lunch is served!" she announced, dropping the bags onto the nearest table with a triumphant sigh.

Her co-workers descended on the food like a pack of hungry wolves, barely muttering thanks as they grabbed their orders and retreated back to their desks. Stephanie stood there for a moment, watching them all, before finally retreating to her own desk with the last untouched bag, a simple sandwich she had picked up for herself.

As she unwrapped her lunch, her mind wandered back to the terrier she had seen. There was something about that dog... something that felt important, even if she didn't know why.

Maybe it's just the stress, she thought, taking a bite of her sandwich. *I've been running around all day. I'm probably just imagining things.*

But deep down, she couldn't shake the feeling that the little brown and white dog wasn't just any ordinary dog. And something told her she hadn't seen the last of it.

Max limped down the alleyway, his once-proud terrier strut reduced to a defeated shuffle. His fur was matted with grime from the day's misadventures, and his body ached from head to tail. It had been one of *those* days, the kind where everything seemed to go wrong, and by the time it was over, all you could do was collapse in a heap and hope tomorrow would be better.

As he rounded the corner, the familiar scent of the alley behind the old pub drifted toward him. Normally, the smell of stale beer and rotting garbage wasn't something to look forward to, but tonight, it felt like a welcoming embrace. This alley was his haven, his safe spot, at least, until evening came.

Max padded over to his usual spot behind the dumpsters, wincing as a sharp pain shot through his paw. He'd stepped on something earlier, probably a broken bottle or a rogue bit of glass, and now every step was a reminder of how spectacularly terrible his day had been.

He slumped down onto the pavement with a heavy sigh, resting his head on his paws. The chaos of the day replayed in his mind: the blanket couple who hadn't appreciated his interest in their non-picnic activities, the angry shouts, the kicks, and the cigarette butt he had somehow managed to step on. And to top it off, Roger was nowhere to be found.

His usual companion, the obnoxious seagull, had been missing for most of the day, leaving Max to navigate the city's madness alone. It was typical, really. When things got tough, Roger had a way of disappearing, probably off somewhere bothering some poor soul for fish.

"Just my luck," Max muttered to himself as he rested his tired body against the cold, hard pavement. "This day couldn't end soon enough."

But despite the aches and pains, there was something to look forward to. Tonight wasn't just any night, it was one of the nights he worked at *The Raj of Persia*, his favourite restaurant. They served the kind of Dal that could soothe even the weariest soul, thick, spiced, and so full of flavour it felt like a warm hug in a bowl. Just thinking about it made Max's tail, or rather what would soon *not* be a tail, twitch with anticipation.

The transformation was still a few hours away, but Max could already feel the familiar tingling in his bones, the slow, unmistakable build-up of energy that signalled the shift from dog to man. Or, as he liked to think of it, *from Max to Max*. Becoming human again wasn't without its own set of headaches, but it had its perks, two hands, for one, and the ability to enjoy a proper meal without having to eat it off the ground.

Then there was *The Raj*. It wasn't just about the food, though that was reason enough to keep going back. The owners were good people, the kind who didn't pry or make assumptions. They didn't need to know why Max only worked the night shift, and he didn't need to explain. That unspoken understanding made them *decent folk* in his book, and Max had come to cherish people like that.

He couldn't put his paw, or hand, soon enough, on why, but Max just knew he'd dealt with enough bad people in his time. He couldn't remember the details, but the feeling stuck, like an old scar that aches in the rain. Cruelty, greed, deception, he'd seen it, felt it, endured it, and it had left its mark. But *decent people*? They stood out like stars in a cloudy sky. They didn't want anything more than what you could give in the moment, and they treated you with respect. People like that were rare, and when Max found them, he stuck around.

His thoughts drifted to the warm, comforting aroma of spiced lentils and the soft, golden naan that came fresh out of the tandoor. Being human again meant indulging in those simple pleasures, food, conversation, the ability to sit at a table instead of under it. He stretched out on the pavement, trying to ease the tension in his tired muscles.

The sun had dipped below the horizon, painting the sky in soft purples and pinks as the city shifted into its evening rhythm. The streets were still busy, but there was a different energy now, slower, calmer, the kind of energy Max found soothing after the chaos of the day.

"Just a little longer," Max muttered to himself, closing his eyes and letting the city's sounds wash over him. The distant rumble of traffic, the chatter of people heading home, the rustle of the wind through the alley, all of it blended into a background hum that felt almost meditative. The aches of the day melted away, replaced by a quiet anticipation for what the night would bring.

Soon, he'd be on two legs again, navigating the night as a man instead of a dog. It would be a different kind of chaos, but at least it would come with a change of perspective, and a delicious meal. Max couldn't wait.

As the sky began to darkened and the sun began its journey into the dark, Max closed his eyes, letting the sounds of the city lull him into a light sleep. The transformation was coming, but until then, he'd take whatever peace he could find. Even if it was in the middle of a dirty alley, bruised and battered from the day's adventures, Max knew that tonight would be better. And that was enough to keep him going.

Because no matter how tough the day had been, there was always the promise of something good around the corner. And for Max, tonight, that something was a hot bowl of dal and the quiet satisfaction of working at a place where, for a few hours, he could just be himself, play with numbers and of course earn a few coins.

Chapter Eight

The rest of Stephanie's day unfolded exactly as she'd predicted: an endless parade of meetings that could have been emails, emails that could have been ignored, and a mounting pile of unreasonable demands from Alistair, whose concept of deadlines seemed to exist in an entirely different reality from everyone else's.

By mid-afternoon, Alistair returned from a long, boozy lunch with one of their more obnoxious clients. They both smelled faintly of stale alcohol and overpriced cologne, a combination that wafted through the office like a warning siren. Settling into Alistair's office, they began a conversation that was both overly loud and entirely self-congratulatory, punctuated by bursts of laughter that were designed to make sure the rest of the office knew how much fun they were having.

From the snippets Stephanie could hear, the conversation seemed to consist mainly of inside jokes and exaggerated anecdotes, each man outdoing the other with increasingly absurd tales of their own brilliance. The effect was like a pair of peacocks trying to out- preen each other, their booming voices carrying through the thin walls and solidifying in everyone's minds the very impression they were clearly desperate to cultivate: that they were not only the funniest people alive but also the most important.

Stephanie sighed and turned back to her computer, tuning them out as best she could. She'd learned long ago that attempting to reason with Alistair, especially post-lunch-Alistair, was as productive as arguing with a hurricane. Best to keep her head down, meet the latest absurd deadline, and wait for the inevitable lull when he retreated to his office sofa for his late-afternoon "power nap."

She glanced at the clock. Three more hours to go. It was going to be a long day.

Stephanie sat at her desk, her eyes tired from hours of staring at her computer screen, sifting through the endless stream of emails that had piled up over the past few days. She had just finished replying to a particularly tedious message when she noticed a new email notification pop up in the corner of her screen. The subject line caught her attention: "Shipping Confirmation: Puma."

Her brow furrowed as she clicked on the email, her curiosity piqued. The email wasn't addressed to her, it seemed to have been forwarded accidentally by Alistair. The message contained a series of shipping details, various dockets, and logistical information, all centred around the transport of a live puma. Her breath caught as she scrolled through the email, her mind racing to make sense of it.

The shipment was scheduled to arrive in the next few days, and the documents included a detailed breakdown of the animal's care requirements, customs forms, and even a list of permits, most of which seemed highly questionable, if not outright illegal. Stephanie's heart began to race. Why would Alistair be involved in something like this? And how on earth had this ended up in her inbox?

Before she could process any further, the door to Alistair's office swung open, and he strode out, one of his top clients who Stephanie remembered as a Mr. Marchand being politely escorted out of the offices with the utmost of grace

Returning to where Stephanie sat a with a broad smile plastered across his face. Alistair looked more than pleased with himself, practically glowing with self-satisfaction as he adjusted the sleeve of his suit jacket, revealing a sleek, new watch on his wrist.

Stephanie quickly minimized the email, her mind whirling as she tried to compose herself. "Afternoon, Alistair," she greeted him, trying to keep her voice steady. "You look like you've had a good day."

Alistair's grin widened as he sauntered over to her desk, casually resting a hand on the back of her chair. "Ah, Stephanie, you wouldn't believe it. Just got back from the most delightful lunch appointment with Mr Merchand. Picked up this beauty," he said, holding up his wrist to showcase the watch. The light caught the face of the timepiece, making it gleam.

She forced a smile, though her thoughts were still tangled around the email she had just read. "It's a very handsome watch," she said, trying to sound genuinely interested.

Alistair's eyes lit up, clearly eager to share. "This, my dear, is a Patek Philippe. One of very few in the world. It's not just a watch; it's a statement, exquisite craftsmanship, a testament to everything I value. It's a piece of art."

Stephanie nodded; her mind still half-focused on the troubling email. But something in Alistair's tone, or perhaps the smug satisfaction in his eyes, compelled her to probe just a little deeper. "It's beautiful, Alistair. Must've cost a small fortune."

For a brief moment, something dark flickered across Alistair's expression. His ever-present smile faltered, and his eyes narrowed, just enough to send a chill through the air. When he spoke again, the warmth in his tone was gone, replaced by something cold and sharp. "It's not about money, Stephanie," he said, his voice clipped. "It's about power. Influence. Having something others can't. When I look at my wrist, I see the culmination of centuries of craftsmanship, something most people wouldn't even dare dream of possessing."

Stephanie blinked, taken aback by the sudden shift in his demeanour. "Of course, Alistair," she replied cautiously, sensing she'd stepped onto dangerous ground. "I didn't mean, "

But he cut her off, his voice rising, tinged with a surprising edge of anger. "It's not just a watch!" he snapped, leaning forward slightly, his eyes locking onto hers with unsettling intensity. "Do you think something like this just happens? That anyone can walk into a store and get one of these? It's a symbol, Stephanie. A symbol of everything I've worked for. Everything I've *earned*."

Her heart skipped a beat, and a cold shiver ran down her spine. Alistair's outburst was as shocking as it was disproportionate. He wasn't just angry, he was consumed, his words heavy with a kind of passion she'd never seen from him before. She'd joked, or maybe just commented, on his expensive taste in watches, but somehow, it had ignited something far deeper, something unhinged.

"Alistair," she said carefully, her voice soft and even as if speaking to a skittish animal. "I didn't mean to undermine its value. It's a stunning piece, truly. I just, well, I guess I've always wondered what makes someone spend so much on something to tell the time."

But that, apparently, was the wrong thing to say. His glare intensified, and his chest rose and fell with shallow, deliberate breaths. "Curiosity," he said slowly, his voice low and razor-sharp, "can be a dangerous thing, Stephanie. It leads people into places they don't belong. It makes them ask questions they shouldn't ask. And sometimes, it gets them into trouble."

Stephanie froze, unsure whether his words were meant as a veiled threat or an exaggerated overreaction. Either way, she suddenly felt as though the air in the room had grown heavier, colder. She nodded stiffly, unwilling to press further. Whatever Alistair's fixation on his watch symbolized, she had no desire to find out where that dark undercurrent might lead.

Stephanie's heart pounded in her chest as she met his gaze, her mind racing. The email, the puma, and now this sudden, inexplicable rage, it all felt connected, somehow, though she couldn't quite piece it together.

She could feel the tension crackling in the air, the unspoken warning in Alistair's words hanging between them like a storm cloud.

Finally, after what felt like an eternity, Alistair seemed to pull himself back from the brink. He straightened, adjusting his suit jacket with a quick, sharp motion, and his expression smoothed back into one of practiced indifference. "I have a meeting to prepare for," he said curtly, turning on his heel and striding toward his office without another word.

Stephanie watched him go, her mind spinning. As soon as the door clicked shut behind him, she let out a breath she hadn't realized she'd been holding. The image of the puma shipment flashed in her mind, along with Alistair's unsettling reaction to what should have been a simple conversation. Something was very wrong, and she couldn't shake the feeling that she had just glimpsed a side of Alistair that he kept carefully hidden from the world.

By the time she finally left the office, she felt as if she had been running on a treadmill all day, lots of effort with little progress to show for it and of course, the run in.

The journey home was its usual blur of crowds and noise, with the packed tube train filled with tired commuters, each lost in their own world. She leaned back against the cold metal of the carriage, trying to block out the hum of the city, her mind drifting off to a far more pleasant place.

When she finally reached her apartment, the sinking realization hit her, she'd forgotten to do the shopping again. With a sigh, she trudged to the fridge, opened it, and was greeted by the depressing sight of a few wilted vegetables, some rather old cheese, a suspiciously unidentifiable jar at the back, and, of course, eight different types of mustard. Because what fridge didn't have an unnecessary collection of mustard taking up valuable real estate?

Dropping her bag by the door, she kicked off her shoes, one landing with a thud and the other bouncing against the wall. Oliver, her ever-attentive cat, immediately leapt down from his usual perch on the windowsill, winding his way between her legs with a loud, insistent meow.

"Don't look at me like that," she muttered, reaching down to scratch behind his ears. "Unless you've developed a taste for Dijon, we're both out of luck tonight."

She padded across the small kitchen, Oliver trailing behind her, and opened a can of cat food. As she scooped it into his dish, she watched him purr in anticipation, his little tail twitching happily.

"You've got it easy, you know," she murmured to him as she leaned against the counter, watching him eat. "No deadlines, no demanding bosses, no endless errands… Just food, naps, and the occasional chase after a stray sock."

Oliver glanced up at her mid-bite, as if to say, *Yes, and isn't it wonderful?*

Stephanie chuckled softly, shaking her head. "Maybe we should think about getting a puppy for company, Oliver? Someone to keep you on your toes?"

She hadn't meant to ask it, hadn't even realized she was thinking about it until the words slipped out of her mouth. A puppy? Where had that come from? She frowned, feeling a strange sense of confusion wash over her. She wasn't even a dog person, really. Oliver was enough of a handful as it was, with his unpredictable mood swings and habit of knocking things off shelves for no apparent reason. Why had she even mentioned a puppy?

Stephanie shook her head again, trying to dismiss the odd thought. Maybe it was just the stress of the day catching up with her, making her think strange things. She hadn't exactly had the most relaxing afternoon, running from one restaurant to the next to collect lunch for the entire office. And then there was that little brown-and-white dog she had seen earlier, just a fleeting glimpse of it racing down the street, but something about it had stuck in her mind.

"A puppy," she muttered to herself as she made her way to the fridge, staring at its meagre contents. "What on earth am I thinking?"

She sighed and resigned herself to throwing together whatever she could find. Eventually, she settled on a bizarre concoction of canned beans, peanut butter spread on crackers, and a few sad olives that had been languishing at the back of the cupboard. It was far from appetizing, but after the day she'd had, she just wanted to eat something and be done with it.

As she spread the peanut butter on the last of the crackers, Oliver sauntered back into the kitchen, his tail swishing with an air of feline superiority. He leapt gracefully onto the counter, settling himself near her with a curious glance at the mess she was making.

"You're lucky you don't have to deal with this," Stephanie said, shaking her head as she assembled her makeshift meal. "Ever wonder what it's like to be human, Oliver? Endless decisions, bad sandwiches…"

Oliver let out a long, slow meow, one that Stephanie had learned to interpret as a mixture of disdain and a firm *"Don't you dare."* His tone carried a warning that only a cat could deliver so effortlessly: *Do not mess with perfection. And certainly don't bring a dog into this.*

Stephanie chuckled, hearing the unspoken message loud and clear. "Fine, fine," she said with a smile, turning to face her feline companion. "No puppies. For now."

Oliver responded with an approving flick of his tail, as if to say, *Good. Let's keep it that way.*

Satisfied that her momentary lapse in judgment had been corrected, Oliver hopped down from the counter and made his way back to the sofa, leaving Stephanie alone with her less-than-appetizing meal.

She sat down at the table and took a tentative bite of her creation. Immediately, she regretted it. The combination of peanut butter, beans, and olives was just as dreadful as it sounded. She forced herself to swallow, grimacing as the strange mix of flavours assaulted her taste buds.

"This is… awful," she mumbled to herself, pushing the plate away with a sigh. Her stomach rumbled in protest, and she knew she couldn't force herself to eat another bite of that disaster.

There was only one solution.

Stephanie glanced at the clock and saw that it was still early enough to make a quick run to Mr. Chan's, the thought of a warm, comforting meal, something actually edible, was too tempting to resist.

She stood up, grabbed her coat and bag, and gave Oliver a quick scratch behind the ears as she headed for the door. "I'll be back soon," she said. "Don't worry, no puppies will be following me home."

Oliver responded with a slow blink and a disinterested yawn, clearly satisfied with his unchallenged role as the sole ruler of the apartment. As if to underscore his indifference to her plight, he promptly began licking himself in a manner that could only be described as far too impolite to print.

-

The familiar bell above the door chimed as Stephanie stepped into Mr. Chan's. The tiny restaurant was cosy, just as she remembered, the air thick with the mouth-watering scent of soy sauce, garlic, and sizzling meat. The place was quieter now, only a few regulars sat at the small tables, eating in comfortable silence.

Mr. Chan stood behind the counter, as always, expertly tossing ingredients into a wok. When he saw Stephanie, he raised an eyebrow, a small smile playing on his lips.

"Back again huh?" he asked with a knowing tone. "Can't stay away, huh?"

Stephanie laughed softly as she approached the counter. "I tried to make dinner at home, but let's just say it didn't go well. You're my last hope."

Mr. Chan chuckled, wiping his hands on his apron. "I suppose I can't blame you. What can I get for you tonight? Sweet and sour again?"

Stephanie opened her mouth to automatically reply with her standard order, but then hesitated. Something about the day had made her feel restless, like she needed a change, even if it was a small one. She thought about the dreadful dinner she had just attempted to make and realized that tonight wasn't a night for routine.

She smiled; her decision made. "Actually... you know what? Let's do something different tonight."

Mr. Chan raised an eyebrow, clearly amused. "Different, huh? What's caught your fancy?"

Stephanie glanced at the menu behind him, scanning the options even though she had seen them a hundred times before. "How about... the black bean chicken instead? And maybe throw in some of those steamed dumplings, too."

Mr. Chan's smile widened as he turned back to the stove. "Ah, stepping out of your comfort zone. Good choice."

Stephanie chuckled. "Yeah, I figured it was time to mix things up a bit."

Mr. Chan worked quickly, the sound of sizzling filling the small restaurant as he prepared her new order. Stephanie watched him with a sense of quiet satisfaction, feeling oddly pleased with her decision. It was just a meal, but changing things up, even in this small way, felt good, like a tiny rebellion against the monotony of her day.

As she waited, her mind drifted back to something she had been meaning to ask. "Actually, I wanted to ask you something…"

Mr. Chan glanced at her, his hands still moving with practiced ease as he stirred the wok. "Oh? What's that?"

"There was this man I met here the other night. Quiet, but nice. I think his name was Max. Have you seen him around lately?"

Mr. Chan paused for a moment; his expression thoughtful. He turned his attention back to the wok, but there was something different in his demeanour, something more reserved. "Max… yes, I know him. Strange fellow, that one, does my books, good accountant, very smart. Comes in at night, usually. Keeps to himself, mostly. Always asks to be paid in coins. Not sure why, but I don't ask too many questions."

Stephanie's curiosity piqued. "Coins? That's odd. Why would he want coins?"

Mr. Chan shrugged, as if it were just one of life's little mysteries. "He says they don't fly away like notes. Bulky, annoying, but reliable. Makes sense, I suppose. But there's… something else about him. Unusual man"

Stephanie tilted her head slightly. "Something else?"

Mr. Chan paused, as if searching for the right words. "Well… he's the best bookkeeper I've ever had. Max does my accounts. Numbers come easy to him, like he sees something the rest of us miss. He's saved my business money on more than one occasion, catching mistakes I wouldn't have even known to look for."

Stephanie blinked, surprised. "Max does your books?"

Mr. Chan nodded, his eyes ever so slightly glazing over. "Every week. Quiet fellow, like I said. Comes in after hours, does his work, takes his payment, and goes on his way. But there's… something about him. I don't know what it is, really. It's like… he's carrying something with him, something heavy, but you wouldn't know it just by looking at him. He's quiet, keeps to himself, but there's this… presence. Like he's lived more lives than he lets on. I don't ask, not my business."

Stephanie found herself intrigued by Mr. Chan's description. There was a quiet reverence in his voice, as though he knew there was more to Max than met the eye, even if he couldn't quite put his finger on what that "more" was. It made her wonder just how much of Max's life was hidden beneath the surface.

"Interesting," she said softly. "Do you think he's okay?"

Mr. Chan looked at her, his gaze steady but unreadable. "I think Max is one of those people who's always okay, even when he's not. You know what I mean?"

Stephanie nodded slowly. "Yeah… I think I do."

Mr. Chan finished preparing her order and slid the takeout containers across the counter with a smile. "Be careful of interesting people," he said, his tone light but carrying an undercurrent of seriousness. "They tend to make life… complicated."

Stephanie laughed softly, but the weight of his words lingered. "Thanks, Mr. Chan. You're a lifesaver."

"Anytime," he replied, watching her as she made her way toward the door.

As she left the restaurant, drawing her collar up around her neck, Stephanie couldn't help but think about Mr. Chan's words. There was something about Max, something that made him stand out, even though he seemed to do everything he could to blend in. And while she didn't know exactly what that something was, she had a feeling she hadn't seen the last of him.

Chapter Nine

Returning home Stephanie realised that Fiona had returned and together they sat on the sofa, sharing the meal, the takeout containers in hand as the comforting aroma of the Chinese food filled the room. For a while, they ate in silence, the tension in the room slowly easing with each bite. A good hearty meal with some flavour always had a way of making things better, even if only for a little while.

Fiona poked at her noodles, she had been crying. the tears leaving faint streaks on her cheeks. She hadn't said much, but the quiet felt companionable, not strained. Stephanie gave her friend time, knowing that sometimes, it was enough just to sit together, to share the moment without forcing any words.

After a few more bites, Fiona finally broke the silence. "Do you ever feel like… I don't know… like you're just waiting for something to happen, but you don't know what it is?"

Stephanie looked up from her dumplings, considering the question. "Yeah," she said slowly. "All the time. It's like… like life is this big waiting room, and you're stuck flipping through old magazines, waiting for your name to be called. And you don't even know what you're waiting for."

Fiona nodded, her expression softening slightly. "Exactly. It's like… I keep thinking things will change, that I'll wake up one day and everything will make sense. But it doesn't. And I'm scared that this is it, that nothing's going to change unless I do something. But I don't know what that something is."

Stephanie reached over and gently squeezed Fiona's hand. "I get it. I really do. But you're not alone, Fi. We'll figure it out together. One step at a time."

Fiona sighed, but there was a hint of relief in her voice as she leaned back against the sofa. "Thanks, Steph. I don't know what I'd do without you."

Stephanie smiled. "Same goes for me. We're in this together, okay?"

Fiona managed a small smile, but the tension in her eyes didn't fully fade. She seemed lost in thought, her gaze drifting to the window as she absentmindedly twirled a noodle around her fork. After a moment, she let out a shaky breath and looked back at Stephanie.

"There's… there's something else," Fiona said, her voice barely above a whisper. "Something I haven't told anyone."

Stephanie immediately sensed the weight of what Fiona was about to say. She set her container down on the coffee table and turned her full attention to her friend. "What is it?"

Fiona hesitated, biting her lip as if struggling to find the right words. "It's David," she finally said, her voice trembling. "You know we were taking a break! Well, we've been kind of dating again, just to see. I found out he's been cheating on me again."

Stephanie's heart sank. She had never been a fan of David, he was arrogant, self-centred, and treated Fiona more like an accessory than a partner. But hearing this, seeing the pain in her friend's eyes, made her blood boil. "Fiona... I'm so sorry. How did you find out?"

Fiona wiped at her eyes, her voice shaking as she continued. "I saw messages on his phone. I wasn't even snooping, he left it out, and a notification popped up. At first, I didn't want to believe it, but... there were so many. He's been seeing someone else for months. He doesn't know that I know, but... I can't un-see it, Steph. I can't stop thinking about it."

Stephanie reached for Fiona's hand again, squeezing it tightly. "Fi, that's awful. You deserve so much better than that. Why haven't you told him you know? More to the point, why are you seeing him again?"

Fiona's eyes filled with fresh tears as she looked down at their joined hands. "Because... because I don't know what to do. I'm so unhappy with him, but... I don't want to end it, either. He's rich, Steph. He takes care of me. I know that sounds terrible, but... I don't know if I can walk away from that. What if I never find someone else? What if I end up alone?"

Stephanie felt a pang of sympathy and frustration all at once. She understood the fear, she really did, but it hurt to see Fiona trapped in a situation where she was choosing security over her own happiness. She didn't want to judge her friend, but she also didn't want to see her settling for someone who didn't deserve her.

"Fi," Stephanie said gently, "you don't have to decide right now. But just… think about what's best for you. I know it's scary, but staying with someone just because they're rich? That's not going to make you happy in the long run. You deserve someone who loves you and respects you, not someone who treats you like you're disposable."

Fiona sniffled, wiping at her eyes with the back of her hand. "I know… I know you're right. But it's just so hard. I don't know if I'm strong enough to leave him."

Stephanie wrapped her arms around Fiona, pulling her into a tight hug. "You are strong enough. And you're not alone. Whatever you decide, I'm here for you."

Fiona clung to her, her body trembling with silent sobs. "Thank you, Steph. I just… I feel so lost."

"You're not lost," Stephanie whispered, holding her friend close. "You're just finding your way. And it's okay to be scared. But you're going to get through this. We'll figure it out together."

For a while, they just sat there, holding onto each other in the quiet of the apartment. Outside, the city buzzed with life, but in that moment, it felt far away, like something that belonged to someone else, not to them.

Eventually, Stephanie pulled back and offered Fiona a small, reassuring smile. "How about we start with dinner? Eat up. Mr. Chan's always makes things better."

Fiona managed a tearful laugh, nodding as she wiped her eyes. "Yeah… that sounds good."

They settled in, the warmth of the food and the comfort of each other's company slowly easing the tension in the room. It wasn't a perfect solution, but for now, it was enough.

-

Max sat in the quiet corner of *The Raj of Persia*, a bowl of steaming dal and a naan in front of him, alongside a modest stack of receipts and ledgers that he half-heartedly promised himself he'd get to. The restaurant was mostly empty at this hour, save for the faint hum of conversation drifting over from a couple seated near the entrance. The warm, spicy aroma of cumin, coriander, and something delightfully garlicky filled the air, wrapping around him like a comforting blanket. This place had become more than just a favourite spot, it was a sanctuary, a small island of warmth and flavour in the sprawling chaos of the city.

He spooned some of the rich, fragrant curry into his mouth, letting the earthy, spiced flavours linger on his tongue. Food was one of life's few joys for Max, a fleeting pleasure in an existence that otherwise felt disjointed and strange. And the dal at *The Raj of Persia*? It was unmatched, the kind of meal that could make a man, or dog, believe the universe wasn't entirely against him.

The difference between eating as a man and eating as a dog, however, was a revelation he never stopped appreciating. For starters, when you're a dog, food is mostly about speed. A quick sniff, a snap of the jaws, and whatever questionable morsel you've found on the street is gone before your brain has time to register what it might have been. Was that a bit of sausage? Or an old shoelace? The line was thin, and often, the regret immediate.

As a human, though, Max got to *taste* things, really taste them. The complexities of a good dahl, for instance, weren't wasted on a quick gulp. The layers of flavour, the subtle kick of chilli, the silky texture of the lentils, he could savour it all without worrying about anyone yelling, "Get away from that!" or "Drop it!" And there was naan, glorious naan. As a dog, bread was just bread, but as a man, it was an edible masterpiece. Soft, warm, and perfect for scooping up every last bit of curry.

And then there was the dignity. Eating as a human didn't involve crouching on the ground or being told off for sniffing someone else's plate. No one glared at you for licking your bowl clean (not that he didn't *occasionally* consider it). He could sit here at a proper table, in a proper chair, and enjoy his meal with utensils, a luxury he'd never take for granted.

Max chuckled to himself, tearing off a piece of naan and dunking it into the dal. "Definitely better than scarfing down leftovers from a bin," he muttered under his breath, earning a curious glance from the waiter passing by. Max gave him a polite nod, then turned his attention back to his meal.

Tonight, with the city's noise muted by the restaurant's comforting hum and the promise of another warm, spiced bite in front of him, Max allowed himself a rare moment of peace. It wasn't much, but it was enough.

Max glanced down at the pile of receipts, his fingers absently running over the worn edges of the papers. Numbers had always come easily to him. They made sense in a way that life often didn't, orderly, predictable, comforting in their precision. But tonight, even the numbers couldn't distract him from the strange heaviness that had settled over him.

As he worked through the accounts, his mind began to wander, drifting into memories that felt both distant and achingly familiar. He wasn't sure if they were from this life or another, he could never quite tell where the past ended and the present began. But tonight, the memories were particularly vivid, flooding his mind with images that made his heart ache.

He could see her clearly now, a woman with bright eyes and a smile that lit up the room. They had met in a park, on a night much like any other. She had been sitting on a bench, reading a book, when he had approached her, drawn to her in a way he couldn't quite explain. Their conversation had been easy, natural, as if they had known each other for years.

He remembered the way she laughed, the way she tilted her head when she was deep in thought, the way her hand felt in his, warm and steady, grounding him in a way he hadn't known he needed. They had built a life together, a life that felt real and solid in a way that his current existence never did. There had been a home, a small cottage at the edge of a forest, filled with the sound of laughter and the warmth of love.

He could see the birth of their children, two bright, joyful souls who had brought light into their world. He could feel the weight of them in his arms, the way they had clung to him as he rocked them to sleep. He remembered the small, everyday moments that had filled their days, the smell of fresh bread baking in the oven, the sound of rain tapping against the windows, the soft murmur of bedtime stories.

But the memories weren't all joyful. As he sat there in the quiet of the restaurant, the darker images began to seep in, the slow, painful decline of his wife's health, the way her laughter had faded, replaced by the shallow gasps of someone fighting for every breath. He remembered the nights spent by her bedside, holding her hand as she drifted in and out of consciousness, her once-bright eyes clouded with pain.

And then there was the moment when she was gone, when her hand had gone limp in his, and the house had fallen silent, the warmth seeping out of it as if she had taken it with her. He had been left with nothing but the echoes of a life that had once been whole, and the empty space where she had been.

Max blinked, pulling himself back to the present, the sounds of the restaurant filtering back into his awareness. His heart was heavy, and there was a tightness in his chest that made it hard to breathe. He wasn't sure how much of it was real, how much of it had actually happened, or if it was just some strange, fragmented memory from a life that might not have even been his.

Was he a man, or was he a dog? Had he lived many lives, or was this just the trick of a mind trying to make sense of an existence that didn't fit neatly into one box?

Max wasn't sure. He never was. All he knew was that the memories felt real, and the grief that accompanied them felt even more so.

He took another bite of his curry, the warmth of the spices grounding him in the present, pulling him back from the depths of his mind. The food was good, really good, and for a moment, it was enough to distract him from the heaviness that lingered in his chest.

The Raj of Persia had always been a place of comfort for him, and tonight, it was no different. But even as he sat there, surrounded by the familiar smells and sounds of the restaurant, Max couldn't shake the feeling that he was drifting, that he was caught between two worlds, two lives, two selves.

He didn't know if he was immortal, if he was trapped in some endless cycle of rebirth and loss, or if he was simply a man whose mind played tricks on him. But whatever the truth was, he knew that he couldn't dwell on it for too long. Life, whatever it was, had to go on.

Max finished his meal and carefully closed the ledger, checking the final numbers one last time. Everything balanced perfectly, as it always did. He stood up and made his way over to the counter, where the owner of the restaurant was busy cleaning up for the night.

Max handed over the ledger with a quiet nod. "It's all done. Everything checks out. I made you a few savings on your VAT on page 11, it's all in there."

The owner, a broad-shouldered man with a thick moustache, smiled warmly and took the ledger from Max. "Thank you, Max. I don't know what I'd do without you."

Max returned the smile, though it didn't quite reach his eyes. "Glad to help."

The owner reached into the cash register and began counting out Max's payment, but Max raised a hand to stop him.

"Coins, if you don't mind, like usual." Max said, his voice calm but firm. "Coins are always useful."

The owner looked at him for a moment, then nodded, gathering up a handful of coins and placing them in a small cloth bag. He handed the bag to Max with a curious look, but he didn't ask any questions. Max had been working for him for a while now, and the request for coins had long since become routine.

Max took the bag, the weight of the coins familiar and reassuring in his hand. "Thank you," he said quietly, slipping the bag into his pocket.

The owner gave him a nod of understanding. "Take care of yourself, Max."

Max nodded in return and turned to leave, returning once again to the streets that were his home. The city buzzed around him, the distant hum of traffic and the soft murmur of conversation drifting through the streets. For a moment, he just stood there, letting the sounds and smells of London wash over him.

The memories still lingered at the edges of his mind, but for now, he could push them aside. He was Max, whoever, or whatever that meant, and tonight, that would have to be enough.

Chapter Ten

Max had barely stepped outside *The Raj of Persia* when he noticed it, a stubborn smear of dal smack in the middle of his shirt. He stopped under the dim streetlights, frowning as the golden yellow stain seemed to glow in judgment. "Brilliant," he muttered, brushing at it uselessly. As he adjusted his stance, his eyes caught another spot on his trousers. "Oh, fantastic. Mucky pup," he grumbled to himself. Apparently, dinner had decided it wasn't quite done with him.

With a resigned sigh, Max adjusted the small cloth bag of coins nestled in his pocket. There was no point lamenting it. He knew exactly what he had to do: head to the laundrette. It wasn't far, and, as luck would have it, he had a decent relationship with the machines there, a no-nonsense place that accepted coins without asking any awkward questions. Coins were always good for situations like this, dependable and untraceable, much like Max himself.

The cool chilly night air brushed against his skin as he made his way through the quiet streets of London. The city felt calmer at this hour; its usual hum softened to a steady murmur. Soon, the laundrette came into view, its small, unassuming storefront wedged between a kebab shop and a newsagent. The flickering neon sign in the window simply read *Laundry*, one of the few places left in London that didn't try to dress itself up.

Max pushed open the door, the bell above jingling softly to announce his arrival. Inside, it was as familiar as ever. The rows of old, dependable machines hummed quietly, their dull rhythm filling the room like a lullaby. The air carried that distinct blend of detergent and fabric softener, the kind of smell that always reminded Max of fresh starts, even if they were temporary.

A few people lingered in the laundrette. An older woman at the far end folded a neat pile of linens with the precision of a drill sergeant, while a man near the entrance flipped through a newspaper, his face hidden behind the broadsheet. Neither spared Max a glance, which suited him just fine.

He wasted no time. Stripping down to an oversized T-shirt that barely grazed his knees and a pair of socks that had seen better days, Max loaded his clothes into one of the machines adding a small cupful of blue and white washing powder. He fished a few coins from his cloth bag and fed them into the slot, the machine roaring to life as water began to slosh inside.

With his clothes on their journey to cleanliness, Max settled into one of the hard plastic chairs by the window. He looked ridiculous, sitting there in a shirt that could've doubled as a tunic, his socked feet stretched out in front of him. But ridiculous was par for the course, and Max was far beyond caring about appearances.

The rhythmic spin of the washing machine held his gaze, the repetitive motion oddly soothing. As he sat there, his thoughts began to wander, drifting back to the night at *The Raj of Persia*. The memory lingered in fragments, the comforting spice of the dal, the warmth of the naan, and the fleeting sense of peace he'd felt in that quiet corner of the restaurant.

And then came something else. A flicker of something deeper. Was it a memory, or just one of those strange tricks his mind liked to play? It was impossible to tell. Either way, it carried weight, an inexplicable heaviness that settled in his chest. Max let out a soft sigh, leaning back in the chair as the hum of the machines filled the room.

This moment, here in the laundrette, wasn't extraordinary. It wasn't dramatic or life-changing. But it was part of his routine, a brief pause in a life that otherwise seemed to shift and tumble like the clothes spinning in the washer. And he was just fine with that.

-

Stephanie had needed to get out of the apartment. After the conversation with Fiona, she felt restless, her thoughts swirling as she tried to make sense of everything. How could Fiona stay with someone like David, knowing he was cheating on her? Was money really worth that much? Could love, or at least, the idea of it, be sacrificed for security?

The questions gnawed at her as she wandered the streets, the familiar hum of the city buzzing around her. She knew life wasn't perfect, that everyone had their flaws, but was it worth settling for someone who made you unhappy just because they offered stability? Could you really justify staying with someone like David, someone who didn't respect you, just because they could provide for you?

She didn't have the answers, but the questions weighed heavy on her mind. Maybe it was the tiredness, or the emotional drain of her conversation with Fiona, but tonight, everything felt more complicated than usual.

As she turned down a quiet side street, she noticed a small bar tucked away in the corner, its neon sign casting a faint red glow onto the pavement. A couple of men stood outside, laughing loudly, drinks in hand. They looked over as she approached, their eyes lighting up with interest.

"Hey, love," one of them called out, taking a step toward her. "Fancy a drink? We're just getting started."

Stephanie's instinct was to walk past without acknowledging them, but the second man joined in, flashing her a grin that was more predatory than friendly. "Come on, we'll be good," he said with a wink. "Just one drink. You look like you could use some fun."

She forced a polite smile, her pace quickening as she tried to brush them off. "No thanks, I'm good."

But they weren't ready to let her go just yet. The first man stepped closer; his tone more insistent now. "Come on, don't be like that. We'll show you a good time."

Stephanie's heart sped up, a familiar knot of unease tightening in her stomach. The light banter had taken on an edge, one that made her uncomfortable. She knew how this went, the way a casual invitation could quickly turn into something else if she wasn't careful.

She kept her eyes forward, her voice firm as she replied, "I said no, thanks."

The men exchanged a glance, but finally, they relented, backing off with exaggerated shrugs. "Suit yourself, love," the second man said, taking a swig from his drink. "Your loss."

As she walked away, the sound of their laughter fading behind her, Stephanie couldn't shake the feeling of disappointment that settled over her. It wasn't just about the encounter itself, though that had left a bad taste in her mouth, but about what it represented. The casual, shallow offers of a "good time," the promise of fleeting pleasure with no substance beneath it. Was this all there was?

She wanted something more. Something deeper. Something real.

But tonight, the city felt more hollow, and she was left wondering if maybe Fiona had the right idea after all. If love was just a fairy-tale, if happiness was fleeting, then maybe it was better to settle for something stable, even if it wasn't perfect. Maybe security was the closest thing to happiness that anyone could really hope for.

Lost in thought, Stephanie turned another corner and found herself in front of a small laundrette. The flickering sign caught her eye, casting a soft glow on the otherwise dim street. Through the glass, she could see a lone figure sitting near the window, his head tilted back against the wall, his eyes half-closed as if lost in thought.

It took her a moment to recognize him, but when she did, a small smile tugged at the corners of her lips.

It was Max.

Stephanie hesitated for a moment, unsure if she should disturb him. But something about the way he sat there, so quietly, so alone, made her want to reach out. She raised a hand and gently knocked on the glass, the sound soft but enough to get his attention.

Max blinked, his gaze slowly shifting to the window. When he saw Stephanie standing there, a look of mild surprise crossed his face. He gave her a small smile, and she took it as an invitation to come inside.

Stephanie pushed open the door, the bell chiming above her head as she stepped into the laundrette. The warmth of the room was a welcome contrast to the cool night air, and she could immediately smell the faint scent of detergent and fabric softener.

As Stephanie walked into the laundrette, she stopped dead in her tracks, her laughter bubbling out before she could even think to suppress it. Max sat there, half- naked in a hard plastic chair, his legs crossed in a way that suggested he thought he belonged there. The oversized Snoopy T-shirt draped over him like a tent, making him look both utterly ridiculous and somehow completely adorable.

"Max," she said, still grinning, "why are you sitting here half-naked in a Snoopy T-shirt that's way too big for you?"

Max glanced down at the shirt, tugging at the hem like he was checking its fit. Then he shrugged, his face perfectly straight. "Laundry day," he said, as though that explained everything.

Stephanie raised an eyebrow, leaning on the table next to him. "Laundry day, sure. But… Snoopy?"

Max leaned back, folding his arms and looking at her with mock indignation. "Snoopy is iconic. Do you even know who you're looking at here? This is *the first dog on the moon.*"

Stephanie blinked, caught off guard. "The first dog on the moon? Are you serious right now?"

Max nodded solemnly. "Absolutely. NASA had Snoopy in training. In fact Buzz Aldrin wanted to say, 'The Beagle has landed,' but Armstrong cut him off with his famous line. Tragic, really. Snoopy never got the credit he deserved."

She stared at him, unsure if he was joking or genuinely convinced of his own story. "You're messing with me."

Max smirked. "Am I? Think about it. They give a silver Snoopy as a NASA endorsement for a reason. The man, I mean, dog, was a pioneer. First proper canine astronaut."

Max muttered something about *Laika* under his breath then continued. "You should be honoured to be in the presence of his greatest fan."

Stephanie laughed, shaking her head as she dropped into the chair next to him. "You're unbelievable, you know that?"

"Unbelievable or underappreciated?" Max countered, tapping the Snoopy logo on his chest. "Much like our boy here. He trained, he dreamed, and he got overshadowed by a giant leap and an eagle. Story of my life."

Stephanie couldn't stop laughing. The absurdity of Max, sitting there in his oversized attire, spinning a tale about NASA's forgotten beagle astronaut, was just the kind of ridiculousness she needed.

"Well," she said, finally catching her breath, "I suppose if anyone can pull off Snoopy at a laundrette, it's you."

"Damn right," Max said with a grin. "When life gives you dirty clothes, wear a shirt that says, 'I'm aiming for the stars.'"

Stephanie shook her head again, the hum of the machines filling the quiet as she settled in next to him. The whole thing was ridiculous, but somehow, with Max, it felt perfectly normal.

Stephanie chuckled; she realised that she was sitting next to him. She glanced around the small laundrette. "Well, you're definitely pulling it off. How's everything been going, anyway? Surviving out there?"

Max leaned back in his chair, stretching slightly. "Surviving, yes. Thriving? Well, that's debatable. The city can be a bit of a grind, you know?"

Stephanie nodded, leaning back as well. "Tell me about it. Work's been… exhausting lately. I've been putting out fires left and right."

Max raised an eyebrow. "I'm guessing you're not a fire-fighter. What do you do again? Professional juggler? Corporate trapeze artist?"

Stephanie snorted. "I wish. I work in a Law firm, as a legal secretary, but I'm trying to get my law degree. You know, the glamorous life of endless emails, deadlines, and clients who think everything can be fixed with a large bill."

Max tilted his head thoughtfully. "Ah, yes; lawyers. Now there's a profession that's been around since... well, since humans realized they needed someone to argue for them without getting their own hands dirty."

Stephanie smirked. "Yeah? So, when did lawyers come into existence, then? Feels like they've been around forever, making mountains out of molehills."

Max leaned back in his chair, his expression turning thoughtful. "Well, technically, they've been around longer than you'd think. Ancient Rome was when things really kicked off. Back then, they were called 'orators.' They'd argue people's cases in front of the Senate, which, let's face it, was probably just a bunch of old men in togas pretending to pay attention. You could say that's when humanity decided it needed a designated talker, someone who could spout big words while everyone else sat there nodding along, pretending to understand."

Stephanie couldn't help but laugh, her grin widening as he spoke. "How do you *know* this stuff? Seriously, Max, you're like a walking encyclopaedia of random history facts."

Max shrugged, a playful glint in his eyes. "You pick things up. Besides, history's full of fun little quirks like that. Orators were basically the first lawyers, and from there, we just kept finding new ways to make life more complicated."

Stephanie leaned forward, resting her chin on her hand as she listened. She was loving the moment. Max talking about the past, weaving little stories that made her feel like she was peeking through a window into another time. He had this knack for making history feel alive, for turning what should have been dry facts into something vibrant and fascinating.

"Exactly," she said with a chuckle. "And now lawyers are making our dreams into nightmares. But hey, at least it pays the bills, right?"

Max gave her a teasing smile. "Bills? In this economy? Are you sure you're not just bartering your soul for rent every month?"

Stephanie laughed, shaking her head. "Feels like it sometimes. Honestly, I'm probably just a few steps away from offering my sanity as a down payment."

They shared a comfortable laugh, and for a moment, the rest of the world faded away. The laundrette felt like their little bubble of warmth and light, a safe corner where time didn't matter and the world outside could wait.

"You really do know a ridiculous amount about everything," Stephanie remarked after the laughter subsided. "It's weirdly impressive."

Max raised an eyebrow, his lips quirking into a smirk. "Stick around, and you'll learn that I'm full of useless trivia. It's my secret talent."

"Not useless," Stephanie said, nudging him playfully. "You make it all sound... fun."

Max chuckled, shaking his head. "Glad someone thinks so. Most people just glaze over when I start rambling."

"Not me," Stephanie replied, smiling warmly. "I could listen to you talk for hours."

Max looked at her for a moment, his expression softening. "Careful, or I might start charging for history lessons."

Stephanie rolled her eyes, laughing again. "Oh, please. I'll pay you in laundry tokens."

"Deal," Max said, and they both laughed, settling into the easy rhythm of their conversation as the washing machines hummed on around them.

As Stephanie looked around, her eyes landed on a small, worn book sitting on one of the benches. She reached over and picked it up, running her fingers over the faded cover. "*The Time Machine*," she read aloud, her voice thoughtful. "By H.G. Wells."

Max glanced at the book, a faint smile tugging at his lips. "Good choice. A classic."

Stephanie turned the book over in her hands, studying it. "It's funny, isn't it? The idea of time travel. How little

119

time we have, and how we're always wishing we could have more of it, or go back and fix things."

Max nodded slowly; his gaze distant as if he were lost in thought. "Yeah… time's a tricky thing. You never realize how much of it you've lost until it's gone."

Stephanie looked at him curiously. "I read this as a child, I'm not sure some of it went in. Have you ever read it?"

Max's smile widened, just a little. "I bought that book when it first came out. Had it signed by the writer, he was a good man, a very interesting fellow, apart from the fascination with snuff."

"Nice try, Max." Stephanie laughed softly, shaking her head. "Do you know when that book was written?."

Max chuckled along with her, though there was something in his eyes, something that made Stephanie pause for just a moment, a depth and sparkle that spoke of ….. it was a look she couldn't quite place, a quiet weight that seemed to linger in the air between them.

He leaned back in his chair, staring up at the ceiling. "You know, people talk about time like it's a currency, like it is something you could save up or spend on things that mattered. In some ways it is, time, after-all is the only thing that you are born with. But it slips through your fingers, no matter how careful you are."

Stephanie listened intently, lost in his words. There was something almost hypnotic about the way Max spoke, like he was recalling memories that didn't quite belong to him. She wanted to ask more, to dig deeper, but the gentle rhythm of his voice lulled her into a sense of comfort. It was as if time itself slowed down inside that little laundrette, making her forget about the world outside.

Max smiled faintly, his gaze drifting to the distance as though he were seeing a world long gone. "It's funny, the things that stay with you. Like how people used to line up for hours just to catch a glimpse of a new invention, or how they'd crowd into parks to hear a gramophone play the latest tune. The world felt... smaller then. Simpler. People had a different kind of patience."

Stephanie tilted her head, intrigued by the wistfulness in his tone. She didn't fully understand the weight behind his words, but she could feel it. "Yeah... things are different now. Everything's about speed, the next big thing, the next deadline. Sometimes it feels like there's no time to just... stop. To breathe."

Max's eyes flicked to the book sitting on the chair beside him, its weathered cover a testament to countless readings. He reached over and gently ran a hand across it, a faint smile tugging at the corner of his mouth. "H.G. Wells. *The Time Machine*. You know, when this first came out, people thought he was the greatest thing since sliced cake. Couldn't get enough of him. His ideas, his vision, they were revolutionary. People were convinced he'd live forever through his works. And in a way, they were right. His stories endured. He, however, did not."

Stephanie watched him carefully, her usual light-hearted teasing replaced by a quiet respect. "That's... kind of bittersweet," she said softly.

Max nodded, his smile tinged with a mix of wisdom and melancholy. "It is. But it's also the way of things, isn't it? The ideas we leave behind have the power to outlast us. What we create, what we give to the world, that's what lingers."

He turned his gaze back to her, his expression soft but intent. "And that's why it's important to breathe, Stephanie. To take a moment, every now and then, just for yourself. The world's rush doesn't mean you have to rush with it. Stop. Feel the weight of your own presence. Be *you*. That's the one thing the world can't take from you."

The hum of the laundrette machines filled the silence that followed, but it wasn't uncomfortable. It was warm, steady, grounding, like the space between his words had given her something to hold onto.

Stephanie nodded, a small smile playing at her lips. "You really know how to make a person think, Max."

Max chuckled lightly, leaning back in his chair. "Just remember to breathe while you're doing it."

Stephanie smiled, feeling a warmth spread through her chest. "I'll try. Thanks, Max."

They continued talking, their conversation light and easy, filled with idle small talk and the occasional joke. The laundrette felt cosy, almost peaceful, as if it existed outside of time, a small bubble of quiet in the middle of the bustling city, their bubble.

Eventually, the drying machine buzzed, and Max's clothes were ready. He stood up, stretching as he went to retrieve them. Stephanie watched him move, slipping back into the role of the man who always seemed to be on the move, always caught between one world and another.

"Well," Max said, pulling on his freshly washed shirt, "I guess this is where we part ways for the night."

Stephanie smiled, standing up as well. "Yeah, I should get going too. But… I'm glad I ran into you."

Max nodded, his smile soft and genuine. "Same here. Take care of yourself, Stephanie. Hopefully we'll bump into each other again soon"

"I'd like that, Max," she replied, watching as he made his way to the door. For a moment, she thought about asking him to stay a little longer, to keep talking, but the words caught in her throat.

And then, just like that, Max was gone, disappearing into the night as quietly as he had appeared. Stephanie stood there for a moment, the warmth of the laundrette lingering around her as she thought about their conversation. There was something about him, something she couldn't quite put her finger on.

But for now, she pushed the thought aside, tucking it away in the back of her mind. There would be time to think about it later. For now, she just needed to find her way home.

As she walked outside, the warmth from the machines lapping at her back, Stephanie couldn't help but glance back at the laundrette, half expecting to see Max still sitting there, his oversized Snoopy shirt and easy smile catching the fluorescent light. But the window was empty, and the quiet hum of the machines faded behind her as the door clicked shut.

Above her, a seagull perched on a lamp post let out a muffled "Caw!" Its gaze followed her as she moved, its black, beady eyes unblinking, almost too focused for a bird. Its head tilted slightly, and it opened its beak, tasting the air as if searching for something just out of reach.

Stephanie paused, staring at it for a moment, feeling an odd shiver creep up her spine. It was just a bird, she told herself, but there was something unsettling about the way it watched her, as though it knew more than it should.

Shaking off the thought, she adjusted her bag on her shoulder and started walking, the sound of her footsteps echoing faintly in the stillness of the night. Above her, the bird remained motionless, its shadow stretching long under the streetlight.

With a small sigh, she turned and began walking, her thoughts drifting back to Fiona, to Max, to the strange sense that time was slipping through her fingers faster than she realized. "Signed copy. " she laughed to herself.

Chapter Eleven

The morning light filtered through the cracks in the blinds of Stephanie's apartment as she sat at the kitchen table, cradling a cup of tea in her hands. The events of the previous night still lingered in her mind, her conversation with Fiona, the unsettling encounter outside the bar, and, of course, running into Max at the laundrette.

She couldn't shake the feeling that there was something unusual about him. Sure, he was a bit quirky, his dry humour, his preference for coins, his oversized Snoopy T-shirt, but there was more to it than that. The way he had spoken about *The Time Machine*, as if he had actually been there when it first came out, left a strange impression on her. She had brushed it off at the time, assuming it was just his sense of humour, but now, in the quiet of the morning, she found herself wondering if there was something more to his story.

"Of course he wasn't there. That's impossible." She mused to herself.

Stephanie sighed, setting her cup down and glancing over at Oliver, who was perched on the windowsill, staring intently at a bird outside. "What do you think, Oliver? Am I overthinking things?"

Oliver responded with a soft, indifferent meow; his attention still focused on the bird. Stephanie chuckled, shaking her head. "Yeah, you're probably right. I should just let it go."

But letting it go was easier said than done. Max seemed so different from the people she normally encountered, the shallow flirtations outside the bar, the cold professionalism at work, the complicated mess of Fiona and David's relationship. Max was… well, he was Max. That alone made her want to know more.

But despite the confusion and questions swirling in her mind, there was something else she felt, contentment. The quiet buzz in her life wasn't grand or earth- shattering, but it was hers, and that meant something. The small moments of peace, like sipping tea in the morning or sharing a laugh with someone like Max, made her feel connected, present, even if the rest of the world seemed to be in chaos. It was enough, at least for now.

Her thoughts were interrupted by the sound of her phone buzzing on the table. She picked it up and saw a message from Fiona.

Hey, Steph. Thanks for last night. I've been thinking a lot about what you said. Maybe it's time I do something about David. I just… I don't know. Let's talk later?

Stephanie's heart ached for her friend. She knew how hard this was for Fiona; how torn she was between the comfort of staying with David and the desire for something better. But at least Fiona was thinking about making a change, and that was a step in the right direction.

Of course, Stephanie texted back. *We'll figure it out. Call me whenever you're ready to talk.*

She set her phone down and took another sip of her tea, trying to push aside the heavy thoughts that seemed to follow her everywhere these days. Maybe she just needed to get out of the apartment, clear her head. The fresh air would do her some good.

With that in mind, Stephanie quickly dressed, grabbing her jacket before heading out the door. The city was already awake and bustling, the sounds of traffic and the chatter of people filling the streets. She let herself get lost in the crowd, the familiar rhythm of London life washing over her in an assuring way as she wandered without any particular destination in mind.

Once Stephanie left the apartment, Oliver remained on the windowsill, his tail flicking lazily as he continued to watch the pigeons outside. They were gathered near a small patch moss on the window ledge, pecking at it with their usual indifference to the world around them.

But today, the pigeons seemed to be in a particularly chatty mood, and Oliver's ears twitched as he overheard their conversation.

Coo coo "You see that cat in there?" it cooed in a low, conspiratorial tone, nodding toward Oliver's perch in the window. *Coo coo* "Thinks he's the king of the world, doesn't he?"

The smaller pigeon, nervously pecking at a crumb on the pavement, glanced up at Oliver and back at the larger pigeon. *Coo coo* "Yeah… but, you know, cats are dangerous, right? They've got claws and everything."

The larger pigeon fluffed up his feathers dramatically, letting out a scoff that was practically theatrical. *Coo coooo* "Please. Dangerous? Cats think they're predators, but they've got nothing on us. We rule this city, mate. They're stuck inside their little boxes, but us? We own the streets."

A third pigeon perched nearby chimed in, his head bobbing enthusiastically. *Coo coo* "Too right! Cats think they're all sneaky, but they've got nothing on pigeons, *coo coo.* We're everywhere! They can't compete with our numbers or our smarts."

The pigeons around them cooed in unison, puffing up their chests and shuffling their feet as if they'd just delivered a victory speech. Their collective self-assurance echoed through the alley, growing louder with every self-congratulatory squawk.

Inside the window, Oliver cracked open one golden eye, his ears twitching faintly. He couldn't understand their language, but the arrogance in their tone was unmistakable. He stretched lazily, letting out a deliberate, jaw-cracking yawn, the picture of indifference as he flexed and stretched out his claws.

The large pigeon narrowed his gaze and flapped his wings in frustration. *Coo coo* "Look at him, just sitting there! Thinks he's so much better than us." He turned to the others, his beak jutting toward Oliver. *Coo coo* "You ever see a cat on every corner? No, you don't! But pigeons? We're everywhere, mate. We're the real kings of this city."

The smaller pigeon bobbed his head in agreement. *Coo coo* "And all he's got is that box. We've got the sky, coo coo!"

The pigeons broke into a chorus of proud coos, their chatter filling the alleyway. Their leader ruffled his feathers triumphantly, as though Oliver's indifference had only solidified their supremacy.

Oliver, now fully awake, blinked at them once, slowly, before turning his back and curling up with deliberate ease. His tail flicked dismissively, a silent but pointed *You wish*.

The larger pigeon squawked indignantly. *Coo coo* "See that? Ignoring us! That smug little fur-ball thinks he's above it all!"

Coo coo "He's just jealous," muttered another. *Cooo coo* "Jealous of our freedom. Coo cooo."

Their voices rose again in triumphant agreement, echoing their supposed victory, while Oliver settled into a nap, thoroughly unimpressed by the feathered commotion outside.

Oliver, clearly unimpressed, lazily flicked his tail and turned away from the window, his message clear: *You can have your streets. I've got more important things to do, like nap.*

The pigeons, satisfied with their victory, returned to pecking at the crumbs on the pavement, their small talk fading into the background as they resumed their daily routine. Oliver, meanwhile, jumped down from the windowsill and sauntered over to his favourite spot on the sofa, curling up into a comfortable ball.

After all, whether pigeons ruled the streets or not, Oliver knew that the real apex predator was the one who didn't need to prove it.

-

Max sat by the window of the small café, sipping his coffee and watching the city outside as it slowly shifted from the stillness of the late night to the quiet stirrings of early morning. The café, too, was beginning to hum with life. The barista wiped down the counter, preparing for the morning rush, and the soft strains of jazz were joined by the distant clatter of dishes from the kitchen.

He'd lost track of time. It happened sometimes, especially when he let himself get lost in his thoughts, memories that weren't always his, fragments of lives he wasn't sure he'd actually lived. But now, as the first hint of dawn threatened to creep over the horizon, Max's stomach tightened with a familiar worry.

He glanced down at his watch, a small, antique piece that had seen better days. The time caught him off guard he had stayed too long. He was cutting it too close to sunrise, if he didn't hurry, he wouldn't make it back to his usual hiding spot in time.

Panic sparked in his chest as he quickly finished his coffee, leaving a few coins on the table before rushing out of the café and into the cool morning air. The city was still quiet, but not for long. Soon, the streets would be filled with people going about their day, and he needed to be out of sight before that happened.

Max darted down side streets and narrow alleyways, the familiar route to his usual spot playing out in his mind. But as he ran, he could feel the slow, inevitable pull of transformation creeping up on him, the way his body began to feel lighter, more agile, more… canine.

He cursed under his breath. He wasn't going to make it. He needed to find somewhere, anywhere, to hide before it was too late.

As he rounded a corner, his vision blurred for a moment, the world spinning as his legs began to shorten, his hands shifting into paws. In a matter of seconds, he was no longer Max, the man rushing through the alleyways of London, he was Max, the small, scruffy brown-and- white terrier with a wonky tail.

Max stood in the alley, now fully transformed, his tail twitching with frustration. The pile of clothes he had just been wearing lay crumpled on the ground, and his mind raced as he tried to figure out what to do. He had been too late, again.

He couldn't just leave his clothes and watch lying around, but the more immediate problem was his small sack of coins, which had tumbled out of his pocket during the transformation. The worn, cloth pouch sat in the middle of the alley, gleaming faintly in the dim light.

Max padded over to the small purse, nudging it with his nose. He couldn't leave it behind, not when he had worked so hard to collect those coins. Without a second thought, he gently picked up the purse in his mouth, the weight of the coins swinging slightly as he held it between his teeth.

With the purse secured, Max turned his attention back to his clothes. He needed to hide them, and quickly. His eyes scanned the alley, finally landing on a stack of cardboard boxes near a dumpster. It wasn't perfect, but it would have to do. Max trotted over to the boxes and began pushing his clothes into the space between them, using his nose and paws to tuck them out of sight.

It started to rain.

Chapter Twelve

The small sack of coins dangled from Max's mouth as he trotted through the early morning streets, the city slowly waking around him. The weight of the coins felt familiar and reassuring, a tangible reminder of the world he was tied to, this strange, chaotic world where he existed both as man and dog, constantly shifting between the two.

But the weight of the coins wasn't the only thing pressing down on him. His mind buzzed with fragments of memories, flashes of places and faces that seemed to blur together. It was as if his life, his many lives, were all layered on top of one another, creating a confusing tangle of moments that he couldn't fully untangle.

And through it all, one thought kept circling back to him: *Where was Roger?*

Roger had always been there. For as long as Max could remember, that scruffy old seagull had been a constant presence in his life. Roger would perch on the edge of a rooftop, cawing and flapping his wings as he complained about the state of the world. Sometimes, Max would catch sight of him scavenging for food near the fish market, or perched by the docks as the boats came in with their catch. Roger was a fixture, a part of the city as much as the cobblestones and the lampposts.

But Roger wasn't just a seagull. Max knew that, though he couldn't quite explain how. There was something more to him, something that lurked just beneath the surface of those beady eyes and ragged feathers. Roger wasn't like the other animals Max encountered. He was different. He *felt* different.

Max didn't know exactly what Roger was, but he had always sensed that the old bird knew more than he let on and that deep down there was a connection between them. There were times when Roger's gaze seemed almost too knowing, too sharp, as if he could see right through Max, to the man, to the dog, to the strange tangle of lives that made up his existence.

Max shook his head, trying to clear the fog of his thoughts. He couldn't afford to let himself get swept away in those strange, half-formed memories, not now. He needed to focus on the present, on the immediate problem of finding somewhere to hide until he could retrieve his clothes. But the images refused to leave him, lingering like whispers on the edge of his mind.

Faces, places, lives. They drifted in and out, unbidden, fragments of experiences he couldn't explain. He had seen cities he didn't think he'd ever visited, felt emotions tied to people he was certain he'd never met. How could he remember something he hadn't lived? As far as he knew, this was his only life, yet the memories came anyway, insistent and haunting. And lately, they were becoming sharper, more vivid, as though they were desperate to be noticed.

There was always love in those memories, or at least the search for it. An endless yearning, a need that ran so deep it felt like part of his very being. It was a feeling that tugged at him constantly, a quiet but relentless reminder that something was missing. Did he truly remember searching for love in another life? Or was it simply a need born out of his strange existence, a way to make sense of the ache he carried?

Max didn't know, and that was the part that unsettled him most. He couldn't be sure if these fragments were real or the creations of a restless mind trying to fill the gaps. Yet the more he thought about it, the more he was convinced that love was the key. Not just any love, but something pure, something deep enough to transcend the boundaries of who, or what, he was.

But love wasn't simple. It wasn't as easy as just finding someone and holding on. He thought he had loved before, he could feel it in the depths of his chest, but the memories were slippery, like trying to hold water in his hands. Had he truly loved, or was it just another trick of his fractured mind? And why, no matter how deeply he felt, did it always seem to slip away?

Every time, it seemed, he ended up back here. Not in this exact city, there had been so many cities, but always in this state, caught between two selves, a man and a dog, searching for something he couldn't quite name. And each time, the cycle began again, as if he was running a race with no finish line, only the faintest hint of what he was chasing.

The city around him was waking up, its hum of activity growing louder. Max closed his eyes for a moment, letting the noise blur into a distant murmur. Answers.

135

He needed answers. And if his memories wouldn't give them to him, perhaps the living would.

Tonight, he decided, he would go to the park. He'd watch people, couples holding hands, friends laughing, strangers meeting for the first time. Maybe, in their gestures and connections, he could find a clue. If he could understand what made them whole, perhaps he could figure out what he was missing. Maybe, just maybe, he could finally stop searching.

Max pushed himself up from where he had been resting, the purse of coins still secured in his mouth. But even as he began to move through the city once again, his mind drifted to the evening ahead. Tonight was Alfredo's Deli, a place where the food was always fresh, the atmosphere warm, and the pasta divine. The best Italian on this side of the Thames, they said. It was a place that reminded him of simpler things, of comfort.

And right now, Max could use a little comfort.

-

Once he was satisfied that his belongings were as safe as they could be, Max took a moment to collect himself. The city was now fully awake , the distant rumble of traffic, the soft murmur of voices, and the occasional clatter of a bin being emptied. He had survived another night, but something felt different. As he stood there, the purse of coins dangling from his mouth, a strange sense of déjà vu washed over him.

Has this all happened before?

The thought floated to the surface of his mind, unbidden but persistent. There was something familiar about it all, the alley, the clothes, the constant shifting between man and dog. It wasn't just this night. It was every night. There were memories, fragments of other lives, other people and places that flickered at the edges of his consciousness. They were just out of reach, like shadows that dissolved the moment he tried to grasp them.

The book. Those memories.

Max blinked, his head tilting slightly as he tried to make sense of it. He remembered something, someone, a long time ago. But the details were hazy, blurred by the passage of time, or perhaps by the strange nature of his existence. Had he lived through this before? Was this all part of some endless cycle, repeating over and over again? And if so, what was the point of it all?

The questions swirled in his mind, but no answers came. Just that nagging sense of familiarity, of something he couldn't quite place.

As he navigated the narrow streets, the weight of the memories, the déjà vu, and the uncertainty pressed down on him. The world was shifting, changing, and Max couldn't shake the feeling that something was about to happen, something big, something he couldn't quite see yet.

For now, all he could do was keep moving. Keep surviving. And hope that, somewhere along the way, the pieces of the puzzle would start to fit together.

As he wandered down the street, deftly sidestepping a group of American tourists loudly debating between Madame Tussauds and the Tower of London, his thoughts drifted to Stephanie. It was rare to meet someone so genuinely kind. *I'd very much like to see her again,* he thought.

The sun started to hang lower in the sky, casting a warm golden hue over the park as Max nestled into the grass beside a cluster of bushes. His small purse of coins sat beside him, an unusual sight for a scruffy terrier. The park was alive with activity, families, joggers, and of course, couples. Couples, Max observed, were everywhere.

People passed by Max with casual indifference, while others took a moment to notice the curious little dog sitting there with his purse, a small sign read "A penny for the pup?" Max had many signs, hidden away all over the city. London was his city, in fact, the thought came to him, all cities had been his city…he shook his head.

A woman walking her dachshund paused, her eyes lighting up at the sight of Max. "Aren't you adorable!" she exclaimed, rummaging through her bag before producing a few coins and dropping them in front of him. Her dachshund, however, was far less impressed. The little dog stopped short, stiffening like an aristocrat confronted with a particularly unwashed commoner. With its nose tilted skyward, it gave Max a look of pure disdain, as if to say, *Really? Begging on the street? How utterly pedestrian.*

Max raised an eyebrow at the dachshund, resisting the urge to roll his eyes. "Don't look at me like that," he muttered under his breath, though to the woman it would have sounded like a soft whine. The dachshund sniffed dramatically, clearly unimpressed, before looking away with the aloofness of royalty.

The woman glanced around, presumably searching for Max's owner, then shrugged as if deciding it didn't matter. "Poor thing," she murmured, giving the dachshund's leash a gentle tug. The snooty little dog gave Max one last disdainful glance before trotting off, tail held high, its attitude firmly intact.

Max waited until they were out of sight, then nosed the coins into his purse. Plink, plink. The sound was familiar, comforting in its own way. "Snobs," he muttered under his breath, casting a glance down the street where the dachshund had disappeared. *At least I have better manners,* he thought with a small, satisfied grin.

But Max's real focus was on the couples. He had come here to learn, to watch, and to understand something about the elusive thing that he had yearned for through countless lives; love.

He turned his gaze to a bench nearby, where a couple in their late thirties sat side by side. They were dressed casually, their bodies angled slightly away from each other. They weren't arguing, but there was a stiffness in their postures, a quiet tension that hung between them like an invisible wall.

The man scrolled through his phone, barely glancing at the woman next to him. She sat with her arms crossed, staring off into the distance, her expression distant and tired. They exchanged a few words, but their conversation was clipped and devoid of warmth, more of an obligation than a desire to connect.

Max could sense it, the weight of their shared history pressing down on them. They were together, but it was clear that whatever had once connected them had faded over time. They stayed because leaving would be too hard, too complicated. Max imagined the mortgage, the bills, the countless practical reasons that kept them tethered to each other, even though the love had long since faded.

A jogger slowed down as he passed by Max, pulling out a few coins from his pocket. "Here you go, mate," he said with a grin, dropping the coins onto the ground. Max waited for the jogger to move on before nudging the coins into his purse. *Plink, plink.* Another addition to his collection. He paused for a second, 'A jogger carrying money, whatever next?' he thought to himself.

Max's attention shifted to another couple, sitting on a blanket spread out on the grass. They were younger, perhaps in their early thirties, and they held hands tightly, their fingers intertwined as if they were clinging to each other for dear life. The woman leaned into the man's shoulder, and he rested his head on top of hers, their bodies folded into one another in a way that suggested they were trying to find solace in each other's presence.

But Max could sense the tension between them, like an unspoken weight pressing down on their shoulders. His ears twitched as their voices floated toward him in hushed tones, the kind people used when discussing matters too delicate to say aloud.

"It's been six months," the man murmured, his voice tight with frustration masked as reassurance. "These things take time."

The woman let out a shaky breath. "But what if... what if it's me? What if I can't..." She trailed off, her voice cracking under the strain.

"It's not you," the man replied quickly, though there was a heaviness to his words, an unspoken fear that echoed hers. "We'll keep trying. We just need to stay strong, together."

Max lowered his head slightly, pretending to be focused on a patch of dandelions as he listened. He didn't mean to eavesdrop, well, not entirely, but their voices carried a mix of hope and despair that was impossible to ignore.

He could see it now, the strain etched into their faces, the tightness in their smiles. They were trying to have a baby. Desperately. And failing.

The woman's red, puffy eyes and the man's furrowed brow told the rest of the story, even without the words. They clung to each other like their connection was the only thing keeping them from falling apart. Max had seen this before, the fragile hope, the unyielding pressure, the way the dream of a child could bring people closer or drive an impossible wedge between them.

He let out a quiet sigh, his gaze softening. The hope and fear radiating from the couple were almost tangible, like a current flowing between them, keeping them tethered but straining the bonds at the same time. They had poured everything into this dream, this singular hope of creating a family, and now they were left grappling with the reality that it might not happen.

Max watched as the man tightened his grip on her hand, leaning in to press a kiss to her temple. "We'll figure it out," he whispered.

The woman nodded, though her face betrayed her uncertainty. Max turned his gaze away, giving them a sliver of privacy, even if it was only symbolic. He'd seen this struggle so many times, in so many lives. Hope, fragile as glass, could cut just as deeply when it shattered.

A young mother with a stroller stopped in front of Max, smiling down at him. "Oh, look at you with your little purse!" she cooed, reaching into her wallet and pulled out a five-pound note. She placed it on the ground next to him before continuing on her way. Max stared at the note for a moment, then carefully sat on it, waiting until he could stash it safely later. Notes were tricky. They could blow away, and people noticed them more than they did with coins.

His gaze moved to another couple, walking arm in arm down the path. They were in their forties, dressed in expensive clothes, with an air of confidence that suggested they were used to getting what they wanted. But there was something hollow about the way they moved, something empty in the way they spoke to each other. Their conversation was filled with talk of business deals, vacations, and the latest gadgets they had purchased, but there was no real connection between them, no warmth, no joy.

They were career-driven, focused on success and status, and it had hollowed them out. Max could see it in their eyes, the way they barely looked at each other as they talked. Their relationship was built on money and possessions, but it was devoid of the deeper connection that made love meaningful. They were together, but only in the most superficial sense.

Max shifted slightly, the weight of his purse pressing against his side. As he watched these couples, he felt a strange mix of emotions, sympathy, curiosity, and a lingering sense of confusion. Was this what love looked like? Was this all there was? People clinging to each other out of habit, out of desperation, or out of the desire for something that wasn't love at all?

A small child toddled up to Max, giggling as she dropped a few pennies in front of him. Her mother called her back, smiling apologetically as she scooped the child into her arms and walked away. Max nosed the pennies into his purse, the familiar *plink, plink* momentarily returning him to the present.

But his mind continued to wander, drifting through the lives of the people around him, trying to make sense of it all. The park was filled with love, fragile, complicated, imperfect love. And yet, as Max sat there, he couldn't help but wonder if he was missing something. Something that went beyond the fleeting connections and the quiet despair he saw in so many of the people around him.

Tonight, he would work at Alfredo's, where the smells of garlic and fresh pasta filled the air, and the laughter of customers created a warm, welcoming atmosphere. Alfredo's was a place that made him feel grounded, even if only for a little while. And maybe, just maybe, he would find some clarity there, something to help him understand the strange, tangled web of love that seemed to elude him at every turn.

But for now, Max stayed where he was, watching the people of the park and collecting his coins, trying to piece together the puzzle of love, one observation at a time.

Chapter Thirteen

Before heading to Alfredo's Deli, Max knew he had one more task to complete. He retraced his steps back to the alley near the dumpster where he'd hidden his belongings earlier that day.

As Max approached the familiar alley, his heart gave a small leap of relief when he spotted his clothes tucked behind the stack of cardboard boxes, just as he'd left them. He paused for a moment, glancing up at the darkening sky. He didn't need a clock; as soon as the sun dipped below the horizon, the transformation began.

The shift was as natural as breathing now, though it never stopped being strange. Max felt his body stretch and his senses recalibrate, the world twisting slightly as he moved from fur to flesh. It always left him a little off balance, like stepping onto solid ground after hours at sea. But as disorienting as it was, he was used to it by now.

Still, he couldn't help but wonder why it worked that way, why a man at night and a dog by day? Why not the other way around, or why not just one form all the time? There must be some grand design behind it, surely. Someone, somewhere, must have planned it this way for a reason. Then again, maybe not. Maybe it was just another peculiar quirk of the universe.

"Oh well," he muttered, brushing the thought aside as he stepped forward and began to dress.

He slipped on his shirt, jacket, and trousers, feeling more like himself with each piece of clothing. But as he looked around for his shoes, he noticed something was missing. Max frowned and checked the surrounding area, but it was clear, they were gone.

For a moment, he simply stared at the spot where his shoes had been. They had been good shoes, solid, comfortable, and practical. Most dogs didn't care much for shoes, often seeing them as chew toys, but Max had always appreciated a sturdy pair.

Rather than feeling annoyed, Max found himself hoping that whoever had taken them was getting good use out of them. Shoes were a valuable thing when you lived on the streets, and if someone needed them more than he did, then perhaps it wasn't such a loss after all.

Straightening up, Max chuckled softly to himself. It was just another minor inconvenience in a life full of oddities. Barefoot, he slung his small purse of coins into his pocket, remembering the five-pound note that had blown away earlier. The memory made him smile wryly, paper money never seemed to stick with him for long.

With his clothes on and his purse secured, Max left the alley behind and made his way toward Alfredo's. His bare feet padded softly on the pavement, but he didn't mind. The streets of London were familiar, and there was a certain comfort in feeling the ground beneath him as he walked. Alfredo's was waiting, and there was work to be done.

Max approached Alfredo's Deli with the familiar scents of garlic, fresh tomatoes, and baked bread filling the air. The red, white and green awning over the entrance made the small deli feel warm and inviting, like a hidden gem in the heart of the city. Max had always felt at ease here, a brief respite from the strangeness of his existence.

He pushed open the door, the bell jingling softly as he entered. Inside, the deli was buzzing with life. Customers chatted at the small tables, and the sound of clinking dishes echoed from the kitchen. The atmosphere was warm and lively, a sharp contrast to the quiet streets outside.

Lorenzo, the broad-shouldered, moustachioed owner of the deli*, spotted Max as soon as he walked in. A grin spread across his face, and his booming voice filled the room. "Ah, Max! There you are! Come in, come in! We're just getting started for the evening rush."

Max returned the smile, feeling the warmth of Lorenzo's welcome. He nodded, slipping into the comfortable routine of work, even as the complexities of his life loomed in the background. Tonight, there would be time to think, to learn, to observe, just as he had done in the park. But for now, there was something grounding about the smells, the sounds, and the simple work of balancing the books at Alfredo's Deli. The rather oversized slice of lasagne didn't make matters any worse.

* No-one actually knew who Alfredo was, but the name seemed to match the business too well to change it.

147

Stephanie arrived home just as the last of the day's light was fading. She unlocked the door to her small flat, pushed it open with her shoulder, and was greeted by Oliver, who was perched on his favourite spot on the windowsill. The cat gave her a slow, lazy blink as she set down her bag and kicked off her shoes.

"Hey, Ollie," she mumbled, rubbing her eyes. "Long day."

Oliver responded with a half-hearted meow before resuming his watch over the street below. Stephanie smiled at his indifference as she dragged herself to the kitchen. She was exhausted, the kind of tired that seeped into bones and made even simple tasks feel monumental. She glanced at the fridge but didn't have the energy to make anything complicated, so she settled for a quick sandwich. The bread was a bit stale, and the cheese was on the verge of turning, but it would do.

As she slumped onto the couch, her phone buzzed in her pocket. She pulled it out and saw Fiona's name flashing on the screen. Stephanie hesitated for a moment before answering, Fiona's calls were always unpredictable, and after the conversation they'd had last night, she wasn't sure what to expect.

"Hey, Fiona," Stephanie said, trying to sound more cheerful than she felt.

"Steph!" Fiona's voice crackled through the line, practically vibrating with excitement. "You're not going to believe this, David proposed!"

Stephanie froze, her exhaustion from the day momentarily forgotten. She shifted in her chair, gripping the phone tighter. "Wait… what? He proposed? Like, marriage? With a ring?"

"Yes!" Fiona squealed, her voice pitching so high Stephanie had to pull the phone away from her ear. "A beautiful ring, so sparkly! He took me to that fancy French place downtown. Then, right in the middle of dinner, he got down on one knee and asked me to marry him! Of course, I said yes!"

Stephanie blinked, trying to process the words. David proposed? Marriage? This was the same David who Fiona had spent months venting about, his selfishness, his wandering eyes, the texts from that *"friend"* Fiona had been too afraid to confront him about. And now, suddenly, she was engaged? It felt like whiplash.

"That's… wow, Fiona. That's huge news. Congratulations," Stephanie said, forcing the words out with a cheerfulness she didn't feel. Her mind was already spinning.

"Thank you! Oh my God, Steph, I'm so excited. I can't even believe it. It all feels like a dream!" Fiona's voice bubbled with giddy energy.

Stephanie hesitated, searching for the right words, but her scepticism pushed to the surface. "I'm glad you're happy, Fiona, really. But… are you sure this is what you want? I mean, after everything we've talked about with David… are you absolutely sure?"

There was a pause, just long enough for Stephanie to hear the shift in Fiona's tone when she replied. "What do you mean? Of course, I'm sure. He proposed, Steph. That means he loves me. He wants to spend his life with me."

"I know," Stephanie said carefully, softening her tone. "But you've been so conflicted about him lately. I mean, not long ago, you weren't even sure if you wanted to stay with him. I just… I just want to make sure you're making the right decision. You deserve to be truly happy."

Fiona's excitement dimmed further, her voice cooling noticeably. "Why can't you just be happy for me, Steph? This is what I've been waiting for. David's finally committing, and now you're telling me to be cautious? What, do you think I'm making a mistake?"

Stephanie took a breath, steadying herself. She didn't want to hurt Fiona, but she also couldn't ignore everything they'd discussed before. "It's not that, Fiona. I just don't want you to feel rushed into this. I mean, you deserve someone who's all in, no doubts, no hesitations. You've been through so much with him, and I, "

"Steph," Fiona cut in, her voice clipped now. "David loves me. People make mistakes, okay? But he's shown me he's serious about us. Why can't you see that?"

Stephanie bit her lip, feeling the tension rising on the line. "I *do* see it, Fiona. I'm just saying it's okay to take a moment and really think about this. Marriage is a big step, and I just want to make sure you're doing it for the right reasons, not because, "

"Not because *what*?" Fiona snapped, the irritation in her voice sharp now. "Because I don't deserve to be happy? Because I should just sit around and wait for some perfect fantasy relationship that doesn't exist? You don't get it, Steph. I love him, and he loves me. That's all that matters."

Stephanie sighed, realizing she was only pushing Fiona further into her defences. "You're right. I just... I just want the best for you, that's all."

"I already have it," Fiona said firmly, her excitement dimmed but her conviction unwavering. "David is the best thing for me. You'll see."

Stephanie didn't argue. She just nodded, even though Fiona couldn't see it. "Okay. If you're happy, that's what matters."

"I *am*," Fiona said, her tone softening just a little. "Thanks, Steph. I know you're just looking out for me, but this is real. I've never been more sure of anything in my life."

"Alright," Stephanie replied, a faint knot of unease settling in her stomach. "If you're happy, then I'm happy for you."

But as Fiona launched into a bubbly description of wedding ideas and Pinterest boards, Stephanie couldn't help but wonder, was Fiona truly happy, or just desperate to believe she could be?

"Anyway, I'll see you tomorrow," Fiona said, her tone still guarded. "I'll talk to you later, okay? I need to call my mum and tell her the good news."

"Yeah, of course. Take care, Fiona."

The call ended, and Stephanie sat there on the couch, staring at her phone. She had wanted to be supportive, but the unease gnawing at her wouldn't go away. Fiona might be happy now, but Stephanie couldn't shake the feeling that this engagement was more about David making a grand gesture than actually fixing the problems in their relationship.

She leaned back against the cushions, letting out a long sigh. It seemed like everyone around her was moving forward, making decisions, taking big steps, while she was still here, stuck in the same routine, with the same doubts and questions swirling in her mind.

Oliver jumped down from the windowsill and padded over to her, rubbing his head against her leg. Stephanie smiled faintly and reached down to scratch behind his ears. "What do you think, Ollie? Am I overthinking things again?"

Oliver responded with a soft purr, pressing his warm body against her side. Stephanie chuckled softly, grateful for the small comfort. "Yeah... maybe I should just let it go."

But even as she tried to push the conversation with Fiona out of her mind, the uneasy feeling lingered, settling deep in her chest like a weight she couldn't quite shake.

She sat on the couch staring at the half-eaten sandwich in her hands. The bread was stale, the cheese was questionable, and the whole thing tasted like disappointment. She sighed, her stomach twisting with a mixture of hunger and frustration. This wasn't how she had imagined unwinding after a long day.

She took one last, hesitant bite before grimacing and tossing the sandwich into the bin. "That was dreadful," she muttered to herself. "Why do I even try?"

Her stomach growled in protest, reminding her that she hadn't eaten a proper meal. She needed something real, something warm and satisfying, something that didn't taste like a chore. Maybe getting out of the flat for a bit would help clear her mind, too. Anything to shake off the unease from her conversation with Fiona.

With a sigh, Stephanie grabbed her coat and headed out the door. The familiar sounds and smells greeted her as she stepped onto the street, a welcome change from the stifling thoughts that had been swirling in her head. She had no particular destination in mind, just a vague hope that she'd stumble upon something that would lift her spirits.

As she walked further down the road, lost in thought, a feeling of happiness for her best friend but also a feeling of *oh god this isn't going to end well is it? T*he scent of something amazing hit her. It was a mouth-watering aroma, savoury, rich, and full of promise. Her head turned instinctively toward the source, and she saw a man walking by with a sandwich that looked like it had been made by the gods themselves. Thick slices of fresh bread, golden brown, with layers of delicious-looking fillings peeking out. The smell alone was enough to make her stomach rumble with renewed hunger.

Unable to resist, Stephanie quickened her pace and caught up with him. "Excuse me!" she called out, a bit more eagerly than she had intended. The man turned to her with a curious look.

"Sorry to bother you," she said, offering an apologetic smile. "But that sandwich smells amazing. Where did you get it?"

The man grinned, clearly pleased with his choice. "Oh, this? It's from Alfredo's Deli, just down the road. Best sandwiches in the city, hands down."

"Alfredo's," Stephanie repeated, nodding as she made a mental note of the name. "Thanks. I think I'll head there."

"Good choice," the man said with a wink before continuing on his way, taking another satisfied bite of his sandwich.

Stephanie watched him go; her decision already made. She needed that sandwich, needed that moment of indulgence to replace the frustration of the day. And if Alfredo's was as good as it smelled, it might just be the perfect way to lift her spirits.

With new purpose in her step, Stephanie turned and headed toward Alfredo's Deli, her hunger leading the way. But was it only her hunger, there was something else, something inside her telling her, that, tonight, she had to be there.

Stephanie walked down the dimly lit street, her anticipation growing with every step. The enticing aroma of fresh bread and savoury fillings guided her toward Alfredo's Deli, she could already feel her mood lifting. The random stranger from earlier hadn't exaggerated, if the food was as good as it smelled, this might be exactly what she needed to turn the day around.

Chapter Fourteen

Stephanie arrived at Alfredo's, the little deli exuding warmth and charm even before she stepped through the door. The Italian-style awning, striped in the familiar green, white and red, cast a soft glow under the light of the streetlamp, while the faint flicker of candles from inside hinted at an old-world cosiness. She paused for a moment, taking it in, the handwritten chalkboard signs out front advertising *Today's Specials* and the cheerful clatter of plates and silverware filtering through the glass.

When she opened the door, a wave of comforting aromas enveloped her: garlic sizzling in olive oil, the sharp brightness of fresh basil, and the rich tang of simmering tomatoes. The scent was like a warm embrace, easing some of the tension she'd been carrying all day. Inside, Alfredo's was everything you wanted a family-run Italian eatery to be. The room was small but inviting, with chequered tablecloths draped over mismatched wooden tables. Old Chianti bottles, their necks wrapped in wicker, served as candleholders, wax dripping in uneven streams down their sides to form little sculptures of time gone by.

The deli was alive with energy but managed to feel intimate at the same time. Couples leaned across their tables, speaking in hushed tones or laughing over shared plates of pasta, while a cheerful waiter darted between them, balancing a tray laden with steaming dishes.

Stephanie let her eyes roam the room, scanning for a table, when her gaze landed on someone unmistakable. Max. He was seated at a small table by the window, bathed in the warm light that filtered through Alfredo's slightly fogged glass. His bare feet were tucked neatly under his chair, an old cloth purse of coins resting beside him.

But he wasn't his usual laid-back self, charming strangers with an offhanded quip or indulging in idle chatter. Instead, Max's attention was fixed on a ledger spread out in front of him, his brow furrowed with an intensity that seemed out of place in the carefree atmosphere. His pen moved quickly, jotting down notes with a precision that felt almost business-like.

Stephanie hesitated for a moment, watching him work. The concentrated look on his face was so unlike the Max she'd come to know, the easy-going man who always seemed to be two steps ahead of the chaos around him. What could he possibly be working on here, in the middle of Alfredo's? As the flickering candlelight danced across his features, Stephanie felt a flicker of curiosity. Whatever it was, it seemed important.

She stepped forward, weaving carefully between tables as she approached, the soft hum of conversation and the clink of glasses fading into the background. She wasn't entirely sure why she felt the need to interrupt, but something told her that if anyone was worth sitting down with tonight, it was Max.

He hadn't noticed her yet, so she took a moment to observe him. There was something endearing about the way he was so absorbed in his work, even in the midst of the lively atmosphere of the deli. And then, as if sensing her presence, Max looked up from his ledger and spotted her entering. He didn't call out, but a small smile tugged at the corners of his mouth.

Stephanie smiled back and walked over to his table. "Mind if I join you?" she asked, her voice light and hopeful.

Max gestured to the empty chair across from him. "Not at all. Please, have a seat."

She sat down, feeling a little more relaxed now that she was with someone familiar. "Looks like I've interrupted some important work," she said, glancing at the ledger.

Max shrugged, closing the book and setting it aside. "Just some numbers. They can wait. How's your evening going?"

"Better now," Stephanie admitted, leaning back in her chair. "I've had one of those days where everything feels off. I needed something to lift my spirits."

"You've come to the right place," Max said, a hint of amusement in his voice. "Alfredo's never disappoints."

They ordered together, sharing a large bowl of Alfredo's famous pasta, fresh bread and a plate of olives on the side, and two glasses of wine. As they waited for their food, Stephanie glanced once again at Max's bare feet under the table. She raised an eyebrow, a playful smile creeping onto her face.

"No shoes tonight?" she asked, teasingly.

Max chuckled, glancing down at his feet. "Ah, yes. My shoes and I have sadly parted ways. Someone else needed them more, I suppose."

Stephanie laughed, the sound light and genuine. "I've heard of kicking off your shoes after a hard day, but losing them altogether? That's a new one."

Max grinned, enjoying the easy banter between them. "Well, let's just say I've got a complicated relationship with footwear."

Their conversation flowed naturally from there, shifting from light-hearted teasing to humorous anecdotes about life in the city. Max shared a story about a run-in he'd had with an overly enthusiastic pigeon who tried to steal his lunch, and Stephanie countered with a tale of her cat Oliver's on-going battle with the neighbourhood squirrels *

The food arrived, steaming hot and smelling heavenly. They both dove in, sharing bites of pasta and tearing off pieces of bread to dip into the rich sauce. It was a simple meal, but somehow it felt like the perfect way to end the day.

*Squirrels are nothing, they are just the attack dogs of the Pigeons, have you ever seen a pigeon and a squirrel together at the same time? No, I though not.

As the bowl of pasta grew emptier, Stephanie glanced at the last few strands left behind and smiled, a memory bubbling to the surface. "This reminds me of *Lady and the Tramp*," she said with a soft laugh. "You know, the scene with the spaghetti?"

Max frowned slightly, tilting his head. "*Lady and the what?*"

Stephanie blinked, momentarily caught off guard. "You're joking, right?"

"Not even a little," Max replied, a grin tugging at his lips. "What's *Lady and the Tramp*? A book? A movie?"

Stephanie let out an incredulous laugh. "It's a classic! It's this old Disney movie about a fancy dog, Lady, and a street-smart stray called Tramp. They fall in love, and there's this really famous scene where they share a plate of spaghetti in an alleyway. They accidentally slurp the same strand of spaghetti and end up kissing."

Max raised an eyebrow, looking at her with mock seriousness. "So, let me get this straight. A romantic dinner, some pasta, and then... surprise dog kiss? And this is a thing people love?"

"It's adorable!" Stephanie insisted, playfully nudging her fork toward him. "How have you not seen it? It's iconic!"

Max chuckled, leaning back in his chair. "I guess I've missed out on some cultural milestones. But now I have to ask, how would you feel about dating a dog?" His tone was light and teasing, but there was a flicker of something deeper in his gaze.

Stephanie smirked, twirling a strand of pasta around her fork. "Well," she began, playing along, "I suppose it would depend on the dog. Is he house-trained? Loyal? Does he, I don't know, steal spaghetti in charming ways?"

Max laughed, his voice warm and genuine. "Sounds like a high bar. But for the right person, or dog, I think it's worth trying to meet expectations."

Stephanie laughed with him, her shoulders relaxing in the glow of the moment. "You're ridiculous," she said, but there was a fondness in her voice that softened the words.

They lingered over the last few bites of pasta, letting the conversation flow easily. They talked about city life, the strange characters, the unexpected joys, and the overwhelming loneliness that could creep in even when surrounded by millions. In those moments, the bustling city outside seemed to fade away, leaving just the two of them in Alfredo's warm glow.

When it was time to leave, they stepped out into the cool night air, the crisp breeze a refreshing contrast to the cosy atmosphere of the deli. They strolled side by side, the rhythm of their steps matching as they navigated the quiet street.

At the corner where their paths would part, Stephanie paused, turning to look up at Max with a soft smile.

"Thanks for tonight. I didn't expect it, but I'm glad it happened."

"Me too," Max said, his voice genuine. "It was a good night."

Stephanie tilted her head slightly, her tone light but teasing. "You know, Max, we do seem to keep bumping into each other."

He smiled; his eyes warm. "Ah, the fates. They've got a plan for everything, don't you know?" He shrugged, his grin widening. "Not that I'm complaining."

They exchanged a look, something unspoken passing between them, before Stephanie gave a small wave and turned to head home. Max watched her go for a moment before continuing on his own way, his steps a little lighter than before.

Neither of them said it out loud, but both felt certain that this wouldn't be the last time they found themselves sharing a meal, a laugh, and a quiet moment in the middle of the bustling city.

Chapter Fifteen

Max trotted through the back-streets of the city; his nose low to the ground as he searched for a familiar scent. Roger had been missing for days now, and Max couldn't shake the uneasy feeling that something was wrong. Roger never disappeared for this long without a reason, and it left him feeling unsettled.

As Max prowled through the shadowed alleys of London, his senses on high alert as he ventured deeper into the city's underbelly. The familiar sounds of bustling streets and honking taxis faded away, replaced by the distant hum of machinery and the occasional drip of water from forgotten pipes. This was a side of London that few ever saw, a labyrinth of narrow passageways and hidden corners where the light rarely reached. Perfect for a dog like Max, who knew the city's secrets better than anyone.

He moved cautiously, his paws making barely a sound on the damp cobblestones. The air here was thick with a mix of scents, old oil, rotting food, and the faint, unmistakable tang of sea salt that suggested he was getting closer to the docks.

As Max sniffed around a rusted metal grate, he caught the scent of something fishy, literally. It was faint, but distinct, like the remnants of a meal left behind by a careless seagull. Max's ears perked up, and he followed the trail, weaving through a maze of alleyways that grew darker and narrower the further he went. The buildings here loomed overhead, their windows boarded up or broken, casting long shadows that stretched across the ground like the claws of some unseen predator.

Despite the eerie atmosphere, Max pressed on, his determination unwavering. He'd been in tougher spots than this before, and he wasn't about to let a few creepy alleys stop him from finding his compadre. Besides, there was something thrilling about exploring these forgotten corners of the city. It was as if he were uncovering a London that existed just beneath the surface, a world of secrets and mysteries waiting to be discovered by those brave enough to search for them.

Making his way through a narrow alley, he picked up a faint, earthy scent. He paused, sniffing the air carefully, before following the trail to a small mound of dirt near the edge of a wall. He gave a low bark and waited, his ears perked up and alert.

After a moment, the ground stirred, and a pair of small, beady eyes peered up through the dirt. A mole popped its head out, twitching its whiskers as it regarded Max with an air of cautious curiosity.

"Oh, good morning to you, sir!" Max said cheerfully, lowering his head until he was at eye level with the tiny creature. "I don't suppose you've seen an odd-looking seagull called Roger around here, have you?"

The mole blinked up at him, its whiskers twitching furiously, then let out a high-pitched squeak and began digging at a frantic pace.

Squeak, squeak, dig dig, intoned the small creature. Fortunately, Max had long since mastered the peculiar art of understanding moles.

"Ah, I see. Near the docks, you say?" Max muttered, watching the mole's enthusiastic paw movements throw up tiny sprays of dirt. "Well, that tracks. Roger never could resist a good fish-and-chip wrapper."

The mole let out another squeak, throwing in a series of energetic noises that Max understood to mean something like, *Squeak squeak,* "Watch out for that Seagull, he's a strange one*" squeak!*

"Noted, my friend. Much appreciated," Max replied with a nod.

"Oh, and while I've got you," he said conversationally, "how's the family? The little ones keeping you busy?"

The mole paused mid-scratch, then squeaked a long series of sounds, punctuated with a dramatic flick of its paws.

"Twins?" Max repeated with a grin. "No wonder you're out of breath. I imagine they're running you ragged, or burrowing you ragged, I suppose."

The mole's next squeaks carried a note of pride, mingled with exhaustion, as if it were saying, *Squeak squeak* "non-stop chaos *though I wouldn't change them for the world," squeak squeak!*

Max chuckled. "Parenthood, eh? It's a full-time job no matter what species you are. And Mrs. Mole? How's she doing?"

The mole paused again, this time letting out a quieter, more reflective string of squeaks, accompanied by a delicate paw shuffle.

"Ah, the usual, then," Max said, nodding sagely. "Well, they say relationships are like digging tunnels, hard work, but worth it when you strike gold."

The mole squeaked softly, as if in agreement, its tiny paws still for a moment before resuming their busy motion.

They continued to make small talk for a few minutes.

"Well, I won't keep you any longer," Max said, rising to his feet. "If you see Roger, let him know I'm looking for him. And good luck with the twins, they grow up fast, you know!"

During a flurry of squeaks Max's ears raised suddenly, a look of joy on his face. "Oh my, that's fantastic. Thank you very much." He offered

The mole gave a final emphatic squeak, its little nose bobbing in acknowledgment, before it vanished back into the earth in a flurry of dirt. Max stood for a moment and smiled. Even in the smallest encounters, there was always a little wisdom to be found, and this was good wisdom.

Max stood up and resumed his search for Roger, weaving through the bustling streets with a growing sense of frustration. Despite the mole's tip, there was no sign of the elusive seagull. It was as if Roger had simply vanished, leaving Max to chase shadows.

As he passed a newsstand, something caught his eye, a newspaper, its bold headline shouting from the rack: *"Earthquake in Peru: Death Toll Rises Beyond Initial Estimates."* Max paused, his brow furrowing as he stared at the paper. The words stirred a memory, uninvited but persistent. The last time there had been a disaster, a tsunami, if he recalled correctly, Roger had disappeared too, gone without a trace for weeks.

He stopped for a moment, considering the coincidence. "Probably nothing," he muttered to himself, brushing the thought aside. Roger was unpredictable at the best of times, and Max had learned not to put too much stock in his absences. Still, the timing gnawed at him, like a loose thread he couldn't quite bring himself to pull.

With a sigh he continued down the street. Whether Roger's disappearance was tied to the news or just one of his many eccentricities, there was no point dwelling on it now. Max's job was to find him, not unravel whatever strange mysteries the seagull always seemed to attract.

As the hours passed, Max found himself distracted by another scent. It was subtle at first, but it grew stronger as he followed it down a side street. The scent of leather, mixed with the unmistakable smell of human feet, led him to a pair of shoes sitting just outside the back door of a small shop.

Max's tail wagged with excitement. They were good shoes, sturdy, well-made, and just the right size. He approached them cautiously, giving them a tentative sniff before gnawing on the heel of one. It was an old habit, a remnant of his dog instincts, but it felt satisfying nonetheless.

After a few chews, Max stopped himself, realizing that he would need these shoes later. With a reluctant sigh, he picked them up in his mouth and carried them to a small hiding spot behind a nearby dumpster. He carefully tucked the shoes away, making sure they were safe for later when he would need them.

With the shoes stashed and his search for Roger going nowhere, Max decided it was time to head to one of his usual spots to wait out the rest of the day. The sun was beginning to waver, and soon enough, he would be back in his human form, ready to face whatever the night had in store.

-

Across the city, Stephanie sat at her desk, staring blankly at the piles of paperwork in front of her. The hum of the office buzzed around her, but she felt disconnected from it all, like she was floating above it, observing but not fully participating.

Adrian had spent the morning barking orders at everyone, his overbearing presence making the atmosphere even more oppressive than usual. He had just returned from yet another one of his business luncheons, and instead of diving into the mountain of paperwork that awaited him, Adrian was busy showing off his latest acquisition.

"This," he announced, striking a pose in the centre of the office, "is a So-and-So & Son original." Stephanie couldn't be bothered to remember the name, it was always "Mr. Something", or the creation of "Someone and son. " Custom-made, of course." He tugged at the lapels of his suit jacket, ensuring that everyone could see the fine stitching and perfectly tailored fit.

"Fit for an ass", she thought.

Amy and the junior staff gathered around him, their expressions a mix of awe and forced admiration. "Wow, Adrian," Amy gushed, clearly playing along. "Very smart! I've heard those suits are incredibly hard to get."

"Oh, they are," Adrian replied with a smug grin. "But when you know the right people, anything's possible."

The juniors nodded eagerly, murmuring their agreement as Adrian spun in place, showing off every angle of his expensive new suit. Stephanie couldn't help but roll her eyes as she watched the scene unfold. It was the same old story, Adrian, ever the narcissist, basking in the attention of his adoring underlings. He thrived on their flattery, and they, in turn, played along to stay on his good side.

Stephanie, however, had no interest in fawning over Adrian's latest vanity project. She had too much work to do and too little patience for his theatrics. Still, it was hard to tune out his voice as he continued to brag about the suit, recounting every detail of the purchase, from the fabric selection to the final fitting.

"And the best part?" Adrian added with a conspiratorial whisper. "Because I know the people that I know, I got it for half price."

The juniors laughed, and Amy clapped her hands together, delighted by the story. "You always know how to get a good deal, Adrian."

Adrian beamed, clearly pleased with himself. "Well, it's all about timing and connections. Remember that, and you'll go far."

Stephanie let out a quiet sigh, turning her attention back to her work. Adrian might be proud of his newest acquisition, but it did nothing to ease the growing pile of tasks she had to complete. The never-ending legal documents on her desk loomed over her like a dark cloud, and every time she thought she was making progress, something, or someone, would set her back.

It wasn't just work that weighed on her, though. Fiona's constant stream of texts about the wedding were wearing her down. Stephanie wanted to be supportive, but the nagging feeling that Fiona was rushing into something she wasn't ready for made it hard to celebrate the news. The tension between wanting to be a good friend and being honest about her concerns left Stephanie feeling conflicted and drained.

She sighed, rubbing her temples as she tried to focus on the task at hand. But no matter how hard she tried, her mind kept drifting, back to last night's dinner with Max, to the easy conversation and the warmth of his presence. It had been a small moment of peace in the chaos of her life, and she found herself longing for more of that calm.

The afternoon dragged on, with emails piling up and Adrian's voice echoing in her ears as he continued to prattle on about his suit. By the time the day was over, Stephanie felt completely spent. She packed up her things, barely acknowledging her colleagues as she headed for the door. All she wanted was to get outside, breathe in some fresh air, and shake off the weight of the day.

As she stepped out of the office building, the crisp evening air wrapped around her, easing her frayed nerves. She chose to take the longer route home, meandering through the city's quieter streets in search of clarity.

And that's when she saw him, Max, sitting on a park bench near to her apartment, looking as calm and collected as ever, his gaze staring off into the distance as if lost in an imaginary world.

Chapter Sixteen

The city had settled into its usual evening rhythm as Max sat on the bench, idly admiring his new shoes. They were a perfect fit, sturdy, well-made, and much better than the old pair he had lost. He shifted his feet slightly, feeling the soles press comfortably against the ground. It was the little things like this that made his strange existence a bit more bearable.

The moles had been surprisingly helpful today. Not only had they tipped him off about Roger's whereabouts near the docks even if that had born no fruit, but they had also provided him with Stephanie's address, something he hadn't asked for directly, but appreciated nonetheless. Moles knew everything, apparently. Max had long ago stopped questioning how or why they knew so much, but he had learned to trust their odd wisdom.

They had also insisted, as they always did, that he must carry two coins. "Squeak squeak, dig dig squeak!" they'd said, their tiny paws emphasizing the point with fervent precision. To them, it seemed like the cardinal rule of existence.

Max chuckled softly, their earnestness warming him in a way he couldn't quite explain. Of course, he already understood the importance of coins, better than most, in fact, but he wasn't about to dampen their enthusiasm by pointing it out. He simply nodded along, letting their advice wash over him. In a life as unpredictable as his, it didn't hurt to heed even the quirkiest bits of wisdom now and then. Besides, who knew more about the underworld than moles?

It was comforting in a strange way. The moles might not know why their insistence mattered so much, but there was something reassuring about their persistence. A little reminder, perhaps, that even the smallest voices in the world had something worth listening to.

Max adjusted his jacket, glancing up at the darkened sky. It was around eight o'clock, and most people were either home or heading there now. But he had chosen this spot for a reason, this park was along Stephanie's route home. Maybe, just maybe, she'd pass by. If she did, perhaps she'd notice him sitting here. Max liked chance encounters, if they didn't happen then better luck next time, but if they did, it made them feel like the universe was saying to you "I'm okay with this sort of thing."

He hadn't planned to see her again so soon, but after their dinner last night, Max couldn't help but hope for another chance encounter. There was something about Stephanie, something grounding and kind, that made his fragmented existence feel a little more whole. And tonight, as the cool evening breeze whispered through the trees, he found himself waiting for her, hoping for a glimpse of that warmth once more.

As he sat there, lost in thought, footsteps approached from the direction of the street. Max's heart skipped a beat as he looked up, and sure enough, there she was,

Stephanie, walking home after what seemed like another long day at work.

She looked tired, her shoulders slightly hunched, her red hair falling loose from the messy bun she had tied it in that morning. Her work clothes were a bit rumpled, and she had the look of someone who had spent the day battling the grind of office life. But when her eyes landed on Max sitting on the bench, her expression softened into a smile.

"Max?" she called out, her voice a mixture of surprise and relief. "What are you doing here?"

Max grinned, standing up from the bench and gesturing to the park around them. "Just enjoying the evening air," he said, as casually as he could manage. "Thought I'd take a walk and ended up here. I didn't expect to run into you, but I'm glad I did." The twinkle in his eye suggesting that everything had turned out in the best of possible ways.

Stephanie approached him, the weariness of the day still visible on her face, but there was a warmth in her eyes that made Max's heart feel lighter.

"I could say the same," she replied, coming to stand beside him. "It's been a long day. I needed some air before heading home. You picked a nice spot."

Max nodded thoughtfully, then, almost on impulse, he said, "How about some dinner? There's a great burger place not too far from here. Thought it might be... fitting."

Stephanie raised an eyebrow, a teasing smile forming at the corners of her mouth. "Burgers, huh? How could I possibly say no to that?"

Her tone carried just the right balance of curiosity and amusement, and Max couldn't help but grin, pleased by her reaction. "Perfect," he said, his voice warm with enthusiasm. "Let's go."

With an easy confidence, he gestured for her to follow, and together they set off, the casual rhythm of their steps mirroring the unexpected comfort they seemed to find in each other's company.

They strolled through the quiet streets together, the tension from the day slowly ebbing away. The burger bar was a small affair tucked away on a side street, with warm lighting and a welcoming atmosphere. A chalkboard signs out front proudly proclaimed the owner's commitment to Battersea Dogs Home and his commitment to gifting them a portion of their profits. Below, text with the day's special: "The Big Dawg Burger."

They found a small table near the window, and after placing their orders, Max settled in, enjoying the casual comfort of the place. Stephanie seemed to relax as well, her tired expression softening as they chatted.

"So," she said with a playful glint in her eye, "Shoes tonight? "

Max chuckled, glancing down at his feet. "Yeah, someone snagged my old pair, but you know that. It's not a big deal, better shoes always turn up eventually."

Stephanie tilted her head, intrigued. "That's a pretty optimistic way to look at it. You don't seem too bothered by the whole thing. Is that how you look at everything?"

Max shrugged, a smile playing on his lips. "I've learned not to get too attached to things. Shoes come and go, but if you keep your head up, you'll find what you need when you need it. Besides," he added, leaning in slightly, "most things in life are okay if you have a few coins."

Stephanie laughed, her eyes lighting up with amusement. "Coins? Are we talking about good luck charms here?"

"Something like that," Max said, grinning. "It's a bit of advice I got from an old friend. Always carry at least two coins. You never know when they'll come in handy."

She looked at him curiously, a smile still lingering on her lips. "You're a bit of an enigma, Max. I like that about you. You're not like most people I meet."

He chuckled softly, feeling a warmth spread through him at her words. "I'll take that as a compliment."

Their food arrived, two towering burgers with all the fixings, accompanied by generous portions of fries. As they dug in, the conversation flowed easily, filled with light-hearted banter and stories about their day-to-day lives.

Max couldn't help but feel a sense of contentment as they talked and laughed over dinner. There was something about Stephanie that made the world feel less complicated, less fragmented. And as they shared their meal in that little burger bar, he realized that this, these moments of connection, were what he had been searching for all along.

By the time they finished eating, the night had grown late, but neither of them seemed in a hurry to leave. They lingered over their drinks, enjoying the quiet comfort of each other's company.

Eventually, Stephanie glanced at her watch and sighed softly. "I should probably get going. It's been a long day, and I've got another busy one tomorrow."

Max nodded, standing up with her. As they walked outside the conversation slowed, replaced by a comfortable silence between them. When they reached the end of the street, where their paths would part, Max hesitated for a moment.

Stephanie turned to face him, a soft smile on her lips. "Thanks for tonight, Max. It was just what I needed."

Without thinking too much, Max stepped closer and opened his arms. "You look like you could use a hug," he said softly.

Stephanie didn't hesitate. She moved into his arms, wrapping hers around him in a warm, genuine embrace. It wasn't the kind of hug that was fleeting or awkward. This was something more, something heartfelt, full of gratitude and connection. For a moment, they simply stood there, holding onto each other as if the world around them didn't matter. Time stopped*

Max could feel the weight of her day melting away in that embrace, and he closed his eyes, savouring the quiet closeness. It wasn't a kiss, but it was something just as meaningful, a sign that they were both finding comfort in each other.

When they finally pulled apart, Stephanie looked up at him with a soft smile. "You give good hugs, Max."

He chuckled, feeling a warmth spread through him. "As do you."

With a final squeeze of his hand, she turned and walked away, leaving Max standing there with a sense of contentment that had been missing from his life for far too long. For the first time in a long while, he felt like he was moving in the right direction, toward something meaningful.

As he turned to make his way back through the quiet streets, Max couldn't help but smile to himself. Better shoes always turn up, and with two coins in his pocket, life seemed just a little bit brighter.

---

*It had in fact slowed a tiny fraction, but that is a story for another time.

Chapter Seventeen

The night air was cool but pleasant as Stephanie and Max walked in opposite directions, their footsteps softly echoing through the empty streets. The evening had gone surprisingly well, more comfortable than either of them had expected. They had spent hours talking and laughing, and when the time came to say goodbye, neither was quite brave enough to take the next step. So, Max had hugged her, just a hug, but it was warm, meaningful, and hinted at the possibility of more to come. In that moment, it felt perfect.

As they parted ways, both found their minds spiralling with a torrent of thoughts, an endless stream of *what ifs*, *self-doubts*, and *if onlys* that refused to be silenced. Each step they took in opposite directions carried the weight of unspoken questions and unacknowledged fears, their thoughts tangled in a web of possibilities they couldn't quite escape.

Stephanie couldn't stop smiling. The whole night felt like something out of one of her favourite romance novels, unexpected, sweet, and just the right amount of awkward. She replayed the evening, savouring the moments that had made her heart skip. The way Max had looked at her when she talked about her love of old books, the crinkle in his eyes when he laughed, and the nervous way he fiddled with his jacket before finally pulling her into that hug.

She could still feel the warmth of his embrace, the solidness of him. There had been a brief, breathless moment when she thought, hoped, he might kiss her. But instead, they parted with smiles and a promise to see each other again soon.

Was that a good sign? Stephanie wondered as she walked. *Or did I misread the whole thing?* She sighed softly, kicking a stray pebble along the pavement. Her mind was a whirl of excitement and doubt. *Why does romance have to be so complicated?* She let out a little laugh at her own thoughts, shaking her head. *Stop over thinking everything, Steph.*

Meanwhile, Max was lost in his own thoughts. He had enjoyed the evening more than he ever thought he would. Stephanie was charming, kind, and funny in a way that caught him off guard. But as much as he had wanted to kiss her at the end of the night, something had held him back. Maybe it was fear, fear of complicating things, fear of his secret, fear that she would eventually find out who he really was, or worse… what he was.

He glanced up at the moonlit sky, his hands shoved deep into his pockets. Part of him longed to give in to the simple joy of the evening, to let himself believe that things could be easy. But the other part, the part that knew he wasn't just a man, but also a terrier, reminded him that things were never easy for him. Not for someone who lived two lives. Two very different lives.

She deserves more, he thought, a knot of worry tightening in his chest. *She deserves better than someone who can only be with her at night, who spends his days chasing pigeons and avoiding street sweepers.*

But even as those thoughts swirled in his mind, Max couldn't deny the pull he felt toward Stephanie. She had a way of making him feel… well, like he wasn't just a man with a strange curse if that's what this existence was, but like he was someone worth knowing. Worth caring about.

Maybe it could work, he thought, though doubt still lingered at the edges of his mind.

-

The days and weeks that followed were a whirlwind of dates, meet-ups and chance encounters each one more charming and awkwardly delightful than the last. Stephanie and Max explored the city together, venturing into quaint bookshops, wandering through local markets, and even spending an evening at an old-fashioned cinema that played black-and-white films. Every moment seemed to bring them closer, though there was always an undercurrent of mystery about Max that Stephanie couldn't quite put her finger on.

Their dates took on a rhythm. They would meet in the evenings, sometimes for dinner at a small, quiet restaurant or a walk along the Thames. Max was always on time, never early, never late. And though they shared many laughs and meaningful conversations, Stephanie couldn't help but notice something odd: Max never once pulled out a phone.

It wasn't until their third date, over drinks at a charmingly rustic pub, that Stephanie finally decided to broach the subject and to ask him about it.

"So," she said, swirling her glass of wine and giving Max a teasing smile, "I've noticed something."

Max raised an eyebrow, leaning back in his chair with an amused expression. "Oh? Do tell."

Stephanie grinned, leaning in conspiratorially. "You never seem to check your phone. Not even once. In fact… I don't think I've ever seen you with one."

Max chuckled, taking a sip of his drink. "You caught me."

Stephanie tilted her head, intrigued. "So… why don't you have one? I mean, who doesn't have a phone these days?"

Max smiled, a mischievous glint in his eyes. "You see, I like to live dangerously. A man without a phone is like a dog without a leash, free to roam, free to chase after whatever catches his eye."

Stephanie looked slightly abashed, "Free to chase whatever catches your eye?"

Max noticed that she looked awkward upon saying this.

"Like other women?" she ventured. *Why, why had I asked this* she thought, *he owes me nothing, I don't want to sound pushy.*

Max looked physically hurt, "Never!" He, let out, louder than he meant, "Sorry, never." He said in a more hushed tone. "Loyalty is everything to me, very few people in this world are loyal. To me it matters, maybe above all else"

A quietness descended upon them for a few moments, Stephanie decided to swing the conversation back on track.

Stephanie laughed, shaking her head. "Seriously, though. How do you survive without one? A phone, I mean. What if someone needs to get in touch with you?"

Max shrugged, his smile softening. "I guess I just like being off the grid. Fewer distractions, you know? Plus, it gives me an excuse to be more… present. Besides, I always seem to find a way to be where I need to be."

Stephanie considered that for a moment, her curiosity deepening. "So, what, you just live your life without GPS, without texting, without… memes?"

Max chuckled again, leaning forward. "I think I manage pretty well. And who needs memes when you've got real life to keep you entertained?"

Stephanie rolled her eyes playfully, but she couldn't help but smile. "Okay, I get the whole off-the-grid thing, but what about emergencies? Or… I don't know, what if I wanted to call you? Do I just… send out a carrier pigeon?"

---

*They are not in fact unreliable, the truth of the matter is that they will go out of their way to sabotage their orders, but this is something that Max though better to keep to himself for now, so 'unreliable' would do.

Max's eyes twinkled with amusement. "Ah, see, that's where you've got it wrong. Pigeons are notoriously unreliable. * You'd be better off sending a crow. They're much more resourceful and reliable to a fault."

Where was Roger? he mused, gazing out of the window.

Stephanie laughed, shaking her head. "You're impossible."

Max grinned, clearly enjoying the banter. "But seriously, if you ever need me, just trust that I'll be around. And if not… well, I've always believed that life has a funny way of bringing people together when it's meant to."

Stephanie couldn't help but be charmed by his response, even if it left her with more questions than answers. There was something enigmatic about Max, something that made him seem both incredibly together and strangely elusive at the same time. But as frustrating as that mystery was, it also intrigued her. It made her want to know more, to peel back the layers and understand the man behind the easy-going smile.

-

Despite the fun they had on their evening dates, there were times when Stephanie wanted to see more of Max during the day. It seemed natural to her, the next step in their growing relationship. One evening, after a particularly nice dinner at a snazzy new bistro, she suggested it.

"Hey," she said, a little hesitantly, "I was thinking… maybe next time we could do something during the day? Like a picnic or maybe breakfast somewhere?"

Max paused for a split second before giving her one of his signature smiles, that mix of charm and something a little too quick to deflect. "Ah, breakfast! I'm going to have to take a rain-check on that, busy time of the year and I'm afraid the coins won't collect themselves."

Stephanie frowned, confused by his answer. "What do you mean?"

Max chuckled, waving it off with a joke. "Let's just say I'm more of a night owl. Mornings and I aren't exactly on speaking terms."

Stephanie smiled at his joke, but she couldn't shake the feeling that there was more to it than just his dislike of mornings. Still, she didn't press the issue. Max was charming, and she enjoyed their time together. If he wasn't a morning person, that was fine… for now.

But it happened again. A week later, after a lovely evening walk, she tried again. "How about a picnic in the park this weekend? We could pack some sandwiches, maybe bring a bottle of wine…"

Max grinned, but there was that same hesitation. "Sounds lovely, but unfortunately, the weekend is when I do my best… work."

Stephanie couldn't help but laugh, though there was an edge of frustration in her voice. "Work? You mean coin collecting again?"

185

Max nodded, his eyes twinkling with amusement. "Yep, those coins won't jump into my pockets on their own. Besides, people count on me"

Stephanie stared at him for a moment, trying to understand. She appreciated that Max had a quirky sense of humour, but the more he deflected her suggestions, the more it began to nag at her. Finally, she decided to push a little further.

"You know," she said slowly, "most of the work you do is at night, in restaurants. I'm sure you could find time for something during the day. Maybe even… I don't know… a weekend off?"

Max smiled again, but there was a flicker of something in his eyes, something that made Stephanie wonder if she had touched on a subject he wasn't comfortable discussing. He leaned back in his chair, rubbing the back of his neck as if considering his answer.

"I guess you could say I'm in a bit of a… routine," he said, his tone light but evasive. "The night work suits me. Always has. Besides, the world's a different place when most people are asleep. It's quieter. I like that."

Stephanie's brow furrowed, not entirely satisfied with his answer. "But you're so good at what you do, accounting, managing finances. Why haven't you ever thought about getting a higher-paying job at a firm? I mean, it doesn't make sense to work so hard at night when you could be making a lot more money during the day."

Max's smile faltered for just a moment before he recovered with another joke. "Ah, but where's the fun in that? Corporate life isn't for everyone. I prefer a more… flexible schedule. Plus, it's not about the money for me. I like to keep things simple."

Stephanie stared at him, her curiosity deepening. It wasn't just his evasiveness about daytime activities; it was the whole picture. The coins, the reluctance to spend time together on weekends, the way he seemed so comfortable in the shadows but hesitant to step into the light.

"Simple," she repeated softly, more to herself than to him. She smiled then, trying to shake off the uneasy feeling creeping up on her. "Well, if you ever change your mind, I'm always up for a picnic."

Max reached across the table and took her hand, giving it a gentle squeeze. "I'll keep that in mind," he said warmly, though there was still a hint of something unreadable in his eyes.

Chapter Eighteen

Stephanie sat in her living room, absentmindedly stroking Oliver, who purred loudly in her lap. His tail flicked occasionally, slicing the air with deliberate precision, as if sending a silent message to the pigeons perched outside the window: *Don't even think about it. I may look asleep, but my radar is always on.*

Her thoughts, however, weren't on Oliver or the pigeons. Instead, they circled around Max, specifically, his peculiar habit of always paying in coins. It didn't matter if they were at a café, a restaurant, or even buying tickets to a show. Max always seemed to have an endless supply of loose change jingling in his pocket.

At first, she hadn't thought much of it. London was a city where coins changed hands constantly, and small transactions were just part of life. But as time went on, the pattern became impossible to ignore.

The night before, when Max had paid for their drinks entirely in coins, again, Stephanie hadn't been able to resist teasing him.

"You know," she said with a playful smile, resting her chin on her hand, "most people carry notes. Or cards. Or, you know, just use their phones these days."

Max had grinned, flipping a coin into the air and catching it with a casual flourish. "What can I say? I'm old-fashioned. Besides, isn't there something satisfying about the sound of coins clinking together?"

Stephanie had raised an eyebrow, leaning back in her chair. "Sure… but where do you *get* all of them? Are you secretly raiding a wishing fountain on your way to our dates?"

He had laughed, that easy, dismissive laugh of his, shaking his head. "Nothing so dramatic, I promise. Let's just say I have a knack for finding them."

And that was it. He'd left it at that, giving her one of his enigmatic smiles before smoothly changing the subject. It wasn't the first time he'd sidestepped her curiosity, and Stephanie had let it go, for the moment.

Now, sitting in her cosy living room, the memory nagged at her. *What are you hiding, Max?* she wondered, her fingers absentmindedly brushing Oliver's fur. Her mind flitted to something else, how he'd reacted when the topic of loyalty had come up. His response had been almost visceral, his voice firm, his expression resolute. Whatever his secrets were, she was certain they didn't involve betrayal. No, it was something else entirely.

Her lips pressed into a determined line. She liked Max, more than she cared to admit, but if he wasn't willing to let her in, to truly open up, then what was the point? She wasn't interested in chasing shadows or playing guessing games. If Max wasn't ready to commit, then she had no business wasting her time.

Stephanie glanced out the window, the pigeons fluttering away as Oliver's tail gave another decisive flick. With a sigh, she set her mind on one thing: she would get to the bottom of Max's mysteries. One way or another.

-

An unspoken tension built within Stephanie with each date, each deflected suggestion of a midday lunch or afternoon coffee, and each handful of coins that Max used to pay for their outings. Despite the small mysteries, Stephanie found herself growing closer to Max, even as she couldn't shake the feeling that there was more to him than met the eye and something very wrong.

One evening when they were walking through one of their favourite parks. The sun had set some time earlier, the night was warm, with the brightest of full moons to illuminate the quiet corner in which they sat. As they sat. watching the world go by, Max turned to her, his expression serious and bashful, he looked almost silly in his obvious shyness..

"Stephanie," he said softly, his voice a little rough around the edges. "There's something I've been meaning to do for a while now."

She looked up at him, her heart pounding in her chest. "What is it?"

For a moment, he hesitated. But then, with a deep breath, he leaned in and kissed her. It was gentle at first, hesitant, as if he wasn't quite sure if he was allowed.

But when Stephanie kissed him back, all that hesitation melted away, and the kiss deepened, filled with all the unspoken emotions that had been building between them for weeks.

As they kissed, Stephanie felt a rush of warmth and joy that took her by surprise. She had been on dates before, had even been in love before, but this… this was different. Despite the oddities and unanswered questions, she had never felt so safe in someone's arms. Max, with all his quirks and mysteries, made her feel alive in a way she hadn't felt in years. There was something about him that brought out a side of her she hadn't known she was missing, a side that was more spontaneous, more open, more willing to take risks and more……. more..

Yes, she thought to herself as the kiss deepened. *There's something strange about him, something I can't quite figure out… but for all his oddities, he's making me happy. And isn't that what matters?*

When they finally pulled apart, they coyly smiled at each other, soft, shy smiles that said more than words ever could. Stephanie's mind raced with thoughts of everything she had been feeling lately, the loneliness of the weekends, the unanswered questions about Max's life, but in that moment, none of it seemed to matter. He was here, with her, and she was happy.

But before either of them could speak, a familiar squawk broke the moment.

Caw caw!

Stephanie jumped slightly, turning to see a seagull perched on a nearby bench, watching them with beady-eyed intensity, for a few moments it pecked idly at a bush beside the seat before turning its head and gazing directly at Max.

Caw Caw "I'm pleased for you old friend" Roger squawked; his gaze fixed on Max. *Caw Caw* "However you understand that she will now have to make a choice. You remember the choice don't you Max?"

Max stiffened, his grip on Stephanie's hand tightening ever so slightly. His eyes met Roger's, and for a long, tense moment, he didn't say anything. Stephanie watched the exchange in confusion, her brow furrowing as she glanced between Max and the seagull.

Finally, Max let out a heavy sigh. "No," he said quietly, his voice strained and so quiet as to be virtually inaudible. "I never have."

Roger tilted his head, his beady eyes gleaming with something like pity, or perhaps it was amusement. *Caw Caw"* Oh…..oh! Well, you always get there in the end, one way or another." Roger replied cryptically before flapping his wings and taking off into the sky, leaving Max and Stephanie standing there in bright moonlight..

Stephanie blinked, turning to Max with a puzzled expression. "Did you just… talk to a seagull?"

Max let out a soft chuckle, though there was an edge of tension in his voice. "Ah, Roger's a bit of a character. Likes to pop in with his philosophical musings from time to time."

Stephanie stared at him for a moment, clearly not satisfied with the explanation. "Philosophical musings? From a seagull?"

Max grinned, trying to lighten the mood. "Well, you know how it is. Some people have therapists, I have Roger."

Stephanie laughed, though confusion still flickered in her eyes. She had so many questions, about Roger, about Max, but something about the way he looked stopped her from pressing. His shoulders were tense, and while he smiled, it didn't quite reach his eyes. She didn't want to ruin the moment, didn't want to push him away just when it felt like they were finally getting closer.

So instead, she squeezed his hand and teased, "Well, as long as your seagull therapist is giving you good advice."

Max's smile softened, becoming more genuine. "He tries his best. Not always the most reliable, though. A bit bird-brained, if I'm honest."

Stephanie chuckled, leaning into Max slightly as they continued their walk through the park. But after a few moments of comfortable silence, she hesitated, glancing up at him with a playful yet nervous look.

"Can I say something without it getting weird?" she asked.

Max raised an eyebrow, a hint of amusement lighting his features. "That depends. Are we talking mildly weird or full-on awkward?"

"Mildly weird," she said with a laugh, though her voice had a vulnerable edge. "It's just... I started to worry you didn't fancy me. Like, maybe I'd been friend-zoned or something."

Max stopped walking, turning to face her fully. "Friend-zoned?" he repeated, his tone light but his expression thoughtful.

Stephanie shrugged, trying to keep the mood casual. "Well, yeah. I mean, you've never made a move. Not even once. A girl starts to wonder, you know?"

Max's gaze softened, and for a moment, he looked almost solemn. "It's not that I don't fancy you, Stephanie, quite the opposite," he said gently. "It's just... to me, a kiss, it's not something you do just because the moment feels convenient. It has to mean something. The timing has to be perfect."

Stephanie blinked, caught off guard by the sincerity in his voice. "Perfect, huh?"

He nodded, his hand still holding hers. "Yeah. A kiss isn't just a gesture. It's... a promise. And when I kissed you, I wanted it to be at the right time, when there was no doubt about what it meant. Not for me, and not for you. I wanted to know that you are the only person that I will ever kiss again"

Her heart fluttered at his words, the vulnerability in them catching her off guard. She felt her cheeks warm but couldn't stop the small smile tugging at her lips. "That's... unexpectedly poetic, Max. But also, kind of sweet."

"Kind of?" he teased, his smile widening.

"Okay, *very* sweet," she admitted with a laugh, leaning into him again as they resumed their walk.

Despite the oddness of the evening, and the lingering mysteries about Max, Stephanie couldn't help but feel lighter. Safe, cared for, and maybe, just maybe, a little more hopeful about whatever was happening between them. For now, walking hand in hand in the fading light, it was enough.

Chapter Nineteen

In the days following their kiss, Stephanie couldn't shake the feeling that something wasn't quite right. It wasn't just the cryptic encounter with the seagull, though their interaction certainly could be classified under, w*ell that was a bit odd now wasn't it?* Something quieter, but persistent.

It started innocently enough. A pigeon landed on her windowsill one morning, pecking at the glass with a soft tap-tap-tap. Oliver, her tabby cat, immediately leaped onto the windowsill, his wide green eyes fixed on the bird. He pawed at the glass, his tail twitching with excitement as he tried to catch the intruder.

Stephanie had laughed at first, snapping a quick photo of Oliver's antics and sending it to Fiona with the caption *Oliver the bird hunter!* It was just a pigeon, after all, nothing unusual in a city full of them.

But then it happened again the next day. And the day after that.

The pigeons didn't come in flocks, but they came often enough that Stephanie began to notice a pattern. Always one or two at a time, always pecking at the glass, always watching her with those small, beady eyes. Oliver's excitement started to shift into agitation. He became more restless, spending hours at the window, his fur bristling as he tracked the birds with an intensity that Stephanie hadn't seen before.

The unease crept in slowly. At first, Stephanie brushed it off as coincidence, pigeons were everywhere in the city, after all. But as the days passed, the feeling grew. She couldn't quite put her finger on it, but there was something about the way the birds lingered at her window that made her uncomfortable. They weren't just pecking at the glass, they were watching her. And not in the casual, absent way birds usually did. Their gaze felt... deliberate.

One evening, after coming home from another wonderful night with Max, Stephanie found Oliver sitting rigidly by the window, his eyes glued to a single pigeon perched on the ledge. The bird wasn't pecking this time, it was just... sitting there, staring in.

Stephanie frowned, feeling a shiver run down her spine. She approached the window slowly, half-expecting the pigeon to fly off as she got closer. But it didn't. It just stayed there, unmoving, its dark eyes following her as she reached for the curtain.

With a quick motion, she yanked the curtain closed, blocking the bird's gaze. She stood there for a moment, her heart pounding in her chest, trying to shake off the feeling that she was being watched. It was ridiculous, of course, just a bird. But the unease lingered.

"Come on, Steph," she muttered to herself, trying to laugh it off. "You're getting spooked by a pigeon. Get a grip."

But, the pigeons kept coming, and Oliver grew more and more agitated. He spent less time lounging around the apartment and more time pacing by the windows, his eyes constantly darting to the ledges, his ears twitching at every small noise from outside. His once-playful swats at the glass had turned into frustrated, almost frantic attempts to get at the birds that seemed to taunt him from the other side.

Stephanie started to feel uneasy in her own home. Every time she caught a glimpse of one of those pigeons, a chill ran down her spine. It was silly, irrational, even, but she couldn't shake the feeling that something wasn't right. Why did they keep coming back? Why did they keep watching her?

She tried to tell herself it was just her imagination, that she was reading too much into it. But Oliver's growing distress only heightened her own anxiety. Every time he hissed or pawed at the window; she felt her nerves fray a little more.

It's just a coincidence; she told herself repeatedly. *Just a city full of pigeons.*

But deep down, she wasn't so sure.

-

Stephanie was trying to lose herself in her work when she felt the familiar presence of Amy hovering near her desk. With a small sigh, she glanced up, forcing a polite smile as Amy leaned casually against the cubicle wall.

"Hey, Stephanie," Amy began, her tone casual but with that ever-present undercurrent of nosiness. "I was just wondering, who are you taking as your plus-one to Fiona's wedding?"

Stephanie froze for a split second, the question catching her off guard. Fiona's wedding was coming up soon, and she hadn't even fully decided if she was ready to introduce Max to that part of her life yet. But before she could stop herself, the name slipped out.

"Max."

Amy's eyebrows shot up, a grin spreading across her face. "Max, huh?" She gave Stephanie a playful wink. "Didn't realize you were seeing someone seriously enough to bring him to a wedding."

Stephanie felt the heat rising in her cheeks and quickly looked down at the papers on her desk, mentally kicking herself for letting Max's name slip so easily. She tried to recover, forcing a casual tone. "Yeah… we've been going on a few dates."

Amy's grin widened, clearly picking up on Stephanie's embarrassment. "So, what's he like? You know…" She winked again, leaning in closer as if she were about to hear some juicy gossip. "Does he stay over?"

Stephanie hesitated, unsure of how much to share. Her mind was racing, not just with thoughts of Max, but with a sudden, chilling realization. *How does Amy know Fiona?*

Before she could answer Amy's question, she blurted out, "Wait… how do you know Fiona?"

Amy straightened up a bit, her smile shifting to something more self-satisfied. "Oh, didn't you know? David is one of my best friends."

Stephanie's stomach dropped. *David.* Fiona's on-again, off-again nightmare of a fiancé. The same David who had cheated on Fiona, only to come crawling back with an engagement ring. The man who had caused Fiona so much heartache, yet somehow had convinced her to give him another chance. And suddenly, it all clicked. Stephanie remembered Amy mentioning a guy she was seeing, a guy who had a full-time girlfriend.

Could David have been the guy Amy was talking about?

Her heart began to pound in her chest as she tried to piece it together. Fiona's silence over the last few weeks now made sense. She had been avoiding Stephanie, likely tangled up in the mess that was her relationship with David. The realization hit Stephanie like a ton of bricks.

Before she could ask anything more, Amy, perhaps sensing Stephanie's internal struggle, smoothly steered the conversation back to Max, clearly uninterested in diving into the drama with David.

"So," Amy continued, as if they hadn't just touched on something potentially disastrous, "tell me more about Max. Where'd you meet him? What does he do? Is it serious?" Her tone was playful, but there was an edge to it, a subtle pressure to get more information.

Stephanie hesitated, her mind still reeling from the revelation about David. But Amy's persistence brought her back to the moment. "Uh, we met... out, one night. He's got a quirky sense of humour, really thoughtful. Works at night, mostly, helps out restaurants, does some accounting."

Amy raised an eyebrow, clearly intrigued by the mystery. "Working at night, huh? As an accountant? Sounds like there's a story there."

Stephanie forced a laugh, trying to deflect. "Maybe. But it's still early, so we'll see how things go."

Amy didn't seem convinced. She leaned in, lowering her voice to a conspiratorial whisper. "Well, just be careful. You know, if he's that quirky and you haven't... you know... moved things along, you might be friend- zoning him without even realizing it."

Stephanie felt her face grow even hotter. The insinuation made her feel both embarrassed and defensive. She opened her mouth to respond, but Amy was already backing away, giving her a knowing smile.

"Anyway," Amy said, her tone light again, "I'm sure it'll all work out. Just... don't wait too long to make your move, you know?"

With that, she turned and walked away, leaving Stephanie sitting at her desk, her heart still pounding. The knot of anxiety in her stomach had only tightened. Not only had she let Max's name slip too easily, but now there was the unsettling connection between Amy, David, and Fiona.

She sighed, rubbing her temples. It felt like her life was becoming more complicated by the day. Amy was the last person she wished to find out.

"Oh great, now my printer's stopped!". Stephanie exclaimed with a thump.

PART 2

Chapter Twenty

Stephanie stood in her kitchen, nervously chopping vegetables for dinner, glancing at the clock for the third time in ten minutes. Max was due to arrive soon. Though they'd spent so much time together over the past few weeks, this felt different. Inviting him into her home made her feel a new level of vulnerability. She had suggested he come over the last time they met, blurting out the invitation almost impulsively, and now she couldn't help but feel a twinge of anxiety about how the evening would go.

After extending the invitation, she had immediately started planning the night: choosing a recipe that was both simple and comforting, making sure the apartment was tidy, and fussing over the small details like which candles to light. Now, with only minutes until his arrival, she found herself double-checking everything. Was the wine opener out? Were the napkins folded nicely? Did the lighting feel right? She even gave the throw pillows on the couch a final fluff before returning to the kitchen, wiping her hands on a dish towel.

In the corner of the room, Oliver sat perched on the windowsill, his gaze fixed on something outside. His tail flicked back and forth, and a low growl rumbled in his throat. Stephanie glanced over at him and sighed.

"Oliver, what's gotten into you?" she asked as she stirred the sauce on the stove. "You've been on edge all week."

Oliver didn't respond the way he usually did, and she followed his gaze to see another pigeon sitting on the ledge just beyond the glass. It pecked lazily at the window, as if it had all the time in the world.

"Ugh, the pigeons again," Stephanie muttered. "They've been everywhere lately. I don't know what's going on, but they're driving me, and you, crazy."

She shook her head and turned back to the stove, focusing on finishing dinner before Max arrived. She tried to brush off the strange sense of unease that had settled over her apartment ever since the pigeons started showing up. *It's just a coincidence,* she told herself. *Pigeons are part of the city. It doesn't mean anything.*

The doorbell rang, making her jump. She quickly smoothed down her dress and hurried to answer it, trying to push the strange thoughts aside.

When she opened the door, Max was holding a bottle of wine in one hand, a small bunch of hand-picked flowers in the other and offering her his signature crooked smile. He looked effortlessly charming, as usual, dressed in a casual shirt and jeans that somehow still managed to look put together. His presence instantly brought a wave of warmth that eased some of her nervous energy.

"Hey," he said softly, his eyes lighting up as they met hers. "I brought wine. I wasn't sure what you liked, so I went with something classic."

Stephanie returned the smile, stepping aside to let him in. "The wine's perfect. Come on in. And those?" Looking at the flowers.

"Ah yes." They were thrust forward in his usual slightly awkward manner.

As Max stepped over the threshold, Oliver let out a low hiss from his perch on the windowsill. Stephanie shot the cat a look. "Oliver, behave," she muttered, though she couldn't help but notice how the cat's eyes followed Max warily as he entered the apartment.

Max chuckled, glancing at Oliver with amusement. But then, as Stephanie mentioned the pigeons again, she noticed something, just for a second, flash across his face. Concern? Worry? She couldn't quite tell, but it was gone as quickly as it appeared.

"Pigeons, huh?" Max said, trying to sound casual as he crossed the room. "That's... interesting." He then approached Oliver, crouching down to the cat's level as if to try and connect with him. "Hey there, Oliver," he said softly. "You've been on edge too, huh?"

Oliver's green eyes locked onto Max with a kind of narrowed suspicion, his tail swishing back and forth. He let out a low growl, his fur bristling slightly. Then, with a sharp hiss, he turned away from Max, jumping down from the windowsill and stalking off to a corner of the room, glancing back at Max he said, *Meow "I don't want you here! Make no trouble, this is my house!"* With that he continued to his spot by the radiator.

Max sighed, standing up and watching the cat with an almost resigned look. "I guess he has nothing to say to me," he muttered, half to himself.

Stephanie forced a small laugh, trying to shake off the oddness of the moment. "I don't know what's gotten into him lately. He's usually much more easy-going."

Max nodded, though there was a lingering tension in his expression. "Maybe he's just picking up on something... in the air."

Stephanie wasn't sure what to make of that comment, but she let it slide. "Come on," she said, gesturing toward the kitchen. "Dinner's almost ready."

Max followed her, and soon they were immersed in the rhythm of cooking together. The conversation flowed easily, with Max sharing stories about his late-night adventures and Stephanie recounting funny anecdotes from his work. Though she noticed that he never mentioned family or friends. The warmth of the evening began to push aside the strange tension, and for a while, it felt like everything was perfect.

At the small table in the kitchen, with its mismatched chairs, Stephanie set the steaming plate in front of Max with a satisfied smile, the rich aroma of roasted chicken and herbs filling the cosy apartment. The dish was simple but hearty, a perfect meal for a chilly evening. Max's eyes lit up as he inhaled the savoury scent, his stomach rumbling in eager anticipation. Across the room, Oliver, the ever-curious cat, perched by the radiator, his nose twitching as he picked up the delicious smell. He let out an appreciative *meow, h i s* eyes narrowing in on the plate as if silently declaring his approval of Stephanie's culinary skills.

As they dug in, the conversation flowed easily, their voices mingling with the soft clinking of cutlery against plates. "You know," Stephanie began, twirling her fork in the creamy mashed potatoes, "I stumbled across this little bistro last week. They had the most amazing ratatouille, absolutely bursting with flavour. It reminded me of that tiny café we found on that rainy day. Remember?"

Max nodded, a smile tugging at his lips. "I remember. The one with the chipped teacups and the old piano in the corner. They served that incredible beef bourguignon. I swear, I've never tasted anything like it since."

Oliver, now lounging on the back of the couch, let out another contented purr, clearly enjoying the relaxed atmosphere. Stephanie chuckled, glancing over at the cat. "Seems like Oliver agrees with our taste in food. Though, I think he's more interested in stealing a bite of your chicken."

Max laughed, cutting off a small piece and setting it aside. "Well, I can't blame him. But don't worry, Oliver. There's plenty for everyone tonight." They continued chatting, sharing stories of their favourite meals, the conversation light and full of warmth, just like the meal Stephanie had lovingly prepared.

Following dinner, as Stephanie removed the plates and beckoned him to the living room., Max moved to the window. Stephanie watched as he pulled something from his pocket, a coin. It wasn't just any coin, though. It looked old, worn, with intricate designs that had been smoothed over by time.

Max placed it on the windowsill, just where Oliver had been earlier, and gave the cat a pointed look. "Leave this here, Oliver. It's important."

Oliver, now watching from his corner, let out a small, reluctant hiss but didn't move to swat the coin away. Stephanie raised an eyebrow, curious about the exchange. "What's that?" she asked.

Max turned back to her with a mysterious smile. "Just a little something for luck. Oliver knows what to do."

She wanted to press him for more details, but the tenderness in his gaze made her pause. Instead, she smiled and let the moment pass, filing away the strangeness in the back of her mind. For now, she just wanted to enjoy the night with Max.

She moved to the living room, where they settled onto the couch with their glasses of wine. The mood shifted from light and playful to something softer, more intimate. Stephanie found herself leaning closer to Max, drawn in by the warmth of his presence and the way his eyes seemed to hold her captive.

They continued to talk, hopes, dreams, aspiration, about the little things that made them laugh, about the things they loved and feared. As the evening wore on, the conversation grew quieter, the pauses between words filled with a comfortable silence.

At some point, without either of them realizing exactly when, Max's hand found hers, his fingers intertwining with hers in a way that felt both natural and thrilling. Stephanie looked up at him, her heart pounding in her chest, and saw something in his eyes that made her breath catch.

Before she could say anything, Max leaned in and kissed her. It was soft at first, tentative, as if he were testing the waters. But when she responded, deepening the kiss, it became something more, something filled with unspoken emotion and a longing that neither of them could ignore.

The kiss turned into another, and then another, and soon they were wrapped in each other's arms, the rest of the world fading away. They moved together, slowly and tenderly, as if they were both afraid to break the spell that had settled over them.

When they finally made love, it was quiet and gentle, an unspoken connection between them that didn't need words to express. The room was filled with soft whispers and the sound of their breathing, and everything else, Oliver's pacing, the lingering unease, the questions, faded into the background. For now, there was only the feeling of being one and the bliss that it bought.

As they lay together in the quiet of the night, entwined on the sofa, an old patchwork quilt covering them. Stephanie felt a sense of peace settle over her. She had never felt this way with anyone before, this safe, this content, yet this... alive. For all of Max's oddities, for all the questions she still had; he made her happy. And right now, that was enough.

Her head pressed against his chest, the hair brushing gently against her cheek as he breathed, she closed her eyes, awash with emotions, she calmly and contentedly drifted off to sleep.

Chapter Twenty-One

Stephanie was lost in a deep, peaceful sleep when something heavy and furry landed squarely on her chest. Startled, she blinked awake to find Oliver standing on the bed, his green eyes glowing faintly in the dim light of the pre-dawn hours. He meowed insistently, and as her grogginess began to fade, she realized he wasn't just trying to get her attention, his gaze was fixed on Max.

She turned her head slightly and saw Max lying next to her, still asleep, his breathing steady and slow. For a moment, everything felt perfect. The warmth of the blankets, the quiet of the room; until Oliver decided to speak.

In the silent, unspoken language of cats, Oliver looked at Max with a piercing gaze and said, *Meow "Cutting it fine, aren't you?"*

Stephanie felt Max stir beside her, his body tensing at Oliver's words. Slowly, his eyes fluttered open, and the moment they focused on the clock on her bedside table, a look of pure panic, even terror crossed his face.

"Oh no, oh please no!," Max muttered under his breath, sitting up abruptly. His movements were quick, frantic, as he scrambled to untangle himself from the blankets. "I'm late, too late."

Stephanie blinked in confusion, still half-asleep. "Max? What's going on?"

He was already out of bed, hastily pulling on his clothes. "I need to go. Right now." His voice was tight, and there was a sense of urgency in his every movement that sent a ripple of anxiety through her.

"Go? But why?" she asked, sitting up and trying to make sense of his sudden rush. "It's still dark outside."

Max didn't stop to explain. He yanked his shirt over his head, then knelt down to pull on his shoes. "I stayed too long; .I, I….."

Stephanie lay there, becoming more concerned by the second at the look of sheer panic on Max's face. This wasn't 'I'm late for a meeting' or 'I've forgotten to put money in the parking meter' this was wild panic and it was scaring her.

Oliver, now sitting calmly at the foot of the bed, watched Max with a knowing expression. *Meow" Running late are you?,"* the cat said, though to Stephanie this just sounded like Oliver protesting at the abruptness of the current whirlwind unfolding before them.

"Max, please," Stephanie tried again, her voice laced with concern. "What's going on? Why do you have to leave so suddenly?"

Max paused for a brief moment, just long enough to meet her worried gaze. His eyes softened, and for a second, she saw the struggle in him, wanting to stay, wanting to explain, but knowing he couldn't. Not yet. Not like this.

"I'm sorry," he said quietly, his tone filled with regret. "I promise I'll explain everything. But right now, I just... I need to go."

He pressed a quick kiss to her forehead, then turned to Oliver with a look that was almost apologetic. "Thanks for the warning," he murmured, before rushing out of the room.

Stephanie sat there in stunned silence, the warmth of his kiss still lingering on her skin, as she heard the front door click shut. The apartment felt suddenly cold, and the knot of worry in her stomach tightened. What was Max running from? What could possibly be so urgent that he had to leave before dawn like this?

She glanced at Oliver, who was now calmly grooming himself as if nothing unusual had happened. "What was that all about?" she asked, more to herself than to the cat.

Oliver paused mid-lick, casting her a sly glance before hopping down from the bed and padding out of the room without a sound, leaving Stephanie alone with her unanswered questions.

-

Max darted through the quiet, deserted streets of the city*, his heart pounding in his chest. The sky was still dark, but the faint glow of dawn was beginning to creep over the horizon. He had stayed too long, much longer than he should have, and now he was running out of time.

The transformation was coming. He could feel it in the tension of his muscles, the strange shift in his senses. He needed to find somewhere to hide before it was too late.

But the city was waking up faster than he could escape.

As he sprinted down the narrow alleyways, the stillness of the early morning was being replaced by the sounds of life stirring: the distant hum of traffic, the soft thrum of footsteps on the pavement, and the clang of delivery trucks unloading their cargo. Every corner he turned seemed to throw another obstacle in his way.

A delivery bike came speeding out of nowhere, nearly knocking him over. Max stumbled, barely managing to regain his balance as the rider sped past, cursing at him under his breath. He pushed forward, his breaths coming in short, ragged gasps. The narrow streets that had been so empty just moments ago were now filling with early risers, dog walkers, shopkeepers, and cyclists weaving through the streets.

Max was running out of time. He could feel the transformation creeping closer, the tingling in his limbs growing more intense with each step.

His vision blurred, and he stumbled again, narrowly avoiding a crash with a man carrying a stack of newspapers. The man shouted something after him, but Max didn't stop to listen. He couldn't afford to.

*As deserted as London ever could be. To call the streets deserted is akin to describing the quiet musings of Brian Blessed.

The first rays of sunlight began to pierce through the dark sky, casting long shadows across the pavement. Max knew he was out of time. The change was coming, and there was nothing he could do to stop it.

As he reached the middle of a junction, the transformation hit him with full force. His body seized up, the familiar pain of bones realigning and muscles contracting overtaking him. He collapsed onto the pavement, unable to stop the process.

Just as the transformation began, a few early risers rounded the corner, their eyes catching sight of Max in mid-change. A man walking his dog froze in place, his mouth hanging open in shock as he watched Max's human form shift and contort. An elderly woman on her way to buy the morning paper stopped, rubbing her eyes in disbelief. A cyclist skidded to a halt, staring in wide- eyed confusion.

Max's body shrank, his limbs shortening, his clothes falling loose around him. In a matter of moments, the man they had just seen was gone, replaced by a small, scruffy brown and white terrier, panting heavily on the pavement.

The bystanders stood there in stunned silence, too shocked to move. But the more they stared, the more they began to question what they had seen.

"No, that can't be right," the elderly woman muttered to herself, shaking her head. "Must've been my eyes playing tricks on me. Too early to be seeing things like that."

The man with the dog glanced down at his own pet, then back at the terrier that had appeared out of nowhere. "Yeah… must be the light or something," he said, though his voice wavered with uncertainty. "I didn't really see… that."

The cyclist blinked a few times, then rubbed his eyes with the back of his hand. "Yeah, shots were a great idea last night Steve!," he mumbled before pedalling away, trying to convince himself that it had just been his imagination.

Max, now fully transformed into a dog, remained crouched on the pavement, his heart still pounding in his chest. He looked around, his ears flattened against his head as he watched the groggy bystanders slowly move on, each one of them rationalizing the impossible sight they had just witnessed.

Too close, Max thought, his mind racing. *That was way too close.*

He waited until the street had cleared, then cautiously picked up his watch, looking around he darted into the nearest alley, his small paws padding silently on the pavement. He needed to get out of sight; to hide until the city was fully awake and the chaos of the morning could swallow him up.

"Bugger!" as he curled up behind a stack of crates, his heart still thudding in his chest, he looked on as a sweeper lorry swept his clothes away, never to be seen again.

I must be more careful he mused he couldn't shake the fear that next time, he might not be so lucky.

Chapter Twenty-Two

Stephanie spent the day feeling increasingly frustrated and anxious. Ever since Max had rushed out of her apartment before dawn, she hadn't been able to shake the unsettling feeling gnawing at her. She had wanted to call him, to ask him what had been going on, but then she remembered, Max didn't have a phone. Of course, he didn't. What kind of person in this day and age didn't have a phone? She could only stew in her thoughts, left wondering what on earth was happening with him.

By the time she got to work, her frustration had only grown. She tried to focus on her tasks, but her mind kept drifting back to Max, the frantic way he had left, the constant secrecy surrounding him, and the growing number of questions she had that never seemed to get answered. She glanced at her phone out of habit, even though she knew there wouldn't be any messages from him. The fact that she couldn't reach out to him left her feeling even more powerless and on edge.

Across the office, Amy seemed to sense her distraction. She gave Stephanie a few lingering looks throughout the day, smirking as if she knew something Stephanie didn't. It made Stephanie's skin crawl. *What's her deal?* she wondered, feeling more unsettled than ever.

During lunch, Amy approached her with a coy smile, leaning casually against her desk. "You've been awfully distracted today," she said, her tone dripping with fake concern. "Everything okay? Or is it that mysterious boyfriend of yours?"

Stephanie bristled, her patience already worn thin. "I'm fine, Amy. Just busy."

Amy's smirk widened. "Busy… or worried? You know, it's been my experience that when a guy acts shady, it's usually because he's hiding something. Just a thought."

Stephanie forced a tight smile, but inside, she felt her stomach twist. Was Amy right? Was Max hiding something from her? She had always brushed off his quirks as just that, quirks. But now, she couldn't help but wonder if there was something more to it. Something she wasn't seeing.

By the end of the day, Stephanie was done with wondering. She needed answers. When she left the office, she headed straight to the café where she and Max had agreed to meet that evening. She wasn't going to let this drag on any longer. She needed to know what was really going on with him.

As she arrived at the café, she spotted Max sitting at a small table near the window, and her heart lurched at the sight of him. But something was off. He was dressed in mismatched clothes, an old, wrinkled button-up shirt that didn't seem to fit right, paired with a pair of trousers that looked like they had seen better days. His usually charming, put-together appearance was nowhere to be found.

Stephanie approached the table, her emotions a tangled mess of frustration, confusion, and hurt. As she got closer, Max looked up and met her eyes with a sheepish smile, but it did nothing to ease the knot in her stomach. His mismatched outfit only added to her growing unease. This wasn't the Max she knew, the confident, composed man who always seemed to have everything under control. He looked... dishevelled, almost desperate.

"Hey," Max said softly, standing up as she reached the table.

"Hey," Stephanie replied, her voice tight. She didn't bother with pleasantries. She sat down across from him, crossing her arms over her chest. "We need to talk."

Max hesitated for a moment, then sat back down, the nervousness in his posture unmistakable. He tried to give her a reassuring smile, but it didn't reach his eyes. "Yeah, I figured."

Stephanie took a deep breath, trying to keep her voice steady. "Max, what's going on? I've been trying to make sense of everything, but nothing adds up. You won't see me through the day. You don't do weekends, except at night. Then there are all the coins You don't even have a phone. And this morning." She paused, struggling to find the right words. "This morning, you bolted out of my apartment like the building was on fire."

Stephanie instinctively thought of the old movies she's watched with her father about vampires who could only be out at night.... she put that thought out of her head.

Max winced, clearly realizing that his usual deflections weren't going to work this time. "Stephanie, I, "

"No." She held up a hand, cutting him off. "I need you to be honest with me. No more jokes, no more vague excuses. Last night was wonderful, I woke up feeling like life was finally coming good, then boom, all......all that happened. What are you hiding from me?"

Max opened his mouth to respond, but before he could say anything, Stephanie's emotions spilled over. She looked down at the table, her voice trembling as she spoke. "I... I've given myself to you, Max. I've let you in, let myself care about you, and now... now I'm wondering if that was a mistake. I don't even know who you are."

Max's face softened at her words; the guilt clear in his expression. He leaned forward, resting his hands on the table as he looked at her with a sincerity that made her heart ache. "Stephanie, it wasn't a mistake. I swear to you, it wasn't. I know I haven't been fair to you, and I know I've been keeping things from you. But it's not because I don't care. I do. I care about you more than you know."

Stephanie blinked back tears, trying to maintain her composure. "Then why? Why all the secrets?"

Max sighed, running a hand through his hair. "I... I wish I could explain it all right now, but it's not that simple. I've been living with something, something that makes it hard to live a normal life. It's not because I don't want to be with you. I do. But... there are things about me that make it complicated."

"Complicated?" Stephanie echoed, her frustration flaring again. "What could possibly be so complicated that you can't just be honest with me?"

Max opened his mouth, but this time, instead of deflecting with humour, he hesitated. She could see the struggle in his eyes, the battle between wanting to tell her the truth and the fear of what that truth might mean for them.

"I've never met anyone like you, Stephanie," Max said quietly, his voice filled with emotion. "And I don't want to lose you. But if I tell you everything… I'm afraid you'll walk away."

Stephanie's heart ached at his words, but the frustration still burned within her. "Max, you're already pushing me away by not being honest. Whatever it is, I'd rather know than be left in the dark."

Max looked down at the table, his fingers tracing the edge of his coffee cup as he gathered his thoughts. When he finally spoke again, his voice was barely above a whisper. "I can't explain everything right here, right now. But… I promise I'll tell you. I just need a little more time."

Stephanie bit her lip, torn between her desire for answers and the genuine emotion she saw in his eyes. She wanted to trust him, but every instinct in her was screaming that something wasn't right. Still, she nodded slowly. "Okay. But no more running off without an explanation. No more secrets. If we're going to keep seeing each other, I need you to be honest with me."

Max nodded, relief flooding his expression. "I promise. No more secrets."

As they sat there in the café, a fragile understanding seemed to pass between them. Stephanie wasn't fully satisfied with his answers, she knew there was more he wasn't telling her, but for now, she decided to give him the benefit of the doubt. She hoped that whatever he was hiding, it wasn't something that would tear them apart.

But what neither of them noticed was Amy, standing across the street. She had followed Stephanie to the café, curiosity driving her to uncover whatever it was that Stephanie had been so secretive about. She watched the pair intently, her sharp eyes picking up on every detail of their tense conversation.

Amy smirked as she leaned against a lamppost, unnoticed by Max and Stephanie. *There's definitely something going on here,* she thought. *And I'm going to find out what it is.*

Chapter Twenty-Three

Amy had always been the woman everyone wanted to know, beautiful, confident, and seemingly untouchable. She had men chasing after her, eager to shower her with attention and gifts. But beneath the glamorous exterior, Amy was hollow. She was always the mistress, never the bride. Men pursued her, but only in the shadows, always returning to their wives or girlfriends. They wanted her, but never in a way that mattered. She had lovers but no real relationships, admirers but no real friends.

This constant cycle of being desired but never chosen had left her bitter, envious of anyone who seemed to have something genuine. She hated seeing people happy. She couldn't stand the thought of others having the kind of love and stability she had never experienced. It fuelled her, pushed her to expose people's secrets, to tear down their facades. If she couldn't have happiness, neither should anyone else.

Gossip had become her way of maintaining control, of ensuring she stayed relevant in a world that only valued her looks. She lived for the thrill of knowing something no one else did, for the power that came with holding someone's secrets in her hands. So, when she first noticed Stephanie's distraction at work, she couldn't help but dig into it. What was so special about this man that had Stephanie so wrapped up? When she began to follow them and realised that Max was hiding something, something big, her instincts kicked in. She wasn't going to let this go. She needed to know what it was, and she needed to use it to her advantage.

It was this bitterness and drive for control that led Amy to the street corner near Stephanie's apartment that night, watching from the shadows as Max and Stephanie walked together. She had been following them for days, sensing that something was about to happen. But she needed more than just her intuition, she needed proof. Something tangible. Something she could use.

As Max and Stephanie walked into a small market on their way home, Amy spotted a guy loitering on the corner, the kind of guy who looked like he was always up for making a quick buck. She approached him with a sly smile, holding out a crumpled £20 note.

"Hey," she said, glancing over at Max and Stephanie. "See that guy over there? I need you to slip this into his pocket. Can you do that for me?"

The guy raised an eyebrow, clearly intrigued. "What is it?"

"Just an Airtag," Amy replied, showing him the small, discreet tracking device. "It won't hurt him. I just need to know where he goes."

The guy hesitated for a moment, then shrugged and took the money. "Alright Luv."

Amy watched from a distance as the guy casually bumped into Max as he exited the store, expertly dropping the Airtag into the pocket of his coat. Max didn't seem to notice, and soon he and Stephanie were walking back toward her apartment, unaware of the tracker that was following Max's every move.

Satisfied, Amy pulled out her phone and opened the tracking app. A small blip appeared on the screen, signalling that the Airtag was active. She smiled to herself, feeling the familiar rush of power.

"He's married; I know the type" Amy said to herself in a quiet tone. "Besides if he is and I tell her I'm actually doing her a favour."

"I'm nice like that!" She smirked.

-

Her apartment was immaculate, styled in the latest trends and filled with expensive things. Designer furniture sat in pristine condition, untouched except for the occasional visitor she tried to impress. The sleek, modern sofa in her living room was covered in decorative pillows that had never been moved, and the coffee table was stacked with glossy books she'd never read. The walls were adorned with abstract art, pieces chosen for their ability to impress rather than any personal connection to them.

The apartment was filled with labels and baubles, but nothing of meaning. Everything was carefully curated, designed to project an image of success and control. Yet behind it all, Amy knew there was something missing. There was no warmth in her space, no sign of a life truly lived. It was all surface-level, just like her relationships.

Always the mistress, never the bride. Always envied but never loved.

She hated it. Hated that for all her beauty and success, she couldn't have what others seemed to find so easily, genuine happiness, real connection. She couldn't stand seeing people like Stephanie, who seemed so effortlessly content. It burned inside her, fuelling her desire to tear it all down. She wasn't going to let anyone else have what she couldn't.

It was just before dawn when Amy watched the dot on her phone's screen begin to move. Her heart raced as she saw it leaving Stephanie's apartment, heading down the quiet streets. She threw on her coat, slipping out into the early morning air, the city still cloaked in the soft silence of pre-dawn. This was her chance, she was finally going to get the answers she craved.

That's why she was here, following Max in the early hours of the morning, determined to uncover his secret. *'What do you do? How does Stephanie find so much happiness in you?!?'* She thought, and now, with the Airtag she had planted in Max's pocket, she had the upper hand. She had control. She wasn't going to let this slip away.

She followed the tracking signal through the still streets, her breath visible in the chilly air. She was tired, but the caffeine she had downed earlier kept her wired, her mind buzzing with anticipation. She stayed at a distance, letting the blip on her phone guide her until it stopped in a small park just down the road from Stephanie's apartment.

Amy slipped into the shadows of a towering oak tree, her movements deliberate and silent. She positioned herself carefully, her back pressed against the rough bark as her sharp eyes followed Max emerging from the park's entrance. He looked different tonight. His mismatched clothes hung loosely on his frame, and the usual easy confidence she found so irritating was gone, replaced by an almost frantic unease. The jittery tension in his movements sent a thrill through her.

What are you hiding, Max? she wondered, her lips curling into a faint, predatory smile as she crouched lower, her body concealed by the thick trunk and the veil of shadows. Her fingers tightened around the phone in her hand, the camera app already open and recording.

Max paused in the middle of the park, glancing around with a nervous energy that made her pulse quicken. He seemed to be scanning the empty paths, his gaze darting to the trees and bushes as if searching for unseen eyes. *Too late for that,* Amy thought smugly, her position cloaked in darkness and distance. She watched his every movement with laser focus, feeling the simmering anticipation of a hunter waiting for the perfect moment to strike.

And then, it happened.

Max's body began to shift, the transformation so sudden and grotesque that even Amy, with all her scepticism and cynicism, felt her breath hitch. His limbs contorted unnaturally, his spine arching and shrinking. His clothes slipped from his frame and pooled at his feet like discarded skin. Amy's mouth fell open as she watched his form melt away, defying all logic, until the man was no more.

In his place stood a small, scruffy brown-and-white terrier, panting heavily on the ground.

Amy didn't blink. Her phone stayed steady, capturing every second. Her chest rose and fell in shallow breaths, her mind struggling to reconcile what she had just seen. But shock quickly gave way to something darker, an excitement that buzzed in her veins like an electric current. Slowly, a wicked grin spread across her face, her teeth catching the dim light as she whispered to herself, "Got you."

The video on her screen was clear, undeniable proof of what Max really was. No rumours or vague suspicions, this was extraordinary. Amy's mind raced with possibilities, each more tantalizing than the last.

What are you, Max? she thought, her eyes narrowing as she zoomed in on the dog, who now stood shaking his head as though trying to clear it. The same nervous energy remained, even in his animal form. Max, if that was even his real name, was hiding something far bigger than she could have ever guessed. And now she had the power to uncover it, and exploit it.

"Oh my," Amy murmured under her breath, her tone dripping with malice as she continued recording. "Imagine what someone would pay for *you,* little fella." Her fingers tightened around her phone, the thought making her almost salivate. The possibilities were endless, money, influence, power. What she had just witnessed wasn't just a freak occurrence. It was an opportunity.

Amy licked her lips, her heart pounding with the thrill of it all. No one else knew about this, and that gave her a dangerous edge. She had the upper hand. As she watched Max sniff at the ground cautiously, oblivious to her presence, Amy's mind began plotting. Selling the footage, controlling Max, using him, whatever it took to turn this bizarre secret into something that served *her*.

"You've been running from something, haven't you, Max?" she whispered to herself, her voice low and taunting. "Well, guess what? The game's over. And now, you're mine."

She tucked her phone into her pocket, careful not to stop the recording. Then she slipped further into the shadows, her smile widening as she watched Max skitter away into the darkness, unaware of the storm that was about to descend upon him.

Amy backed away from the scene, keeping her eyes on Max as she retreated into the shadows. She knew what she had to do next. She had to tell Alistair. He would know how to make this work to their advantage. They could control Max, leverage his secret for all it was worth. And with this video, there would be no denying it.

As she slipped away, she couldn't help but feel a rush of satisfaction. Finally, she was the one with something real, something no one else could touch. And she couldn't wait to see how it all played out.

Chapter Twenty-Four

The next morning, Amy sat in her meticulously curated apartment, her mind buzzing with the events of the night before. She couldn't stop replaying the transformation in her head, Max changing from a man into a dog, right before her eyes. She had undeniable proof, and now she was ready to act.

But this wasn't just about the thrill of holding someone else's secret. No, this was about money. Serious money. Max wasn't just some oddity, he was a potential goldmine, and Amy knew exactly who would be interested in such a rare find.

She picked up her phone and dialled Alistair's number, her fingers trembling with excitement. When he answered, she wasted no time.

"Alistair, we need to talk," she said, her voice brimming with urgency. "I've found something... unbelievable. And it could make us both incredibly rich."

Alistair's interest was piqued immediately. "What are you talking about?"

"Not over the phone," Amy replied, her tone sharp. "Meet me at the usual place. You'll want to hear this in person."

There was a brief pause on the other end of the line, and then Alistair agreed. "Alright. I'll be there in an hour."

When Amy arrived at the café where they usually met for their private discussions, she could barely contain her excitement. She ordered a coffee and sat at a corner table, rehearsing her pitch in her head. Alistair, always one to sense an opportunity, arrived on time, his usual self-assured smirk in place. He slid into the seat across from her, raising an eyebrow as he took in the look of barely-contained excitement on her face.

"This better be good," he said, leaning back in his chair.

Amy didn't waste any time. She pulled out her phone, opened the video, and handed it to him. "Watch this."

Alistair's smirk faded as he watched the footage, his expression shifting from curiosity to disbelief. His eyes widened as he saw Max's body contort, shrink, and finally transform into a small, scruffy terrier. When the video finished, he stared at the phone in stunned silence.

Finally, he looked up at Amy, his voice filled with awe and greed. "Is this real?"

Amy nodded; her smile triumphant. "It's real. And it's going to make us very rich."

"Wait, what? I mean who, who is this?" Alistair asked, still in a state of disbelief.

"Oh" said Amy with a tone that suggested that this was nothing out of the ordinary, "this, this is Max."

"Max?" Queried Alistair. "Do I know this Max?"

"Max, is Stephanie's boyfriend." She offered.

"Stephanie? Wait, what? My, I mean our Stephanie? From the office?"

Amy nodded in affirmation.

"Does Stephanie know?" Alistair queried.

Amy shook her head with a caustic smile.

Alistair leaned forward, his mind clearly racing with possibilities. "This… this is huge. If we capture him, we could sell him for a fortune. We just need to find the right buyer."

Amy grinned, knowing exactly where his mind was headed. "I already have someone in mind. Remember that client of yours? The one who collects rare antiquities and hunts endangered species for sport?"

Alistair's eyes gleamed with recognition. "Of course. Lucien Marchand. He's always looking for something unique, something no one else can get their hands on. And this… this is right up his alley."

Lucien Marchand was more than just a wealthy collector. He was an eccentric billionaire with a taste for the rare and exotic. He wasn't satisfied with simply owning beautiful objects, he craved the thrill of the hunt, the excitement of capturing something elusive. Whether it was ancient artefacts or endangered animals, Lucien would spare no expense to add it to his collection. And Max, with his unique condition, would be the ultimate prize.

Amy leaned back in her chair, crossing her arms with satisfaction. "If we play this right, Lucien will pay millions for Max. All we have to do is capture him, and we'll be set for life."

Alistair nodded, his sharp eyes glinting as his mind worked through the logistics. "We'll need to be careful. I'm sure this Max is no idiot. Stephanie, well could complicate things if she catches wind of what we're doing. We can't afford any slip-ups. We'll have to lure him in, play this smart, make sure he doesn't see it coming."

Amy leaned back in her chair, a slow, calculated smile spreading across her face. "Don't worry about Stephanie," she said, her voice dripping with confidence. "She doesn't have a clue. And Max... he's already paranoid, jumping at shadows from what I have seen All we have to do is let them continue as normal, let him think everything is still under his control. Trust me, he'll walk right into our hands."

Alistair smirked, his earlier hesitation melting away as Amy's enthusiasm fuelled his own. "This isn't just a big job, Amy. This is *the* job. Bigger than anything we've ever pulled off. Oh this is going to be big!"

Amy's fingers tapped rhythmically against the edge of the table, her mind racing with the thrill of the scheme. For the first time in years, she felt truly powerful. This wasn't just about the money, though that was a delicious bonus, it was about finally stepping out of the shadows, about proving to herself and the world that she wasn't some bystander in other people's stories. She was in control now, and everyone who had underestimated her was about to regret it.

"Imagine it," Amy said, her voice low and charged. "Once we have Max, we deliver him straight to Lucien. The pay-out? Millions. That kind of money means freedom, real freedom. We can disappear, live however we want, and never look back."

Alistair leaned forward, his elbows resting on the table, his expression intense. "Exactly. But we have to stick to the plan. Max won't be easy to catch, not if he realizes we're onto him. We can't give him an inch. No hesitation, no second-guessing."

Amy nodded; her eyes gleaming with adrenaline-fueled determination. "I'll handle getting close to them. Max trusts Stephanie, and she doesn't suspect a thing. I'll make sure she stays oblivious, and he stays on edge. When the time comes, he won't even know what hit him."

The two of them leaned over the table, their empty coffee cups pushed to the side as they sketched out the finer details of their plan. Each step was calculated, precise, leaving no room for error. Capturing Max wasn't just about the pay-out, it was about finally seizing control of their lives.

As the café began to clear out and the hum of conversations dimmed, Amy and Alistair exchanged a final look. For them, this wasn't just a scheme; it was their shot at rewriting their futures. And for Max, it was the beginning of the end.

Chapter Twenty-Five

Max and Stephanie's relationship had been a whirlwind of late-night encounters and whispered conversations, but recently, it had begun to shift. Despite the tension that still lingered between them after Stephanie's confrontation, they had started to find a new rhythm. Max had become more present, more attentive, and Stephanie found herself drawn even closer to him, even though his odd behaviour still left her with questions.

Stephanie spent her days at work thinking about Max, replaying their conversations in her head, trying to piece together the puzzle that was his life. And at night, when they were together, she couldn't deny the connection between them. There was something about him, something beyond his charm and humour, that made her feel alive in a way she hadn't felt in years.

But even as their relationship deepened, a sense of unease hung over her. She couldn't shake the feeling that Max was still holding something back, something important. Every time she brought it up, he would deflect, turning the conversation back to lighter topics. It frustrated her, but she couldn't bring herself to push too hard. She didn't want to scare him off. Not when things were finally starting to feel real.

Max stood in Stephanie's kitchen, the soft glow of the evening moon filtering through the windows. As Stephanie prepared a simple dinner, he noticed a small bowl on the counter where she kept her keys, spare change, and other random items. His eyes landed on something familiar among the clutter: the coin he had left on her windowsill days ago.

Max frowned slightly, reaching into the bowl and plucking the old coin from its new resting place. He held it in his hand for a moment, feeling its weight and the smooth, worn surface beneath his fingers. Without a word, he walked over to the window and placed the coin back on the sill, exactly where he had left it.

Stephanie turned around, catching the movement out of the corner of her eye. "What's that?" she asked, curious.

Max glanced at her, a small smile tugging at the corners of his lips. "Just an old habit," he said softly, not offering any further explanation. The coin seemed insignificant, but to Max, it was a small gesture to keep things in balance, an attempt to realign with the greater forces at play, forces he knew all too well but couldn't yet explain to her.

They sat down to dinner a little while later, the conversation light and easy at first. But as the evening wore on, Stephanie couldn't help but bring up the question that had been weighing on her mind. She looked at Max with a mixture of affection and concern.

"You know," she began, her voice soft, "I've never met anyone like you. You're… different."

Max smiled at her, though there was a flicker of something deeper in his eyes, something more than just amusement. "Different, huh? I hope that's a good thing."

"It is," Stephanie replied, reaching out to take his hand. "But sometimes, I just wish you'd let me in a little more. I feel like there's this whole side of you that I don't know."

Max's smile faltered as he looked down at their intertwined hands, his thumb brushing lightly over her knuckles. For a moment, he seemed lost in thought, the weight of unspoken truths casting a shadow over his features. When he finally spoke, his voice was quiet but deliberate, each word chosen with care.

"Stephanie... there are things in this world, no, in this existence, that are bigger than any one person. Some paths aren't just roads we walk; they're rivers that shape the land, the skies, and everything in between. They become points in time and space where countless other paths converge. They're not just about one life; they ripple outward, affecting everything around them."

Stephanie furrowed her brow, confusion flickering in her eyes. "Max, what are you trying to say? I don't understand."

He sighed deeply, his gaze lifting to meet hers. "The universe... it's not as chaotic as it seems. It has a rhythm, a design, even if it's too vast for us to comprehend. And the gods, whether we believe in them or not, they have their hands in that design.
Sometimes, the plans they weave are so complex, so far-reaching, that the ones caught up in them don't even

realize it. They don't know their purpose, or why they've been chosen. They're just… there, playing their part."

Stephanie's confusion deepened, but she remained silent, sensing that he wasn't done.

Max's voice softened, taking on an almost reflective tone. "Think of a seed," he said. "It falls from a tree, carried by the wind or swept up by a stream. It doesn't know where it's going or why, it has no say in the matter. The current carries it, depositing it on a patch of soil it didn't choose. And there, it grows. Centuries later, that tree changes everything around it. Its roots shape the land, its branches shelter countless lives, its very presence alters the world. Yet it was just a seed, Stephanie. It didn't have a choice. It simply *was*."

Stephanie blinked, her mind racing to keep up with his words. She didn't fully understand, but she felt the weight of them, the sense of something far larger at play. It was as though Max was trying to tell her that his secret wasn't just his own burden to bear, it was part of something vast, something ancient, something that stretched far beyond their lives.

Max gave her hand a gentle squeeze, his gaze searching hers. "Some of us are like that seed, Stephanie. Swept up in currents we can't control, planted in places we didn't choose. We don't always know why we're there, or what our purpose is, but that doesn't make our role any less important. Sometimes, it's not about understanding, it's about existing. Being. And trusting that the reason will reveal itself when the time is right."

Her chest tightened, and she felt a strange mix of emotions, confusion, awe, and something that felt uncomfortably like fear. "Max, is this about you?" she asked softly. "Is that how you feel? Like you're just… swept up in something you don't understand?"

Max's smile returned, faint but genuine, tinged with a sadness that she couldn't quite place. "Maybe," he admitted. "Or maybe I'm just beginning to understand. But if there's one thing I've learned, it's that some secrets, some paths, are bigger than us. They don't just shape who we are. They shape the world, the people we meet, the choices we make. And sometimes… sometimes, all we can do is trust the flow."

Stephanie didn't respond, but her grip on his hand tightened slightly, as if anchoring herself to his presence. She couldn't shake the feeling that Max wasn't just speaking in metaphors. There was something real, something monumental, hidden beneath his words. Something he wasn't ready to say outright but that she could sense, like a shadow lurking just beyond her understanding.

Whatever it was, she realized, it wasn't just Max's secret. It was something far greater, something that could change everything.

"So… are you saying that your secret… it's part of some bigger plan? Something that affects more than just you?"

Max nodded slowly. "Yes and no. It's not something I can't explain easily. In fact. I'm not entirely sure what the *secret* is really" He let out a small sigh, "B u t I promise, Stephanie, I will tell you everything soon. You deserve to know the truth. I just… need a little more time. Time for me to discover the entire truth."

Stephanie squeezed his hand gently, her heart torn between wanting to know and fearing what the truth might mean for them. "Okay," she whispered. "But don't wait too long. I need to know what we're up against."

Max looked into her eyes, the weight of his secret heavy in the space between them. "I promise, I won't."

They sat in silence for a while, the unspoken words hanging in the air. But even in that silence, there was an understanding between them, a fragile connection that had grown stronger despite the mysteries that still lingered.

-

Later that night, wandering the streets, his thoughts a jumble of emotions and questions. He knew he couldn't keep hiding the truth from Stephanie much longer. The time was coming when he would have to reveal everything, no matter the consequences.

As he walked through a quiet alley, he heard the familiar *Caw* of Roger, the seagull who always seemed to show up at the most inconvenient or was it convenient times. Max looked up and saw Roger perched on a lamppost, his beady eyes gleaming in the dim light.

Caw! "Cutting it a little fine, aren't you?" Roger said, his voice carrying a mix of amusement and reproach as he perched on the edge of the park bench. His feathers shimmered faintly in the moonlight, a stark contrast to the weight in his tone.

Max sighed, dragging a hand through his hair. "Yeah, I know. I'm working on it," he muttered, his frustration barely contained.

Roger tilted his head, his beady eyes narrowing with an almost human intensity. *Caw Caw! "You do realize that if she finds out, she'll have to make the choice, right?"* His voice dipped; the playful edge replaced with something mournful. Ca*w Caw "... The Choice."*

Max froze, the words cutting deeper than he cared to admit. His chest tightened, and for a moment, he couldn't bring himself to respond. When he did, his voice was hoarse. "The choice? You're always going on about it. You talk about it like it's inevitable, but you never explain what it actually *means*. How can she make a choice if I don't even know what it is?"

Roger let out a low, rasping caw, the sound more like a chuckle than a bird's cry. *Caw Caw "Oh, Max... you know what I mean. The gods have their plans, their rules, their endless schemes. But mortals? Mortals have free will. They have to choose their path. And once she knows the truth... you can't take it back. That choice will be hers to make, and it will change everything."*

Max clenched his fists, his frustration boiling over. His voice rose, sharp and raw. "I don't *know*, Roger! You talk to me like I should understand all of this, rules, choices, gods! But I don't! I don't know why I'm here, who I am, or who I *was!*"

The last word echoed in the still night air, carrying the weight of years of confusion and anger. Roger remained silent, watching him with a calmness that only fuelled Max's agitation.

Max's breath hitched as an image flashed through his mind, unbidden and vivid. He staggered slightly, gripping the bench for support as the memory washed over him.

A vast gate loomed before him, towering, ancient, terrible in its enormity. The iron bars twisted like serpents, their patterns both intricate and grotesque. The air around it shimmered with a heat that wasn't natural, a searing intensity that seemed to burn his very soul. Shadows danced across the ground, though there was no light to cast them, and a low, guttural hum resonated from the gate, like a heartbeat from another realm.

Max's pulse quickened, his throat tightening as the memory faded just as suddenly as it had come. He snapped back to the present, the night air cool against his skin, grounding him.

A long moment passes. The bird looking down at him blinking slowly.

"I can't keep lying to her," he said finally, his voice barely above a whisper. "But how? How do I even begin to explain… this?" He gestured at himself, frustration bleeding into his every word. "How do I make her understand who I am when I don't even understand it myself?"

Roger fluffed his feathers, his head bobbing as he regarded Max with what almost looked like pity. *Caw caw"... Maybe ask her if she likes dogs?"* he said with a hint of dry humour. Then his tone turned serious again, his voice softer but no less firm. *Caw caw "Just remember, Max... every choice has consequences. And once the truth is out, you can't undo it. Be ready for what comes next."*

With a powerful sweep of his wings, Roger lifted off the bench, his silhouette cutting through the night sky as he disappeared into the shadows.

Max stood there, staring after him, his thoughts churning. Roger's words lingered; each one heavy with implication. He knew the seagull was right. Once Stephanie learned the truth, everything would change. And the choice she would face, whatever it was, wouldn't just alter her life. It would ripple out, affecting them both in ways neither of them could yet imagine.

Max exhaled shakily, running a hand over his face. He glanced at the moonlit path ahead, knowing that when he faced Stephanie again, it would mean stepping into the unknown. For both of them.

Chapter Twenty-Six

Amy and Alistair had always been opportunists, but this was different. This was bigger than anything they had ever imagined. As they began to put their plan into motion, both were acutely aware of the stakes, and the potential for an unimaginable payday.

Amy had always been good at getting close to people, at playing the role of the concerned friend or the confidante. Now, she turned those skills on Stephanie, embedding herself deeper into her life. She knew that to keep Max under her watchful eye, she had to stay close to Stephanie, close enough that neither of them would suspect her true intentions.

The first step was to subtly weave herself into Stephanie's day-to-day routine. She began showing up at the office with coffee for Stephanie, acting like the thoughtful co-worker who just wanted to be friends. She invited Stephanie out for drinks after work, suggesting they have a "girls' night" to relax and unwind. And, of course, she made sure to drop hints that she was genuinely interested in getting to know Max better.

"Why don't you bring Max over for dinner sometime?" Amy suggested one afternoon as they chatted over lunch. "I mean, we work together every day, but I barely know the guy. And if he's important to you, then I want to get to know him too."

Stephanie, caught up in the whirlwind of her deepening relationship with Max, didn't suspect a thing. She was flattered by Amy's sudden interest in her personal life, seeing it as a sign that they were becoming closer as friends. The idea of introducing Max to more of her world seemed like the next logical step, especially since he had been so elusive about other parts of his life.

"Sure," Stephanie said with a smile. "That sounds nice. I'll talk to Max about it."

As Amy smiled back, her mind was already calculating. She knew that every interaction brought her one step closer to getting what she wanted. The more she could ingratiate herself into Stephanie's life, the easier it would be to keep tabs on Max and set the trap when the time was right.

While Amy worked on the ground, Alistair was busy behind the scenes. He had made contact with Lucien Marchand, the eccentric billionaire who had been his client for years. Lucien was no ordinary collector, his passion for rare and exotic items went beyond art and artefacts. He was a hunter, a man who thrived on the thrill of the chase and the ownership of things that no one else could possess.

Alistair had been careful not to reveal too much too soon. Lucien was a man of power, and he didn't react well to half-baked promises. Alistair knew he needed to approach this carefully, to build up the anticipation without giving away the full scope of what he had in mind. The key was to pique Lucien's curiosity, to make him hungry for more.

Lucien Marchand was a man of many layers, each more complex and enigmatic than the last. Born on the sun-soaked island of Malta to a French father and a Dutch mother, Lucien's early life was steeped in a blend of cultures, each influencing his taste for the exquisite. From a young age, he was surrounded by beauty, whether it was the rugged coastline of Malta or the finely crafted antiques his parents collected. Yet, even as a child, Lucien's interests ran darker and deeper than simple admiration for the finer things in life.

As he grew older, his appreciation for art and luxury evolved into an obsession with the rare and the untouchable. By the time he inherited his family's vast fortune, a conglomerate of shipping, mining, and manufacturing industries, Lucien had already established himself as a connoisseur of the world's most coveted treasures. His homes, scattered across the globe, were veritable museums, each filled with priceless artefacts and artwork. But it was the estate in the British countryside, an isolated stately home of some history surrounded by dense forests, that housed his most private and treasured collection.

Lucien's public persona was that of a cultured, refined billionaire, known for his impeccable taste in wine, art, and fashion. He frequented the world's most exclusive events, his presence always marked by an air of quiet authority and elegance. Yet beneath this polished exterior lay a man driven by a primal urge, a need to dominate, to possess, and ultimately, to conquer. His true passion was hunting, not merely as a sport, but as a manifestation of his desire to assert control over the wildest, most dangerous aspects of nature.

The walls of his chateau were adorned with the heads of exotic animals, a lion from the African savannah, a Bengal tiger from India, a polar bear from the Arctic. These trophies were not just symbols of his wealth and status, but of his ability to conquer the untameable. However, these public displays were only a prelude to the real secrets that lay within the chateau.

Hidden deep within the estate, accessible only through a series of heavily secured corridors, was Lucien's "special" room, a place that few had ever seen, and even fewer had lived to talk about. This room was the culmination of Lucien's darkest desires. The walls were lined with glass cases, each housing a piece of his private collection: stolen masterpieces from history's greatest artists, rare and endangered species preserved in lifelike poses, and, most disturbingly, a series of human skulls, each one meticulously catalogued and displayed as if it were another rare relic.

These skulls were not mere curiosities; they were the trophies of a man who viewed life, human or otherwise, as something to be owned, dominated, and ultimately, extinguished for his pleasure. Each skull had a story, a tale of a life snuffed out to satisfy Lucien's insatiable hunger for the extraordinary. The room was a macabre gallery of his conquests, a shrine to his belief that anything, no matter how rare or sacred, could be acquired, if one had the resources and the will to take it.

Lucien's obsession with the exotic and the forbidden had led him to the darkest corners of the world, where he trafficked in the most illicit of goods. He dealt in black-market art, rare animals, and, some whispered, even people. His connections ran deep into the underworld, where money could buy anything, and where Lucien thrived. To him, the world was a vast hunting ground, and he its apex predator, always on the prowl for his next great prize.

During a private lunch at an exclusive club in Mayfair, Alistair broached the subject delicately. He leaned back in his chair, sipping a glass of wine as he spoke with calculated precision.

"Lucien, you're always looking for something unique, something that no one else can get their hands on," Alistair began, his tone casual but with an undercurrent of excitement. "Well, I've come across something recently. Something... extraordinary."

Lucien, a man in his mid-50s with salt-and-pepper hair and a gaze that could cut through steel, raised an eyebrow in interest. "Extraordinary, you say? You've piqued my curiosity, Alistair. What is it?"

Alistair smirked, leaning in slightly. "Let's just say it's a rare... find. Something that goes beyond artifacts and antiquities. Something living."

Lucien's eyes gleamed with intrigue. "Go on."

"I can't give you all the details just yet," Alistair said, playing the game of suspense. "But imagine this, an ancient, almost mythical being, hiding in plain sight. Something that defies science and logic. A creature that has lived among us without detection for who knows how long."

Lucien's smirk mirrored Alistair's. "And you know where to find this... being?"

Alistair nodded slowly. "I do. But here's the thing, Lucien, this isn't going to be cheap. Capturing it won't be easy. But I know he will be exactly what appeals to you."

Lucien's gaze sharpened, the gears in his mind turning. "He? You know me too well, Alistair. I'm intrigued. Tell me more."

Alistair leaned back in his chair, satisfied with Lucien's response. "I will. But first, let me make sure everything's in place. I'll contact you with the details when the time is right."

Lucien raised his glass in a silent toast, his expression one of anticipation. "I look forward to it. Oh, and as for the price. You know that has always been a secondary concern for me."

As they finished their lunch, Alistair's mind raced with plans. He knew that Lucien was hooked, and now it was just a matter of delivering the prize. But capturing Max would require careful planning and flawless execution. There could be no mistakes, no room for error. Too much was at stake.

Chapter Twenty-Seven

Stephanie had noticed the oddities about Max almost from the beginning, but in recent weeks, they had grown harder to ignore. His habit of leaving before dawn, no matter how late they stayed up talking or how close they were the night before. The way he deflected her questions about his daytime whereabouts with that same maddeningly charming smile and a vague, "I'll explain soon."

At first, she had told herself it didn't matter. Maybe he just needed his space. Everyone had secrets, right? And Max... well, he had a way of making her feel so cherished, so seen, that she had convinced herself she could live with his quirks.

But over time, the doubts began to pile up, small but insistent, like stones in her shoe. She found herself replaying their conversations, scrutinizing his every excuse. His kindness, his humour, and the way he made her feel like the centre of his universe, were they real, or just distractions?

By now, she had heard "soon" more times than she could count. It had become his favourite word, the shield he used to fend off her growing frustration. And she was tired of it. Tired of waiting, tired of being fobbed off, tired of pretending that his secrets didn't matter when they clearly did.

That morning, when Max slipped out of bed with his usual quiet urgency, Stephanie watched him go, her heart heavy with resolve. She had tried to be patient, had given him more time than she knew she should. But enough was enough.

As the front door clicked softly shut behind him, Stephanie sat up, throwing off the covers. She quickly dressed, tying her hair back with determined efficiency. Whatever Max was hiding, it was time to find out. She wouldn't sit around waiting for "soon" any longer.

With a final glance in the mirror, she grabbed her coat and stepped outside, the early morning chill biting at her cheeks as she hurried after him. Max might have thought he could leave his mysteries behind with the sunrise, but Stephanie was done being kept in the dark.

She kept her distance as she trailed him through the early morning streets, the city still quiet and bathed in the soft light of dawn. Max moved with purpose, but there was a nervousness in his step, as if he were trying to avoid being seen. Stephanie's heart pounded in her chest, a mixture of fear and curiosity driving her forward.

As Max turned a corner into a narrow alley, Stephanie hesitated. She ducked behind a nearby building, watching as Max glanced around, making sure he was alone. And then it happened, something she could never have prepared herself for.

Max's body began to shift and contort, his limbs shortening, his posture collapsing in on itself. His clothes fell loose around him, and within moments, the man, she had been following was gone. In his place stood a small, scruffy brown and white terrier, panting heavily as it looked around with familiar, human-like eyes.

Stephanie's breath hitched in her throat as she watched Max's body contort and shift, his human form dissolving into that of a small, scruffy terrier. The transformation happened right before her eyes, and yet her mind refused to process it. Her heart raced, and a cold wave of disbelief washed over her. This couldn't be real. It couldn't be happening.

But it was.

The man she had fallen for, the man she had spent so many nights with, shared so many laughs and tender moments with, was now standing before her as a dog. A small, brown and white terrier, panting nervously as his clothes lay crumpled on the ground beside him.

For a moment, Stephanie just stood there, frozen in place, her mind racing to make sense of what she had seen. And then, without warning, the dam inside her broke.

She collapsed to her knees on the cold pavement, her body shaking as sobs wracked her frame. Tears streamed down her face, blurring her vision as she struggled to catch her breath. Everything, her world, her sense of reality, was crashing down around her.

Max, now in his terrier form turned in alarm to see her kneeling on the ground, he let out a panicked whine as he saw Stephanie break down. He padded over to her, his small paws clicking against the concrete, and tried to nudge her with his nose. When that didn't work, he licked her cheek, desperately trying to comfort her in the only way he could. But it wasn't enough. Stephanie was inconsolable.

Her sobs grew louder, more frantic, and Max's panic grew with them. He circled her, his mind racing with helplessness. He wanted to explain, to tell her that everything would be okay, but there were no words, only barks and whines. He couldn't communicate, couldn't tell her what she needed to hear. All he could do was watch as her world crumbled before her eyes, knowing that he was the cause of it.

Above them, the city seemed to come alive with a new, unsettling presence. On the rooftops surrounding the alley, pigeons began to gather. They perched in clusters, cooing and flapping their wings, their black eyes gleaming in the early morning light. It was as if they were mocking the scene below, their incessant coos echoing off the walls in a way that felt almost like laughter.

Max glanced up at them, his panic deepening. The pigeons… they always seemed to be watching. Always lurking on the edges of his world. And now, as Stephanie sobbed in the alleyway, they were here, laughing at him, mocking his failure. He let out a low growl, but the pigeons only cooed louder, their presence unnerving him even more.

"This is insane," Stephanie choked out between sobs, her voice thick with disbelief. "This… this can't be real. I must be losing my mind. I must have gone mad."

Max whimpered, circling back to her side. He had to do something, anything, to get her to calm down, to help her understand that she wasn't crazy, that this was real. But how? How could he communicate with her when he couldn't even speak?

Then, in a moment of desperate clarity, an idea came to him. He spotted a piece of string lying near a pile of trash at the edge of the alley. It wasn't much, just a frayed piece of rope, discarded and forgotten. But it was enough.

Max trotted over to the string, picked it up in his mouth, and brought it back to Stephanie. He gently placed the string in her lap, then nudged it toward her, looking up at her with pleading eyes. When she didn't respond, he did the only thing he could think of: he placed the string around his own neck and sat there, waiting, hoping she would understand.

Stephanie blinked through her tears, her gaze drifting down to the string in Max's mouth. It took a moment for her mind to register what he was doing. He wanted her to lead him. He was giving her control, trying to show her that he trusted her, that he was still Max, still the man she loved, even in this strange and terrifying form.

With trembling hands, Stephanie picked up the other end of the string and looped it around her fingers. She looked down at Max, her breath shaky as she tried to calm herself. "Okay," she whispered, her voice barely audible. "Okay... let's go home." She bundled his clothes under her arm, slipping his watch into her pocket.

Max let out a small, relieved bark and stood up, ready to follow her. Slowly, shakily, Stephanie got to her feet, clutching the makeshift leash in her hand as she led him out of the alley. The pigeons continued to coo and flap above them, but she ignored them, too overwhelmed to process anything other than the fact that her entire world had just been turned upside down.

They walked in silence, the weight of unspoken words crushing down on both of them. Stephanie's mind was a chaotic storm, a whirlwind of emotions that she couldn't seem to control. Shock, disbelief, betrayal, fear, and an overwhelming, all-consuming hurt churned inside her, each emotion fighting for dominance. Her hands trembled at her sides, her fists clenching and unclenching as if grasping for a stability that eluded her.

Her chest tightened with every step, the ache in her heart growing unbearable as the memory of what she had just witnessed played over and over in her mind. *Max... Max is a...* She couldn't even finish the thought. Her brain rebelled against the very idea, the sheer impossibility of it all. And yet, there he was, trotting beside her in silence, a scruffy, nervous little terrier where the man she loved had been only moments before.

She glanced down at him, her vision blurring as tears welled in her eyes again. The sight of him, so small, so vulnerable, made her stomach twist. The man who had held her hand, laughed with her, made her feel seen and safe, was now padding beside her on four legs. The absurdity of it all made her feel unmoored, like the ground beneath her feet had vanished.

When they passed a small café, a builder standing outside with a coffee in hand called out, "Cute pup, love!"

Stephanie's head snapped forward, her jaw tightening as fresh tears spilled down her cheeks. *Cute pup?* she thought bitterly. *This isn't a dog. This was...* Her breath hitched. *This was my lover.* The thought hit her like a punch to the gut, her stomach churning violently. She quickened her pace, desperate to put distance between herself and the casual, unknowing comment.

Max kept close to her side, his small body tense, his ears flicking nervously at every sound. He didn't speak, couldn't speak, but Stephanie could feel his fear radiating from him, a palpable thing that only added to the tension choking the air between them. He knew. He knew everything had changed.

He had lost control of the one thing he had fought so hard to protect: the truth. And now, he had nothing left but hope. Hope that Stephanie wouldn't walk away, that she wouldn't see him as some kind of monster.

But Stephanie's thoughts were a tempest, and hope was nowhere to be found. She wanted to scream, to demand answers, to make sense of the madness that had turned her world upside down. But she couldn't. Her throat felt raw, constricted by the weight of everything she couldn't say.

As they turned onto her street, the quietness of the early morning seemed almost mocking. The familiar sidewalks and buildings now felt alien, as if she were seeing them through a cracked lens. And still, the pigeons lingered, more every moment, like a crowd jostling for position at a lynching. Perched on lampposts, rooftops, and window ledges, they were silent observers, their dark, glassy eyes following the pair with unnerving intensity.

Stephanie wiped at her cheeks with the back of her hand, her steps faltering as she reached the entrance to her apartment building. She looked down at Max, her chest heaving as her tears returned with renewed force. "How... how could you?" she whispered, her voice breaking.

Max looked up at her, his tail still, his body tense, his ears flat back against his head. He wanted to say something, anything, but all he could do was look at her with those sad, knowing eyes.

The pigeons cooed in mocking tones, their presence a reminder that the world was watching. That whatever had brought them to this moment was bigger than either of them. That the universe had plans, plans that couldn't be avoided, couldn't be undone.

Stephanie pushed the door open and stepped inside, her legs shaking as she led Max into the apartment. She didn't look back, afraid that if she met his gaze again, the fragile thread holding her together would snap.

Max followed silently, the weight of her pain crushing him with every step. He didn't know how to fix this, didn't even know if he could. All he knew was that everything had changed, and the path ahead was one he could no longer navigate alone.

Chapter Twenty-Eight

In her apartment, Stephanie moved through the day like a ghost. She had no energy left, no tears, no emotions that she could name. Everything inside her felt hollow, as though her very sense of reality had been ripped away, leaving behind only emptiness. She couldn't bring herself to look at Max, who sat quietly in the corner in his dog form, his head hanging low in shame.

Max had tried, several times throughout the day, to get closer to her, to offer her comfort in the only ways he knew how. But each time, she had gently pushed him away, whispering, "Not now. I need to talk to you one-on one." He understood, even though it hurt. He could feel the weight of everything that had happened pressing down on both of them, and all he could do was wait.

Stephanie sat on the edge of the couch, staring blankly at the wall. She didn't know how much time had passed, hours, maybe more. Her mind raced with thoughts she couldn't control, and every time she tried to make sense of it, she was pulled deeper into confusion. What she had seen... it didn't fit into any world she knew. It didn't make sense.

As the afternoon light faded and the shadows in the room grew longer, Stephanie turned her gaze toward Max. She studied him for a long moment, her heart aching with the weight of it all. And then, in a soft voice, she spoke the thought that had been forming in her mind all day.

"It's a night-time thing, isn't it?" she said quietly, more to herself than to him. "You change at night… and during the day, you're this…. A dog."

Max's ears perked up slightly, but he didn't move. He simply watched her, waiting, knowing that the moment of truth was approaching.

The minutes dragged on in agonizing silence, until finally, as the last light of day disappeared and the apartment was swallowed by twilight, it happened. Max's small, furry form began to shift and contort, growing taller, more human. His fur receded, his limbs lengthened, and soon, he was no longer a dog but a man, sitting on the floor of her apartment, naked and vulnerable.

Max wrapped his arms around himself, his head bowed in shame. He couldn't bring himself to look at her, couldn't face the hurt and confusion in her eyes. He felt exposed in more ways than one, and the weight of his secret pressed down on him like never before. He had no answers, only questions, questions that had haunted him for as long as he could remember.

Stephanie, still sitting on the couch, watched him with wide, tear-filled eyes. She had guessed the truth, but seeing it happen before her very eyes made it real in a way she still couldn't fully comprehend. For a long moment, neither of them spoke. The silence between them was heavy, thick with everything that had been left unsaid.

Finally, she broke the silence. "Max… what are you?" she asked, her voice trembling. "I need to understand."

She barked out a loud but brief laugh at this, at the absurdity of what was happening, yet there was no joy in it.

Max took a deep breath, lowering his hands from his face, his shoulders slumping as if the weight of the universe had pressed down on him. When he finally looked up at Stephanie, his eyes weren't just filled with sorrow, they held a deep, aching confusion, like a man staring into a vast chasm and finding only more questions.

"I... I don't know," he whispered, his voice trembling with something that felt like defeat. "I've been like this for as long as I can remember. But the thing is... I don't remember being a child. I've never had a childhood. No parents, no first memories. Nothing. I've always been... this. A man at night, a dog during the day. And no matter how many times I've lived, I don't know why."

Stephanie blinked, her lips parting in disbelief. She tried to speak, but the words wouldn't come. Max continued, his voice barely rising above a murmur, as if saying it out loud might make it all unravel.

"I've tried to figure it out. God, have I tried. But it's all just... fragments. Shadows of memories, flashes of things I can't place. Faces I've never met but feel like I've known forever. Places I recognize but have never been to. It's like... like I've lived this life over and over again, but I can't make sense of it. And the worst part?" He paused, his jaw tightening. "The worst part is that it all feels deliberate, like strings being pulled just out of sight. Like someone's playing a game with me, and I'm just... stuck."

Stephanie's heart broke at the anguish in his voice. "So…
you have no past? No future? You just… exist?"

Max let out a bitter laugh, his head bowing slightly.
"Yes," he said softly. "That's it. I just exist. No origin, no
destination. Every time, it's the same. I wake up as a dog,
live through the day, and then I'm a man again when night
falls. There's no beginning, no end. Just this endless
cycle. And I can't escape it."

Stephanie reached up, brushing away a tear that had slid
down her cheek. She wanted to say something, to offer
comfort, but what could she say to that?

"And Roger?" she asked instead, her voice shaky. "The
pigeons, why are they always following you? What do
they have to do with this?"

Max's gaze darkened, his brow furrowing deeply. "I
don't know," he admitted after a long pause. "Roger… he
knows things. More than I do, I'm sure of it. He's always
there, in every life I've lived. Always watching, always
talking in riddles that seem to lead nowhere. He shows up
when things are about to go wrong or when I need him
most, but I don't know if he's helping me or just keeping
me in check. It's like he's bound to me somehow, like
we're tied together by something I can't understand."

Stephanie shivered, but she wasn't sure if it was from his
words or the way his expression shifted when he
mentioned the pigeons.

"And them?" she pressed.

Max exhaled slowly, his voice dipping lower. "The pigeons are different. They're... unsettling. They're everywhere, watching, following. Every time I look up, they're there, on rooftops, streetlights, wires. And there's something in their eyes, Stephanie. Something... wrong. Like they're not just birds. It's like they *know* me, like they're part of this too, but not in a good way. There's a darkness to them. They're not like Roger. With him, I feel like there's at least a flicker of intent, a purpose. But the pigeons..."

He trailed off, his gaze distant, as though he could see them even now, staring back at him through the veil of the night.

"Like they're malevolent," he finished, his voice barely a whisper. "Not overtly, not in a way you can pin down, but it's there. They linger, always just out of reach, always watching. They remind me that none of this is random. That someone, somewhere, is pulling the strings. And me? I'm just the puppet."

The silence between them stretched, heavy and oppressive. Stephanie's chest tightened, her mind struggling to process everything Max had said. She wanted to dismiss it, to chalk it up to some fantastical delusion, but the raw anguish in his voice made it impossible to ignore.

"Max," she said finally, her voice cracking, "if you're the puppet... then who's the puppeteer?"

He met her gaze, his eyes haunted and hollow. "That's the question, isn't it?" he said bitterly. "And I've been asking it for lifetimes, I think. But the gods don't answer, Stephanie. They just… watch. Like the pigeons."

His words hung in the air, filling the room with a suffocating sense of inevitability. Whatever was happening to Max, whatever forces had bound him to this cursed existence, Stephanie realized with a shiver that it wasn't just about him anymore. It had never been. Something far larger, far darker, was at play, and now, she was caught in its web too.

Stephanie sat back, trying to process everything he was saying. It was so much, too much. She didn't know what to think, what to feel. This man she had fallen in love with, who had been such a huge part of her life, was something she couldn't even begin to understand. And yet, despite everything, despite the confusion and hurt, she still cared about him. She still loved him.

"Why didn't you tell me?" she asked, her voice breaking. "Why did you let me fall in love with you, knowing… knowing that this was what you were?"

Max looked up at her, his eyes filled with regret. "I didn't mean to hurt you, Stephanie. I never wanted to cause you pain. But… I didn't know how to tell you. How do you explain something like this? How do you tell someone you love that you're… not like them?"

Stephanie's tears flowed freely now, but she didn't look away. "But I love you, Max. And you… you let me love you without telling me the truth."

Max crawled across the floor to her, kneeling at her feet, his hands trembling as he reached for hers. "I know," he whispered. "And I'm so sorry. But I never meant to hurt you. All I've ever wanted... all I've ever known... is that I want to protect you, to treasure you. To love you. You're the only thing that matters to me, Stephanie. You always have been."

Stephanie looked down at him, her heart breaking for the man who knelt before her, so lost and confused in his own life, yet so determined to love her. She could see the sincerity in his eyes, the raw emotion that he was struggling to express. And despite everything, despite the pain and the shock, she couldn't help but feel the same way.

"I don't know what to do," she whispered. "I don't know how to... how to make sense of any of this."

Max squeezed her hands gently, his voice filled with quiet desperation. "You don't have to make sense of it right now. Just... please don't walk away from me. I'll give you all the time you need, but please... don't leave my life."

Before Stephanie could respond, a familiar noise filled the air, a low, mocking cooing sound that sent a shiver down her spine. She turned her head toward the window and saw them again, pigeons, hundred, thousands of them, gathering on the rooftop across the street, their black eyes gleaming in the dim light.

Max tensed, his gaze shifting to the window. "Not them... not now," he muttered under his breath.

Stephanie furrowed her brow, confused. "What?" she asked, but Max didn't respond.

A sudden commotion shattered the tense silence. A deafening screech tore through the air as Roger the seagull swooped down from the sky with a burst of feathers, scattering the pigeons in a chaotic flurry. His wings flapped with determined fury, and his voice rang out, sharp and commanding.

Caw! "*Get out of here, you lot!*" Roger bellowed, his tone dripping with disdain. "*This is not your place to be!*" He drove the pigeons away with relentless determination, his movements deliberate, almost violent.

As the last of the pigeons reluctantly retreated to the safety of the rooftops, Roger turned his gaze on Max. His eyes were dark and impenetrable, holding none of the usual sharp humour or warmth. They seemed lifeless, like black mirrors reflecting something ancient and unknowable.

"*Caw, caw...*" Roger whispered, his voice low and eerie. *Caw* "*The choice, Max. Now she must choose. With the truth comes the choice.*"

Max stood motionless, his jaw tightening as the words hung in the air. His fists clenched at his sides, frustration bubbling to the surface. He didn't look at Roger; he didn't need to. He already knew what was coming.

Caw "*... the choi,* "

"Enough!" Max's voice exploded, cutting Roger off mid-sentence. His fists were trembling, his eyes blazing with barely contained anger. "Yes, I know about the bloody choice!" he snapped, his voice sharp and cracking with emotion. "You've been going on about it for *lifetimes,* Roger. But do you ever tell me what it means? Do you ever actually *explain* it? No! You just circle above me like some damn harbinger, throwing riddles and cryptic nonsense while I'm the one stuck living this, this *half-life!*"

Stephanie flinched at the sudden outburst, her confusion deepening as she looked between Max and the seagull. Her heart raced, her mind grasping for something, anything, that could make sense of what was happening.

"Max…" she began, her voice barely above a whisper. "What choice? What is he talking about?"

Her words hung between them, unanswered, as her eyes darted from Max to Roger and back again. Roger's head tilted slightly; his gaze now fixed on Stephanie. There was something unnerving in the way he regarded her, as though he could see far more than she ever wanted anyone to see.

Max glanced at her, his expression pained, but he said nothing. His silence only added to her mounting dread; the pieces of a puzzle she didn't understand swirling chaotically in her mind.

"Max," Stephanie pressed, her voice firmer now. "What choice? What truth?"

Roger fluffed his feathers and let out a soft, almost mocking caw. *Caw "She wants answers, Max. They always do. But once she knows, there's no going back."*

Before Stephanie could say another word, Roger spread his wings and took off, vanishing into the dark sky as quickly as he had appeared. The silence that followed was suffocating, the weight of unspoken truths pressing down on them both.

Stephanie turned to Max, her voice trembling. "What did he mean? What choice? Tell me, Max."

Max's shoulders slumped, his anger dissipating into something far heavier. "It's not that simple," he said quietly, his gaze dropping to the ground. "And once you know... you can't un-know. It changes everything."

Stephanie's stomach turned as his words sank in, her heart pounding in her chest. Whatever this was, whatever *he* was, it was more than she had bargained for. And yet, she couldn't walk away. Not now. Not without knowing the truth.

Something shifted inside Max's mind. Memories, half-formed, fragmented images, began to flood back to him. He saw flashes of himself in different times, different places, always making the same decisions, always facing the same impossible choices.

"The choice..." Max whispered, his voice trembling, his gaze set somewhere far from her small living room. "It's always the same. Three choices. The same options... over and over."

Stephanie's heart pounded in her chest as she watched the realization dawn on him. "What are you talking about?"

Max's memories drifted back through the centuries, each recollection tinged with a mixture of love, loss, and the mysterious choices that had shaped his path. These were not just fleeting romances; they were connections that had left indelible marks on his soul, only to be torn away by forces beyond his understanding.

The first memory took him to ancient Egypt, where the sun cast long shadows over the golden sands. He stood beside her, Nefret, an Egyptian queen whose beauty rivalled the brilliance of the Nile at dawn. Her laughter, soft and melodic, would echo through the cool stone halls of her palace as she gazed out over the horizon, lost in thought. Yet even in those moments of joy, there was always a shadow, a weight in her eyes that Max couldn't quite decipher. One day, as they walked along the banks of the Nile, a majestic ibis appeared, its white feathers gleaming in the sunlight. The bird seemed to watch them with a knowing gaze, its presence a harbinger of the choice that would soon follow. Nefret's smile faded, and when she turned to Max, there was pain in her eyes. The words she spoke were soft, filled with regret, and though Max never understood the choice she had made nor knew what it was, the hurt lingered long after the ibis had taken flight.

The scene shifted to ancient Rome, the bustling heart of the empire, where Max found himself at the side of Livia, a noblewoman as sharp and cunning as she was beautiful. They would stroll through her villa's gardens, her hand resting lightly on his head as they discussed matters of state and strategy. But one evening, as the last rays of the sun bathed the garden in gold, a peacock appeared, its iridescent feathers shimmering like a thousand jewels. The bird strutted before them, its gaze piercing, as if demanding something unspoken. Livia fell silent, her usual confidence wavering. When she finally spoke, her voice was laced with sorrow, the choice she had made leaving a rift between them that could never be mended. Max never knew what the peacock had signified, but the pain of that moment was etched in his memory, as vivid as the bird's brilliant plumage.

His thoughts then turned to the cold, vast Russian countryside, where he had once lived with Anya, a peasant girl whose warmth and kindness had been a balm to his weary soul. They shared a small cabin, its walls barely keeping out the winter's chill, but inside, the fire burned bright, and Anya's love was like the warmth of the hearth. But one fateful day, as the snow began to fall, a great snowy owl perched on the roof of their cabin, its wide eyes seeming to pierce through the walls, through time itself. Anya saw the owl and fell into a deep, troubled silence. When she spoke again, her voice trembled with the weight of the choice she had been forced to make. The sadness in her eyes was unbearable, and though Max pressed close to her, he felt her slipping away, lost to a decision that tore at both their hearts. The owl's haunting call echoed in the distance as Anya's warmth faded, leaving Max with nothing but the cold and the memory of her gentle touch.

Each woman had made a choice, one that Max could never fully comprehend but that had left him with scars that time refused to heal. The presence of these majestic birds, the ibis, the peacock, the snowy owl, each perfectly suited to their surroundings, had always marked the moment of decision, a silent witness to the choices that led to pain and separation. Max had loved them all deeply, but in the end, they had all slipped away, their decisions shrouded in mystery, leaving him to wander alone through the ages.

Now, as he stood beside Stephanie, listening to Roger's ominous words, that old familiar ache returned. Another choice loomed on the horizon, another path that could lead to love or heartbreak. He looked at Stephanie, saw the kindness in her eyes, and felt a flicker of hope. Yet, he knew, as always, that nothing was certain. The presence of the choice was a looming shadow, and even though he could not see the bird this time, he knew it was there, waiting.

Max's eyes filled with a strange mix of clarity and confusion as the memories resurfaced. "You have to choose, Stephanie. I live this life, hoping for love, an overwhelming yearning to be a part of something, always alone, always cold and outside. If I ever find the warmth of another soul and they find out about my true self......You have to make the choice. There are three... three paths, and none of them are easy."

Stephanie gripped his hands tighter, her mind racing. "What choices?"

Max took a deep breath, steadying himself as he prepared to explain, the memories flooding his brain, all that had come before and in many ways what was always to come, with them came the Choices.

"The first choice." He glared at Roger" ... you can choose me as I am now. Max. a man, I will be in my human form at all times, I will love you, comfort you, we can have a normal life, full of joy and happiness..... but my lifespan will be that of a dog. Ten more years, maybe twelve at the most. We can be together, but… it will end in heartbreak. You'll lose me far too soon."

Stephanie's breath hitched in her throat, but she didn't let go of his hands. "And the second choice?"

Max's gaze turned distant, as if he were seeing the choice play out before him. "The second choice… you keep me as a dog. I'll live a long life, a man's lifespan, fifty years or more. I'll be the most loyal, loving companion you've ever had. Always by your side, always protecting you. But… I'll never be human again. I'll never be the man you fell in love with."

Tears welled up in Stephanie's eyes as she tried to process the impossible decisions laid before her. "Well, that would piss Oliver off…. And the third?"

Max swallowed hard; his voice barely audible. "The third choice… you choose to forget me. And if you do that… I'll be gone, gone from your life, you will forget me and eventually… I'll come back somewhere and somewhen else. But you won't know me. You'll never know me again or know that you ever had."

Stephanie's world spun; her knees weak as Max's words sank in like lead. Three choices. Three impossible, unfathomable choices. Each one felt like a door slamming shut on a part of her life she wasn't ready to lose. Whatever she decided, she knew, would change everything, her, Max, the very fabric of their existence.

Max's hands trembled in hers, his grip tight but desperate, as if trying to anchor himself to her. His voice broke when he spoke, the pain evident in every word.

"Stephanie, I need you to believe me, I didn't know about the choices. Not until now." His eyes searched hers, pleading for understanding. "I've never tried to deceive you. Never. I didn't keep this from you on purpose. I didn't even understand my own life, my own existence, until... until this moment."

Stephanie blinked, her tears blurring his face, but she could still see the raw honesty in his expression. "I... I thought I had time to figure it out," he continued, his voice cracking. "I thought I could protect you from this, but... I've been caught in this cycle for so long, Stephanie. I didn't know the rules, didn't know the truth. I only knew that I loved you, and that... that felt real, more real than anything I've ever had."

His words were a knife to her heart, cutting through her anger and confusion with a sharpness she couldn't deny. "I never wanted this for you," he whispered, his hands trembling in hers. "But I do love you. I've always loved you. And whatever you choose... I'll understand. I'll stand by it. I'll stand by *you.*"

Tears streamed down Stephanie's cheeks as she gazed into his eyes. Her heart was breaking, shattering under the weight of what lay before her. She didn't know how to make this decision. She didn't know what was right, or if there even *was* a right choice. But one thing was undeniable, her love for Max. It was real, it was raw, and it was worth fighting for, even if the battle seemed impossible.

A sharp, relentless tap at the window pulled her from her thoughts. *Tap. Tap. Tap.* She turned toward the sound, and there was Roger, perched on the ledge, his beady eyes locked on her.

The tapping ceased, but Roger didn't move. He stared at her, and Stephanie felt her stomach turn. It wasn't just a look. It was a presence, dark, probing, as if the seagull wasn't just seeing her but exploring her, his gaze sinking into the corners of her mind where her deepest fears and desires hid.

"You have three days to choose," Roger said, his voice echoing in her head like a dark chant, not that of a bird, that of a man. It wasn't just a command, it was a promise, cold and absolute. "Choose wisely. Choose well. I will return here at midnight on the third day."

Stephanie's breath hitched as Roger stretched his wings, the span of them unnervingly large, shadowing the window like a monstrous omen. For a moment, he didn't look like a seagull at all, but a creature far older, far darker, with an unrelenting power behind his every movement.

Before he launched himself into the night, Roger turned his head slightly, fixing her with one last, piercing look. "Do not run," he warned, his voice sharp and final. "Never run."

And with that, he was gone, soaring into the darkness, leaving Stephanie trembling in the silence he left behind.

Her heart pounded as she turned back to Max, who was watching her with eyes filled with sorrow and fear. The reality of it all crushed down on her, suffocating her with the enormity of what she had to decide.

"I don't know how to do this," she whispered, her voice breaking.

Max reached for her hands again, his grip steady despite his own trembling. "You don't have to do it alone," he said softly. "No matter what happens, I'm here. And if it's me you're choosing against... I'll still understand. I'll always understand."

Stephanie bit her lip, her mind spinning with fear, love, and the weight of the unknown. Three days. Three choices. And somehow, she would have to find the strength to face them all.

Chapter Twenty-Nine

Alistair Castel was not a man who gambled. He had built his reputation on precision, on the ability to identify and seize opportunities with ruthless efficiency. And the secret Amy had uncovered, the impossible transformation she had witnessed, wasn't just an opportunity. It was a once-in-a-lifetime jackpot, a chance to secure the kind of power and wealth that others could only dream of. Alistair had no intention of letting it slip through his fingers.

For the past week, his meticulous planning had consumed him. Every detail had been scrutinized, every variable accounted for. He had made discreet calls to his network, ensuring that the pieces fell perfectly into place. His wealthy client, Lucien Marchand, was ready to pounce the moment Max was secured. Marchand wasn't just rich, he was a collector of the rare and extraordinary. To him, Max wasn't a person or even an anomaly; he was a trophy. Something to possess, to display, to feed his insatiable hunger for control over the unique and unattainable.

Amy, meanwhile, had played her role brilliantly. She had woven herself deeper into Stephanie's life, the ever-supportive friend, always there with a kind word or a helping hand. But beneath her facade, she was a predator, feeding Alistair every scrap of information he needed. Max's habits, Stephanie's routines, even the small details of their private conversations, Amy handed it all over without hesitation.

The plan itself was deceptively simple. Isolate Max. Catch him in his dog form during the day, when he was most vulnerable, and neutralize him before anyone could interfere. The transformation schedule had given them a predictable window of opportunity, and Alistair had ensured that they would strike when the odds were in their favour.

But there was one thing Alistair hadn't accounted for, human emotion.

Amy had begun to notice cracks forming in the perfect picture she had painted. Stephanie had grown distant at work, her focus slipping, her demeanour changing. She seemed distracted, her thoughts clearly elsewhere, and it was unsettling. At first, Amy had dismissed it as a side effect of the deepening connection between Stephanie and Max. But now, she wasn't so sure.

It was in the small, subtle signs that Amy began to sense something was wrong. Stephanie glanced over her shoulder more often, her eyes darting toward shadows as if expecting someone to be there. Max, too, had changed his patterns, taking longer routes, avoiding places he had once frequented. It was as if they had caught a whiff of the danger closing in, their instincts sharpening.

Amy reported these changes to Alistair, her tone laced with irritation. "They're being careful, more careful than they should be. It's like they *know* something's up."

Alistair's brow furrowed as he considered her words. He didn't believe in coincidences, and this sudden shift in behaviour set his teeth on edge. "They're suspicious," he said, his voice cold and calculating. "But suspicion isn't proof. If anything, it means we need to move faster. They're trying to stay ahead of us, but they don't know how far we've already come."

Amy hesitated, something in her gut twisting. She had done her part, had played her role perfectly. But now, as the pieces began to fall into place, the reality of what they were planning started to feel heavier. Stephanie wasn't just a target to her anymore, she was a person. A person with emotions, fears, and a life that would be irrevocably shattered when this was over.

"You're sure this will work?" Amy asked, her voice quieter than usual.

"It will work," Alistair snapped, his tone brooking no argument. "Marchand is expecting results, and I don't fail."

Amy nodded reluctantly, though the doubt in her chest didn't dissipate.

For Alistair, this wasn't just about capturing Max, it was about solidifying his power, proving that nothing was beyond his reach. But for Amy, the lines between loyalty, ambition, and humanity were beginning to blur.

As the plan hurtled toward its conclusion, both of them knew that one misstep could send everything spiralling out of control. And yet, Alistair remained steadfast, his mind focused on the prize. In his world, there was no room for second-guessing. Max and Stephanie might suspect danger, but it didn't matter. He would have Max. And with Max, he would have everything.

But even the most calculated plans could crumble when the human heart was involved, and the heart, be it Max's, Stephanie's, or even Amy's, had a way of defying even the most ruthless of strategies.

-

The air in Stephanie's apartment was heavy with unspoken words, but after everything that had happened, there was an unspoken understanding between them. Max sat on the floor near the couch, his head resting against her knee, while Stephanie absentmindedly stroked his hair. The weight of the choice hung in the air, but for now, neither of them wanted to speak it aloud.

Finally, Stephanie broke the silence. "So," she said, trying to force some lightness into her voice, "I guess I'm dating a werewolf... kind of. Except, you know, you're a dog during the day instead of a full moon."

Max chuckled softly, the sound a mix of amusement and sadness. "Well, if you want to think of it that way... I guess it's better than sprouting fur and fangs every night and chewing on the local citizens,.... right?"

Stephanie smiled, but there was sadness in her eyes that she couldn't hide. She turned her gaze toward the window, staring out at the street below. "It's just... so much, Max. I don't even know where to start. How do you even begin to make a decision like this? How do you even begin to work any of this out in your head?"

Max looked up at her, his expression gentle but serious. "You don't have to decide right now, Stephanie. And I don't want you to feel pressured. All I want is for you to choose from the heart. Whatever decision you make… I'll accept it."

Stephanie let out a soft sigh, leaning back against the couch. "That's what makes it so hard. I don't want to lose you, Max. But no matter what I choose, I feel like I'm going to lose something."

Max reached up and took her hand, giving it a gentle squeeze. "I know. But I trust you, Stephanie. Whatever happens… we'll face it together."

For a moment, Stephanie allowed herself to relax into the moment. Max was right, this wasn't something she had to decide immediately. They had time, and they could face it together but ultimately it was her choice! She took a deep breath, trying to push aside the weight of her decision, if only for a little while.

As she padded over to the window Stephanie smiled, but her mind was elsewhere. She turned to the window, looking out at the quiet street below, her thoughts drifting back to the past few weeks. She had been trying so hard to piece everything together, but now that she knew the truth, certain things stood out in a way they hadn't before.

Stephanie stood by the window of her apartment, absentmindedly sipping her tea as she gazed out at the city below. The late afternoon light bathed the streets in a soft, golden glow, and everything seemed peaceful. She let out a small sigh, trying to unwind after the longest of days, her mind a turmoil of thoughts.

As she scanned the familiar sights, people hurrying home, cars crawling along the streets, the occasional dog walker, a figure caught her eye. Standing across the street, just outside the entrance to the pawn shop, was Amy.

Stephanie's breath caught in her throat. Amy was standing perfectly still, her face partially obscured by the collar of her coat, but there was no mistaking her. She was just... staring. Her eyes were fixed on Stephanie's building, her gaze sharp and unsettling, as if she was waiting for something, or someone.

For a moment, Stephanie wondered if she was imagining it. She blinked, hoping that when she looked again, Amy would be gone, just a trick of the light or her mind playing tricks on her after all the stress of the past few days. But Amy was still there, rooted to the spot, her eyes locked on the apartment as if she could see straight through the walls to where Stephanie stood.

The cup in Stephanie's hand trembled slightly, the warm ceramic suddenly feeling too hot against her skin. She stepped back from the window, her heart beating faster. What was Amy doing here? How long had she been standing there, watching?

Stephanie swallowed hard, forcing herself to think. Should she go down and confront her? Or would that only escalate things further? But as she hesitated, Amy seemed to sense that she had been noticed. Her head tilted slightly, and for just a second, Stephanie thought she saw a small, almost imperceptible smile curl the corners of Amy's lips.

As Amy turned she moved across the pavement and disappeared into the shadows of the alley. The unease she left behind clung to Stephanie's apartment like a heavy fog, the tension in the air almost palpable.

Stephanie sat on the edge of the couch; her arms wrapped around herself as her mind churned. "Amy..." she whispered, the name slipping out almost unconsciously.

Max, sitting cross-legged on the floor and leaning against the couch, looked up sharply. "What about her?"

Stephanie hesitated, her brow furrowing as pieces of the puzzle began to click into place. "She's been... everywhere lately. Hovering. Ever since we started getting serious, she's been there. Always inviting me to dinners, asking about you, checking in. At first, I thought she was just being friendly, but now..." Her voice trailed off, the realization dawning.

Max straightened, his expression darkening as he processed her words. "How could they know, though?" he asked, his voice laced with frustration.

Stephanie looked at him, her heart racing. "Could she have followed you?"

Max frowned, his mind racing through the possibilities. "I guess I wouldn't know," he admitted reluctantly, the thought twisting uneasily in his chest. "I don't exactly spend my days watching over my shoulder, well except for wardens and larger dogs."

Stephanie's mouth opened to respond, but before she could speak, Oliver padded into the room. He paused, fixed Max with a glare, then let out a practiced hiss before swatting at one of the pockets of Max's trousers.

"Seriously, Oliver?" Max muttered, trying to pull his leg away, but the cat was relentless, clawing and pawing with exaggerated indignation.

"Oliver, quit it," Stephanie scolded half-heartedly, her focus still on the conversation.

Then came the sound of something small clattering to the floor.

Both Max and Stephanie turned their attention to the source of the noise. Oliver, looking immensely pleased with himself, was now flicking a small, round disk across the hardwood with his paw.

"What is that?" Stephanie asked, leaning forward.

Max reached out and picked up the object, holding it up to the light. It was a smooth, round tag, faintly etched with a symbol that looked like a piece of fruit, an apple. He turned it over in his hand, his stomach sinking.

Stephanie's eyes widened as recognition set in. "That's... that's not yours, is it?"

Max shook his head slowly, his voice tight. "No. It's not mine."

Their eyes met, the gravity of the situation crashing down on them. Stephanie's mind raced as she pieced it together. "She must have planted it," she said, her voice trembling. "Amy must've slipped it onto you somehow, your coat, your bag. That's how they've been tracking you. That's how they knew where you were."

Max's jaw clenched as anger and frustration surged through him. "A tracker," he muttered, his grip tightening on the tag. "They've been following me this whole time."

Stephanie's heart pounded as the weight of their realization settled. "They've been waiting for the perfect moment," she whispered, her voice barely audible. "And now... they're close."

Oliver meowed innocently and trotted off, leaving the two of them staring at the small tag as if it were the harbinger of their doom.

Max stood up, pacing across the room as the gravity of the situation hit him. "They've been watching us this whole time. Following me, how much does she know? They are Waiting for us to slip up."

Stephanie's stomach twisted with guilt. She had trusted Amy, believed that her co-worker was genuinely interested in being her friend. But now she could see the truth, Amy had been playing a game, and she had unwittingly given her the information she needed to set them up.

"I can't believe I didn't see it sooner, that bitch" Stephanie said, her voice trembling. "All the signs were there, and I just... I ignored them. How could I be so stupid."

Max crossed the room to her, taking her hands in his. "This isn't your fault, Stephanie. You couldn't have known. They were careful, calculated. But now that we know, we have to be even more careful."

Stephanie nodded, but the fear in her chest only grew stronger. She felt like the walls were closing in on them, that every move they made was being watched. And now, with the truth out in the open, the danger felt more real than ever.

Max's voice was calm but firm as he spoke. "We need to stay one step ahead of them. We can't let them catch us off guard."

Stephanie clung to his hands, her mind racing. "What do we do? How do we stop them?"

Max's gaze was determined. "We can't confront them directly, not yet. But we can make it harder for them to find us. We'll have to change our routine, keep moving. And we can't trust anyone."

Stephanie's heart pounded as she nodded in agreement. Everything she thought she knew had been turned upside down, and now she realized just how dangerous their situation had become. Amy and Alistair weren't just after information, they were after Max. And if they succeeded, she didn't even want to think about what would happen to him.

As they sat together in the small apartment, Stephanie and Max both knew that the worst was yet to come. The growing unease that had been simmering beneath the surface was now impossible to ignore. They were being hunted, and the clock was ticking.

Chapter Thirty

Stephanie couldn't stop pacing. Her mind was spinning with everything she'd realized, every piece of the puzzle falling into place with horrifying clarity. The sense of dread that had taken root in her chest only deepened as the implications settled over her like a dark cloud. How had she missed it all? The puma email, Alistair's sudden influx of money, the expensive watches, the way he had been acting so erratically lately, it all made sense now, and yet, it was terrifying.

Max sat against the sofa, his worried eyes following her every movement. He had tried to console her earlier, offering his usual mix of humour and calm logic, but there was little comfort in words when both of them knew the truth, they were in real danger. His usual playful behaviour had faded, replaced by the seriousness of the situation. He could see the gears turning in Stephanie's head, trying to connect the dots.

"We need to stay ahead of them," Max said again, his voice calm despite the storm swirling in his mind. He was a planner by nature, always thinking several steps ahead, but this… this was something he couldn't fully control. There were too many unknowns, too many pieces that could shift at any moment.

"But how?" Stephanie asked, stopping mid-pace to look at him, her eyes wide with fear. "We don't know what they're planning or when they're going to strike. We're just… waiting."

Max sighed, running a hand through his hair, frustration evident in his posture. "That's the problem. We have to think like them, figure out what they're after and stay out of their reach until we can figure out our next move."

Stephanie sat down heavily on the couch, burying her face in her hands. The weight of everything was pressing down on her, suffocating her thoughts. She could feel a headache forming, the pressure building behind her eyes. "They want you, Max. They see you as some… thing they can use. But why? Why go through all this trouble?"

Max shook his head, the confusion evident in his eyes. "I don't know. Maybe they see me as something valuable. Maybe they think they can sell me to the highest bidder or use me for something. But whatever it is, it's not good."

Stephanie's stomach twisted at the thought. Her boss, her co-worker, people she had trusted, were now plotting to capture the man she loved. The realization hit her like a tidal wave, knocking the breath out of her. And she had been too blind to see it. The signs had been there, but she had brushed them off as quirks, as oddities in the daily grind of corporate life.

"I should have known," she whispered, her voice trembling with guilt. "I should have seen it sooner."

Max moved to sit beside her, his presence a small comfort in the midst of her turmoil. He took her hand in his, squeezing it gently. "You couldn't have known, Stephanie. They played their cards right. But now we know, and we can stop them."

Stephanie nodded, but the fear didn't go away. It lingered in the back of her mind, gnawing at her like a relentless beast. She looked out the window, half- expecting to see Amy lurking across the street again, but the street was quiet, too quiet. The usual bustle of city life seemed muted, as if the world was holding its breath, waiting for something terrible to happen.

"We have to leave," she said suddenly, her voice firm with newfound resolve. "We can't stay here. It's not safe."

Max nodded in agreement, his expression mirroring her determination. "You're right. We need to get out of here, at least for a while. Somewhere they won't think to look."

Stephanie stood up, the urgency of the situation propelling her forward. "Let's pack a few things. We'll leave right away. I don't care where we go, as long as it's far away from here."

Max stood up as well, a sense of urgency settling over them both. He could feel it in his bones, a primal instinct warning him that time was running out. The trap was closing in on them, and if they didn't move quickly, they'd be caught.

As they hurriedly packed their bags, Stephanie couldn't shake the feeling that they were being watched. The thought of Amy, the way she had been following them, the strange behaviour that had gone unnoticed until now, it all felt like a piece of a larger, more sinister puzzle. Alistair's sudden wealth, the extravagant purchases, the way he had flaunted that new watch, it all pointed to something dark, something dangerous.

"Max," she said, her voice trembling as she zipped up her bag. "What if Alistair's sudden wealth is connected to this? The puma email, the watches, everything, what if it's all tied together?"

Max paused, his brow furrowing in thought. "It's possible. He could be involved in something much bigger than we imagined. Smuggling exotic animals, selling them to the highest bidder... it would explain a lot. The money, the secrecy, the way he's been acting."

Stephanie's heart pounded in her chest as she considered the implications. "But why you? Why would they target you? Unless they know!" She added with a look of horror.

Max hesitated, the weight of the question hanging in the air. "I don't know," he admitted, his voice barely above a whisper. "But whatever it is, it's not something we can take lightly. We need to get out of here and figure this out before it's too late."

He stopped, "If they do know the truth. The actual truth. I'm probably the rarest creature on the planet right now!"

Stephanie nodded, her resolve hardening. "We'll go to the countryside. Somewhere remote, where they won't think to look for us. We'll figure out our next move from there."

Max agreed, but his mind was still racing. "And we'll need to stay connected to what's happening here. We can't lose track of them, or we'll be walking blind."

Stephanie grabbed her laptop and phone, her hands shaking slightly as she packed them into her bag. "We'll stay ahead of them, Max. We have to."

But even as she said the words, a nagging doubt lingered in the back of her mind. Were they already too late? Was the net already closing around them?

-

Across the road, Amy watched from the shadows, her sharp eyes fixed on Stephanie and Max as they hurriedly packed their bags. She had been tailing them for days, her presence a ghostly spectre just beyond their awareness. Every step she took was calculated, every movement precise. This was her moment, the culmination of days spent waiting, planning, and staying just out of sight. Alistair's patience was wearing thin, but mistakes were not an option. They only had one chance, and it had to be flawless.

The street outside Stephanie's apartment was unnervingly still, the faint hum of distant traffic the only sound breaking the silence. Amy's senses were razor- sharp, her nerves attuned to every flicker of light, every shadow stretching across the pavement. The air felt charged, thick with anticipation. She slipped her phone from her pocket, her fingers trembling ever so slightly as she typed out a single word: *Now.*

The message sent; Amy felt a surge of adrenaline ripple through her. The net was closing in, the game reaching its crescendo. Max was almost within their grasp. Stepping deeper into the shadows, she allowed a small, satisfied smile to creep across her face, her heart racing with the thrill of the hunt.

Across the city, Alistair Castel's phone buzzed on his desk. The room around him was dimly lit, the heavy curtains drawn tight to block out the world. He picked up the device, reading Amy's message with a faint smirk tugging at his lips. The moment he had been orchestrating for weeks had finally arrived.

He dialled quickly; his voice steady despite the adrenaline coursing through him. "Lucien, it's time. We're moving now."

Lucien Marchand's response was smooth, almost lazy, yet it carried the unmistakable weight of authority. "Excellent. Don't fail me, Alistair. I'm paying handsomely for this... acquisition."

Alistair's smirk deepened, his tone laced with confidence, though an edge of something darker lingered beneath. "You'll get what you paid for. By morning, Max will be yours."

As the call ended, Alistair allowed himself a moment of satisfaction. The plan was unfolding perfectly, each piece falling into place with surgical precision. Soon,

Max would be delivered to Lucien, and the spoils of success would be his to savour.

It wasn't just the money, though the promise of wealth had already begun to transform Alistair's life. The bespoke suits, the rare watches, the sleek, exotic car gleaming in his garage, these were mere symbols of his growing power. What truly fuelled him was the control, the intoxicating thrill of bending people and events to his will.

And Max? Max wasn't just a payday. He was a rarity, a curiosity, a trophy unlike any other. Alistair relished the thought of pulling the strings that led to this moment, the subtle manipulations and careful deceptions that had brought them to the brink of triumph. As the clock ticked toward their final move, Alistair's confidence only grew.

Amy waited silently in the shadows, her breath steady, her pulse quick. The tension of the hunt had reached its peak, and soon, the prey would fall. Across the city, Alistair's smirk widened, his eyes gleaming with anticipation. The game was almost over, and he intended to win.

But as Alistair prepared for the final phase of their plan, a small, nagging doubt crept into his mind. Stephanie had proven to be more resourceful than he'd anticipated. If she managed to slip through their fingers, if she managed to escape…

No. He couldn't allow that to happen. Not when he was so close to completing the deal of a lifetime.

He made another call, his voice cold and commanding. "There is a possibility that they know. I don't want them getting out of the city. If they try... well, you know what to do."

The men who answered the call were no ordinary enforcers; they were specialists in handling the shadowy transactions that defined Alistair's empire. Over the years, they had moved everything from live, endangered species, smuggled from rainforests, deserts, and oceans, to priceless antiques ripped from their rightful owners. Rare artefacts, stolen from ancient sites, and fragile artworks carefully extracted from private collections were their everyday cargo.

They had perfected the art of transporting the unthinkable, knowing how to keep a snow leopard sedated just enough to survive the journey, or how to pack a centuries-old vase so it wouldn't so much as crack. Their vehicles were modified for stealth and containment, equipped to deal with any scenario, hidden compartments, air-regulated cages, and even soundproofing for more... vocal shipments.

To them, it didn't matter what the cargo was, as long as Alistair paid well, and he always did. Live creatures, stolen heirlooms, even the occasional high-value human target, it all blurred into a single, unspoken mantra: *Get it done. Don't ask questions.*

Now, as they prepared for their latest acquisition, the men didn't flinch at the unusual nature of their task. If Alistair wanted this peculiar creature, this man-dog anomaly, they would handle it like they handled everything else, with precision, efficiency, and an utter lack of concern for the morality of it all.

For them, it was just another job. But even they couldn't shake the strange unease that clung to the edges of this particular assignment. Something about Max, about the way Alistair had spoken of him, felt different, more volatile, more... alive. Still, they wouldn't question it. They never did.

They were experts in dealing with the exotic and the dangerous, and Max was no different in their eyes. To them, he was just another specimen, another rare asset to be secured and delivered.

"Understood," came the gruff response. "We'll take care of it."

These men were hardened, used to the risks and the rewards that came with trafficking in the illegal trade of the world's most rare and endangered creatures. They had transported everything from snow leopards to black-market falcons, and the complexities of handling such dangerous cargo were second nature to them

Alistair hung up the phone, feeling the weight of the plan settling into place. He could see it all unfolding: the team moving in on Stephanie's apartment, the swift, precise capture of Max, the smooth handoff to Lucien. He glanced at his watch, the expensive timepiece gleaming in the dim light of his office. It was more than just a symbol of his success, it was a reminder of what he was willing to do to maintain his power. The sacrifices he was willing to make.

But even as he admired the watch, a flicker of unease twisted in his gut. Stephanie had surprised him. Her tenacity, her intelligence... he would not underestimate her, it could cost him dearly if he did.

He picked up the phone once more, hitting redial. "I want extra men at her apartment. Make sure they're the best we have. And if they try to run... make sure they understand there's nowhere they can go."

The response was immediate, efficient. "We'll handle it, sir."

As he ended the call, Alistair felt the adrenaline surge through him again. The game was in motion, and there was no turning back now. He could already see the headlines, the whispers of his triumph echoing through the elite circles he frequented. This was his moment, his victory. All he had to do was make sure that nothing, and no one, got in his way.

Chapter Thirty-One

Max and Stephanie moved quickly, stuffing clothes and essentials into backpacks. Max's mind was racing with possible routes, safe places to hide, anything that would keep them off the radar for long enough to figure out their next step.

Stephanie's hands were shaking as she zipped up her bag. She tried to stay calm, but the fear was creeping in again, threatening to paralyze her. "Where will we go?"

Max slung his backpack over his shoulder, his expression focused. "We'll head out of the city for a bit. Maybe the countryside, somewhere remote, where we can lay low for a few days."

Stephanie nodded," Though we only have three days Max" she followed his lead as they made their way out of the apartment. As they reached the dimly lit hallway outside her front door, something stopped her, an instinct, a feeling that made her freeze.

"Wait," she whispered, pulling Max back. "Something's wrong."

Max stopped, his eyes scanning the hallway ahead. It was quiet, too quiet. The hairs on the back of his neck stood up as he realized they weren't alone.

Before he could react, the door at the end of the hallway burst open, and two men dressed in black rushed in, blocking their exit. Their faces were expressionless, eyes focused with a cold precision that told Max this wasn't their first job. Every muscle in his body tensed, and without thinking, he grabbed Stephanie's hand, pushing her back toward the apartment door.

"Max!" Stephanie cried out, fear flooding her voice.

Max's mind raced, but there was no time to think, only time to act. He positioned himself in front of Stephanie, ready to defend her at all costs. The two of them backing to the apartment and the safety that it promised.

Their retreat however was cut short. More figures appeared behind them, closing in from the opposite end of the hallway. They were surrounded.

Stephanie's breath caught in her throat as she realized the extent of the trap. Panic surged through her, and she clung to Max's hand, her heart racing. The reality of the danger they were in crashed down on her all at once.

Max's eyes darted around the hallway, searching for any possible escape, but there was none. His mind raced, and he instinctively moved around in front of Stephanie, in an attempt to shield her with his body. He wasn't going to let them take her not without a fight.

At that moment Amy stepped into view, emerging from behind the men with a calm, almost casual façade. She stood there, arms crossed, her face devoid of any warmth or emotion. This was no longer the friendly co-worker Stephanie had thought she knew, this was someone else entirely.

"Going somewhere?" Amy asked, her voice dripping with mock sweetness. She tilted her head slightly, watching them both with a cold, calculating gaze.

Stephanie's heart sank, the betrayal cutting deeper than she had imagined. "Amy, please," she begged, her voice breaking. "You don't have to do this."

But Amy's smile faded, replaced by a look of thinly veiled disdain. "Oh, Stephanie… you really are naive, aren't you? Of course, I have to do this. You have no idea what's at stake here. Do you know how much Max is worth? We're talking millions. And you…" Her gaze flicked over to Stephanie, cold and indifferent. "You're just an inconvenience."

Max glowered, stepping forward to put himself between Stephanie and Amy. His eyes locked on Amy with fierce intensity. "You won't get away with this."

Amy's expression didn't waver. She shrugged; her tone casual. "I already have!."

In an instant, the men at Amy's side sprang into action. One lunged at Max, and Max reacted on pure instinct, deflecting the blow and sending the man crashing into the wall. But the other men were quick, too quick, and within moments, Max found himself grappling with two of them at once.

Stephanie screamed as she watched Max fight for his life. Her heart pounded in her chest as fear threatened to overwhelm her. She tried to run to him, to help in any way she could, but before she could take more than a few steps, strong hands grabbed her from behind, yanking her backward.

"Let me go!" she cried, struggling against the grip of one of the men. Her eyes darted to Max, who was still fighting with everything he had, but the odds were against him. She could see the desperation in his eyes, the fear that he might lose this fight.

Max broke free for a brief moment, managing to land a solid punch on one of his attackers. But just as he turned to make his next move, he felt a sharp pain at the back of his head. The world spun around him, and he stumbled forward, his vision blurring. He tried to steady himself, but his legs gave out beneath him, and he crashed to the ground.

"Max!" Stephanie screamed; her voice filled with terror as she saw him fall. She fought harder against her captor, tears streaming down her face as she tried to break free, but the man's grip on her only tightened.

Stephanie's arms were wrenched painfully behind her back, and the cold, unyielding bite of the zip ties cut into her wrists. She twisted and struggled, but the men holding her were unyielding, their grip like iron. The realization of her helplessness hit her like a tidal wave, there was no escape, no way to stop what was happening. The man she loved was being taken from her, and all she could do was watch.

Max lay crumpled on the floor a few feet away, his breathing shallow. His head throbbed, the world around him a distorted blur. He could vaguely hear Stephanie's desperate cries, but his body refused to respond. His mind screamed at him to get up, to fight back, but the blow to his head had left him dazed, his strength sapped.

"Get him up," one of the men barked, and two others roughly hoisted Max to his feet. His knees buckled, and they dragged him upright, securing his arms with thick ropes that dug into his flesh. He winced in pain as another heavy blow landed on him, "Quit struggling or you'll get another!" A gruff voice stating coldly.

"No!" Stephanie screamed; her voice raw with anguish as she thrashed against her restraints. "Please, don't do this! Don't take him! He's done nothing to you!"

Amy stepped forward, her heels clicking ominously against the hardwood floor as she crouched in front of Stephanie. A twisted smirk played on her lips; her eyes gleaming with cruel amusement.

"Oh, Stephanie," Amy said mockingly, tilting her head as if Stephanie's suffering was some kind of spectacle. "This isn't about you. You were never part of the plan. Max is the prize. You? You're just collateral damage."

Stephanie's tear-streaked face twisted in anger and despair. "He's not a prize! He's a person! He's *everything* to me!" Her voice cracked as she pleaded, desperation lacing every word.

For a fleeting moment, Amy's expression flickered, softening as if Stephanie's words might have reached her. But it vanished as quickly as it came, replaced by icy detachment. She rose to her feet, brushing invisible dust off her clothes as if ridding herself of an inconvenience.

"Love is messy," Amy said coolly, her voice devoid of any warmth or humanity. "But this isn't about love. It's about business. And business, Stephanie, is booming."

She turned toward the men holding Max, nodding toward the stairs. "Let's move. We don't have time for this melodrama."

Max's vision began to clear, just enough for him to see Stephanie struggling on the floor, her wrists bound and tears streaming down her face. His heart ached at the sight. Mustering every ounce of strength he had left, he tried to push back against the men dragging him, but his efforts were futile. His body was too weak, too broken.

"Stephanie..." he whispered, his voice barely audible, each word a struggle. "I'm... sorry."

"Max!" Stephanie cried, her voice filled with despair as the men began dragging him down the corridor and her back into her apartment. "Don't do this! Please don't take him!" Her screams echoed through the apartment, raw and desperate, but the men didn't stop.

Amy followed them, her stride confident and unhurried. At the top of the landing, she turned back, her eyes locking onto Stephanie's. "Don't bother trying anything," she said with a chilling smile. "You won't get far."

With that, she nodded to one of the men, who pulled the door shut. Stephanie heard the sharp, final *click* of a lock sliding into place, and her heart sank even further.

She was trapped. Alone.

The silence that followed was deafening. Stephanie sagged against the wall, her sobs wracking her body as she tried to process what had just happened. Max was gone, taken by people who saw him as nothing more than a commodity. And she was powerless to stop it.

Outside, the faint sound of tires screeching marked their departure. Stephanie clenched her fists against the biting plastic of the zip ties, her tears falling harder. But even through her anguish, a spark of determination flickered in her chest.

They had taken him.

Stephanie's heart pounded in her ears as she slumped against the wall, the tears still flowing as the reality of what had just happened began to sink in. Max was gone. They had taken him, and she had been powerless to stop it.

But as the minutes ticked by, something shifted inside her. The fear and despair that had consumed her began to morph into something else, something stronger. She couldn't let this happen. She couldn't let them take Max away from her, not like this.

Her mind raced as she began to work on freeing herself from the restraints. The zip ties cut into her wrists, but she didn't care. She couldn't afford to care. All that mattered was getting to Max, saving him before it was too late.

With a surge of determination, Stephanie wiggled her hands free, the plastic ties snapping with a sharp sound, blood welling where the sharp plastic restraints had been, the skin white. She pushed herself to her feet, her body trembling from the adrenaline coursing through her veins. She had to move quickly, every second counted.

As she stumbled back into her apartment to gather her things, she knew one thing for certain: she would do whatever it took to get Max back. No matter the cost, no matter the danger, she wasn't going to lose him.

Not now. Not ever.

Chapter Thirty-Two

Stephanie stood frozen in the middle of her apartment, her wrists raw and burning from where the zip ties had bitten into her skin. The dull ache in her arms was nothing compared to the storm raging in her chest. Her heart pounded so violently it felt like it might burst, the echo of her own pulse roaring in her ears. Max was gone, ripped away right in front of her. The helplessness she had felt in that moment still clung to her, a suffocating weight.

But even as tears threatened to blur her vision again, that helplessness began to turn into something that she could use; Determination. She couldn't let it end like this. She wouldn't.

Her trembling hands reached for her phone and keys as her thoughts spiraled into a chaotic whirlwind. What could she do? Who could she call? Her breathing quickened as the memory of Amy's smug face and cold words came rushing back. Amy. Her co-worker. Her *friend.* The betrayal hit her like a physical blow, leaving a bitter taste in her mouth. And then there was Alistair… The pieces clicked together, each one sharpening her anger.

How could she have trusted them? She replayed every interaction, every moment she had brushed off her instincts. The way Amy had hovered, the way Alistair had seemed distant but watchful. It had all been so carefully orchestrated, and she had walked right into it. Her stomach churned with a mixture of anger, disgust, and regret.

But regret wouldn't help her now. There was no time to dwell on her mistakes. She needed to act.

Stephanie's eyes darted around the room, searching for answers as if they might somehow materialize. For a moment, she felt like she was drowning, grasping at nothing but air. And then, a thought cut through the chaos. Fiona. Her best friend. The one person she could trust without question.

She grabbed her phone, her fingers shaking as she dialled the number. Each ring felt like an eternity, her chest tightening with every passing second until finally, Fiona's groggy voice came through the line.

"Steph? What's going on? Are you okay?"

Stephanie took a deep breath, trying to steady her voice, but the panic broke through. "Fiona, listen to me. Max… he's been taken. I need your help."

The line went silent for a moment, and Stephanie held her breath. When Fiona spoke again, her voice was sharp, all traces of sleep gone. "Taken? What do you mean? Are you okay? Where are you?"

"I'm at my apartment," Stephanie said, her voice cracking. She pressed a hand to her forehead, trying to keep herself grounded. "I can't explain everything right now, but I need you to come over. Please, Fiona. I don't know what to do."

"I'm on my way," Fiona said without hesitation. "Stay put, Steph. I'll be there soon."

The call ended, and Stephanie lowered the phone, her hand trembling. She exhaled shakily, but the relief was fleeting. The fear, the anger, the helplessness, it all came surging back, threatening to overwhelm her. She couldn't just stand there. She needed to move.

She began pacing the small apartment, her bare feet silent against the floor. Her mind raced with worst-case scenarios. What were they going to do to Max? Where had they taken him? And how could she possibly stop them?

The image of Max, bound and helpless, flashed in her mind, and her stomach twisted painfully. She had seen the fear in his eyes, the vulnerability he rarely showed. And now, he was gone, taken by people who saw him as nothing more than a commodity.

Her hands balled into fists at her sides as her pacing quickened. She couldn't lose him, not like this. Max had always been there for her, a steady presence when everything else felt uncertain. And now it was her turn. She had to find him, no matter the cost.

Stephanie glanced at the clock, willing time to move faster, willing Fiona to arrive. She needed someone by her side, someone to help her think clearly. But even as she waited, the determination inside her solidified.

They had taken Max. They had underestimated her. And

they were going to regret it.

It wasn't long before Fiona burst through the door of Stephanie's apartment, her expression filled with worry. "Steph, what's going on? You're scaring me."

Stephanie ran to her, pulling her into a tight hug. The moment she felt Fiona's familiar embrace, the dam broke, and everything came rushing out. "They've taken Max... they've taken him, Fiona," Stephanie said, her voice trembling with fear and anger.

Fiona pulled back slightly; her brow furrowed with concern. "What do you mean they've taken him? Who took him? And... why Max?"

Stephanie took a shaky breath, her hands wringing as she paced the room, her thoughts spinning. "It's Amy... and Alistair," she began, her voice trembling. "They've been after Max this whole time. I didn't see it, Fiona. I didn't realize what they were planning. Amy, she was pretending to be my friend. But it was all fake. She just got close to me to get to him."

Fiona, sitting on the edge of the couch, leaned forward, her brows furrowed in disbelief. "Amy? *Your* Amy? That's... I mean, I knew she was nosy, but this? This is insane."

Stephanie stopped pacing, turning to face her friend, her eyes red and glistening with tears. "I trusted her, Fiona. I told her things, about me, about Max. And she used all of it against us. She was feeding everything to Alistair, and now they've taken him."

"Taken him?" Fiona repeated, her voice sharp with confusion and alarm. "Why would they take Max? What's going on, Steph? You're not making any sense."

Stephanie's breath hitched, and she pressed her trembling hands to her face. How could she explain this without it sounding ridiculous? But Fiona was here. Fiona was her best friend, the one person she trusted. She had to try.

"Max..." she started, her voice barely above a whisper. "He has a rare condition. Something that makes him... valuable. To the right, or wrong, people."

Fiona blinked, sitting straighter. "Valuable? What do you mean? Steph, this is getting weird. You're not giving me much to go on here."

Stephanie dropped her hands, meeting Fiona's gaze with desperation in her eyes. "He's not like other people, Fiona. He's... different. At night, he's a man. But during the day..." She swallowed hard. "He's a dog."

Fiona froze, her mouth opening and closing as she tried to process what she'd just heard. "A dog," she repeated flatly, her voice almost disbelieving.

Stephanie nodded quickly, her voice cracking. "Yes. I know it sounds insane, but it's true. I've seen it happen, Fiona. And now Amy and Alistair know. They've taken him because they think they can use him, or sell him, or... I don't even know what. But I can't just sit here and let it happen."

Fiona leaned back, her expression shifting between disbelief and concern. "Steph... are you okay? Are you sure about this? I mean..." She trailed off, clearly struggling to find the right words.

"I *know* how it sounds," Stephanie snapped, her voice tinged with desperation. "But I'm telling you the truth. Max isn't just some guy with secrets. He's cursed, Fiona. He's been like this for as long as he can remember, and now he's in danger because of it."

Fiona exhaled deeply, shaking her head as she tried to wrap her mind around what Stephanie was saying. "Okay... Let's say I believe you. Let's say Max is, what, a man-dog hybrid or something? What do we do? Where do we even start?"

Stephanie bit her lip, her gaze darting around the room as she fought to think. "I don't know yet. But Alistair has connections, resources. He wouldn't have taken Max far, not yet. We just need to figure out where they'd go."

Fiona rose from the couch, placing a firm hand on Stephanie's shoulder. "Alright. We'll figure this out. Together. But you need to calm down and focus. Where could they have taken him?"

Stephanie took a deep breath, her friend's grounding presence steadying her for a moment. "They'd need somewhere private, secure... somewhere they wouldn't risk being seen. Maybe..." She trailed off, her mind racing.

"Maybe we don't guess," Fiona said firmly. "Let's think this through. Who else knows about Alistair? His habits? His places? Anything?"

Stephanie's eyes darted around the room, her mind racing as the enormity of the situation hit her. "We have to figure out where they've taken him," she said, her voice trembling but determined. "There has to be a way to track them."

Fiona stood beside her; her expression resolute. "You're right. But we can't just rush into this blind. We need something to go on."

Stephanie's breath hitched as an idea struck her. "Amy... she's been all over me for weeks, trying to get close. She must have her phone on her. If we can track her, we might figure out where they've taken Max."

Fiona pulled out her phone, already typing as her mind worked. "I know someone who can help with that. He's a tech genius, good with tracking, hacking, that sort of thing. If anyone can figure out where Amy's been, it's him."

Stephanie nodded, a flicker of hope breaking through her despair. "Call him. Please. We don't have time to waste."

Fiona dialled the number, her tone brisk as she explained the situation. Stephanie paced nervously, her heart pounding as she caught fragments of Fiona's conversation. Words like "urgent" and "real-time tracking" made her stomach twist, but also gave her a fragile sense of hope.

After what felt like an eternity, Fiona hung up and turned to Stephanie. "He's in. He's going to work on tracking Amy's phone. Once we pinpoint her we'll know where Alistair and Max are. We'll know soon enough."

Stephanie exhaled shakily, her hands trembling slightly. "Thank you, Fiona," she said, her voice trembling. "I don't know what I'd do without you right now."

Fiona reached out, placing a steadying hand on Stephanie's shoulder. "You'd figure it out. But you don't have to. I'm here, and we're going to get him back."

Stephanie felt a surge of determination building within her. "We have to. Max... he's more than just someone I care about. I can't let them do this to him."

"We won't," Fiona said firmly, her tone leaving no room for doubt. "We're not letting them win. They think they're clever, but we'll outsmart them."

They waited for the call from Fiona's friend, the tension showing on them both. Soon enough however a grin crept onto Fiona's face, "So, you're dating a dog?"

Stephanie cast her a glance, "Shall we discuss your track record.... hmmm?" They smiled at one another, the smile of friends who have been through a lot in their time.

The room was still heavy with tension, but there was an undercurrent of resolve now, a shared purpose. As they waited for updates, Stephanie felt the weight of her fear shifting slightly, making room for the burning determination to see this through.

No matter what Amy and Alistair had planned, no matter what it took, Stephanie wasn't going to let them win. She would bring Max home, and she would make them pay.

Chapter Thirty-Three

Max's world was a blur of pain and confusion. His head throbbed from the blow that had knocked him down, and his body felt heavy, as though weighed down by something far more than the restraints that bound him. He was vaguely aware of being dragged into a van, of rough hands lifting him, throwing him into the back, but everything was hazy. He fought to stay conscious, to cling to some sense of awareness, but the darkness kept pulling at him.

Eventually, the van stopped, and he was hauled out and dragged into what felt like a cold, industrial space. His senses were dull, but the harsh scents of oil and metal still cut through the fog. He tried to open his eyes, but his vision was blurred, his body uncooperative. The bite of bindings around his wrists made him wince. The clank of steel against concrete echoed around him as he was forced into a chair, his arms shackled to its sides.

Slowly, the fog in his mind began to lift, and Max became aware of his surroundings. He was in a large, dimly lit warehouse, the walls lined with cold steel and concrete. The distant hum of machinery echoed in the background, a low, ominous sound that filled the space.

As his vision cleared, Max saw a figure standing in front of him, a man with sharp, calculating eyes, the kind that could weigh a situation in an instant and know exactly how to exploit it. Alistair Castel wasn't what one might expect of a man pulling the strings behind something like this. He wasn't brooding or maniacal. He was calm, composed, almost clinical in his movements, like a surgeon preparing for a precise operation.

Alistair looked down at Max with a faint smile, more of a polite mask than anything resembling warmth. "Welcome back to the land of the living," he said with an almost conversational tone. "I was beginning to think you'd be out for hours."

Max blinked up at him, his mind still fuzzy from the blow. He tugged at the restraints, testing their strength, but they held firm. He took a deep breath, trying to gather his thoughts. "What do you want from me?" he asked, his voice hoarse.

Alistair stepped closer; his hands casually tucked into the pockets of his tailored coat. "I want what any reasonable person would want, Max, an opportunity. And you, my friend, represent a very rare and valuable opportunity."

Max narrowed his eyes, trying to read the man in front of him. There was something about Alistair's demeanour that unsettled him, not the wild arrogance of a typical villain, but the cold pragmatism of someone who saw people as nothing more than assets to be manipulated.

Alistair smiled, noticing Max's scrutinizing gaze. "Something tells me you've been alive a long time, haven't you? Seen things most of us could never imagine. That makes you special. Unique." He paused, letting his words sink in. "And to some, to me, very valuable."

Max's fingers curled tighter around the cold steel arms of the chair, the pressure biting into his palms as he fought to keep himself composed. His memories, once scattered fragments, had become a deluge since the night he'd confessed his curse to Stephanie. Now, under the harsh lights of Alistair's makeshift interrogation room, those memories surged like a tidal wave. Flashes of agony, betrayal, and survival clawed at his mind, centuries of torment and endurance, all leading him to this moment.

"Valuable?" Max's voice dripped with contempt, his lips curling into a defiant smirk despite the pounding in his skull. "You think I haven't been here before? You think you're the first person to try and break me, to turn me into their little experiment, their prize?"

Alistair's smile didn't falter, but his eyes narrowed, watching Max intently.

"I've lived through hell, Alistair," Max continued, his voice hardening as he leaned forward in the chair. "I've been tortured by the Shah of Persia, strung up like an animal for his amusement. I've been ripped apart by a Viking king's hounds because I refused to kneel. Burned alive by an emperor who wanted to test the limits of immortality." He spat the last word as if it were poison.

"And you?" Max's gaze locked onto Alistair's, his voice dropping into a low growl. "You're just another suit in a long line of sadistic egomaniacs who think they've found the ultimate trophy. You're nothing new. Just another pawn who doesn't realize he's playing a much bigger game. Yes I'm old, I have no idea how many lifetimes I've lived."

Max levelled his gaze at Alistair, staring at him with all of the hatred and defiance that he had, "You think you have what it takes to control me!"

For a moment, the room was silent, save for the hum of fluorescent lights overhead. Alistair tilted his head slightly, his expression almost amused as he began to circle Max like a predator toying with its prey.

"Bravado," Alistair said finally, his tone soft and deliberate. "That's what this is. A survival mechanism. You talk big, make yourself sound invincible, because deep down, you're terrified. You're clinging to the belief that your past makes you untouchable." He leaned closer, his voice lowering to an almost intimate whisper. "But it doesn't, Max. It just means you've had the privilege of suffering longer than most."

Max's jaw tightened, but he refused to look away. He wasn't going to give Alistair the satisfaction of seeing his fear, even as his stomach churned with unease.

"And that's the problem with men like you," Alistair continued, his smile taking on a cruel edge. "You've been through so much; you think you've seen the worst the world has to offer. But you haven't, Max. You haven't seen me."

Max swallowed hard, willing himself to keep his composure. "I've faced worse than you, Alistair. Don't flatter yourself."

Alistair chuckled, the sound low and unsettling. "You think so? Perhaps you have. But there's always something worse waiting, isn't there? Always something around the corner, just when you think you've found solid ground." He straightened; his hands clasped behind his back as he studied Max like a specimen under a microscope.

"You're an anomaly, Max. A creature of contradictions. A man cursed to live between worlds, yet stubbornly trying to play the hero. Do you even know what you are? Or has the weight of your existence finally blurred the lines?"

Max opened his mouth to respond, but Alistair cut him off, his voice dropping to a razor's edge.

"It doesn't matter," Alistair said, his tone suddenly cold. "Because everyone breaks, Max. Even you. And when you do, I'll be there to pick up the pieces."

Max clenched his teeth, his body taut with defiance. But inside, he could feel the cracks beginning to form, the weight of centuries pressing down on him, the truth he couldn't escape. Alistair's words clawed at the dark corners of his mind, and for the first time in a long time, Max wasn't sure he could win.

But he wouldn't give Alistair the satisfaction of seeing him crumble. Not yet.

Max kept his gaze locked on Alistair's, refusing to flinch. But internally, he was battling the doubts creeping into his mind. He had survived horrors beyond imagining in his countless lifetimes, but that didn't mean he was invincible. He could be broken, he had been broken before. And the thought of it happening again, of losing himself in the process, terrified him more than he cared to admit.

Alistair straightened, his casual stance never slipping. "I don't need to threaten you, Max. You already know what's at stake. You can pretend all you like, but sooner or later, you'll come to see things my way. It's just a matter of time."

Max gritted his teeth, his mind racing. He had to find a way out of this, before it was too late. But for now, all he could do was buy time, keep Alistair talking, and hope that Stephanie could somehow find him.

Because despite his best efforts to project strength, Max knew one thing for certain: he couldn't do this alone.

Chapter Thirty-Four

Stephanie paced the living room, her hands fidgeting with the frayed hem of the cushion she clutched tightly. The familiar warmth of her apartment did nothing to soothe the storm raging in her mind. She couldn't focus. Every second that passed felt like an eternity. Max was out there somewhere, captured, vulnerable, and she had no idea how to find him.

"Come on, Chris, pick up," Fiona muttered from the couch, tapping her foot impatiently as she held her phone to her ear. "We don't have all day."

Stephanie glanced out the window, where the sky was growing darker, heavy clouds casting a shadow over the street below. A strange tension hung in the air, almost as if the city itself was holding its breath.

Finally, after what seemed like an eternity, Fiona let out a relieved sigh. "Chris! About time! Did you find anything?"

She listened intently, her brow furrowing in concentration. Stephanie watched her anxiously, trying to read her expression. Then Fiona's face fell, and she closed her eyes in frustration.

"Damn it," Fiona muttered, pulling the phone away from her ear and placing it on speaker. "Tell her, Chris."

Chris's voice crackled through the phone, low and calm but laced with the seriousness of the situation. "Amy's phone is still at the law firm, Steph. Castel & Fink. She probably left it there to throw us off, either way, unless they are there we can't use that."

"But she had a phone when she was here!" Stephanie stated.

"I'd imagine it was a burner, you don't use your own phone for things like this!" Chris stated matter of factly.

Stephanie felt her heart sink. All that hope she had clung to, gone, just like that. She slumped into the armchair, feeling utterly defeated. They had nothing to go on, no leads, no way to track Max.

"Great," Stephanie muttered, rubbing her temples. "Just great. So now what? We're back to square one?"

Fiona bit her lip, glancing at her phone as if willing it to give them the answers they needed. But it stayed silent, offering no solutions. The heaviness of the moment pressed down on Stephanie, and she was about to lose all hope when a sudden thought hit her like a bolt of lightning.

"The Airtag!" Stephanie blurted out, sitting upright. "There was an Airtag, help me find it."

They searched the living room and found nothing, Oliver sat on the windowsill, casually gazing over, *Meow "I slipped it back in his pocket, thought it might help the mangy mutt!"*

"It's not here" said Fiona, "do you think he's got it on him?"

"It must be, if he has it we can trace it! Right Chris?" Stephanie clamoured in desperation Chris, still on the line, jumped in immediately. "Airtag? That's perfect. If you can give me the serial number, I can track it."

Stephanie nodded, her mind racing. "The serial number... It'll be on Amy's phone, right? She used it to set up the tag."

"Most likely," Chris replied. "If we can get access to her phone, I can trace the Airtag and find Max."

Fiona looked at Stephanie, determination replacing the earlier frustration in her eyes. "Then we need to get to Castel & Fink and get that phone."

Stephanie nodded, feeling the urgency of the situation settle into her bones. "Let's go. Chris, stay where you are. We'll call you when we're there."

They rushed out of the apartment, Stephanie barely stopping to grab her keys before locking the door behind them. As they hurried down the stairs and out onto the street, the chill of the evening air hit them, but Stephanie barely noticed. Her mind was racing with plans, possibilities, and the desperate need to save Max.

But as soon as they stepped outside, the air seemed to shift, thickening with an oppressive energy. They froze in their tracks, their eyes drawn upward.

Pigeons. Thousands of them.

The sky churned with their frenzied movements, a mass

324

of dark, fluttering shapes that spiralled in unnatural, chaotic patterns. The birds darted low over rooftops, then ascended as one, forming jagged, swirling shapes against the fading light. Their wings beat in eerie synchronization, and yet their path seemed aimless, as though driven by a force that neither woman could see.

Their cries filled the air, not the usual coos and caws, but something deeper, harsher, a discordant symphony that reverberated through the street like a warning. The sound crawled under their skin, making Stephanie's chest tighten.

"What the hell?" Fiona whispered, her voice barely audible over the rising din. Her wide eyes stayed fixed on the spectacle above.

Stephanie shivered as a cold dread settled over her. Something wasn't right, this was more than just an unusual flock of birds. The pigeons moved with purpose, their chaotic spirals too deliberate, as if following some silent, sinister order. Her eyes traced the spiralling vortex they formed, its twisting column seeming to rise from the street near her apartment and extend endlessly into the sky.

And then she saw it. Something even more disturbing.

Some of the pigeons weren't just flying, they were dripping. Dark, viscous drops fell from their feathers, splattering against the pavement. At first, Stephanie thought it was droppings, disgusting but harmless. But when the drops hit the ground, they hissed, releasing tiny wisps of smoke as they burned into the asphalt.

Stephanie stumbled back, her hand covering her mouth as

bile rose in her throat. "That's... that's not normal," she managed to whisper, her voice shaky. "That's *definitely* not normal."

Fiona took a cautious step forward, squinting at the dark, glossy liquid pooling in tiny, sizzling craters on the ground. Her face was pale, her voice unsteady. "What the hell are we looking at, Steph? This isn't... this isn't natural."

Stephanie's mind raced as she tried to make sense of the scene. The birds, the spirals, the burning liquid, it all felt wrong, like a nightmare bleeding into reality. The pigeons above seemed agitated, their movements growing wilder as they spiralled higher and higher, their calls building to an unbearable crescendo.

And then, just as suddenly as it began, the vortex of birds shifted. The pigeons veered sharply away from the apartment, their chaotic patterns coalescing into a single, purposeful direction. It was as if they had been summoned elsewhere, leaving behind only the acrid scent of the sizzling pavement and the echo of their haunting cries.

Stephanie exhaled a shaky breath, her knees threatening to give out. "I don't... I don't understand," she murmured, her voice hollow.

"Whatever this is, it's not random. This is," She hesitated, searching for the right word. "This is something *else.*"

Stephanie's head swam her thoughts tangled in fear and confusion. "And whatever it is... it's not finished," she said softly, her gaze falling to the ground where the corrosive droplets still hissed and steamed.

For a moment, neither of them moved, the silence pressing down on them like a physical weight. Stephanie could feel it in her bones, this wasn't over. Whatever force had driven those birds was still out there, watching, waiting.

Staring up at the sky. "What are they doing? Why are they,"

And then Stephanie saw him. Roger.

Perched upon a lamppost just to the side, Roger seemed otherworldly. His feathers, once scruffy and dull, now shimmered with an almost ethereal glow. Each plume caught the dim light and refracted it with an intensity that made him look larger, more magnificent than ever before. He stood apart from the chaos of the pigeons swirling around him, their erratic movements starkly contrasted by his still, commanding presence.

Roger wasn't part of their frenzied mass. He was above it, watching with an unnerving calmness, his sharp gaze cutting through the tumult like a blade. The keen intelligence in his eyes sent a shiver down Stephanie's spine, as if he knew far more than he let on.

And then, with a single, deliberate movement, Roger turned his glowing eyes to her.

Stephanie's breath caught in her throat. The connection was undeniable, a pull she couldn't quite understand but couldn't ignore. Roger's beady, luminous eyes locked onto hers, holding her in place, and for a brief moment, she felt as though he could see right through her, into her thoughts, her fears, her soul.

Slowly, Roger tilted his head upward, gesturing toward the sky with a deliberate motion of his beak.

The swirling pigeons above seemed to intensify their spirals as if responding to an unseen command. Their movements became sharper, more focused, the cacophony of their cries growing louder.

Stephanie's mind raced, her heart pounding in her chest. The pigeons... Roger... The corrosive liquid raining down... It was all connected. Somehow, they were trying to tell her something.

And then, suddenly, it clicked.

Her gaze snapped back to Roger, who now seemed to stand even taller, his luminous feathers radiating an almost divine light. This wasn't just a bird. He was a sentinel, a messenger. The chaos above wasn't random, it was a warning.

The weight of realization settled over her, heavy and suffocating. Whatever was happening, it was bigger than her, bigger than Max. The universe was stirring, and Roger was its herald.

"We have to follow them," Stephanie said, her voice steady despite the fear bubbling inside her. "We have to follow the pigeons."

Fiona blinked at her, looking both sceptical and alarmed. "Are you serious? Follow the pigeons? Steph, they're literally burning holes in the pavement!"

But Stephanie's mind was made up. She wasn't sure how or why, but she knew, deep in her gut, that this was the way to find Max. The pigeons were leading them to him.

"Yes," Stephanie said firmly. "We have to follow them. It's the only way."

Fiona hesitated for a moment longer, then let out a resigned sigh. "Alright, fine. But if I get pooped on, you owe me."

Stephanie cracked a small, nervous smile as they both rushed to the curb. A taxi was idling nearby, and they flagged it down. The driver, a middle-aged man with tired eyes, rolled down the window and gave them a questioning look.

"Where to, love?" he asked, glancing between the two of them.

Stephanie pointed up at the sky, where the pigeons were still swirling in their strange, chaotic dance. "Follow those pigeons!" she said, the urgency in her voice unmistakable.

The driver raised an eyebrow "Follow some pigeons? In London? Look love I love a good joke me, but let's not be silly now." The driver said, "what is this some kind of prank?"

Stephanie pointed up. He craned his neck and looked up through the window and there, above them was a swirling mass of tens of thousands of pigeons, all heading East in a huge procession.

"Right, erm, yeah" he said, "follow them pigeons it is then!" His face a mix of curiosity and bemusement, and pulled away from the curb, the taxi joining the stream of traffic as they set off after the birds.

As the taxi weaved through the streets of London, following the path of the pigeons above, Stephanie couldn't help but feel a strange mix of fear and hope. The pigeons were leading them somewhere, somewhere important. And she could only pray that wherever it was, it would bring them one step closer to saving Max.

Fiona fixed Stephanie a quizzical look as they bounced around in the cab, a realisation hitting her," dog?" she said with a raised eyebrow.

Stephanie looked at her flatly, smiled, tilted her head slightly to the right and replied, "Dog!"

"Huh!" Said Fiona, her eyes fixed on the dark sky.

The taxi sped along, the driver clearly unnerved by what was transpiring, it weaved in and out of the light traffic as it followed the chaotic swarm of pigeons overhead. Stephanie sat on the edge of her seat, her heart pounding in her chest. Every glance out the window showed the darkening sky filled with birds, their eerie, unnatural movement sending chills down her spine. They weren't just flying, they were darting, diving, and spiralling in a coordinated chaos that made the hairs on the back of her neck stand up.

And Roger… Roger was keeping pace with them.

From her window, Stephanie spotted the familiar seagull weaving in and out of the pigeon swarm with precision and purpose. But something was different about him. His feathers were darker now, almost black, and there was an intensity in his movements that Stephanie had never seen before. He looked… fiercer, more focused, like a predator goading its prey.

"Do you see that?" Stephanie muttered, more to herself than to Fiona, as she watched Roger dive low and then rise again, almost as if he were corralling the pigeons, keeping them in line. The sight was both mesmerizing and terrifying. This wasn't the Roger she knew. This was something else, something much more dangerous.

Fiona, noticing Stephanie's fixation, glanced out the window as well. "What the hell is he doing? He looks like he's… hunting."

Stephanie nodded; her throat dry. "I don't know, but whatever it is, it's not normal."

As if to punctuate her words, Roger suddenly swooped down with a burst of speed, slamming into a pigeon with a wet *thud*. The unfortunate bird dropped to the ground, lifeless and Roger barely hesitated before diving back into the swarm, his sharp beak and talons working with terrifying efficiency to bring down more of the pigeons.

"What the" Fiona began, her voice rising in alarm, but Stephanie cut her off.

"Keep following them!" she urged the driver, who had noticed the unsettling spectacle outside. The man nodded wordlessly, his face pale, and pressed harder on the accelerator. They sped through the city, leaving the familiar streets behind as the pigeons led them toward the outskirts of town.

After what felt like an eternity of twisting and turning through the labyrinth of London's streets, Stephanie noticed a change in their surroundings. The tall buildings and bustling shops gave way to industrial landscapes, rows of warehouses, shipping containers, and cranes looming against the skyline. The air smelled of oil, saltwater, and the distant hum of machinery. They were heading toward the docks.

"Fiona," Stephanie said quietly, her voice trembling with a mix of fear and determination. "They're leading us to the docks."

Fiona's eyes narrowed as she looked out the window, scanning the area. "I see it. Look, over there,"

Stephanie followed Fiona's gaze and saw what she was pointing at: a cluster of dark shapes at the far end of the container yard. As they got closer, the shapes became more distinct, Land Rovers, sleek and black, parked beside a row of expensive-looking cars. The vehicles stood out against the bleak industrial backdrop; their presence unmistakably ominous.

"Alistair," Stephanie breathed, her heart sinking as she realized what this meant. "He's got to be here. And if he is Amy will be too. They're all here."

Fiona clenched her fists, her jaw tight with anger. "And they've brought company," she added, nodding toward the luxury cars parked alongside the Land Rovers. "Looks like Alistair's buyer has arrived."

The driver slowed the taxi as they approached the entrance to the container yard, pulling over to the side of the road just outside the gates. The pigeons were still circling overhead, but their movements had grown more erratic, their numbers thinning as Roger continued to dive and strike with ruthless precision.

"We'll get out here," Fiona told the driver, handing him a wad of cash. "Keep the change, and... stay safe."

The driver nodded quickly, grateful to be leaving the strange situation behind. Without a word, he drove off, leaving Stephanie and Fiona standing at the edge of the container yard. The shadowy warehouses loomed ahead, their presence heavy and foreboding under the dim industrial lights.

Fiona immediately hit speed dial, her fingers trembling slightly as she brought the phone to her ear. Chris answered on the first ring.

"Chris," she said, her voice sharp with urgency. "We're here. Alistair and Amy are inside, and they have Max. Can you track the Airtag now?"

There was a brief pause, followed by the faint sound of typing on Chris's end. "I'm on it," he said. "Give me a second…"

The silence that followed was filled with tension, broken only by the distant hum of machinery and the unsettling caws of pigeons circling above. Stephanie's heart raced, her mind spinning with images of Max, bound, hurt, and surrounded by Alistair and his buyer. She clenched her fists, forcing herself to focus.

Chris's voice finally crackled back through the phone. "I can't give you precise details without the serial number or MAC address, but there's definitely an Airtag pinging from the large building to your east. It's right next to the container stacks."

Stephanie swallowed hard; her mouth dry as she turned to look at the building Chris had described. "Thanks, Chris. We'll take it from here."

"Be careful," Chris said, his tone serious. "I wish I could do more."

She ended the call and looked at Fiona, her resolve hardening. "Max is in that warehouse. I'm going in to get him."

"Wait," Fiona said, her voice firm. "You can't just rush in there. Let's call the police, call anyone who can help. We need backup."

"Then *you* call them," Stephanie replied, her tone unyielding. "Call the police, call everyone. Tell them someone's been kidnapped, and you're outside the warehouse."

Fiona hesitated, her face a mixture of frustration and determination. "I'm coming with you," she said, standing her ground. "You need me."

"I do," Stephanie admitted, her voice softening for a moment. "But I need you out here more. Someone has to make sure the police come, and make them *hurry*. If anything happens to me, Max still needs someone fighting for him. Promise me, Fiona. Call them. Make them come now!"

Fiona stared at her for a long moment before nodding, her expression hardening with determination. "Fine. But you'd better come back out, Steph. Both of you."

Stephanie gave her a brief, fierce look of gratitude. "I will."

Without another word, she turned and set off at a run toward the warehouse, her heart pounding with fear and resolve. The imposing building loomed larger with each step, and as she reached the edge of the container yard, Stephanie whispered to herself, *I'm coming, Max. Just hold on.*

Approaching the container yard's entrance, staying low and moving cautiously. The pigeons overhead were beginning to coo in unison, their strange mission unknown to all but themselves. Stephanie came to one of the exterior walls of the warehouse. Glancing around she could see some odd-looking containers with rows of bars along one side, signs of animals stirring inside.

Further along waited large articulated trucks with container flatbeds, their engines rumbling away idly as they   waited.

"What the hell is going on here?" she muttered to herself, "It's like a mobile zoo" She could hear some of the men, similar in appearance to the ones that she had seen outside her apartment. Some, checking manifests, others keeping a watchful eye out. Every now and then she could hear a clang of bars, a low rumble or a road. There were definitely animals in these containers and from what she had seen thus far and by the actions of Alistair's men they were undoubtedly rare and illegal to trade in.

As the two women slipped into the shadows of the containers, the warehouse loomed closer, its massive steel doors like the gaping maw of some great beast. Stephanie's heart raced as she prepared herself for what was to come.

Whatever was waiting for them inside, she knew one thing for certain: she wasn't leaving without Max.

Chapter Thirty-Five

Max's head still throbbed, his temples pulsing with every beat of his heart. The rough fabric of the hood covering his face scratched against his skin, suffocating him in darkness. He could barely move, his arms bound tightly behind his back, wrists raw from the ropes that dug into his skin. The cold, damp air in the warehouse wrapped around him like a second skin, chilling him to the bone. His muscles ached from sitting in the same hunched position for what felt like hours.

But it wasn't the darkness or the cold that unnerved him the most, it was the sounds.

Somewhere close by, the clanging of metal echoed in the cavernous space. It was an unsettling sound, like a cage door slamming shut, followed by the low growl of something feral. Max strained to listen, his heart racing as he tried to make sense of the cacophony around him. The heavy thud of large animals shifting in their enclosures reverberated through the floor, rattling his bones. Every few moments, there'd be the unmistakable scrape of claws on metal, followed by deep, primal snorts.

He knew where he was, or at least, he could guess. From what he had gleaned from his earlier conversation with Alistair this was Lucien Marchand's warehouse. A place infamous for housing things that didn't belong in polite society. Trophy animals, some rare and endangered. It wasn't just a warehouse. It was a holding pen for the grotesque desires of a man who collected living creatures like one might collect fine art. The thought of it made Max's stomach churn.

Somewhere to his left, something heavy shifted, letting out a menacing growl that sent shivers down his spine. It was close, too close. The sound of the iron bars shaking as the creature moved made Max's throat tighten in fear. Whatever it was, it was pacing, restless. His mind raced with images of lions, tigers, pumas… creatures with sharp teeth and dead black eyes.

Another clang echoed through the space, louder this time. The metal of a cage door slamming shut reverberated in the darkness, followed by the sound of footsteps, human footsteps. Two sets. One heavy and purposeful, the other light and steady. Max's pulse quickened. He knew those steps wouldn't be bearing good news. Alistair and Lucien paced deliberately towards the bound figure.

The footsteps grew louder, drawing closer. Max held his breath, his senses on high alert. He could feel the presence of the two men standing over him before they even spoke. The pungent smell of expensive cologne mixed with the musty odour of the warehouse. He could almost taste the tension in the air.

Then, without warning, the hood was yanked off his head.

The sudden brightness of the fluorescent lights stung his eyes, and he blinked rapidly, trying to adjust to the harshness. His vision swam for a moment before focusing on the two figures standing before him. Lucien

Marchand, the billionaire industrialist, towered over him with a look of cold satisfaction. His tailored suit was immaculate, and his sharp blue eyes gleamed with malice. Alistair stood beside him, arms crossed, a smug grin playing on his lips.

"Well, well," Lucien drawled, his voice dripping with cruel amusement. "Look who finally decided to join us."

Max's mouth was dry. His tongue felt thick, but he managed to croak out a few words. "What... what is this?"

Lucien chuckled softly, kneeling in front of Max. His expression was one of mock sympathy. "This, my dear Max, is where you'll be staying for just a little while, at least until I take you to your.....permanent accommodation. I must say, you've been quite the elusive prize. Alistair here has done a splendid job of finally bringing you to me."

Max's heart pounded in his chest, his mind racing. "Prize? I'm not some animal for your collection," he spat, his voice rough with anger.

Lucien's smile widened; his eyes gleaming with amusement. "Ah, but you're wrong, Max. You see, you're far more than just a man. You're... unique. Something special." He leaned in closer, his voice dropping to a whisper. "And special things belong to collectors like me."

Lucien paused for a moment and slipped his phone out of his pocket. "Let me show you how 'special' you are."

He hit play on the device and the video started to play, the video that Amy had taken days earlier.

There for the first time, Max saw himself change, it was funny, he thought, all those lives and he'd never seen himself transform from one self to another as someone else would, it really was quite unsettling he realised.

"What are you Max? Where did you come from? How do you do the things that you do?" Lucien hissed, "We will have plenty of time to discuss all this, plenty of time."

Max recoiled, his body tensing against the ropes. He struggled to keep his composure, his mind flashing with images of all the creatures Lucien must have trapped in this place. The clanging of cages, the growls, it all made sense now. He was nothing more than another rare prize for Lucien's twisted collection.

Alistair stepped forward, his smirk widening. "You should be honoured; Max. Lucien doesn't just collect animals. He collects the rarest, the most... extraordinary. You're in good company."

Max glared at him, anger flaring in his chest. "You're both insane," he growled. "I'm not going to be part of whatever sick game this is."

Lucien's smile faded, his expression hardening. "Insane? Perhaps. But I'm a man who gets what he wants. And right now, what I want is you." He stood up, his voice cold and sharp. "You'll learn, in time, that there are worse fates than being part of my collection."

The sound of something large crashing against the metal bars echoed through the warehouse, sending a jolt of fear through Max's body. Lucien glanced over his shoulder at the noise, his smile returning. "And don't worry, Max. You'll have plenty of company. In fact, some of them are quite eager to meet you."

The low growl of a predator rumbled through the air, closer now, as if whatever was in the cage had sensed the tension between the men. Max felt the weight of the situation pressing down on him. He was trapped, surrounded by cages and predators, with no way out.

Lucien turned to Alistair, his tone casual, as if they were discussing a business deal. "I trust everything is ready for transport?"

Alistair nodded, glancing at Max with a look of contempt. "Everything's in place. Once he's... prepared, we'll move him to the estate."

"Good. Good!" Lucien gave a little clap of his hands before his gaze shifted back to Max. "You've been brought here for a reason. I do suggest you get comfortable with the idea that you're not going anywhere." He leaned down, his voice low and threatening. "You belong to me now."

Max's heart hammered in his chest as the two men turned and walked away, their footsteps echoing in the vast, empty space. The sound of the cages rattling, the distant growls of the animals, and the finality of Lucien's words weighed heavily on him.

He was no longer a man or a dog. He was a prisoner.

Chapter Thirty-Six

The dimly lit interior of the warehouse was eerily quiet, broken only by the occasional creak of metal and distant animal noises. Stephanie slipped through the open doorway, pressing herself against the cold steel wall. The weight of the moment bore down on her shoulders as she crept closer, her breath shallow. Somewhere inside this industrial maze, Max was waiting, and she wasn't about to let him down.

A soft, rhythmic cooing drifted to her, gentle in volume yet overwhelming, as if it pressed against the very air around her. She hesitated, glancing upward toward the massive steel joists overhead. There, perched in eerie stillness, were hundreds, no, thousands of pigeons. Feathers fluffed, bodies unmoving, yet every single one fixed its gaze on the same unseen point. The sheer weight of their collective focus sent an icy ripple down her spine, the tiny hairs on the back of her neck standing on end. She swallowed hard, forcing herself to look away, to shake the unsettling image from her mind. There was no time for distractions. She had a mission to complete.

Peering around the corner, Stephanie spotted Alistair's men. Their sharp eyes scanned the room as they patrolled methodically between the rows of shipping containers, unaware of her presence. The rattling of cages from hidden corners confirmed what she had feared, there were animals here, and this operation was much more than just about Max. She was about to take down something far bigger than she had imagined.

As she crouched low and moved silently through the shadows, Stephanie heard a familiar voice, muffled but unmistakable. Max. Her heart leaped, and she quickened her pace, following the sound. She rounded a corner, and there, bound to a chair, was Max. His hands were chained, his face bruised, but his eyes still held that defiant spark she had come to know so well.

Alistair stood in a dimly lit recess with Lucien Marchand, a tall, impeccably dressed man with silver hair and a cold, calculating expression. Lucien glanced around the space with casual disinterest, as though the rare and exotic animals caged around him were nothing more than commodities.

Alistair handed Lucien a sleek tablet, displaying a final contract and the payment details. "As agreed, Mr. Marchand. £3.2 million, transferred in three parts. I trust everything is in order?"

Lucien smirked, nodding as he skimmed the contract. "Yes, quite. You've outdone yourself this time, Alistair. A fine collection of specimens." His eyes flicked toward a large cage nearby, where a panther paced restlessly, its eyes gleaming in the dim light. "Most of them will be quite a thrill for my... guests."

Alistair raised an eyebrow, intrigued. "Your farm in Oxfordshire, yes? I hear it's quite the exclusive retreat."

Lucien chuckled, his voice low and smooth. "Indeed. It's become something of a tradition among my... acquaintances. We gather a few times a year for a hunt. Nothing like taking down a truly wild beast with your own hands, wouldn't you agree? There's something primal about it. And some of these creatures..." He gestured around at the cages. "… will provide excellent sport."

Alistair's lips curled into a smirk, though a flicker of unease darkened his gaze. "Hunting them? Seems a bit… theatrical, even for you, Lucien."

Lucien waved a dismissive hand, his demeanour one of practiced indifference. "Theatrical? Perhaps. But let me assure you, it's a spectacle worth every penny. My guests are not your ordinary socialites, Alistair. They are the movers and shakers of Europe, the untouchables. And what do such men desire? Not mere possessions or power; they already have those. No, they crave something money can't buy: the raw thrill of danger, the primal rush of the hunt. Exclusivity, risk, triumph, it keeps them coming back. You should join us sometime. It's… invigorating."

Alistair hesitated, carefully masking his disdain. "Perhaps," he said coolly. "Though I have other… interests. Speaking of which," he added, gesturing toward a container at the far end of the room, "So Max isn't part of your hunting party?"

Lucien's eyes gleamed with a dark hunger, his smile spreading like a slow, predatory ripple. It wasn't a smile of amusement but one of sheer possession, and it made Alistair's stomach tighten. "Oh, Max?" Lucien drawled, his voice oozing satisfaction. "No, my dear Alistair, Max is far too… special for such trivialities. He's not a beast to be hunted. He's a treasure, one that demands a far more… refined approach."

Alistair's gaze flickered toward the container where Max was confined, his discomfort growing. "You're sure about this, Lucien? He's… unpredictable. His history alone makes him volatile. He's not like the others."

"That's precisely why I want him," Lucien said smoothly, his tone laced with a sinister confidence. "Max isn't merely a creature to control. He's a challenge, Alistair. A puzzle, a mind to dismantle piece by exquisite piece. It's rare to encounter something so unique, so... layered. I intend to savour every moment of his undoing."

Alistair frowned, the weight of Lucien's obsession settling uncomfortably in the pit of his stomach. "As long as the money's good and the transaction remains clean, he's your problem now. Handle him however you see fit, but don't let it come back to me."

Lucien chuckled, a soft, chilling sound as he pocketed his tablet, the glow of a completed transaction disappearing into his tailored jacket. "Oh, Alistair, you worry too much. It's all under control, as always. Now, about that offer... You really should join me at the farm. There's a jaguar in the next shipment, magnificent creature. I think you'd find it quite... exhilarating."

Before Alistair could formulate a reply, the steady echo of footsteps interrupted them. One of his guards approached, his stance rigid with deference. "Everything's ready, sir. Just waiting on your final approval to load the cargo."

Alistair turned his gaze to Lucien, who offered a satisfied nod. "Proceed," Alistair said tersely.

As the guards moved to oversee the transfer, their heavy boots clanging against the steel floor, Alistair turned back to Lucien. His expression was carefully neutral, but a thread of unease lingered in his voice. "Enjoy your acquisitions, Lucien. Especially… Max."

Lucien's smile widened, his eyes glittering with an almost manic glee. "Oh, don't worry, Alistair. I intend to enjoy him thoroughly. Max will be… cherished."

The word hung in the air, its meaning warped by Lucien's malice, and for a fleeting moment, Alistair wondered if he'd just sold far more than he'd bargained for.

As the final arrangements were being made, the eerie stillness of the warehouse was shattered. A deafening roar reverberated through the cavernous space, immediately followed by the metallic crash of a cage door swinging open. Both Alistair and Lucien turned in unison, their eyes widening in disbelief as a massive tiger sprang from its enclosure, its muscles rippling with raw power.

The cage door stood open behind them, its hinges creaking as it swung further. Stephanie, crouched out of sight behind a collection of stacked boxes, held her breath as she watched the chaos unfold. She had taken a gamble opening that door, it had swung outward, toward the two men, giving her a precious few seconds to slip back into the shadows undetected.

The tiger, sensing its chance at freedom, let out another bone-rattling roar and charged forward, claws raking across the ground as it tore through the maze of crates and containers. Shouts erupted as Alistair's men scrambled in every direction, tripping over each other in their panic. Lucien, stepped aside with unnerving composure, his sharp eyes scanning the chaos even as the massive beast barrelled past him, smashing through crates and upending cargo.

Above them, Roger swooped down, his feathers glowing with an almost spectral radiance in the dim light. His piercing screech cut through the air, a sound that seemed to amplify the panic.

With his usually palmated feet now razor-sharp talons, Roger dove toward the tiger, striking its flank with savage precision. But instead of lashing out in fury, the great cat halted mid-step, muscles coiled, its deep golden eyes locking onto his.

Roger settled onto the floor before it, his talons clicking against the concrete. His avian form loomed larger than it should, his presence something more than flesh and feather. The tiger's breath came slow and heavy, its body taut with instinct, yet it did not attack. Instead, it took a cautious step backward, shifting its weight onto its hind legs. Then, ever so slightly, it dipped its head a gesture of acknowledgment, of deference.

For a long moment, neither moved. The air between them buzzed with something ancient, something understood but unspoken. Then Roger lifted his gaze toward the rafters, his ember-like eyes reflecting the countless pairs staring back. He opened his beak wide and let out a shrieking *CAW*, a sound that was neither purely avian nor entirely earthly, a cry that reverberated through the vast space with an unnatural force.

At once, the tiger sprang forward, its powerful form surging toward its former captors with renewed purpose. Above, the pigeons erupted from the steel joists, a hurricane of wings, beaks and flashing eyes. The air filled with the deafening sound of beating feathers, a storm of creatures descending upon those who had thought themselves untouchable.

In the midst of this pandemonium, Fiona burst through the side door, her face a mask of determination as she wielded a large blue fire extinguisher. Without hesitation, she unleashed a torrent of foam, spraying wildly across the area in front of her. The thick white spray coated the floor and walls, causing men to slip and crash into each other while desperately clutching their weapons as they fell.

Lucien's calm façade finally cracked, his face twisting in rage as he surveyed the disaster unfolding before him. His voice, sharp and commanding, cut through the noise. "What in *hell* is going on here?" But his tone betrayed the simmering panic underneath.

The tiger let out another earth-shaking roar, crashing through a row of crates and sending splinters and shattered wood flying across the warehouse floor. Scattered among the wreckage lay antiques and artifacts, treasures that had no rightful owner, never meant to be hoarded by a single man. They were a testament to Lucien's insatiable greed, his need to claim and collect what was never his to keep.

The other animals, sensing their chance, joined the chaos. As Stephanie opened more of the cages, monkeys chattered wildly as they escaped and proceeded to swing from the rafters, wolves prowled between toppled boxes, and exotic birds screeched, their colours blurring as they took to the air in a flurry of feathers.

Alistair grabbed Lucien by the arm, his face pale and taut with urgency. "We need to get out of here! Now!"

Lucien wrenched his arm free, his fury barely contained. "This isn't over, Alistair! I *paid* for this shipment! I expect it intact!"

"Let's just get out of here!" Alistair shot back, as he nervously looked around the warehouse, instinctively following the screams.

The warehouse had plunged into pure bedlam. The air was a swirling haze of foam, feathers, and the acrid stench of burning guano sizzling against the metal floor. Shouts of panicked men clashed with the bellows of the tiger and the piercing cries of unseen creatures, merging into a deafening symphony of chaos. Crates toppled like dominoes, spilling their contents across the ground, gleaming curiosities, shattered glass, and desperate animals scrambling for freedom.

Above it all, the pigeons descended in a spiralling storm, their bodies twisting and diving with unnatural precision. They tore into Lucien's men in a coordinated frenzy, their beaks lashing, wings battering, claws raking at exposed flesh. But their movements weren't wild or uncontrolled; they were deliberate, guided by an unseen force, as if following the sweeping hand of a conductor.

And at the heart of it, above the carnage, something soared, a resplendent form cutting through the darkness. A seagull, but something more. His feathers shimmered, ghostly light rippling across them like sunlight on water, an ethereal beacon amid the chaos. He glided through the maelstrom, unshaken, untouchable. His eyes burned with purpose, watching as the storm he had summoned tore through the corrupted people below.

From her hidden vantage point, Stephanie's heart raced. Her trembling fingers dug into the edge of the container she was crouched behind, but she forced herself to stay focused. She had done this, unleashed the chaos and there was no turning back.

A fresh burst of foam erupted across the warehouse floor as Fiona unleashed another spray from her fire extinguisher. Guards slipped and crashed into each other, their weapons clattering uselessly to the ground. Stephanie took the opportunity to dart between two stacks of crates, her eyes scanning the frenzied scene. The tiger prowled nearby, its amber eyes fixed on the guards, who scrambled to keep their distance.

The sound of crashing metal drew her attention to the far side of the warehouse. Amidst the chaos, she looked over at Max, slumped in a heavy metal chair, his arms still bound with chains. His face was pale, streaked with dirt and blood, but he was alive. Relief surged through Stephanie's chest, but it was quickly tempered by the urgency of the situation. He needed her, and there wasn't a second to lose.

"Fiona!" Stephanie called; her voice sharp but quiet enough to avoid drawing unwanted attention. Fiona turned, her fire extinguisher still in hand, and followed Stephanie's gaze to Max. Without hesitation, the two women moved in unison, slipping through the chaos with deliberate steps.

As they approached, a guard staggered into their path, his face smeared with blood and foam. Fiona didn't hesitate, she swung the fire extinguisher with surprising force, the metallic clang echoing as it connected with his head. The guard crumpled to the ground, clearing their way forward.

"Max!" Stephanie called out as they reached him, dropping to her knees beside the chair. His head lolled to one side, but he lifted it weakly at the sound of her voice. His eyes, though weary, lit up with recognition.

"Steph," he croaked, his voice hoarse but filled with relief.

"I'm here," she said, her voice trembling with both fear and determination. "I'm getting you out of here." She reached for the lock binding the chains around him, her fingers fumbling as the adrenaline coursed through her veins. "Fiona, help me!"

Fiona knelt beside her, glancing around warily. The chaos around them was still escalating, guards shouting, animals screeching, the tiger roaring as it cornered a group of men. "Hurry," Fiona urged, keeping one hand on the fire extinguisher as she scanned their surroundings.

Stephanie's hands shook as she worked at the lock, her sweaty fingers struggling to find purchase. "Damn it!" she hissed, her frustration mounting. There was no sign of any keys, and time was running out.

Fiona gave her a sharp look, then hefted the fire extinguisher. "Move," she said firmly. Stephanie scrambled aside as Fiona brought the heavy metal cylinder down with all her strength. The lock broke with a deafening clang, the sound momentarily cutting through the noise of the warehouse.

They worked together to uncoil the chains from around Max, their movements quick but careful. Stephanie's hands trembled as she gently pulled his arms free, wincing at the angry red welts the chains had left on his

351

wrists. "Max, can you stand?" she asked, her voice laced with urgency.

Max nodded weakly, but the moment he tried to rise, he cried out in pain and collapsed back into the chair. Stephanie caught him just in time, her hands trembling as she steadied him. "Max, what's wrong?" she asked, panic rising in her voice.

"My ankle," Max gasped, his face pale and slick with sweat. "I think… I think it's broken."

Stephanie glanced down and immediately recoiled. His ankle was swollen and discoloured, an angry purple spreading over the twisted joint. A deep bruise snaked up his leg, and her stomach churned at the sight. She tore her gaze away and looked back at his face, her heart breaking at the pain etched into his features.

"Oh my God," she whispered, the full weight of his suffering hitting her like a blow. The bruises on his face, the raw red marks around his wrists from the chains, every wound told a story of what he had endured. "They… they did this to you, if you were such a prize why treat you this way?" she said, her voice shaking with a mix of horror and anger.

Fiona knelt beside her; her jaw tight as she surveyed Max's condition. "We don't have time to feel sorry," she said firmly, though her voice wavered slightly. "We have to get him out of here before they come back."

Stephanie nodded, swallowing hard to push her emotions aside. She gently wrapped an arm around Max's waist, careful not to jostle his injured ankle. "Fiona, I need you," she said, her voice strained. "We can't do this alone."

Fiona moved quickly, slinging Max's other arm over her shoulder. "We've got you, Max," she said, her voice steady but urgent. "You're not staying here a second longer."

Max's head lolled slightly as they lifted him, his body trembling with effort. "I'm sorry," he murmured, his voice barely audible. "I'm slowing you down."

"Stop," Stephanie said sharply, her grip tightening around him. "You've been through enough. You don't have to do this alone anymore."

As they began to move, Max winced with every step, the pain in his ankle forcing him to lean heavily on the two women. Fiona kept scanning their surroundings, her eyes darting toward the chaotic shadows of the warehouse. The sound of guards shouting grew closer, cutting through the din of roaring animals and clanging metal.

"We need to pick up the pace," Fiona hissed, adjusting her grip on Max. "They're coming."

Stephanie bit her lip, her heart pounding. "We'll make it," she said, more to herself than anyone else. Her gaze flicked back to Max's battered face, and a surge of determination swept through her. She wasn't going to let them take him again.

Together, they moved as quickly as Max's injury allowed, weaving through the chaos of the warehouse. Every step was a struggle, but Stephanie's resolve never faltered. Max was hurt, broken, but he was alive, and she was going to make sure he stayed that way.

"Hold on, Max," she whispered as they neared the exit. "We're almost there."

Together, they began to move, weaving through the pandemonium toward the nearest exit. The tiger roared once more, its massive form tearing through another stack of crates, providing them the cover they needed. The fight wasn't over, not yet, but Stephanie's resolve burned brighter than ever. She wasn't leaving without Max.

As they neared the exit, they heard a voice behind them, Lucien Marchand, shouting orders at Alistair's men. He was furious, his overtly calm exterior completely shattered as he tried to salvage what was left of his operation.

"Get those animals under control! Do you hear me?" Lucien bellowed, his voice rising above the chaos. "I will not lose this shipment!"

The chaos inside the warehouse was reaching its crescendo. The air was thick with foam, feathers, and the acrid stench of sweat and fear. The sounds of wild animals mingled with the shouts of panicked men, creating a chaotic symphony that echoed off the metal walls. But amidst it all, another sound began to rise, faint at first, then growing louder: the distinct wail of approaching sirens.

Lucien froze, his head snapping toward the entrance as the piercing blue and red lights spilled through the warehouse windows. "What the….." he began, but his words were cut short by the unmistakable screech of tires and the heavy slam of car doors outside.

"Police!" a voice bellowed from outside, followed by the pounding of boots on concrete. Officers moved in, their figures dark silhouettes against the flashing lights. The first wave stormed the entrance, weapons drawn and voices commanding.

"Everyone on the ground! Hands where we can see them!"

The guards closest to the entrance hesitated, their panic-fuelled instincts at odds with the barked orders. Some dropped their weapons, raising their hands shakily, while others bolted deeper into the warehouse, hoping to lose themselves in the chaos.

Lucien turned to the retreating Alistair, his face a mask of fury and disbelief. "This is your doing! Your incompetence!"

Alistair's composure cracked under the weight of Lucien's accusation, his jaw tightening. But he wasn't about to stick around and argue. He had always been a pragmatist, and in that moment, his survival instincts kicked in. Without a word, he turned on his heel and bolted toward the back of the warehouse.

"You coward!" Lucien roared after him, his voice echoing above the din.

Alistair didn't look back. He weaved through the maze of boxes, his polished shoes skidding on the slick floor as he pushed his body to its limits. The shouts of officers grew louder behind him, their presence pressing closer with each second.

At the same time, another team of officers fanned out, sweeping through the chaos. One group moved to secure the perimeter while others focused on rounding up the remaining guards and calming the loose animals. The sight of a roaring tiger pacing near the centre of the warehouse gave them pause, they notified their colleagues yet they pressed on, their training overriding their fear.

Meanwhile, Alistair ducked behind a towering stack of crates, his breath coming in ragged gasps. His shirt stuck to his back with sweat, and his mind raced. *Think, think!* He scanned his surroundings, looking for an escape route, but all he saw were endless rows of containers and the harsh glow of floodlights overhead.

The sound of heavy boots rounding the corner froze him in place.

"Going somewhere?"

Alistair turned slowly, his hands instinctively raising as he faced two officers, their weapons trained on him. A Taser glinted menacingly in the dim light; its prongs aimed squarely at his chest.

His face went pale, his bravado draining away. "Wait… we can talk about this," he stammered, his voice barely audible over the noise of the warehouse.

"On the ground. Now!" one officer barked, his tone leaving no room for negotiation.

Alistair sank to his knees, his hands still raised. As he hit the floor, the weight of his decisions, and their consequences, settled heavily on him. He had gambled everything, and now it was over.

Back near the entrance, Lucien's fury turned to desperation. He watched as his carefully curated empire crumbled before his eyes. The tiger that had been meant as a centrepiece for his twisted hunts prowled restlessly, its presence a cruel reminder of how thoroughly he had lost control.

An officer stepped toward Lucien; his voice sharp. "Hands in the air!"

Lucien hesitated, his gaze darting toward the shadows as if weighing his chances of escape. But the cold steel of a night stick, glinting in the dim light left little room for delusions of grandeur. Slowly, reluctantly, he raised his hands, his face twisting in a grimace of defeat.

Chapter Thirty-Seven

Outside the warehouse, a sleek black Mercedes idled just beyond the loading docks, its engine purring softly. Inside, Amy sat rigid in the driver's seat, her nails tapping nervously against the leather-wrapped steering wheel. Her sharp eyes flicked between the warehouse entrance and the rear-view mirror, the tension in her body palpable. She was waiting for Alistair's signal, ready to hit the gas and vanish into the night as soon as the deal was finalized. But deep down, a gnawing unease had begun to take root.

The distant wail of sirens sent a chill down her spine. Her heart thudded against her ribcage as flashing blue lights appeared, bouncing off the steel walls of the port. Police cars screeched to a halt in front of the warehouse, and Amy's stomach dropped. The deal had gone horribly wrong.

"Oh no, no, no," she muttered under her breath, gripping the steering wheel tighter. Her mind raced, calculating her options. Alistair had been adamant that everything was under control, but the scene unfolding before her told a different story. She had to leave, now.

Slamming the car into gear, Amy stomped on the accelerator. The Mercedes roared to life, its tires screeching against the slick dock pavement as she sped toward the port's exit. Her hands were trembling, but she kept her focus on the road ahead, her mind screaming at her to escape before it was too late.

Her heart sank as a police car suddenly swerved into her path, skidding to a stop and blocking her way. The piercing red and blue lights reflected off the glossy hood of her car, blinding her momentarily. Amy slammed on the brakes, her tires screeching again as the Mercedes jerked to a halt mere feet from the Police car.

"Step out of the vehicle NOW!" an officer barked, his voice cutting through the hum of the idling engine.

Amy froze, her knuckles white as she gripped the wheel. Her gaze darted to the rear-view mirror, but her escape route was gone, another police car had boxed her in from behind. She was trapped.

Swallowing hard, she reached for the door handle with shaky fingers, her mind racing for some last-ditch plan. But there was no way out. Slowly, she pushed the door open and stepped out, raising her hands above her head in surrender.

"Face the vehicle and place your hands on the roof," another officer commanded, his standard issue Taser trained on her.

Amy complied, her breath coming in shallow gasps as cold steel cuffs snapped around her wrists. She was spun around and marched toward the waiting police car, her heels clicking against the pavement in a mockery of the confidence she had exuded earlier.

As she was pushed into the backseat, Amy caught sight of movement at the warehouse entrance. Her heart twisted as she saw Alistair being dragged out in handcuffs, flanked by two officers. His immaculate suit was rumpled, and his face, usually smug and self-assured, was pale and hollow. Their eyes met for a fleeting moment, his filled with fury and hers with a desperate, silent apology.

The door slammed shut behind her, cutting off the view of the chaos outside. The interior of the police car was suffocating small, the sound of the engine a distant hum compared to the roaring panic in her mind. Everything they had built, every carefully orchestrated plan, had unravelled in an instant. And now, all she could do was sit and wait, her fate no longer in her hands.

-

Stephanie, Max, and Fiona made it to the exit. They stumbled out of the building, the adrenaline surging through their bodies, Max leaning heavily on both women. The police had the area surrounded, and medics were already on site, rushing over as soon as they saw Max's condition.

"Over here!" Fiona called out, waving to the medics. "He's hurt, his ankle's broken."

The medics quickly moved in, helping Max over to the waiting ambulance. Stephanie watched, her heart still racing, as they carefully examined his injuries. He was bruised and battered, but he was alive. That was all that mattered.

She was impressed, Fiona, in the short amount of time had managed to amass the Police, Ambulance service and the Fire brigade, she half expected the Coast Guard to show up at any minute.

As they lifted Max into the ambulance, he reached out and took Stephanie's hand, squeezing it weakly. "You saved me," he whispered.

Looking at her with a sense of urgency he added, "Though I think in a very short while these guys are going to get one hell of a shock and I'll be needing a Vet" The sky was starting to lighten, the dark blues giving way to purple and the tingling was starting to form in his limbs.

Stephanie nodded, tears welling up in her eyes. She smiled at him "No you won't", she said staring at him so hard he could feel it. "I've made my choice; a doctor will do just fine"

Max could feel the tingling subside, a strange feeling of completeness encompassing his. He slumped back and in the time-honoured tradition; and passed out.

Fiona stood beside her, covered in foam and looking exhausted but relieved. "We did it," she said, her voice filled with a mix of triumph and disbelief. "I have no idea what has happened tonight Steph, but I'm glad I was there for you."

Stephanie nodded, her eyes fixed on the scene as the police swarmed the warehouse, handcuffing the last of Alistair's men and securing the area. The chaos was finally subsiding, replaced by the hum of engines and the crackle of police radios. It was over. The nightmare that had consumed her life was finally over.

She turned to Fiona, pulling her into a tight embrace. "Thank you, Fi," she whispered, her voice thick with emotion. "I couldn't have done this without you."

Fiona gave her a reassuring squeeze before stepping back, her usual steady resolve softened by a proud smile. "You're tougher than you think, Steph. I just gave you a push."

Stephanie smiled faintly but said nothing, her thoughts elsewhere. She glanced over her shoulder, her gaze drifting toward a large stack of wooden crates near the edge of the chaos. Amidst the din of sirens and shouted orders, a magnificent gull perched atop a large old steel anchor, preening its feathers with an air of absolute indifference. Roger, as imperious as ever, seemed utterly unbothered by the cacophony around him, his sharp eyes half-lidded as he smoothed an already perfect plume.

Stephanie approached slowly, her steps measured, as if she were afraid to break the strange spell surrounding the bird. "I should thank you too," she said softly, her voice barely rising above the noise. "I'd never have found him without you."

Roger paused his grooming, tilting his head to one side to regard her with an unreadable expression. Then he let out a low, deliberate *caaaw*, the sound both dismissive and approving.

She smiled despite herself. Tentatively, she reached out and ruffled the feathers on his head. Roger bowed slightly, his sharp beak parting as if to say, *Yes, yes, that's acceptable.*

"You're something else," Stephanie murmured, her smile fading as the weight of everything began to settle on her shoulders. She gave Roger one last look before turning back toward the waiting ambulance where Max was being tended to.

Behind her, Roger straightened his feathers with meticulous care, smoothing each one into place. He looked regal, almost ethereal in the glow of the flashing lights, his feathers seeming to shimmer faintly in the dim light.

As Stephanie walked away, the soft *whoomph* of wings stirred the air behind her, and she froze at the sound of a quiet, almost human voice.

"Well done," it said, the words laced with something that felt ancient and knowing. "Now be happy, both of you, for as long as you can."

She didn't turn around. She knew he wouldn't be there if she looked. Instead, she closed her eyes for a moment, letting the words sink in, before continuing toward the ambulance and the man waiting for her inside.

Chapter Thirty-Eight

Max had come too and now sat on the edge of the ambulance; a thin, scratchy blanket draped over his shoulders. His whole body ached, each movement sending jolts of pain through his muscles, his ankle swollen and sore, but it was the shock that kept him awake, his mind buzzing with fragments of the night's chaos. The cold air of the warehouse yard seeped into his skin, making him shiver as he stared blankly ahead, the flashing lights of police cars and emergency vehicles dancing in his peripheral vision. He felt dazed, disoriented, as if the world had tilted on its axis and hadn't quite righted itself yet.

The low hum of voices drifted around him, the hurried chatter of paramedics, the sharp bark of police orders, the distant growl of animals in their cages being handled by zoo personnel who had been roused in the middle of the night at short notice, the majority of whom were employed by London Zoo.

Max had never really been a fan of zoos. Something about them just didn't sit right with him. He'd been to one once, one of those "fun for the whole family" places where kids pressed their faces against thick glass, giggling as animals paced back and forth. But while everyone else saw a fun day out, Max saw something else. To him, it wasn't just a collection of exotic creatures, it was a place full of restless prisoners, stuck in an endless routine with nowhere to go.

As he got older, that uneasy feeling never really went away. Whenever people talked about zoos being good for conservation or education, he bit his tongue. He knew some places did important work, helping injured animals, protecting endangered species, but for the most part? It just felt like fancy cages wrapped up in good PR. The animals might be well cared for, but that didn't change the fact that they weren't free.

There was something deeply unsettling about seeing wild, powerful creatures stuck in small spaces, reduced to living in carefully measured square footage. Max remembered watching a lion once, stretched out under a fake rock, staring into nothing. It was a look he couldn't forget, as if it had given up on the idea of being anything more than a living exhibit.

And after everything that had happened with Lucien and Alistair, Max's feelings about captivity had only sharpened. Seeing animals treated like collectibles, locked away for someone's twisted amusement, made his blood boil. The sound of rattling cages and the low growls of trapped creatures in that warehouse still lingered in his mind.

There was something deeply unsettling about it all, cages, containment, the idea of keeping something locked away. Max couldn't shake the feeling that, once upon a time, he hadn't been the one trapped, but the one standing guard, ensuring something never escaped.

It wasn't a clear memory, more like a whisper in the back of his mind, an instinct woven into his very being. An old duty, long forgotten. But when he focused on it, when he let his thoughts drift in just the right way, fragments began to surface, fleeting images, half-formed recollections that slipped through his grasp the moment he tried to hold onto them. The nagging sense remained, though, undeniable and ever-present: he had once played a role in keeping something contained. Something that was never meant to be free.

Somewhere nearby Stephanie was speaking with the police. He could hear her voice, steady but tinged with fatigue, recounting the events that had led them here. Each word she spoke reminded him that it was over, at least for now. But the tension still clung to his body like a second skin, refusing to let go.

The medic who had been checking his vitals approached him again, gently pressing a cloth to the gash on his forehead. "You're going to need stitches for this," she said softly, her voice kind but professional. "Try to stay still."

Max nodded but didn't respond. His mind wasn't focused on the pain, or the wound, or even the chaos around him. Instead, it kept drifting back to the moment his hood was pulled off, Lucien and Alistair standing over him, smiling like they had won. The primal fear he had felt in that warehouse lingered, tightening around his chest.

Across the yard, Stephanie stood with DCI Clark, her arms crossed tightly over her chest as she spoke with quiet intensity. Max couldn't make out all the words, but he could tell by her posture that she was trying to explain everything, how they had gotten involved, why they had ended up at the warehouse, and how it all spiralled into this nightmare.

The flashing blue lights from the police cars flickered in the corner of his vision, casting long shadows over the warehouse walls. Officers moved purposefully, securing the area while paramedics tended to the injured, their radios crackling with reports from the scene. Beyond the fence, a team of animal control specialists from the London Zoo was working to tranquilize and recapture the exotic creatures that Lucien had illegally smuggled into his grotesque collection. He could hear the tranquilizer guns firing, followed by low growls and hisses from the animals in their cages.

"Max is it?" A voice interrupted his thoughts, and Max looked up to see DCI Clark approaching, a worn notepad in his hand. Clark's face was lined with exhaustion, but his eyes were sharp as he studied Max. "We need to ask you a few questions. I know you've been through a lot, but it's important we get your account."

Max took a deep breath, nodding as he struggled to find his voice. "I'll try," he rasped, his throat dry and scratchy. "But I... I don't even know where to start."

Clark nodded sympathetically and glanced toward the paramedic, who had stepped aside to give them some privacy. "Take your time," he said. "Let's start with why you were there. Why were you in that warehouse?"

Max's mind raced. He could feel the weight of the question pressing on him, the reality of what he'd gotten himself into suddenly crashing down around him. He had no choice but to tell the truth...or at least part of it. "It all started with an email," he began, glancing over at Stephanie, who had joined them and stood beside Clark, her face tense with worry. "Stephanie found it. It was forwarded by accident from Alistair Castel, her boss. There were documents, shipping details, things about a puma being smuggled. It was... illegal. And I couldn't just let it happen."

Stephanie stepped in, her voice steady and clear. "The email showed they were involved in smuggling exotic animals. I didn't know the full extent of it at the time, but when I showed it to Max, we realized they weren't just transporting animals, they were using them for something... something much worse." She paused, glancing at Max for a moment before continuing. "He thought he could stop them, that if he went there, he could find out what was really happening and maybe stop them before anyone got hurt."

Clark's pen scratched against his notepad as he wrote down their statements, his brow furrowing in concentration. "And you didn't think to contact the authorities?" he asked, his tone not accusatory but filled with the weight of what could have gone wrong.

Max shook his head, guilt gnawing at him. "I thought I could handle it. I wasn't even sure it was real. I didn't want to drag anyone else into this. I didn't realize how dangerous it really was until it was too late."

The detective nodded, his expression softening. "You're lucky to be alive," he said quietly. "Lucien Marchand isn't just some rich guy playing around with animals, he's dangerous. We've had an eye on him for a while, but we never had enough evidence to pin him down. Thanks to you, we finally have what we need."

Max swallowed hard, the reality of what he had stumbled into settling like a heavy weight in his gut. Lucien and Alistair had been arrested, but the danger they represented still lingered in the air, like the faint echo of something dark and sinister.

"We're going to need a full statement from both of you,"

Clark continued, his voice more formal now. "But that can wait until after you've been treated. Someone from the station will come by St. Georges tomorrow and take some more details."

Max's body felt like it had been through a war, every inch of him aching, but the thought of being admitted to the hospital made his stomach churn. He wanted answers, closure, something that would make sense of all the chaos. But before he could protest, Stephanie stepped forward, placing a hand gently on his shoulder.

"You need to go, Max," she said softly, her voice full of concern. "You've been through hell. Let them take care of you."

He sighed, knowing she was right. The medics were already moving in to load him into the ambulance, and the idea of sleep, of finally closing his eyes and letting the world slip away, was too tempting to resist.

Max glanced back at the warehouse. He could see the London Zoo team still working, their tranquilizer guns aimed at the cages where the exotic animals had been held. The growls and roars had quieted now, replaced by the calm efficiency of professionals who knew exactly what they were doing. It was a strange sense of relief to know that the animals, at least, were being cared for, even if they had been pawns in Lucien's sick game.

Stephanie stood beside him as he was loaded into the back of the ambulance, her face etched with worry. "I'll be right behind you," she promised, squeezing his hand.

Max met her gaze, exhaustion and gratitude mixing in his eyes. "Thanks... for everything," he managed to say.

She smiled softly, her eyes filled with the same mixture of relief and sadness that he felt. "Always."

As the ambulance doors closed, Max allowed his body to sink into the stretcher, his eyes closing as the weight of everything that had happened, not just that day, but what seemed like an eternity finally overcame him.

Back at the warehouse, the London Zoo team worked swiftly, securing the last of the animals and loading them into transport crates. The night air was thick with the scent of hay, animal musk, and the faint tang of chemicals from the tranquilizers. The once chaotic scene was slowly being brought under control, but for Max, the chaos of what had been set in motion would not end with Lucien's arrest. Was he destined to be hunted forever?

As the ambulance pulled away, sirens cutting through the still night air, the warehouse behind him faded into the distance. But the memories, the fear, and the strange, haunting events of the past few days would stay with him for a long time to come. And somewhere, in the dark corners of his mind, Max couldn't help but wonder, what would come next?

Chapter Thirty-Nine

The bright, sterile smell of the hospital greeted Stephanie as she walked down the corridor to Max's room. It had been a long couple of days since the showdown at the docks, and Max had been recovering from his injuries ever since. His broken ankle had required surgery, and the bruises and cuts that covered his body had taken their time to heal. He had been unconscious for two days. But today, finally, he was getting discharged.

She hadn't been able to visit him as much as she wanted to, a mix of meetings with the police, various animal societies and friends meant that this was the first time that she would see Max awake.

Stephanie pushed open the door to his room and found him sitting up in bed, fully dressed, with a mischievous grin on his face. There was something about the way he looked at her that immediately put her on edge.

"Ready to go home?" she asked, trying to ignore the feeling. A huge smile plastered across her face.

Max opened his mouth, but instead of answering, he let out a loud, exaggerated bark.

Stephanie blinked, caught off guard. "What...?"

Max barked again, this time louder and more insistent, wagging an imaginary tail and panting like a dog. Stephanie stared at him, speechless for a moment, before bursting into laughter.

"Are you serious?" she managed to say between giggles. "You've been out of it for two days, and this is how you greet me?"

Max barked once more, then grinned, his eyes twinkling with amusement. "Well, I thought I'd have a little fun before getting out of here. I needed to see you smile after everything that's happened."

Stephanie rolled her eyes, still smiling as she walked over to his bed and playfully swatted his arm. "You're ridiculous. Come on, let's get you out of here before you start chasing squirrels."

Max laughed, the sound warm and genuine, a rare moment of lightness after the chaos of the past days. He grabbed his crutches and carefully pushed himself upright, his movements slow but steady. Stephanie moved to his side, ready to help if needed, but he managed on his own. "I'm serious," he said with a smirk, his eyes twinkling with mischief. "For the next week, I'll only communicate through barking. Barks are a great way of simplifying things."

Stephanie rolled her eyes, chuckling as they walked down the hospital hallway. "Simplifying things, huh? Well, don't expect me to scratch your ears."

He grinned. "Aw, but you'd do it so well."

The playful banter carried them down the elevator and through the hospital's automatic doors. The sharp noon air greeted them, a welcome contrast to the sterile hospital atmosphere. Stephanie flagged down a cab, helping Max into the back seat before sliding in beside him. She watched him carefully, noting the strain etched into his features, though he was clearly trying to hide it behind his usual use of humour.

As the cab pulled into traffic, Max leaned back against the seat, his crutches propped awkwardly between them. His eyes darted toward the window, and without warning, he reached for the handle and cranked it down. The window slid open, letting in a rush of cool air that whipped around the taxi's interior.

"Max!" Stephanie exclaimed, half-laughing, half-scolding. "What are you doing?"

He didn't answer immediately. Instead, he shifted, leaning toward the open window. The city lights blurred and shimmered as the cab picked up speed, and Max tilted his face into the wind, closing his eyes. His shoulders relaxed, and for the first time in hours, he looked like he wasn't in pain, or maybe just like he was somewhere else entirely.

Stephanie shook her head, bemused. "You're taking this a bit far, aren't you?"

He cracked one eye open, his grin broad and unapologetic. "Have you ever tried it? Feels incredible."

"You're not a dog right now, Max," she said, her voice laced with affection despite the exasperation.

He popped back in and looked at her in a questioning manner.

"The dog thing. Head out of car windows." She said as if he should know exactly what she meant.

He smiled softly at her, "It's not that, I've never seen this place as a man in the daytime before. It's amazing."

The driver looked at them in the mirror with a confused expression, rolled his eyes and went back to his task at hand.

Stephanie nestled into his arms.

The lightness of their banter followed them back to Stephanie's apartment, a small bubble of normalcy in the chaos of their lives. The night was cold and the city had quietened somewhat, as if the world itself was finally taking a breath.

Inside, Stephanie helped Max settle onto the couch, carefully adjusting a cushion under his injured leg. He leaned back with a contented sigh, his crutches propped against the armrest. For a moment, it was easy to forget everything, the danger, the fear, the uncertainty. They were just two people, together, sharing a rare moment of peace.

Stephanie dropped into the chair opposite him, her body sagging with exhaustion. The last few day's events pressed down on her like a heavy weight, but being here with Max brought a strange sense of comfort. He closed his eyes briefly, a faint smile playing on his lips, and the sight made her chest ache in a way she couldn't quite explain.

"You okay?" Max asked, his voice soft, his eyes opening to meet hers.

Stephanie nodded, brushing a stray hair out of her face. "Just tired," she admitted. "It's been… a lot."

Max's expression softened. "Tell me about it. But hey, we're here. Right now, that's enough."

She smiled faintly, leaning back in her chair, letting her gaze rest on him. The room was quiet except for the hum of the city outside, a peaceful backdrop to the moment they shared. Stephanie let her eyes drift closed for a second, her breathing slowing. Despite everything, being here with Max felt like the calm after a storm, a fragile reprieve they both desperately needed.

Her phone buzzed, and she saw a message from her boss flash across the screen. She had been avoiding this conversation for days, but she knew it was inevitable. Sighing, she opened the message.

Stephanie, we need to talk. The firm's reputation has taken a hit after what happened with Castel & Fink. The owners are furious, and they're convinced you had something to do with it. You're being let go. I'm sorry.

Stephanie stared at the words, feeling a hollow ache in her chest. She had known this was coming, but it still hurt. Everything she had worked for, everything she had built, was gone in an instant. She put the phone down, rubbing her temples as the reality of the situation sank in.

Max noticed the change in her expression immediately. "Steph... what's wrong?"

She sighed, looking at him with weary eyes. "I lost my job. They're letting me go. The owners are furious with what happened with the Alistair and Amy. They think I had something to do with it as Amy mentioned me."

Max frowned, reaching out to take her hand. "I'm so sorry, Steph. I know how much that job meant to you."

"It's not just that," Stephanie admitted, her voice tinged with frustration. "I'm worried about money, Max. Rent, bills... everything. I don't know how we're going to make it."

Max was silent for a moment, his brow furrowed in thought. Then, slowly, a smile spread across his face. "You know... I've been thinking."

Stephanie raised an eyebrow, curious but still feeling the weight of her worries. "About what?"

"About us. About everything we've been through. What if we didn't stay here?" Max suggested, his tone thoughtful. "What if we moved to the country? Somewhere quiet, away from all of this."

Stephanie blinked, surprised by the suggestion. "The country? Max, how would we even afford that? I just lost my job. This is the real-world Max, as people we have bills to pay, responsibilities!" She immediately bit her lip. "Sorry, I didn't mean..."

Max's smile grew, and he leaned in closer, his voice lowering conspiratorially. "Well, you see... I have some money."

Stephanie's eyes narrowed playfully. "Money? Where?"

Max's grin turned into a smirk. "*In* the city."

Stephanie raised an eyebrow, waiting for him to elaborate. "In the city?" she repeated. "What are you talking about?"

Max leaned back; his expression smug as he finally revealed his secret. "I have investments. Savings. Let's just say... I'm not as broke as I appear. I've been holding onto some funds, waiting for the right moment. And I think this is it, Steph. We can start fresh. Somewhere new. Away from all the chaos."

Stephanie stared at him, processing his words. The idea of leaving the city, of starting over in the countryside, was both scary and hugely exciting. After everything they had been through, maybe a new beginning was exactly what they needed.

"You're serious?" she asked, her voice filled with a mix of disbelief and hope.

Max nodded, his eyes warm and reassuring. "Absolutely. We can make this work, Steph. You and I... We'll figure it out together. What do you say?"

Stephanie looked at him, at the man who had been through so much with her, who had faced down danger and come out the other side. She thought about the possibilities, the peace and quiet of the countryside, the chance to rebuild their lives without the past hanging over them. It was a risk, but maybe it was exactly what they needed.

Slowly, a smile spread across her face. "I say... let's do it."

"Great!" Exclaimed Max, "We'll need some wheelbarrows for the coins."

Stephanie just looked at him and smiled.

The next few days were a whirlwind of plans, preparations, and tying up loose ends before leaving the city. Stephanie and Max were determined to start fresh, finding a cottage in the countryside where they could leave the chaos and heartache behind. The thought of waking up to birdsong and crisp morning air, rather than the ceaseless hum of city life, filled them both with cautious excitement.

Fiona, meanwhile, was dealing with her own emotional fallout after discovering David's betrayal with Amy. To Stephanie's relief, Fiona seemed almost buoyant. "Honestly, it's like I dodged a flaming cannonball," she'd said more than once, tossing items into boxes as she helped Stephanie pack.

"Well, at least one good thing came out of all this," Fiona said with a wry smile, stacking books into a crate. "No wedding, no David, and no more Amy. That's a hat trick in my book."

Stephanie chuckled, appreciating Fiona's ability to find humour in the aftermath. "I'm just glad you're okay with how everything turned out. And I'm even more glad you're coming with us."

"Are you kidding?" Fiona replied, placing a dramatic hand on her chest. "There's no way I'm letting you two run off to paradise without me. I need a little countryside adventure too. Fresh air, rolling hills, maybe even a rugged farmer or two to keep things interesting." She winked playfully, earning a laugh from Stephanie.

But before the move could happen, there was the small matter of Max's coin collection. Stephanie had rolled her eyes when Max insisted they pay for the cottage outright in cash, specifically, coins. "You've been collecting these for how long, exactly?" she'd asked, eyeing the neatly stacked piles in her apartment. It wasn't just a few stacks mind you, there were thousands of them. The entire apartment looked like a gigantic coin pusher machine that you would find in an arcade.

There was one pile though that stood out from the others. Stephanie had found a number of coins that had historical relevance and were to be appraised, chiefly and of greatest interest was a pair of 1933 George V pennies.

"A while," Max replied with a sheepish grin. "Coins are reliable. They're not like cards or digital money, no banks freezing accounts or losing passwords. Besides, they jingle."

"Max," Stephanie said, pinching the bridge of her nose. "The cottage is perfect, but the seller isn't going to take a barrel of change. You need to exchange these."

Which was how they found themselves at the city's largest bank, wheeling in a dolly loaded with sacks of coins. The teller's expression shifted from polite indifference to outright disbelief as Max unloaded the first sack onto the counter with a heavy thud.

"Good morning!" Max said cheerfully. "I'd like to exchange these, please."

The teller blinked, her mouth opening and closing as she tried to process the request. "All... of these?" she managed to say, her voice faint.

Fiona stood to the side, barely holding in her laughter. "Oh, this is priceless," she whispered to Stephanie. "He's going to break the bank. Literally."

The bank manager eventually intervened, overseeing the process as the staff sorted, counted, and double-checked the massive haul. It took hours, but by the end of the day, Max walked out with a cashier's check in hand, looking immensely pleased with himself.

"That wasn't so bad," he said, grinning at Stephanie.

"Speak for yourself," Stephanie muttered, rubbing her temples. "I thought we were going to be banned for life."

Fiona burst out laughing. "Well, at least you've got the money now. The countryside won't know what hit it."

With the funds secured and the arrangements finalized, they left the city behind. The cottage they'd found was idyllic, nestled in the heart of a quiet village surrounded by rolling hills and lush greenery.

As they stepped into their new home, Stephanie felt the weight of the past few weeks lift, replaced by a sense of hope she hadn't felt in years.

And as they settled into their new life, Max couldn't help but grin every time he heard the jingle of coins in his pocket, a small reminder of the adventure that had brought them here.

-

One day some weeks later, as the sun began to set overhead, Stephanie stood outside in the garden of their new home leaning against the fence watching as a cow wandered by, it's slow ponderous movements at odds with its size. It quietly munched on grass, oblivious to the world around it, she watching the colours fade into the horizon. Max came up behind her, wrapping his arms around her waist and resting his chin on her shoulder.

"Penny for your thoughts?" he asked softly.

Stephanie smiled, leaning into him. "I was just thinking about how far we've come. Everything we've been through... it feels like a lifetime ago."

Max nodded, kissing her cheek. "It does. But we made it through. And now... we get to start over."

Stephanie turned to look at him, her heart full of gratitude and love. "Choosing Mr. Chan's that night was the best decision of my life." She smiled.

Max smiled back at her, his eyes filled with the same warmth and affection that had kept them going through the darkest moments. "We did it. And now, we've got the rest of our lives to figure out what comes next."

They stood together in the quiet of the countryside, the world around them peaceful and calm. For the first time in what felt like forever, the future seemed bright, full of hope, possibilities, and new beginnings. Oliver stood beside them his tail ever so slightly licking at Max's leg, though if you ever asked him, he's say it was an accident.

And as the last rays of sunlight disappeared behind the hills, Stephanie knew that whatever challenges lay ahead, they would face them together.

But the clock had started to tick.

Epilogue

To those paying attention, though few ever do, they might have noticed a glimmer in the sky, like a distant star streaking across the horizon. If they had looked closer, they would have seen an incredibly beautiful seagull, flying faster than any creature of the earth has reason to, leaving a vapour trail behind as it sped out of the city. But this was no ordinary bird.

He flew at the speed of thought and imagination, leaving London far behind, racing westward across the counties. A whirlpool of pigeons followed in his wake as if being dragged by an imaginary net, squawking and cooing in protest and panic, their feathers scattering in every direction like confetti caught in a storm. He paid them no mind.

The seagull cleared the coast of England effortlessly, skimming over the Severn River with a slight, almost imperceptible smirk on his beak. He soared over the rolling hills of Wales, where the occasional sheep lifted its head to bleat a feeble *baa* in response. But he paid them no heed either.

As the land fell away beneath him, he reached the open ocean, many miles he covered gliding above the waves, at a point known only to him the seagull suddenly dove, cutting through the water's surface like an arrow. The pigeons behind him, still squabbling and flapping, were pulled into the depths, helpless to resist the force that dragged them along. The water grew darker as they descended, the world above disappearing into a distant memory. Strange, deep-sea creatures glowed with an eerie light as the seagull passed, and they, the Anglers, the bottom dwellers and the cephalopods, prostrated themselves before him in reverence.

Ahead of him, far below the ocean's surface, was a tear in the very fabric of reality, a rent in the silt. A shimmer in the deep, like a dream half-remembered, it was a place that no living thing dared approach. But the seagull, the beautiful and majestic looking seagull, dove straight into it, pulling the protesting flock of birds behind him.

Time stopped.

Roger emerged from the tear, his wings spreading wide as he surveyed the cavern before him. The space was impossibly vast, stretching far beyond what should have been its limits. Lava cascaded from fissures in the walls, the glowing rivers twisting and writhing as though alive, pooling into vast, simmering lakes of molten fire. The oppressive heat pressed against him, but Roger didn't falter. This was not a place that could intimidate him, he had crossed into this realm too many times, and the creatures within knew better than to challenge him.

Above, winged horrors circled in the heated air, creatures with leathery wings, too many eyes, and grotesque forms that defied reason. They flitted in and out of the shadows, their screeches reverberating off the jagged walls. But as Roger glided further in, the creatures scattered like leaves in a storm, their cries muted as they gave him a wide berth. One particularly large beast, its talons glinting in the fiery light, paused mid-flight to regard him. A single, sharp caw from Roger sent it diving back into the shadows, its malformed wings folding in submission.

Below, the ground teemed with tormented figures, their shapes barely human. Their bodies twisted and broken, they stumbled aimlessly, their moans of despair rising like a mournful dirge. Some clutched at the glowing chains that bound them, their blistered hands trying futilely to break free. The sound of rattling iron echoed through the cavern, blending with the distant roar of lava flows. Every so often, one of the wandering figures would glance upward, their hollow eyes locking onto Roger's silhouette before quickly averting their gaze, as though the sight of him brought a terror deeper than their suffering.

The cavern walls were marked with ancient scars, symbols etched deep into the rock, some glowing faintly with an otherworldly light, others charred black as though burned into existence. Smoky tendrils seeped from the cracks, curling and twisting in the air, carrying whispers that seemed to come from nowhere and everywhere at once. Even the lava seemed to react to Roger's presence, bubbling more fiercely as if agitated by his arrival.

Roger perched on a jagged ledge, his feathers gleaming in the molten glow. He preened deliberately, smoothing each feather with care, his movements unhurried. Despite the chaos around him, he was unbothered. This was a domain that feared him, a place where even the darkest entities hesitated to challenge his presence.

One of the grotesque winged creatures dared to edge closer, its many eyes watching him intently. Roger's head turned sharply, his gaze locking onto the creature. The beast quivered, its form trembling under his scrutiny, before retreating with a guttural hiss, disappearing into the shadows from which it had emerged.

He adjusted his wings and peered into the distance, where an obsidian bridge stretched across a chasm of glowing fire. The bridge's surface gleamed like a mirror, reflecting the tortured faces of the souls trapped below, their mouths open in silent screams.

With a powerful beat of his wings, Roger took to the air again, gliding over the chaos below. The tormented figures, the winged monsters, even the walls themselves seemed to shrink back as he passed. He had no fear of this place, it was the realm that feared him.

As the pigeons tumbled out of the tear and landed on the cavern floor, their feathers dissolved into ash. Where each bird had been, there now stood a moaning, humanoid figure, their forms twisted and misshapen, lost souls among the uncountable number of others that inhabited this domain.

The cavern floor was dotted with massive plateaus of smooth, polished black marble. Towering beasts of burden, their bodies smouldering with heat, carried enormous palanquins atop their shoulders. High above, more winged creatures watched over the cavern's denizens with ever-vigilant eyes.

The chorus of mournful wails from the newly transformed creatures echoed through the cavern, a dissonancy of despair that would drive a mortal mind to madness. But the seagull was unmoved. He set down on a central aisle, his form shifting as he landed. Wings became arms, talons became feet, and in an instant, the seagull was gone, replaced by a tall, severe-looking man in an exquisitely tailored suit of midnight black. His white hair was slicked back against his scalp, and a red handkerchief peeked from his breast pocket, matching his deep crimson shirt he wore.

The moaning creatures parted before him as he walked, their protests growing quieter, though none dared approach him. The cavern itself seemed to defy logic, its scale and angles twisting in impossible ways. A normal person would lose their sanity trying to comprehend it, but the man moved through it with ease.

Above him hung a vast chandelier, the size of an entire country, its chains ancient and thick. Globs of wax, each the size of a village, dripped from it, sizzling as they hit the floor far below. The man paid no attention to the grandeur or the grotesqueness of the cavern around him. To him, this was home.

Ahead, looming like a monument to all things beautiful and terrifying, stood a gate, it sad slightly ajar. A gothic edifice of staggering proportions, the gate was both exquisitely crafted and deeply unsettling, its intricate carvings evoking awe and fear in equal measure. Before it stood a lone figure, a small, pale man with an internal glow that seemed to radiate from within him. The denizens of the cavern kept their distance from him, pacing in a wide perimeter, hissing and snarling but never daring to come closer.

The glowing figure of Zeus glanced up as the man in black approached, a wistful smile playing on his lips. His gaze drifted downward to the worn patches in the ancient stone, deep grooves, perfectly spaced, where Cerberus had stood guard since time itself had meaning. The marks spoke of endless vigilance, etched not by the passing of years, but by the patient shifting of massive paws. He could almost hear the soft scrape of claws against rock and the low, rumbling growl that once greeted all who dared draw too close.

Cerberus had been more than a guardian. He was a sentinel, a living boundary between worlds, his presence an unspoken warning to those who thought they could cheat their fate. The very air around those worn grooves seemed heavier, still carrying the faint, lingering echo of his growls, a ghost of a sound that sent a shiver through even the bravest souls.

Hades, dressed in his dark suit smiled back, a genuine smile that softened the severity of his features. "I think he'll be happy," he said quietly. He hesitated for a moment, then added, "I hope he'll be happy."

The glowing figure studied the man for what felt like an eternity. When he finally spoke, his voice was soft and filled with genuine curiosity, as if he hadn't spoken in a million years. "Why?" he asked simply.

Hades's smile grew, a hawkish look to him, there was a warmth in his eyes that had not been there for eons. "Because," he said after a long pause, his voice filled with devotion and love, "He's a good boy. Faithful for all eternity, he deserves this. A brief moment of happiness as a thank you from me."

For a moment, they stood in silence, gazing at each other. There was no hatred between them, no malice. Those emotions had long since passed, worn away by the endless passage of time. Eventually, the glowing figure turned and walked through the enormous gate, the weight of eternity on his shoulders. As he crossed the threshold, he looked back one last time, a faint smile on his lips, before disappearing into the darkness beyond.

Hades stood there for a moment longer, watching the gate until it was still once more. Then, looking at the prints in the hard stone with a final, satisfied smile, he turned away and disappeared into the underworld's endless expanse, leaving behind only the echo of his footsteps and the faint, mournful wail of the souls that lingered in the darkness.

About the Author

Stafford grew up with a life as transient as the stories he now crafts. Born into a family that moved frequently, his schooling was a patchwork of different schools and home tutoring. With friends hard to come by, he cultivated a vivid imagination, one that became his constant companion and, eventually, the foundation for his writing.

An avid reader of both science fiction and horror, Stafford has been inspired by authors like Terry Pratchett, Robert Rankin, Larry Niven, and James Herbert. Their works fuelled his passion for exploring the unknown and weaving stories that delve into the darker corners of human existence.

Now in his early fifties, Stafford is pouring his creativity into his debut novel, Max A passion piece drawn into existence by endless hours mulling over the important questions in life, such as what would it be like to be a Were-duck? Beyond writing, his greatest passion is animals. He lives in Crawley, West Sussex, with his Manchester Terrier, Dino, who keeps him active with daily two-hour walks, whether or not inspiration is striking. Dino's boundless energy and loyalty serve as a constant reminder of the beauty and joy animals bring to life. (Manchester Terriers are truly an awesome breed, after all!)

Having travelled the world during two decades in aviation, Stafford is no stranger to adventure and meeting many people from all cultures and all walks of life. But these days, he dreams of settling in the countryside, where he can write, reflect, and draw inspiration from the quiet beauty of nature.

In addition to this current work, Stafford is penning a new series. This series will take readers to Shadowpine, a fictional town nestled in the mountains of Montana, a nexus point where the veil between worlds is thin, and strange, malevolent forces are always at play.

Whether you're a fan of gripping horror or dark speculative fiction, Stafford promises stories that will keep you up late, leaving the lights on and questioning what lurks in the shadows.

Printed in Great Britain
by Amazon

58619122R00218